This Magnificent Desolation

This Magnificent Desolation

A Novel

Thomas O'Malley

B L O O M S B U R Y

New York   London   New Delhi   Sydney

Lines from *The Undertaking: Life Studies from the Dismal Trade* by Thomas Lynch. Copyright © 1997 by Thomas Lynch. Used by permission of W. W. Norton & Company, Inc., and by kind permission of Thomas Lynch.

From *A Fortunate Man* by John Berger and Jean Mohr, copyright © 1967 by John Berger. Used by permission of Pantheon Books, a division of Random House, Inc., and by kind permission of John Berger.

Reprinted with permission of Scribner, a division of Simon & Schuster, Inc., from *Autobiographies: The Collected Works of W. B. Yeats*, volume III, by William Butler Yeats; edited by Denis Donoghue. Copyright © 1972 by Michael Butler Yeats and Anne Yeats. All rights reserved.

From *Estrangement: Being Some Fifty Thoughts from a Diary Kept by William Butler Yeats in the Year Nineteen Hundred and Nine*, by William Butler Yeats (The Cuala Press: Dublin, 1926; Shannon: Irish University Press, 1970). Reprinted by kind permission of Gráinne Yeats.

From *Duino Elegies* by Rainer Maria Rilke, translated by J. B. Leishman/ Stephen Spender. Copyright 1939 by W. W. Norton & Company, Inc., renewed © 1967 by Stephen Spender and J. B. Leishman. Used by permission of W. W. Norton & Company, Inc.

From *The Greatest Secret in the World* by Og Mandino, copyright 1972 by Og Mandino. Used by permission of Bantam Books, a division of Random House, Inc.

And with thanks to Eric Jones for his kind permission to reprint excerpts from the Apollo Lunar Surface Journal.

Published by Bloomsbury USA, New York

All papers used by Bloomsbury USA are natural, recyclable products made from wood grown in well-managed forests. The manufacturing processes conform to the environmental regulations of the country of origin.

LIBRARY OF CONGRESS CATALOGING-IN-PUBLICATION DATA

O'Malley, Thomas, 1967–
This magnificent desolation : a novel / Thomas O'Malley.—1st U.S. ed.
p. cm.
ISBN 978-1-60819-279-3 (hardcover : alk. paper)
1. Abandoned children—Fiction.   2. Mothers and sons—Fiction.
3. Loss (Psychology) in children—Fiction.   4. Loneliness in children—
Fiction.   5. Imagination in children—Fiction.   6. Vietnam War, 1961–1975—
Veterans—Fiction.   7. Minnesota—Fiction.   8. San Francisco (Calif.)—
Fiction.   9. Psychological fiction.   I. Title.
PR6115.M347T55 2013
823'.92—dc22
2012025659

First U.S. Edition 2013

1   3   5   7   9   10   8   6   4   2

Typeset by Westchester Book Group
Printed in the U.S.A.

When we suffer anguish we return to early childhood because that is the period in which we first learnt to suffer the experience of total loss. It was more than that. It was the period in which we suffered more total losses than in all the rest of our life put together.

—JOHN BERGER

Grief has no borders, no limits, no known ends . . . Some sadnesses are permanent.

—THOMAS LYNCH

To : H. R. Haldeman

From: Bill Safire   July 18, 1969.

IN EVENT OF MOON DISASTER:

Fate has ordained that the men who went to the moon to
explore in peace will stay on the moon to rest in peace.

These brave men, Neil Armstrong and Edwin Aldrin, know
that there is no hope for their recovery. But they also know that there
is hope for mankind in their sacrifice.

These two men are laying down their lives in mankind's
most noble goal: the search for truth and understanding.

They will be mourned by their families and friends; they
will be mourned by their nation; they will be mourned by the people of
the world; they will be mourned by a Mother Earth that dared send two
of her sons into the unknown.

In their exploration, they stirred the people of the world to
feel as one; in their sacrifice, they bind more tightly the brotherhood
of man.

In ancient days, men looked at stars and saw their heroes in
the constellations. In modern times, we do much the same, but our heroes
are epic men of flesh and blood.

Others will follow, and surely find their way home. Man's search will not be denied. But these men were the first, and they will remain the foremost in our hearts.

For every human being who looks up at the moon in the nights to come will know that there is some corner of another world that is forever mankind.

PRIOR TO THE PRESIDENT'S STATEMENT:

The President should telephone each of the widows-to-be.

AFTER THE PRESIDENT'S STATEMENT, AT THE POINT WHEN NASA ENDS COMMUNICATIONS WITH THE MEN:

A clergyman should adopt the same procedure as a burial at sea, commending their souls to "the deepest of the deep," concluding with the Lord's Prayer.

The knowledge of reality is a secret knowledge; it is a kind of death.

—W. B. YEATS

December 1980

UPON A VAST, snow-covered plain in the Minnesota wilderness in the late hours of the night, Duncan Bright and Brother Canice sit by the woodstove in the monastery's kitchen with the wind howling through the cracks in the stone and mortar, and the ancient oak and pine joists that hold the slate roof above their heads moaning like an old sleeping animal. The rest of the children will have long been bathed and placed in their beds; there may be an odd creaking or grumbling upon the ceiling wainscoting as they shift and shudder in their halfsleep, but they will be the only two awake, thin slivers of red and orange flame flickering from the woodstove's grate and moving across both their faces in the dark. Brother Canice is a squat, rotund

1

little man with wispy orange-red sideburns that cover the entirety of his jaws. The rest of his face is shaven so severely and stringently that it shines like a pink, polished stone and Duncan is often surprised he has not drawn blood. On a shelf lined with canned goods—Bristol's peaches, Hammond baked beans, Labrador sardines—Brother Canice's black Vulcanite transistor radio glows amber, humming lightly with static and the odd pip or squeak, as if it were searching out the void for some signal from the stars.

Tell me, Duncan asks him. Tell me again how I came to be here.

Brother Canice picks at something at the front of his teeth: the sunflower seeds he always seems to be chewing. The flameglow is orange on his yellowed caps, which replaced his front teeth a decade ago; he likes to say that he lost them when he challenged the bishop of St. Paul to a fight when they were both young prelates, but the truth is less rebellious and less heroic and perhaps more beautiful. After being bedridden with influenza for three weeks, he'd climbed the tower's stairs to inspect the bells, to greet them, he says—he was responsible for their tone and timbre and when dust and grime built upon them they lost not only their luster but also their pitch. As he leaned forward—his face widening and shimmering familiarly in the ancient brass—a novitiate pulled on the heavily wound cottonstave ropes from below and the bell's lip suddenly came up to greet Brother Canice's face with a violent kiss, slicing into his gums and severing his two front teeth at the root. He laughs as he spits seeds. Just like that, he says, just like that. Two resin-stained teeth spiraling down into the darkness of the bell case. Like bloody yellow pearls.

Tell me what you remember, Duncan, he says now.

I remember being born, Duncan says, and God speaking to me.

And what did he say to you?

I can't remember.

Shadows seem to find the narrow lines of Brother Canice's weathered face, until only the regal cheekbones, the large, moist eyes, and his mouth are visible. His breath smells slightly of wood, a damp teak, as if he's been chewing on bark. Duncan finds it a comforting smell.

And you have no memory of anything else? Brother Canice asks.

Duncan shakes his head and Brother Canice grunts and pokes at the grate, stirring the coals with the ornate, cast-iron poker.

This, then, shall be your story.

Duncan looks at him questioningly and although Brother Canice cannot see the boy's expression in the dark, he shrugs. Brother Canice runs his tongue along the gums of his front teeth and spits sunflower seeds into the stove's grate with impressive accuracy. They watch the seeds boil and hiss and pop and then dissolve, and in the hiss of evaporation Brother Canice says: Until something better comes along, Duncan. Only until something better comes along.

Wood is splintering in the woodstove but the room grows cold and the light from the grate dims. Brother Canice shifts on his stool, opens the grate, and a square of orange-colored light pushes back the darkness. As he leans forward to poke the embers and lay another log on the flames, his pale arms and face are turned crimson by firelight. He closes the grate and the room is in darkness once more; slivers of amber light from the grate flickering on his face and sending shadows dancing around the room.

Brother Canice settles himself comfortably against the kitchen wall and sighs. It was the winter of 1970 and there was a terrible storm, he begins, and Duncan closes his eyes and listens to the wood crackling as it burns and the children murmuring in their dreamsleep in the coffin-dark above them. Brother Canice's ancient voice box seems to wheeze in cadence with the wind beneath the window clasps and the sound of the frames shuddering and cracking with shifting splays of ice and the sense of morning still many hours away.

At dusk the sky above the farms and pastureland of Stockholdt, Minnesota, roils as if it were a living thing, twisting and writhing toward the northeastern horizon, where, briefly visible are small towns, windows glinting nacre in the tallow light, and black ash, yellow birch, and evergreen-lined slopes upon which rust-colored buildings, tin mining shacks, logging camps, and pyramids of dead timber bloom. Above the glacial Iron Range, the sky is a sheet of flat gray steel and the mountains merely an outline stamped upon this background: a picture taking shape, trembling momentarily, and then becoming fixed in its bath of silver halide. Animals, sensing the storm, are still. Not a thing moves. And then at the farthest edges of the sky, a slight undulation begins like a wave far out at sea, and with it comes a slow, rushing blackness as of night. A great wind rises up from the north, and from the deep, leaded bellies of clouds, it begins to snow.

The annual Festival of Lights Holiday Train, a vintage 1928 Great Northern Railway Empire Builder steam engine, leaves Holdbrundt with the first strakes of snow drifting across the tracks, white billows of steam venting from the engine's exchange as the hydraulic rods and pistons stretch and contract and, in ever shortening revolutions, turn the great wheels, and move them forward toward the wide plains of St. Paul.

During the last leg of its four-hundred-mile journey across Minnesota, the train tows two flatbeds upon which bands and other performers have played, three boxcars filled with donated food, clothes, and children's toys, and ten red-and-green turn-of-the century Pullman railcars decorated with wreathes and lit by a hundred thousand miniature Christmas lights. It is two days before Christmas, and meteorologists in St. Paul and Duluth predict a few inches of festive snow covering for those leaving school and work, with heavier snowfalls in the distant mountain and valley ranges of Stockholdt and Thule.

Father Magnusson, who attends this pilgrimage every year from the Capuchin monastery, the Blessed House of the Gray Brothers of Mercy, in Thule, settles into a wide horsehair chair aboard the tenth Pullman and watches the land stretching into darkness beyond the lights of the train, the snow spiraling gently down in shimmering electric, incandescent light. He imagines how this train must look to children and adults waiting on various closed station platforms along the Holiday Train's route: mere way-stations now, boarded-up grain sheds for local villages and towns, gone the way of the train age itself but for this one night, as the Holiday Train, burning coal from its tender at a rate of one hundred pounds per mile, steams along the old Great Northern Railroad, a hundred thousand miniature lights aglow about its fifteen trailing cars like the bright curving tail of some glorious Christmastime comet hurtling across the snow.

For a moment the sound of a transistor radio playing Handel's *Messiah* occupies the stillness and the measure of the train's wheels striking the divides. A young boy bedecked in a Great Northern service coat from another century dims the lamps in the carriage. Father Magnusson says a prayer to the patron saint of his Capuchin order, a benediction for those less fortunate and in need of God's blessing, and finally, because he is away from home and because his mother always made him do so before his bed hour as a child, he says the Lord's Prayer.

From within the darkened glass, the reflection of the lamps: flames flickering in miniature, twisting and bending with the rocking of the train. Peering from his window Father Magnusson recognizes nothing, the distance of the plain foreshortened by falling snow so that not even the lights of nearby Lac qui Parle can be seen.

He leans his head, with its tonsure of white hair, fine as a dandelion clock bristle, upon his pillow. Snow taps the glass, wind moans beneath the windows, and the engine's whistle sounds out the long depths of the dark Minnesota countryside. Father Magnusson closes his eyes and sleeps.

Where the wind abates and the shifting drifts momentarily cease, the land—hills and valleys and mountains—becomes visible, and against it, the small outcrops of the living: pinpricks of light flickering and fading abjectly upon the plain as the storm pushes and heaves its indeterminate way across the Northland. Throughout the night the storm buries the land and the people with it. The temperature continues to plummet until, at Mount Cascade, it is the lowest recorded since the great blizzard of 1908. Winds, gusting at eighty miles per hour, press snow into drifts fifteen feet high. The newspaper accounts of that winter will describe tragedy after tragedy, of man and woman and animal lost and frozen in the worst winter blizzard in seventy years.

At Madelia, Alice Walker goes in search of her husband, Gerald, and both succumb, alone, to the cold, never having found each other.

Thomas Johnson, a farmer tending to his cows, freezes to death near Evansville in the north. His two hundred Holsteins freeze as well. In all, some twenty thousand head of livestock will be lost during the storm.

At New Ulm, Robert Kitchner ventures the storm seeking a doctor for his wife, Bonnie, and newborn baby boy, Joshua Michael Kitchner. All three freeze to death on the road to Perdition.

Sixteen schoolchildren, four parents, and a bus driver freeze to death on a bus stranded between Fort Ridgely and Beaverton Falls. The bus is headed toward Raleigh, one of the last way stations from which they can view the Holiday Train's passing.

No one will know the final death count of the storm until the first thaws two months later, when dozens more bodies are recovered in the snowmelt, like the drowned bodies of swimmers emerging from the sea.

When the Festival of Lights Holiday Train is found, an hour or so before dawn, rescuers see the train from far off in the night, its ten vintage Pullman cars outlined by the hundreds of thousands of glittering Christmas lights, the flickering light from the carriage windows casting a hazy and uncertain light through the swirling snow.

As they draw closer, they see the dark bulk of the train and its carriages, its roof and sides bristling with cables and wires that hold still burning bulbs, and the engine stack outlined against the unmoving gray sky.

Narrow bars of amber light spill from the carriage windows and curve across the high rounded snowdrifts pressed against the doors. The engine is cold and has been for most of the night. Everyone appears to be in a slumber, bodies knitted together and joined wherever space allows, beneath the dining car's tables, in the wide berthed carriage seats, their hands clasped in final rigor and in seeming prayer. Father Magnusson lies curled in his seat, his ligature contracted and rigid, his body pulled into itself in the position of a newborn. The transistor radio continues to play, its static, tinny music sounding hollowly throughout the silent carriages.

The thousands of Christmas lights continue to burn, powered by the four Cat diesel generators in the final boxcar, and only in the hours after the rescuers' grim discovery, as more rescuers arrive aboard mechanized snowcats and make their way toward the train from Shilo and Eden, do the generators fail. The lights flicker and then extinguish themselves, blinking out slowly, car by car, until only one car remains illuminated. And then that too fails and the rescuers are plunged into the skipping, fragmented darkness and shadow of their own slashing flashlights and broad headlights, disembodied shapes, voices, hollers, and cries. The absence of wind is broken at intervals by a sudden soft sobbing as a rescuer discovers, among the frozen bodies, a family member, a relative, a friend.

In Thule, at the Blessed House of the Gray Brothers of Mercy, a bell tolls the hour of five A.M., the morning hours of the Divine Office, and a woman appears through the snow. Where Duncan's mother has come from or what roads she has traveled to reach the Capuchin monastery alive, no one knows. This in itself some call a miracle. A portent of something divine amidst the human tragedy.

She rings the night watchman's bell, and then when there is a stirring from within—through the leaded windows a hazy light illuminating the hall—she lays the baby upon the flagstone. The night watchman catches only a glimpse of her through the swirling snow, and if there is a car waiting for her, he sees no sight of it. She is simply gone, lost in the swirling white; the wind is shearing the frozen surface of Lake Cunburnt and howling across the sound and this baby, bundled and protected in a vast layering of sheepskin blanket, is bawling ferociously at his feet.

There is a moment of cessation, when the storm momentarily abates and the sky clears, and the stars begin to fall from the heavens. Brother Canice says that on the night Duncan's mother arrived with him bundled in her arms, he witnessed from the chapel's tower a meteor shower flaring brightly over the Iron Range, and so distinct and singular was its effect that he swears that he heard each meteor's tail hissing—startling chromatic colors momentarily so brilliant that, when he closed his eyes, he saw them still.

The observatory in St. Paul confirms this. There *is* a meteor shower this night—a Leonid meteor shower; the dust grains of Comet Jacobs-Stein, which, in its return to perihelion, has created a meteor storm the likes of which will not be seen for another thirty years. And for those who might look skyward in the one brief moment when the storm pauses, the stars are falling from the heavens and arcing, fluorescent tails flickering, toward the north and a horizon upon which seems to burn a bright golden ring of incandescent fire. Then the night sky collapses back into itself, the stars disappear, and the blizzard rages once more.

Brother Canice leans back his chair, as if considering the narrative, and Duncan does the same. Two myths entwined together and inseparable from the other. Something akin to the Holy Trinity, yet absent the missing part, that part that contains his parents.

Wind moans in the pipe, breathes upon the embers so that they grow bright. Brother Canice sighs, chews loudly on his sunflower seeds and together they watch the glowing embers of wood in the stove pulsing like a heartbeat in the dark.

.   .   .

When Duncan tells this story to other children in the Home, Julie says that he's got it all wrong, that it was, in fact, *her* mother who arrived amidst a snowstorm, the worst storm of the century. And Julie says that her mother didn't lay her at the feet of just any watchman; rather, it was Bishop O'Connor himself who answered the door and into whose arms her mother pressed the small bundle that he would take as one of his own, before she ran off to her world-famous and final performance at the Humboldt Theater in New York City, never to be heard from again. Julie reminds Duncan that he has no memory and that, in his made-up life, he never knows truth from fiction. Billy shakes his head at the both of them and says they've watched Olivia de Havilland in *Whose Baby Are You Now?* one too many times.

But Duncan's not so sure. He doesn't ever remember seeing *Whose Baby Are You Now?*

In the Beginning, Duncan remembers the sense of cold, so strong it stilled his breath, made him feel as if a great weight were constricting his limbs and pressing upon his chest, and amidst this intense cold there was a brilliant white flash of light, stars exploding supernovae, and then falling collapsing, turning in upon themselves; and God's voice calling to him and so much pain and longing and Duncan—not knowing what those things meant then and having no way to say what he felt—just crying, bawling, his lungs filling with the raw, harsh air that seemed to seize in his throat, and nothing to see but blinding white light.

His mother was sitting with her knees up and apart and the room was dark about them. Through a haze of ice and mist, flickering lights swayed back and forth and Duncan was stuck between his mother's thighs, halfway out and halfway between this world and some other. She bent herself forward so that they were looking at each other for the first time; he could just see her there high above him, so very pale, and suddenly he was calm. His mother gritted her teeth; a purple vein pulsed at her temple. He wonders how he looked to her then: calm or complacent or petulant perhaps, a stubborn little thing refusing to budge and not offering help of any kind.

Breathe! Someone hollered and pleaded. You must breathe!

He stared into her eyes and they were filled with pain. Fine red cobwebs of broken capillaries shot through her eyes like inkblots. Red hair lay frozen in sharp-looking crystalline angles to her head. Her body shook and her jaws trembled. Her face, drained of all color, seemed to glisten and shine. In the darkness someone shouted something about his failing heartbeat, and only then, finally, did his mother at last breathe—a great bellowing, spittle-filled cry that steamed the air before them: Son of a Bitch!

Swaddled in a receiving blanket, Duncan watched in the darkness as they sewed her up. She went into shock as they worked on her, and as someone scrambled to plunge a hypodermic into her shuddering thigh, she turned to look at him one last time before her eyes rolled back in her head.

Duncan watched and listened without a voice, and although he couldn't speak, he knew it was God who had spoken to him at the first moment of his birth, just as he knew it was God's light and music he had been born from, and now—the cold, so very cold, and the dark and his mother's ashen blue, pain-washed face.

Brother Canice says it was all a dream, he couldn't possibly remember being born, that Duncan and his mother never saw each other—such a thing was impossible—and even if he could or had, God certainly didn't speak to him. Duncan reminds him that he's special, they all tell him he's special because he was born the night of the storm, and Brother Canice looks at the ceiling and far away, as if he's listening to the children tossing and struggling and moaning in their dreamsleep against the parents who abandoned them here and their anguish like the caterwaul of distant animals, and says slowly, Oh, Duncan, you're special all right.

Perhaps Brother Canice was right. Perhaps it was all a dream. But that is all Duncan remembers: cold and light and pain and God's voice calling to him, the peace he felt looking upon his mother's face even amidst her terrible struggle, and then something akin to sleepwalking for a long, long time.

Then into this constantly shifting gray—with the sense of things half formed and a brief flickering awareness always dimming into shadow—comes music: the faint, distant sound of an old transistor radio and Elvis Presley singing "Blue Moon." And it is raining. Duncan listens to the sound of raindrops tap-tap-tapping glass. Light trembles and shudders upon a far wall, and the shadow of rain trickles down the paint.

He is in a large room that smells slightly of disinfectant, a room that he would later learn the Brothers called the *pellegrinaro*, or sick room: dark wide-board floors burnished brown and gold with patterns of wear upon which moribund light briefly shimmers as if passing through a bowl of murky water; brightly colored frescoes adorning the walls and showing a narrative of some kind: robed figures journeying though pastureland amidst slanting sunlight, huddled men and women clinging to one another beneath tempestuous black clouds, all leading toward a far hill, where three crucifixes rise in stark silhouette. The image presses at his eyes to rise also, and he cranes his neck toward the ceiling, which, some thirty feet above, curves into a pinioned, gilt dome, bordered by elaborate filigree: a fiery ring in which the faces of the saints and martyrs, in bas-relief, stare down at him.

Panicked, he tries to follow the sound of Elvis's voice, for, with

12

his song, there comes peace and a sense of the divine. The transistor radio momentarily crackles and then its sound reverberates, haunting and thin, as if it were traveling the length of some tiled hallway between distant rooms.

He listens to Elvis's fragile, high, crooning voice and for a moment he closes his eyes and lets the sense of it fill him. If there had been a memory in his head of something other, a thought, or dream, he should have fled there and hid, but there was nothing. Nothing he could evoke and nothing in which he might find comfort besides the sound of Elvis.

A small, wizened old man with a large, almost perfectly rounded skull sits with his eyes closed in a chair opposite him, tapping a white walking stick on the floor in time to the music—or perhaps he is listening to another song, some other music somewhere else, deep inside his head, but it doesn't matter, because there is a big smile on his face and Duncan feels his face and realizes that he is smiling as well. Tall, leaded windows are open to the outside and the smell and sounds of the day drift in; Duncan can hear children laughing and shouting in play, and rainwater hissing through trees. He blinks rapidly and then a girl is standing before him, staring intently.

She is tall and pale and has long dark hair that she repeatedly pushes from her face and from her large, serious brown eyes. She is wearing a blue-and-yellow-flowered dress that seems much too small for her, with the hem resting on her thighs, and a soft-looking velvet belt pinching the material tightly about her waist. She leans forward, hands upon white kneecaps, chin thrust out, and regards him intently.

You're awake, she says and raises both hands off her knees. Finally!

Hello, the girl says, extending a narrow hand. My name's Julie.

Duncan remains still; he doesn't know what to do. Finally, Julie lifts his hand from the chair, places it in her own, and pumps it vigorously.

Julie can talk, and she talks in volumes. She tells Duncan that he's been asleep for a long time—she seems to be the only one able to perceive that he was asleep—as long as she's been here, she says, which is a long, long time. My mother dropped me off here when I was a baby, she says. *She* was a famous actress.

Julie stares intently at his face, her brown eyes searching his mouth, his forehead, and hairline, and lastly his eyes, for something—a defect perhaps?

She touches his hand. It's okay, she says. We're harmless. Her fingers are cool and reassuring and tender. Gradually, Duncan loosens his grip upon the armrests.

How old are you? he asks, and his voice sounds strange to his ears—immense and cavernous. It's as if he has bellowed the words, but the girl doesn't hear him, and he must repeat himself. She leans forward and there is the scent of her hair and the rustle of her clothes as she moves.

The same age as you, Julie says. I'm ten.

And that, that's Billy Bowen, she whispers, and then kicks the old man's stick with her shoe. Hey, Billy, she says. Hey.

Billy opens his eyes and they are large ovals, the dark blue irises occupying all. Billy, Julie tells Duncan, is a nine-year-old boy trapped in the body of an eighty-year-old man—he suffers from the rare disease progeria—and Duncan stares at him and Billy shrugs. It's okay, he says, I'm meant to do something special. This is just my disguise.

Julie pats his knee. Yes, she says, her brow furrowed and her lips pursed with conviction. It's a good disguise, Billy.

The notes of Elvis's "Blue Moon" are fading again, and in the song's echo and reverb there is a tremulous, hesitant quality that makes Duncan pause. And then the song ends and there is silence, and in that silence Duncan wonders if he has merely imagined the song. A delicate wind sighs in the crooked alleys above the windows, and there is a soft slapping sound of sandals on wet concrete outside. A crystalline metal peal breaks the silence: a bell tolling the hour. The sound is oddly familiar, and, with Elvis gone, he finds a strange comfort in that.

I think I'm supposed to do something special too, Duncan says, and Billy smiles at him.

You'll need a disguise, he says.

YOU COULD SEE the Home for miles. It rose upon a hill between farmed valleys and the mining range and looked as if it did not belong to that part of the Midwest at all but rather as if it were a dwelling from Western Europe or Britain of five hundred years before, with its chevet and buttressed bell tower, its Romanesque archways and gilt-roofed chapels, beehive oratories and Cistercian-Gothic chancellery. Turning your gaze east and west on that Thule hillside, in the brisk autumn air, you see the landscape of the Home and of the Minnesota plains: the sweep of terrace and playing field, the perimeter wall with its red bricks glowing as if heated by flame, and, beyond the wall, the farms and rugose hills and highlands of coniferous forests and the far, wide crown of the Iron Range; the red peaks of dairy farms, of galvanized sheet-metal grain silos sparking silver; wooded up-lands, fat white clouds blurring and breaking apart in the blustery twilit pewter-blue sky.

The immensity of the land gathered you in and pressed you toward the monastery's stone walls, covered with hanging ivy whose leaves were a warm burnt orange, curved wide and open at their ends to receive you like welcome arms into the shelter of its mortared and gardened depths. Its halls and courtyards and prayer rooms held the memory and the ghosts of the dead: influenza patients from World War I, and, from later, those with tuberculosis, and later still, mad young men returned home with arms and limbs and minds missing, left behind in parts of Europe and Africa and Asia. Day after day and night after night, amidst the constant low hum of prayer, Duncan can still hear the ghostly echo of these men and their wide-mouthed screams filled with the nightmare of war.

To the Capuchins who ran it, the abbey was known as the Blessed House of Gray Fathers of Mercy. To the children, it was simply the Home, for it was all they knew. The Home held their lives, their bodies and their souls, in its care. They were the children of God, and nothing but nothing could touch them there in that place, not if they were good. God would not let it. Father Toibin used to tell them this, remind them that if they trusted in God and had faith, then they would always be safe, no matter what else had befallen them.

Duncan's dormitory leads off the main hallway on the second floor of the east eave of the Home. It is a small room with eight metal beds—four on either side—and damp: the wallpaper has come away from the wall at the seams and at the top of the ceiling and along the baseboards. The plaster beneath is gray and dark with moisture; in places it is swollen or chalky and soft where it has begun to crumble.

From outside comes the sound of children running upon the flagstones, and laughter. A faint red band of refracted light shimmers like a stain upon the ceiling. Cautiously, Duncan climbs from the bed and peers out the window. A fine latticework of ice frosts the glass like a shattered prism; he scrapes at the ice and, through the fog-bloom of his breath, looks out across the valley. The sun is sinking toward the prairie and there is a thickening of reddish light as everything becomes compressed into that low space above the horizon.

With his face pressed against the cold glass, he continues to stare out at the strange landscape that surrounds him and at the dark walkway that stretches across the courtyard to the chapel. The bell for supper sounds, and a Brother begins to light the lamps throughout the cloister. The lamps on the walkway have yet to be lit, and children are dark shapes passing before slanting bars of amber light cast from the chapel's high arched windows. As they move toward the doors of the dining hall and kitchen, their footfalls clatter upon the stone and their laughter resonates in the chill air—a sound that both scares Duncan and makes him wish that he were one of them.

An hour before sunrise the Brothers stir for Lauds and in the kitchen firewood wheezes and splinters apart in the cast-iron stove. Through its grill Duncan sees twisting flames, sparks of cinder, and the severed stumps, chopped by an ax. From the campanile, Brother Canice tolls the morning bells, and slowly the children emerge from their rooms. One moment the kitchen table is empty of people and then, suddenly, everyone is sitting around it, thumping, scraping chairs, wielding spoons, and, in great shoveling motions, loudly slurping porridge.

And the bells continue to peal, maddeningly, crazily, and Duncan can see Brother Canice beneath the belfry, his wide head and heavy limbs, the great weight of him jumping upon the cottonstave ropes, throwing himself up and down and back and forth against the walls of the bell tower, heaving the bells up and down, and swaying frantically, desperately, from the rope's end, as if, with the effort, he is trying to extinguish something corrupt within himself.

The Brothers stand by the hot stoves in rolled-up sleeves, their white aprons stained with meat juice and offal. A novitiate stirs the contents of a pot over an iron trivet. Another pulls loaves of bread from the oven. There is the steam of cooking, the sounds of clattering pots, scraping plates, and dropped cutlery. One of the Brothers turns on a radio to *The Gardening Hour*, raises the volume over the clanging bells. Old Father Wilhelm trudges slowly through the room to the Great Hall and smiles blearily at the children, as if he has momentarily forgotten who they are and where he is.

Weak rain dribbles down the windowpanes, and two frail lightbulbs hang bare from frayed electric cords sprouting from the cracked plaster ceiling. Sheeting gray upon the wide transom glass, in greater and greater billows, the rain bends and warps the view of the landscape beyond. Duncan shivers and pushes the bowl across the ragged wood. Then he thinks of the hours before supper, the day stretching in such a determinate and yet seemingly endless manner before night, and pulls the bowl back to him. Julie looks up from her own bowl and smiles. Billy nods; his cane taps the floor like the meter of a clock counting the slow minutes of these days.

After breakfast Duncan stands along the stone wall at the rear of the chapel, stomps his worn Sorel boots against the frozen gravel to warm his toes, presses his mittens tightly against his ears, and watches the other children in the yard at play. Then his attention shifts toward the horizon and the pastureland upon the plain that, in undulating valleys, gradually rises toward the hardwood forests of the north and the Iron Range. Turning away from the other children, he journeys the boundaries of the Home, the walls and enclosed gardens, the arbors and the frozen pond with its dusting of snow, upon which he can make out the tracks of a small animal. He walks the grounds and everything seems oddly familiar—it's as if he has been here before in a dream of falling snow and fire.

Later, when he tells Father Tobin of what he sees and hears and feels, Father Tobin will smile and place his hand upon Duncan's chest and Duncan will feel the weight of the hand, callused and hard from years of field labor, against his heart.

But Duncan, he will say, you already know what that is. It is God in everything around you. It's what you've said from the very beginning. It is God talking to you.

And Duncan will laugh inside because Father Tobin understands and because Father Tobin must hear God in his world also, and in these moments it is not so important that he can not always make sense of the words but only that they are.

DR. MATHIAS IS a tall, wiry, shortsighted man; he wears round, thick spectacles that make his eyes seem watery and small, yet when he removes his spectacles, his eyes are voluminous and startled. In occupying so much of his lean, badly shaven face, his eyes seem to take in the entirety of the room as they scan the space before them blindly. There is desperation in those eyes, a panic that Duncan feels he knows, full with the sense of being abandoned and lost and unsure of oneself. Then he returns his spectacles to the bridge of his nose and his eyes recede and float in the dark and murky waters of those thick lenses as he adjusts himself in his seat, his hand pulling at the crotch of his trousers, and regards Duncan from some great, unimpassioned distance.

I wasn't here, Duncan says to him.

They're sitting in Dr. Mathias's office in the dormer that encircles the prayer room. Like all the rooms on the exterior of the Home, it looks out upon the grounds, and beyond, the rolling green pastureland of Thule and Stockholdt. The light and the scented air are dizzying. Duncan feels as if he could sleep.

Of course you were here, Dr. Mathias says. You've been withdrawn for quite some time, I'll grant you, but you've been here, mind and body. I've seen you twice a week for as long as I can remember. I've spoken with you. I've seen you playing with other children about the monastery.

You have to realize, Duncan, that you and so many of the other children here have been dealt a terrible blow. The absence or loss of a parent creates a hole inside us—just as all loss does—that we find all different ways to fill, but we can never fill it fully. And what is left are the echoes of that trauma. Never mind the trauma you experienced when you first arrived as a baby suffering from sever hypothermia, the night of the storm. You may have experienced a simple psychogenic amnesia that is common among children who have suffered some type of trauma, and very common to children of an orphanage. Dr. Mathias slaps his hands upon his knees, where his corduroy pants have worn to a shine, as if they have reached some kind of agreement, and says, But you've definitely been here, Duncan.

Duncan doesn't reply. Instead he focuses on the physical world about him, those things that remind him God is close by: the ribbed stone archways, the steeples, and buttresses of the monastery; the stained rosette glass above the chancel; rain misting the glass and pooling upon the bowed stone; the clatter of the Brothers' sandals in the stairwells, and the thrum of prayer that resonates like a slow, steady wing-beat in the cloister's walkways from the oratories and chapel.

And then there are words, the rounded, fluid, liquid feel of them pouring from his mouth and creating something out of nothing—he trusts in their precision and in the objects they create. He trusts in their imperviousness, and, once uttered, their irrevocable destiny. Father Tobin would say that they are given from God also. In his mind he speaks the words aloud: Rosette. Chancel. Rain. Scapular. Chrysanthemum. Magnesium. Granite. Crucifix. Doctor. Priest. Brother. *Billy. Julie.*

Well, if you weren't here, where were you? Dr. Mathias raises his eyebrows; the question persists.

Duncan stares at his boots.

Somewhere else, he says.

Except Duncan can't remember anything let alone where he was before he was ten, before Elvis's voice woke him up in the Home and Julie was staring at him and knew that he was finally awake. When he tells Julie that he remembers being born and God speaking to him, she says she believes him and he believes that she does and that makes him feel good and as if he doesn't need to worry about explaining it anymore. But he's stopped telling Dr. Mathias that he remembers being born and God speaking to him because he knows he doesn't believe him. Dr. Mathias says that Duncan often experiences night terrors, and that in these night terrors he wakes screaming and sweating with fever. It might take Duncan half an hour or more to calm down and then he would fall back to sleep. In the morning he would remember none of it, but perhaps some of these dreams, these terrors, stay with him. He asks Duncan to think about why God spoke to him when he was born and why he can't remember anything else. *Why?* Duncan has no answer to such questions, and how could he possibly know why God should choose to speak to *him*? What kind of question is that?

THE HOME WAS built in the middle of the eighteenth century by the Capuchin Padre Martin de Lupe and his followers, the last of the Spanish missionaries, a fractured group of friars, brothers, Redemptorists, ascetics, Gnostics, and priests from the Northwest missionary trail who came across the Minnesota plains aboard Conestoga wagons as winter turned to spring, and to them the verdant undulating land seemed touched by the hand of God. They built a small farming community, lumbered the vast evergreens and white pine, planted crops from seeds they'd carried with them almost two thousand miles: wheat, corn, and barley. They ploughed and excavated the prairie of stone and built their first chapel and small grain mill; they dug ditches and silage fields and hewed rock and wood, mined the ore of the Iron Range and, slowly, under the patriarchate of Padre Martin de Lupe, over thirty-six years they built the Blessed House of Gray Brothers of Mercy.

But no one mentions Padre Martin de Lupe anymore. His name

has been stricken from the Litany of Saints and from the blessings and benedictions, but the histories in the library reference him still: a man who might have been beatified if not for the events of 1815, but was instead hanged in the Home's gardens for raping and murdering a local farm girl who had sought asylum there from her father. A black-and-white image of him remained: *The Hanged Priest of the Garden*. In the picture there is no sign of the lake that is there now or the arboretum. Only the tree remains, an ancient elm spotted black with disease.

Duncan thinks of Padre Martin de Lupe often. He is a ravager of children, the Black Angel who lurks in the wine cellar and in the catacombs and labyrinths, in the empty casket hold and charnel house, and who, to this day, haunts the children's graveyard, cradling the worsted, fleshy knot of his broken neck and his head, cantered at a broken angle against his right shoulder, from the back of which hangs a great wing that drags a yard upon the ground, and when he speaks, his voice is a hiss, a gasp, and, quite possibly, the last thing you will ever hear.

The Black Angel will get you—this is what the novitiates tell the children to scare them on nights when the film projector has been set up in the playroom and the cicadas are droning outside in the muggy, tumescent night and the black, glistening trees seem to drip with moisture and insects are falling and crackling on the bug zapper in flashes of strange epileptic light. Later they will hear him making his way from the children's graveyard and then plodding upon the stone toward their bedrooms. The Black Angel who never sleeps and who looks up at the windows of the sleeping children at night just waiting for the right moment to climb the crumbling stone walls like some misshapen spider, to crawl beneath their barely parted window, leaving a viscous trail upon the sill, and into their bedrooms, where he will spread his great maggot-infested wings in a great dihedral before embracing their souls and pulling them to his black breast.

Father Toibin rages whenever he discovers the novitiates have been talking about Padre Martin de Lupe to the children, who are both shocked and pleased by his maddened fits. After hearing of the most recent macabre tale, he comes into Father Malachy's morning classroom and, standing before them, looks upon their ashen faces. His voice resonates off the timbers and about the walls: *In whose care do you entrust your bodies and your souls?*

In God's care, Duncan and other children chant in unison, and Father Malachy joins in as well, his eyes glistening with fervor.

In whose love can darkness never take hold?

In God's love, they chorus. His fire feeds their passion, and they feel lifted from their chairs with it. Had he asked, they would have stormed from the room and yoked the nearest novitiate to the Hanging Tree in the manner of Padre de Lupe and of the Old Testament with the Chosen laying waste to the temples of the Idolaters.

But when the sun goes down and shadows creep across the courtyard and cold comes running from the northern plains, and the lights flicker and the children's breaths steam the crepuscular light, and the lands that surround the Home seem so vast as to be impenetrable and from their windows they see the vastness of that plain upon which here and there a small farmhouse flickers with a light that seems as distant as the stars, then everything changes.

When Brother Wilhelm dampens the lantern wicks with a shaking, palsied hand after they have brushed their teeth and said their prayers and climbed into bed, and all light is extinguished, the only thing that remains is the scent of tallow smoke, ash, and wax, and the crucifix that glows blue from the center of the wall. Duncan listens to the whimper of scared children tossing in their sleep, dreaming of the Black Angel and of mothers and fathers who were once there, perhaps, and are now gone, or of those shadowy adult figures who lurk in the dark of their minds and never leave. Perhaps it is a simple longing for that which they've never had, and such an absence makes them call out in the night.

He imagines what his past must have been like, and there are times when he believes that he can almost will it into existence. He has a mother and even a father, gray, silvery-backed amorphous things that periodically solidify into shapes with limbs and strangely famil-iar, sad features—he sees them standing in some doorway, his bed-room perhaps, the lamp-lit hallway aglow behind them preventing him from seeing them clearly though he is aware that they are look-ing in on him and safeguarding him as he leeps—only to drift apart in the ether so that he cannot draw them together again in his mind. He stares at the ceiling of his room and feels his brow tense with the effort to will them back into some acceptable shape, but it is no use; they are gone and he cannot retrieve them. There is the scent of tal-low and cigarette smoke—perhaps the faint trace of perfume? A man's aftershave or cologne? Of dry wood and bright recently painted walls unlike the damp-mold-spore taint here, with the permanent stains upon the walls and ceilings and the dewy, greasy consistency of the damp pillow beneath his head.

About him the other boys sigh and moan and exhale in their sleep like some great incoming and withdrawing tide—the moan of the relentless sea—and as he listens and closes his eyes, he is rocked by the sound of it and knows that strange comfort that comes with familiar-ity, despite the sadness and fear and emptiness the sounds of their sleep evoke, and why very often he leaves his bed and pads to the kitchen in search of Brother Canice.

TONIGHT DUNCAN WAITS for Brother Canice to toll the bells for Matins, listens to the peal of the bells, their soft rising and falling, and, finally, their ebb—glad on this particular night for Brother Canice's restraint—before he gets up and treads the hall. Like some strange psychic reverberation that reaches out to touch them in the night, they know when the other is awake and this is where they know they'll find each other, placing wood in the stove, stoking the embers, putting the kettle up for tea, or spooning milk warming in a saucepan upon the Titan with the windows frozen and the walls creaking slightly as, outside, ice hardens and shifts, splinters with long, dull cracking sounds upon the stone and clapboard.

Brother Canice has just placed two mugs of steaming milk upon the charred and battered woodblock table and is sitting in the near dark before the woodstove when Duncan patters in upon stockinged feet. The old black-and-white with its rabbit-ear antenna wrapped in tinfoil flickers soundless images, casts them upon the wall.

28

You're not sleeping again? Brother Canice grumbles, his lower lip bunched with sunflower seeds.

Neither are you, Duncan says.

Brother Canice shrugs, spits casually into the grate, then: You're not wearing your slippers either. He shakes his head. You'll end up getting sick walking these cold floors. I won't be responsible for you getting sick.

I'll wear them next time, Duncan says, and when Brother Canice continues to stare at him, he adds, I promise.

Chilblains, that's what you'll get—chilblains. And they're no fun. Trust me. Brother Canice spits into the grate, lifts the hem of his cassock, stoops to pry off his shoes, and then vigorously rubs his feet together, one on top of the other, first the left and then the right, so hard it looks as if it must hurt.

He opens the grate with a soiled dish towel and throws another long onto the flames. His face is momentarily illuminated by flame-light: orange and crimson and then dark sliding down his brow, his wide, full cheeks. He closes the door and sits back with a grunt onto his chair.

What was it like, he asks suddenly, God talking to you?

Duncan looks at him. He's never asked him this before.

I mean, was it a big whooshing sound or something, or did he actually speak?

I thought you didn't believe that God spoke to me.

I'm just asking a question. It doesn't have to mean a thing.

I don't know. It's hard to explain. You just know, that's all.

When I was young, I used to hear the sound of my heart beating on my pillow, you know, through my ear, and I thought it was God.

Brother Canice considers what he has just said for a moment, and adds: Or perhaps it's only now that I think it was God. Do you ever do that? Put your ear up against your pillow and listen to that thumping, like footsteps shaking the heavens.

Brother Canice shakes his head. That's why you can't sleep, he says and keeps at his feet. It's like watching a dog scratching fleas. When he's done, he sighs and stands, pushes the tins aside on the shelf, and lifts down his old Vulcanite transistor radio.

Here, take this, he says and places it on the table. Its black resin is stained and blurred by grime, the back disfigured and partially melted from the heat of its transistor tubes. Brother Canice chews on his sun-flower seeds and stares pensively at it as he spits and his seeds hiss and whistle in the stove. It's a radio, he says and raps his knuckles sharply against its top as if to confirm this.

It's yours. You listen to it and see what it tells you. When I was a boy, I'd listen to it late at night and it told me things, things only I could understand. Once it even told me my future. If that doesn't work, you can always listen to music.

Duncan wants to ask Brother Canice if he is truly a Brother or merely an imposter, and if this is the future that the radio spoke of, but he holds his tongue. Brother Canice stares at Duncan, unblinking, chewing his seeds like cud, holding their edges between the tips of his yellow teeth, and Duncan reaches out and, saying thank you, takes the radio.

Perhaps it will help you sleep, Brother Canice says and shrugs. It never worked for me.

After reciting the rosary again, Duncan climbs into bed and turns the radio's knob low, watching as the deep-set black and gold fre-quency dial fills with warm amber light and, slowly, as the tubes glow through the partially melted back, the hum of electricity buzzing softly through the speakers and the smell of rubber thickening in the room.

He scans across the radio's wavelengths, picking up meager sig-nals here and there, and finally listening to the beeps and squeaks of satellites passing twenty-two thousand miles overhead as he waits for some other sound to emerge from the speakers. He doesn't know what he's waiting for exactly, perhaps the sound of his mother or father or some other ghost from his past to come crackling and spitting through the ether with news of his future.

PARASOMNIAS, OR SLEEP problems, are common in childhood, Dr. Mathias says, and Duncan has to remind himself that the doctor is speaking and he must concentrate on his words. Clouds pass above the skylight in his office and the room turns ashen; the light trembles as clouds thin or thicken and then rain clouds move in and Dr. Mathias switches on a floor lamp next to his desk, illuminating his mahogany desk and turning the finely polished wood a rich, translucent brown.

Dr. Mathias clears his throat and begins again: A distinction is made between problems that are abnormal, such as sleep apnea and narcolepsy, and problems that are behavioral in origin, such as night terrors, somnambulism, and enuresis.

E–N–U–R–E–S–I–S, Duncan speaks aloud. *Enuresis*.

Dr. Mathias frowns, clearly irritated by his intrusion. Duncan, there is no need to do that with your mouth. You do not need to contort it in such a manner. You enunciate your words perfectly well. You speak perfectly well.

And then he sighs. Yes. Bedwetting. But, of course, you do not wet the bed, Duncan. That is not what we're talking about here.

As far as Dr. Mathias is concerned, the only thing wrong with Duncan is that he has suffered from a range of sleeping disorders that many children his age are prone to.

This is nothing to be alarmed about, he exclaims. He tells Duncan that he is an extremely shy and anxious young boy but that, too, is nothing to worry about; it is merely the "type" of boy he is and there is no point in mucking about and trying to make him into something he's not, now is there? Absolutely not.

A few fat raindrops thump the glass and then the clouds are gone and the late-afternoon sun is shining brightly through the windows and Duncan wonders what Billy and Julie are doing and whether Father Tobin is playing baseball with the other kids in the field behind the chapel. Dr. Mathias sighs and switches off the lamp.

These parasomnias that we're talking about, Duncan—and he waves at the air—these sleep disorders, they're episodic in nature and are a reflection of central nervous system immaturity. Thus, they are more common in children than in adults and are generally outgrown with time. There is often a family history positive for them. Perhaps your mother or your father?

I don't have a father, Duncan says. I was born without a father. Just like Jesus. Duncan makes sure not to mention God, but even so, Dr. Mathias's face has a look of displeasure, as if he's sucked on something bitter. Duncan only meant to mention Jesus as a comparison; he knows he is not Jesus, and now wishes he could take it back. But then he is angry. If Dr. Mathias cared at all, he never would have mentioned his mother or father. If he knew him in the way that he says he does and has sat here with him twice a week, every week, year after year, then he would know that his mother abandoned him and that she was alone when she did, perhaps as alone as he is now. Briefly he wonders, as he often does, what his mother might be doing at that moment or whether she is dead, and what she looks like inside her coffin beneath the dirt: pale and still and as beautiful as he remembers from his dreams, twined around in a shroud of white root-tendrils from plants and bushes and small trees above ground.

Dr. Mathias looks at Duncan, pushes out his bottom lip, and rubs at it.

It's not a good or bad thing that you may have inherited this from either one of your parents, Duncan; it just is.

I don't have a father, Duncan says.

Dr. Mathias clears his throat and continues. As a group, these disorders are quite sudden yet predictable in their appearance in the sleep cycle, nonresponsive to environmental manipulation and characterized by—

He stares at the charts around his room, upon the wall, at the hagiography of ebbing sunlight flickering through the bushes outside the warped glass and at play on his fine mahogany desk, and then he looks at Duncan, one eyebrow raised in unflinching and unforgiving appraisal. Parabolas of light curve and slide across his thick spectacles.

Yes, he says, and grunts, strokes the air with a stick of unused chalk, quite naturally characterized by a retrograde amnesia. The origin of your disorder may, indeed, be the trauma we spoke of or a greater traumatic event that we have yet to uncover.

The rain returns and the room darkens and they listen to raindrops pelting the skylight and Dr. Mathias sighs and reaches over to turn on the lamp again.

February 1981

DARKNESS HAS FALLEN and the children are in their beds and it is rapidly growing colder; tonight the temperatures are predicted to plummet to minus twenty degrees, and there has been talk of snow. The children of the Home know the schedule of the furnace as intimately as they do the bell tolling the hours of the Holy Office. They know that if you do not fall asleep before the furnace goes off, you will not sleep because of the cold, and you will not feel a reprieve of warmth again until just before dawn. You learn this, if you are old enough, within your first two weeks at the Home—if you've arrived during the summer, you are already prepared for this divine inevitability by everything else the Home has taught you—and you make sure that you are asleep before the cold touches you, that you are asleep before ten P.M., when Brother Wilhelm turns the thermostat down to forty-five, and you pray that you will be asleep by the hour

Brother Canice tolls the bell for Vigil, at midnight, or else you will be watching your chilled breath smoking the air for hours to come.

Duncan is unable to sleep, and instead listens, waiting for morning and for the electric ticking and then the spark that he knows signals the furnace to ignite. His toes feel numb. He rubs at his nose to dispel the cold and to work the hardened snot. He imagines the final hours of the people aboard the Holiday Train during the winter of 1970, the year he was born, and abandoned to the Home. He begins to shiver with the cold and even when the furnace thumps into life and hot water steams in the pipes he cannot control the chill that has taken hold of him. He pulls the sheets and blankets over his head and curls into a small shape beneath the blankets; when he lifts his head, his breath smokes the air. Eventually he rises and goes downstairs to the kitchen where a fire still burns in the woodstove, but there is no sign of Brother Canice. He sits on a hard-backed chair and listens to the wood crackling and popping in the cast-iron grate.

He falls asleep and wakes to lights shimmering in the distance. He rises and experiences a moment of confusion, a strange disembodiedness as his body betrays him. The flickering lights add to the sense of dislocation. He feels no attachment to the limbs that paddle the darkness before him, rather he is looking upon a boy stumbling, sleepwalking through the snow. On the hill before him, perhaps a quarter mile away, he sees the thirteen cars outlined against the sky and the flickering Christmas lights of the Holiday Train. His feet drag him on as if with a will entirely their own, and though he resists—he wants to turn back toward the retreating lights of the monastery—the distance between himself and the train grows shorter and shorter.

His arms are about him but he can no longer feel them; a sweet calm settles itself upon his thoughts and everything seems to slow. He knows that if only he pushes forward, ignoring the cold, the hollowness of his bones, the emptiness that seems to fill him and that is gradually replaced by a slow liquid warmth, he will discover something wondrous. On the hill before him he is certain there lies illumination and an understanding of the type that only God grants. The drifts rise to his thighs and he seems to sink deeper and deeper with each step forward. He can see the vintage Pullman cars, ice gleaming across their red and green bodies and upon their curved roofs. From the wide windows a strange light casts its glow and the silhouettes of people within the cars move through this light, their shadows elongated and curved upon the snowdrifts, and there is the sound of voices and of laughter, of music crackling through an old radio's tinny speakers.

In front of him a blurred shape appears, becoming more and more distinct as he nears the train. And he knows before he can fully see her that this figure standing before him in the glow of the miniature lights with the storm raging about her is his mother. She stands at the edge of light cast by the Christmas lights, a light so brilliant in its incandescence that it extends twenty feet or so across the wind-polished snow. Her clothes are cloyed and damp with snow and her head is covered with a dark scarf, but how white her face is! How radiant and glowing!

Light fragments, shifts, and fractures through the billows of snow so that at times his mother appears so near that he feels he can touch her and at other times she is a figure retreating, moving away across the plain. She speaks to him, and though it is cold, he does not feel cold, wrapped as he is in the warmth and peace of her presence and the low, soft hush of her voice. But now it begins to snow, heavy and thick, and the wind is gusting, pressing the snow slantways so that she sways and shimmers blurrily and then he can no longer see. All sight and sound is obliterated; only the wind and snow and cold remain and he bends his head into it.

He sleeps again, and wakes sitting in one of the wide chairs of a Pullman carriage, looking out over the frozen landscape and the far glittering bell tower of the monastery. A transistor radio is playing Handel's *Messiah* and he is filled with a sense of exhilaration now, the glorious feeling of no longer being alone, no longer stranded to the wastes of Minnesota with a hundred abandoned children just like him.

The slate-gray sky is slowly turning bluish at the farthest edges of the horizon and the mountains of the Iron Range begin to take shape, white mist rolling from the conifers in the clefts of the valley, snow sheeting the upper peaks. He leaves the train and follows his footsteps back through the snow.

Through the fields he trudges and now, here and there, candlelight sparks in windows of the farmhouses he passes, and he sees movement within. Smoke drifts from chimneys into the cold, clear air, and there is a pain in his heart as he glimpses through kitchen windows the glow of wood fires and tables with families gathered around them for breakfast and the doors closed and frost on the barred windowpanes, and him with nowhere to go but back across the fields to the Home.

Down to the pond, and so through the courtyard, the walkway skinned with a gleaming ice, and by the chapel, deserted and silent so early in the morning before Lauds, window shutters still stamped shut and behind them sleeping girls and boys. He sees them curled up in bed, rows upon rows of them, stretching into infinity, all curled into fetal position as in a time prior to their birth, before their abandon.

Awake now, and a flame to his face, blinding. A dead weight bears him down, his aching back, his blistered feet. Slowly, his senses come back to him. The floor beneath him, cold and hard. Spittle drooling from his mouth. There comes a pressure and pull on his shoulders, urging him up. Fingers, a hand, a face floating pale in the darkness: Billy.

Duncan, are you all right?

Billy, he says. Did you see her? Did you see my mother?

Billy looks into his eyes—each time he sees Billy's eyes in his mind he is reminded of their beauty and the heartbreaking knowledge that each time he stares into them he can never stop himself from thinking, however fleetingly, *He is going to die soon*. Billy considers what to say and is searching for the right words. A mouse is gnawing in the kitchen cabinets. Something—a small tree branch or some other windblown object—skitters down the roof.

Yes, Duncan. I saw your mother. She's beautiful.

The wood in the stove has burned down to crackling embers and the chill of the night creeps quickly into the kitchen. Duncan's feet soon fall numb upon the tiles and he looks down at them. On the floor, tracked from the door at the far end of the vestibule and surrounded by melting snow, dirt, and leaves, his bare footprints glisten wetly.

Duncan, Billy says, staring at the floor, his eyes wide with wonder. Where have you been?

Duncan's fingertips and toes suffer a mild frostbite and develop soft, red, pinched lesions. In a warm room, after coming in out of the cold, they swell as blood rushes brightly into them and then they begin to itch and burn as if he'd been pricked by a needle. Julie rubs a salve over them to help but the only time he feels any relief is at night when Father Wilhelm lowers the thermostat and all warmth leaves the rooms. Brother Canice looks at Duncan's feet when he comes into the kitchen and shakes his head and says I told you you'd get chilblains if you didn't wear your slippers.

The nights continue to shorten; soon there is still light at five o'clock, and when Mass ends and the Brothers are calling the children to supper, the courtyard is lit by the last bright angles of sunlight fading over the hillside and the lamplights come on shining blurrily through a warm mist that drifts slowly across the grounds, altering all sense of distance and space and sound. And so that strange and divine moment in which Duncan had seen his mother passes even before he can really and truly hold it to his heart and, for a little while, he stops thinking about her altogether.

39

I have sometimes dreamed that from time to time hours detached themselves from the lives of the angels and came here below to traverse the destinies of men.

—VICTOR HUGO

April 1981

AFTER FATHER MAGNUSSON's Requiem Mass, in the storm of 1970, his body was placed in the monastery's charnel house, where it lay for two months among the skulls and bones of the past until the thaw of spring, when the ground could finally be hacked at with shovels and pickaxes and gouged open by a backhoe. The novitiates say that the permittivity of the Home's charnel house is unlike any other, that it's a natural conduit for spirits, for demons, and for miracles. Perhaps that is why Billy, Julie, and Duncan find themselves drawn to this place: it has a memory and a sense of what has come

40

and gone, and the spirits here hold on to what remains, much like the children do with their dreams and their wishes.

At the edge of the Garden of Holy Martyrs, the charnel house is a place rarely visited by other children or by priests, and only rarely by Mrs. Bergin, the monastery's Swedish charwoman, but almost every day of the spring, after Father Malachy's class, they come here. Sixteen whitewashed flagstone steps lead down to its arched, Byzantium entranceway. The door is made of maple three inches thick and decorated with the symbols of the lamb and the dove. You push open the door and step within and, as your eyes adjust to the shifting hues of shadow and light, you smell incense of storax and cascarilla, smoky ash and loam, the clear distinct metallic scent of running water.

The charnel house is made up of a dozen or so barrel vaults, each fronted by finely wrought metal bars and gates through which the remains of the dead can be viewed—the bleached and aged skulls arranged facing out so that the Brothers and penitents can stare into the faces of the dead.

In the center of the chamber, beneath the high domed skylight, is St. John's Fountain, made of rough-hewn stone and from which well water gurgles and pools in a font, and then passes back into the stone once more to a natural subterranean cistern. When they are thirsty, they cup their hands and drink from its stone font, where the water is continuously rushing and cold and so clear that they can see the stone bottom of the well, sparkling with mica and quartz, even as the water churns and bubbles and cascades from the stone lip. They clench their teeth with the cold and Billy's eyes seem all the bluer for the pleasurable shock of it.

At the far end of the room, beyond the fountain, stairs lead to storage and to the old refectory, a long, narrow room where the Brothers and the bishop sat for meals a hundred years before the monastery became an orphanage and hospice for children. Along the staircase to the old refectory are niches with the remains of Brothers and Unknowns, children orphaned at the Home with no record and no name and no grieving parent. Some seem to be little more than babies, and Duncan imagines cradling one of their skulls in his hands and gently covering the shattered and as yet unformed fontanele, providing it the protection it never received in life.

Julie dances through sunlight cast from the high-domed glass at the center of the ceiling. She lifts the hem of her dress and her pale legs seems to dissolve as she steps through the shafts of light; the slight muscles in her thighs flex and strain as she pushes off one foot and then the other. As she dances, she recites the tale of her abandonment at the Home and of her mother's stardom. Her words resound in the hollow barrel vaults of the stone room and off the casks, barrels of wax and pitch, the jars of pickled vegetables and meats stored for the long winter.

My mother is a Great Actress, she says, and intones in an exaggerated English accent, a Great Actress who left me here to hone my theatrical skills. Allow me to introduce myself, fellow thespians. I am Madame Julie Preston, of the Royal Thule Academy! And now, let me perform for you my own special rendition of Preston Coldwater's *Patti and Belle*!

Bees drone lazily in the air. Sitting on the floor and leaning against the wall, Billy and Duncan nod sluggishly as Julie dances in the heat, dances until her dress is plastered to her skin, her bare feet slapping the stone. They are the audience to her mother's final dramatic performance at the Humboldt Theater in New York City, a week after Julie was left at the home.

Watching, Duncan feels the air humming at his fingertips as if it is a charged, violent thing, stirred from its sleeping suspension by Julie's emotions. He sits as though entranced and listens to the minute, almost imperceptible reverberations of the charnel house and the Home. Dust motes tumble in frenetic cartwheels in the bright shafts of white light.

When she is done, Julie bows and the white, center part in her hair is visible. Duncan and Billy applaud as she sits, and Duncan's heart quickens at the sight of sweat gleaming upon the insides of her thighs and in the naked, hollow spaces at the back of her knees. She sighs, leans against the cool wall, and looks upward. On the domed ceiling there is a painted sky of varying shades of blue, white clouds, and a thousand silver stars, all arranged in distinct constellations. And in the center of this is the skylight through which the true sky is visible.

Even the children's graveyard can only hold so many bodies, Julie says, sighing, for these are some of the things she knows about the monastery. Often she reminds them that she has been here the longest. Stay with me, she says, mimicking Father Toibin, and nothing will touch you.

She nods toward the barrel vaults and toward the stairs beneath, where the babies are interned. After the corpse has decayed, its remains are brought here, she continues, or to St. Katrine's ossuary in Stockholdt. This is where they brought the dead from the blizzard of '70, the winter my mother abandoned me here.

All those people aboard the train?

The train, the fields, all the homes about Thule. I think it was thirty or forty in all.

The children too?

The children too.

From the far vault a host of blank, grinning skulls stares back. Duncan looks at the hollowed cavities of the eyes sockets, the flared holes of the nostrils, and the bare, gleaming row of cruel-looking teeth on the exposed jawbone, and wonders which ones belong to the dead of the Holiday Train. But of course they are not here—they were placed in the ground as soon as it could receive them that spring.

What about you, Billy? he asks. Duncan must stare at him for a moment until the image of the skulls is gone and there is only Billy before him, pale and wizened and chewing on his cracked lips and looking much like a skull himself. When Julie admonishes him, Billy stops and purses them thoughtfully instead.

My father was a Green Beret, he says. Fought in Vietnam and won the Purple Heart. Got shot—

In the butt, Julie says.

—in the . . ., Billy laughs, in the butt!

Their laughter resounds in the large stone expanse. Water sloshes and ripples and churns in the fountain. Duncan has the sensation of the bones shifting and settling with the vibration of their laughter. The skulls grin back from the dark recesses. Sunlight refracts off the water pooling in the font and shimmers wavily upon the stone floor.

That's why, Billy continues, that's why he couldn't be with me. He was needed in the war. He risked his life saving his platoon at Khe Lhong. If he'd been with me, they would all have died. He nods to himself. Just imagine that, he says, that's got to be thirty men, right?

But what about your mother, Billy? Where was she?

My mother? I don't know. I don't know where she was, but that's not important anyway.

Why?

Billy stares at the skulls as if in silent communion with them. The air smells of ash and loam and of wood smoke from a Brother burning the damp bales of ruined hay cut during last season's topping. There will be leaves and rotted deadfall cleared from the fields for the plow, stones piled atop one another along the wall before the windbreak in preparation of the sowing and planting. A thin thread of black smoke curls above their heads through the ridged, tinctured glass. Duncan can hear children in the playing field. Others helping the Brothers in the gardens.

I hate my mother, Billy says, and for a moment Duncan is convinced that he has misheard him, and he laughs and Billy stares at him.

What are you laughing at?

You, saying you hate your mother. That's funny.

But Billy merely stares at him, and it is the first time Duncan has seen such anger in his eyes. He knows that Billy is suddenly creating a picture of his mother in his mind, the mother who abandoned him, and because his love is so great, so too is his hurt—the betrayal that he believes, wants to believe, he will never forgive. And even as Duncan understands this, he is also confused and startled by it.

Shut your mouth, shit-ass! My mother isn't important. She doesn't matter. It's my dad that's going to come back for me. He's going to be wearing his uniform and his medals and he's going to introduce me to all the men he saved and he'll tell them I'm his son and if it wasn't for them, he would have been with me and just how lucky they are . . . And then, although he continues to glare at Duncan, Billy seems to run out of words.

Billy, Julie begins, and reaches out to touch him, but he slaps her hand away.

Sunlight fades from the room and the darker hues of painted blue upon the ceiling take prominence and Billy, Julie, and Duncan watch, stilled, as the room turns to night. The painted clouds fade into the background and the brushed stars merge in glittering cadence with the sudden nightscape visible through the skylight, the row of twelve double-arched windows that encircle the top of the dome. Duncan feels a thickening in his throat, a constriction as if he might cry. Billy has never been angry at him before.

I'm sorry, Billy, he says.

Why? My dad's coming to get me. Ain't nothing sorry about that, fuckwad. You'll see.

May 1981

AFTER VESPERS AND collation, NBC's *Saturday Night at the Movies* or ABC's *Movie of the Week* plays on the wide color console in the priests' lounge. Officially the children aren't allowed in the priests' quarters except on Movie Night, which is usually on Thursday when there are no Holy Days of Obligation, but Julie, Billy, and Duncan often find a way to sneak behind the large settee that crowds the room before the priests have made their way from chapel or the dining hall, and this is where they'll be when *Saturday Night at the Movies* begins playing.

But this night is different. Instead of a recent release, the television is playing a special on the Apollo lunar landing. They peer from behind the feather-down pillows thick with cat hair at the edge of the settee, and Duncan is struck by the sharp, melancholy black–and–white images on the screen. There is the young President Kennedy before a crowd of students at Rice University, his mouth working without sound. Brother Wilhelm fiddles with the cantankerous, loose knob, and Duncan hears John F. Kennedy's voice:

We set sail on this new sea because there is new knowledge to be gained, and new rights to be won, and they must be won and used for the progress of all people.

We choose to go to the moon in this decade and do the other things, not because they are easy, but because they are hard . . .

Billy nudges Duncan. What is he saying?

Shhhhh. I'm trying to hear.

We shall send to the moon, 240,000 miles away from the control station in Houston, a giant rocket more than 300 feet tall, the length of this football field made of new metal alloys, some of which have not yet been invented, capable of standing heat and stresses several times more than have ever been experienced . . .

Duncan, Billy says, tugging at his sleeve.

It's the moon, Billy. They're sending a man to the moon.

. . . on an untried mission, to an unknown celestial body.

I know, Duncan, Billy says, exasperated. They did this before we were born.

He doesn't remember, Billy, Julie says. He doesn't remember any of this.

But Duncan, they didn't—

Hush, Billy, Julie hisses, and shakes her head at him.

And, therefore, as we set sail, we ask God's blessing on the most hazardous and dangerous and greatest adventure on which man has ever embarked.

The program cuts to footage of the Apollo 11 moon voyage and the launch from Cape Canaveral. Duncan watches transfixed as the *Saturn V* ignites and flame surrounds the base of the rocket's hull. For long moments the rocket seems to hover there, trembling slightly, ponderously upon its pillar of flame, as if it might simply keel over and hurtle, cartwheeling, into the earth, but then slowly, slowly the great rocket begins to move upward, vibrating with the effort of defying gravity, its plating shimmering with shattering ice cascading down the length of its super-cooled hull.

Duncan can feel the thundering vibrations of the rocket's blast as it presses its way against gravity toward the moon. And, at the top of that colossal rocket, the Apollo command module, *Columbia*, with its three astronauts sitting as if upon the head of a combustible needle. Farther and farther the rocket presses, an eight-hundred-foot blazing orange tail arcing northeast across the late autumn sky above the Florida Keys.

And then, the first blurry images from Buzz Aldrin's camera of the lunar surface: desolate, cratered plains strewn with rocks and glinting regolith and the black foreshortened horizon beyond and, farther, the curving plane of the planet suggesting only a greater, absolute darkness. Duncan imagines the moon's coldness and the silence and the absence of color or sound.

Magnificent desolation, Aldrin says, and Duncan murmurs in agreement as his words hang in the vacuum between sensation and thought and as the moon's panorama curves out into blackness. *Magnificent desolation*.

Duncan, Billy begins again, whispering conspiratorially. They never made it. They never made it off the moon. The moon jumper failed to blast off and they were left stuck there. The other astronaut just kept going around the moon waiting for them.

Billy makes a looping motion with his finger and says, Around and around until he died. They all died. What they showed on TV after that, it was all a lie. They'd filmed it before they left.

Hush, Julie hisses. Duncan, don't listen to a word he says. He's making it all up. He's just being silly and spiteful.

The astronauts' ghostly images flit and tremble on the screen as they move back and forth in surreal motion, bounding across the gray, pockmarked surface and stirring silver star dust, which no wind ever moves, imprinting their footsteps forever upon a surface last touched by God.

Brother Wilhelm reaches a palsied and withered hand forward and turns the knob to the left, and with an audible click and hum of transponders cooling, the image of the astronauts and the moon fades slowly from the four corners of the television screen to one single, glowing dot at its center, and then It is gone entirely as if it had never been, and only the shimmering white spark that momentarily impresses itself upon Duncan's sensitive iris, and remains shaking on the inside of his eyelids long after he closes his eyes, convinces him it was real.

Brother Wilhelm is asleep in his armchair, and before they leave, Duncan tenderly touches his hand, which lies trembling upon the armrest. For a moment Duncan stands and listens to Brother Wilhelm's apnea and the long seconds of silence between his shunting and staggered breaths.

When he takes the stairs to bed, one of the boys has already dimmed the lamps. With Brother Wilhelm sleeping, they know they will have an extra hour or two of heat; the hallway is warm with the sound of water bubbling in the radiators and of boys' snoring contently in their sleep. Dressed in his pajamas and wrapped in a blanket, with Brother Canice's radio glowing from his bedside table and crackling and hissing with static, Duncan sits on his bed and stares out at the night sky. High over the prairie shines a full moon encircled by a ring of bluish-white phosphorescence. The ghostly haze of ice and moisture casts its shape in magnified projection: its great maria, those shadowy plains known as seas, and its cratered scars—the illusion of cheek, nose bridge, and brow—creating the sense of some benevolent, slightly curious or confused face, peering down upon and illuminating the snow-covered plains of Thule. From the radio comes a sudden high peak of static and then the disembodied and fractured sound of voices carried by radio waves across the vast distance of space over a decade before:

102:44:45 ALDRIN: 100 feet, 3½ down, 9 forward. Five percent. Quantity light.

102:44:54 ALDRIN: Okay. 75 feet. And it's looking good. Down a half, 6 forward.

102:45:02 DUKE: 60 seconds.

102:45:04 ALDRIN: Light's on.

102:45:08 ALDRIN: 60 feet, down 2½. [Pause] 2 forward. 2 forward. That's good.

102:45:17 ALDRIN: 40 feet, down 2½. Picking up some dust.

102:45:21 ALDRIN: 30 feet, 2½ down. [Garbled] shadow.

102:45:25 ALDRIN: 4 forward. 4 forward. Drifting to the right a little. 20 feet, down a half.

102:45:31 DUKE: 30 seconds.

102:45:32 ALDRIN: Drifting forward just a little bit; that's good. [Garbled] [Pause]

102:45:40 ALDRIN: Contact Light.

102:45:43 ARMSTRONG: Shutdown

102:45:44 ALDRIN: Okay. Engine Stop.

102:45:45 ALDRIN: ACA out of Detent.

102:45:46 ARMSTRONG: Out of Detent. Auto.

102:45:47 ALDRIN: Mode Control, both Auto. Descent Engine Command Override, Off. Engine Arm, Off. 413 is in.

102:45:57 DUKE: We copy you down, Eagle.

102:45:58 ARMSTRONG: Engine arm is off. [Pause] Houston, Tranquility Base here. The Eagle has landed.

102:46:06 DUKE: Roger, Twan... Tranquility. We copy you on the ground. You got a bunch of guys about to turn blue. We're breathing again. Thanks a lot.

102:46:16 ALDRIN: Thank you.

And when Duncan whispers JFK's words, he might have been praying: Dear Lord, *as we set sail, we ask God's blessing on the most haz-*

ardous and dangerous and greatest adventure on which man has ever embarked.
Amen.

He hears Billy's words clamoring in his head again: *They never made it. They never made it off the moon. The moon jumper failed to blast off and they were left stuck there. They all died.* He cannot possibly believe it is true even as he stares up into the night sky and imagines that he sees the small dark shapes of the two men splayed and bent aslant the surface of the moon. But they came home, didn't they? They must have. Mustn't they?

July 1981

A HAUNTING MUSIC reverberates off the stone and echoes in the stairwells as Duncan enters the center hall from the chapel, and with its shifting, fractured quality, it takes him a moment to recognize the voice of Elvis. Rising and then falling, the song materializes fully and then is gone. Duncan walks the halls, moving from room to room, searching for its source.

From Father Toibin's room comes the faint sound of music, and when Duncan passes and finds the door partly ajar, he pauses. A thin slant of light spills across the hallway. A familiar crooning music plays upon a mahogany upright turntable that stands varnished and gleaming in the corner of the room. There is the scent of tobacco and of age—a comforting, spicy, pleasant smell of polished wood floors, ancient carpets, beeswax, and tallow.

Father Toibin's voice calls from the other side of the door, where

Duncan cannot see him: Come in, Duncan, come in. The door is open and I've just made tea.

Duncan pushes against the door and it swings wide slowly. A cat blinks its green eyes at him lazily from its perch upon a red velvet chair covered with its white and black hairs. There is also a red velvet sofa badly in need of new upholstery and above this is a painting of the San Damiano Crucifix, from which, the Franciscans believe, God spoke to St. Francis of Assisi almost eight hundred years ago. From dark wooden tables small lamps with aged, stained yellow paper shades cast their soft glow into the corners of the room.

Duncan closes his eyes to the warmth and to the sound of Elvis's voice and the Brothers' footsteps in the distant stairwells—a rhythm like gently falling rain—reminding him of the first time he opened his eyes after his sleep. The record is spinning on the turntable. The stylus lifts, the tone arm swings out and back, and then the stylus drops once more into the groove and the record begins from its first track. The haunting notes of "Blue Moon" tremble from the aged speakers.

Blue Moon, he whispers and Father Toibin hears him as he emerges from the kitchen carrying a tea tray of clattering crockery.

You like it? This is one of the finest recordings of this song. Bill Black on bass and Scotty Moore on guitar. With the edge of the tray he pushes issues of *National Geographic*, *Time* magazine, and a dog-eared copy of *The Collected Works of Douglas Graham Purdy: Tales of Horror and the Macabre* off a table and onto the floor, and then lays the tray down.

This is what I heard when I first woke up, Duncan says and points to the turntable. I heard this music in the sick room.

Father Toibin nods absently, gestures toward the sofa—Sit, Duncan, please sit—and takes a chair beside the cat. Oh, yes. Will you listen to that, such crooning would put a chanter to shame. He smiles, cocks his head to the side, and scratches idly at his bristles.

It's quite truly a divinely inspired piece of music, he says. And I don't think Elvis would have been afraid to admit that he was singing to God when he sang this.

On the far wall, *The Sacred Heart* with Christ baring his thorn-gouged heart imploringly, and beneath this, lining the baseboard, stacks of old, yellowed newspapers. Father Toibin follows Duncan's eyes and laughs. There you will find every *Minnesota Tribune* and *St. Paul Gazette* for the last twenty years, which is almost as long as I have been here. I really must put them in the compost.

I have trouble letting anything go, he says. It is one of my failings as a Capuchin, I believe, one among many. I ask God's forgiveness all the time, and—he raises a quizzical eyebrow—I think he understands.

From an ornate china teapot, Father Toibin pours steaming brown water into two large mugs and nods to himself. The Brothers that attend to the boys' sleeping quarters tell me of how terribly difficult it has been for you at times, he says. Have you talked to Dr. Mathias? You know that is what he is there for.

There are some things I'd rather not tell him, Duncan says. Is that okay?

Of course, Duncan. Of course.

Can I ask you something?

Yes, yes, yes, Father Toibin says, waving him on as he works to clear the table and his chair of papers, and then sits.

It's about the children who have died here. Do you suppose they all go to God when they die?

Father Toibin harrumphs, clutches at his teacup as brown water sloshes from its tilting rim. He takes a sip and grimaces, as if the liquid has burned his lips. From the campanile comes the sudden discordant ringing of bells and, frowning, Father Toibin glances at his watch. Brother Canice, he says softly, sighs and shakes his head, rubs violently at a point above his eyebrow as if it were causing him sudden and intense pain. For a moment he stares imploringly at Duncan, wide-eyed and helpless, shakes his head in disbelief, and Duncan tries not to smile. Tonight in the kitchen he will tell Brother Canice that Father Toibin is very much taken with his bell ringing.

Well, Duncan, he says, as if trying to think about things other than the bells, children have died here, he says. I wouldn't tell you otherwise. And God has always taken them into his care. I remember how hard the year of that terrible blizzard was—many people died, not just children. And of course many children died aboard the Holiday Train. We weren't even able to break ground to bury the dead. They all remained in the charnel house until spring. And it was late coming that year. I remember the pickaxes they had to use on the ground, and there simply wasn't enough room. We buried them all together: mothers, fathers, daughters, and sons. The other children were all orphans. We buried them in the children's graveyard.

The monastery's record books say that an influenza epidemic took a dozen children in 1902, but still, the blizzard and the Holiday Train, well, it's hard to imagine worse than that. I'd never experienced anything like it. He shakes his head slowly, still unbelieving, and Duncan wonders what he sees upon the plains beyond the monastery's walls. Perhaps mechanized snowcats laden with the Holiday Train's dead rumbling over the snow-covered hills, or the shrouded figures of gravediggers hunched against the wind over their spades and pickaxes, or, at the end of spring, the pallbearers from the chapel carrying the small coffins containing the children from the charnel house to the grave.

I held so many of them during baptism, he says. And so many families begging me to baptize their children, their infants who had died before they could receive the Sacrament of Baptism. All of them so small they weighed next to nothing. The curtains sweep back and Father Toibin is holding up his hands, empty hands cradling the air. Next to nothing, he says again, and then: We baptize dead children with our tears and it is with our tears that they enter heaven.

He comes forward and touches Duncan, not without kindness,

on his arm. Enough of this morbidity, he says. That was a long time ago. He shakes his head. Children have died here, Duncan. Children will always die here. We hold them in God's care and yet they die. This is why we have the children's graveyard. This is why we offer up prayers at Mass. This is why we have faith in God and believe that they are all with him now.

I almost died too, didn't I? Dr. Matthias thinks that's why I can't remember things. Or at least it's a part of why.

You were very sick and we are blessed that you survived, that you are here now.

Duncan thinks of his mother in her coffin wrapped in white roots and her face turning toward him, the pupils of her eyes so large and blue he can see his own longing reflected in them.

Do you think my mother, he says, after she left me here, what do you think happened to her?

Father Toibin purses his lip and considers the question, as if he is weighing what to say, and at first Duncan thinks he will say nothing at all. The children of the Home know that this is the question you do not ask—it is sacrosanct and unwritten but the priests and Brothers will not talk about the children's parents.

Every so often, Father Toibin begins slowly, I used to get a letter from her. They stopped years ago, of course. He waves absently at the air, as if, Duncan thinks, all letters from parents eventually stop when they move on to their new lives and new families or when they simply die.

But she sent money when she could for your support. Even though she could not be a mother to you, Duncan, you were very much in her thoughts. I think, in leaving you here, she felt she was doing what was best.

Duncan looks at him. Instead of feeling pleasure and happiness at the unexpected news, he finds that he is suddenly numb; nausea rolls in his stomach and he fights to settle it.

Finally he says: Can I see her letters?

Father Toibin places his hand on the side of Duncan's head. Let me think about that, okay? I want you to understand that your mother made a choice a long time ago. We don't talk about those choices here and we don't talk about your parents because we don't want to instill the false hope that someday they may return. Sometimes we have to accept what is and then move on in life, otherwise we remain stuck and we fail to thrive. Everything we do here is with that in mind. If I do show you the letters, it will be under the condition that after reading them, you will be able to move on, yes?

Duncan feels the nausea in his stomach subsiding but places his hand there anyway. He wonders what the letters contain and whether or not he really wants to see them at all. Perhaps he should be content for his dreams, of her standing before the Festival of Lights Holiday Train in the snow, for the image of her resting peacefully in the ground.

The cat with the green eyes stretches upon the seat, shakes itself, and then jumps to the floor. Its uncut nails tap the floor as it makes its way out of the room.

It is time you were in bed, Duncan, Father Toibin says, and suddenly he seems very tired. His eyes are red-rimmed and his face pale. I've kept you here much too long.

Duncan whispers: Father, will I die here?

Father Toibin shakes his head and, suppressing a laugh, coughs into his hand. Again, such morbidity! You will not die here, Duncan. We're not a shop of horrors, you know. Besides, doesn't God have other plans for you? Aren't you meant to do something special out there in the world of the living?

IT'S THE SEVENTH game of the World Series and in the playing field beyond the children's graveyard, Father Toibin and three novitiates are umpiring the game. The New York Yankees and the Boston Red Sox are tied 4–4 in the top of the ninth and there are two outs. Billy steps to the plate—someone's folded T-shirt—and with his bat takes two large swipes at the air. He stomps the dirt, toes the T-shirt, and settles into his batting stance, a partial crouch with the bat tight against his shoulder. This is the sixth batter to the plate this inning, and they've already seen Reggie Jackson. A lanky kid with red hair moans at third base, raises his glove to his mouth, and shouts to Duncan, who's about to pitch: He can't be Jackson again.

Jackson's already been up, Duncan calls from the pitching mound, fifteen feet away. Jordan says you can't be Jackson again.

With difficulty Billy straightens his back, points to imaginary bleachers with his bat. I've changed the batting order. I've moved Reggie from third to eighth.

Duncan shakes his head. You've got to be someone else.

Oh, please, does it really matter? Julie shouts. She's standing in the long grass at the farthest edges of the field, wearing a large, tattered floppy straw sun hat that covers her eyes. Her hands are clasped behind her head in boredom. There are three other outfielders and one of them is sitting with his legs crossed Indian-style and flicking stones.

All right, Billy says. I'm Dave Winfield.

Duncan shakes his head again.

Fine. I'm—

Duncan hurls the ball at the center of the plate and Billy swivels his hips, grimacing, and with a loud crack drives the ball directly toward Julie. It strikes the ground and, whispering like a snake, quickly comes to a stop in the grass. Julie doesn't move and already Billy is on his way to second. Julie! the second baseman shouts. Pick up the ball! Pick up the ball!

Julie pouts, pushes the hat back on her head, and trudges to the ball. The other team is cheering.

Hearing the second baseman's shouts, Billy grins, and Duncan watches him, legs thumping up dust, tongue lolling from his mouth like a dog, and laughing. Carefully Billy rounds second, stumbling briefly so that Duncan starts toward him, and then gambols bowlegged around third, raising his hands in celebration, but the ball is sailing through the air in one sharp arc and the catcher has merely to reach out for it. He turns to his left and is waiting with the ball in his glove when Billy comes, tottering and wheezing, to a stop before him.

Goddamn shit! Billy says, and Father Toibin hollers for him to watch his mouth. The children look toward the outfield, where Julie is standing with her oversize leather glove on her hip.

This is the stupidest game I've ever played! she hollers. Is it over yet?

They change sides and Duncan steps up to the plate, scrapes the dirt with his bat, and stares out at Billy. Billy is wild with his pitches and most of the kids are afraid of getting hit by him, even though Father Toibin has warned him to slow it down and take it easy, and they stand way outside the box when they come to bat; Duncan has already struck out twice against him, chasing balls spinning crazily downward into the dirt. This time, though, he wills himself to get as close as he can to the plate and to have patience. He whispers to himself: If it's low, let it go.

Billy throws the baseball from an exaggerated windup and Duncan watches its dirt-sullied cover and its red stitches as it revolves slowly through the air, growing larger and larger like something the astronauts might see from their windows as they hurtled through space in their orbit about the moon. Duncan brings his arms forward, uncorks his weight from his back leg and through his twisting hips like Ted Williams. He sees the ball strike the bat, feels the pleasing tremor in his hands, and then it is gone, past the infield and rising high, high above Julie's head. Julie throws her glove up into the air as it passes but the baseball is still climbing into the sky and she turns to follow the other children's gaze, watching as the baseball rises higher and higher until it is merely a white pinprick in the sky, visible only because of the gray cloud beyond it. At the point at which the height of its arc seems imminent and its trajectory will curve and the baseball will fall back to earth, it continues, shooting upward into those low churning clouds and then rising beyond their ability to see, and is gone.

The children stand, mouths agape, looking up at the sky. A breeze pushes at their shirts and jeans. A spattering of warm raindrops spatter their upturned faces and then there is heat as sunlight flickers in bright splinters from the clouds churning toward the east. The wind sounds in Duncan's ears like waves upon a beach. When he moves his neck, the muscles and tendons creak and crack. Within the clouds strange trembling, violent thrustings, seem to occur—gray shapes flitting back and forth, the vague suggestion of limbs, arms and legs and wings, hands, and of faces pressing and pushing and contorting against the body of the clouds themselves, as if they were merely diaphanous thin-skinned bellies.

As the clouds move, they pass between shadow and light. Disgusted, Billy spits into the dirt and steps off the mound. He reaches into his back pocket and pulls out his Russian wool cap, tugs it roughly down over his wrinkled head. Julie's black hair flows back from her neck and whips about her thin neck. When she looks at Duncan, questioningly, hair finds its way across her eyes and into her open mouth. Duncan shrugs and turns, grinning, as the children from his team clap and pat him on the back.

Together the children pick up baseball mitts and bats, pull sweat-shirts over sweat-dampened T-shirts, and, talking among themselves, allow Father Toibin to march them in staggered columns back to the Home. A young novitiate with olive skin and the dark shadow of stubble on his cheeks and jaw accompanies Duncan, Billy, and Julie down the hill. We must have lost the ball in the sun, he says. Hell of a hit, Duncan.

Duncan knows that they didn't lose the ball in the sun, but he smiles anyway and says thank you. From their height on the hill he looks at the fields falling away so steeply below them to the Home that they—all of them—might have been tumbling from the clouds. Like angels.

In FATHER TOIBIN's office Duncan sits in the large leather-backed chair and looks at the way the light gleams off the rosary beads Father Toibin fingers in his hands. The large sleeves of his hemp-brown robe work their way forward, covering his hands, and he grunts, rolls the sleeves up, pushes them back to his elbows. His forearms are thin, freckled, and thick-tendoned, as Duncan imagines a miner's would be, someone who ate little and yet worked hard: sinew and muscle tightly bound to the bone, a hard, angular body shaped by malnutrition, wasted lungs, and grueling, contorted working spaces. When Father Toibin holds things, the tendons clench and unclench, rise up on his thin arms.

It is a large, high-ceilinged, sparsely decorated room. At the front of it, high upon the pale terra-cotta wall, a wooden cross blackened with age, which, like a sundial, sunlight moves across throughout the day. A beetle knocks in the wall and the room suddenly seems very small.

Are you okay, Duncan? Father Toibin asks, and Duncan nods, looks back down to the letters in his hands and reads them again, as if he might find something more in them. There are eight in all, written on blue-lined stationery. The older ones have yellowed slightly, and the envelopes he pulls them from are dry and translucent. The paper smells of bourbon and stale cigarette smoke and there is a perfume also that in the manner of camphor, storax, and cascarilla—the burnt and smoking incense of Mass—he finds comforting, and yet these are smells that he cannot associate with the image of the woman he has in his head.

His mother has very little to say other than to ask how he is and at other times merely to note that a small check is enclosed and that she will send more when she can. In one of the oldest letters, there's an article from *Opera* magazine praising one of her performances, but no picture of her, and on the bottom, scribbled in the margin in perfect cursive: *So that you know who I was, love, Maggie.* Duncan tries to fight his disappointment and frustration but feels it pressing at him, falling leaden in his stomach and leaving it hollowed-out. Father Toibin was right in telling him not to have false hope or expectation, but that doesn't make it any easier. He wants to smile and assure Father Toibin that everything is fine, that it is exactly as he said it would be, and now he can move on.

As if sensing this, Father Toibin looks at him and Duncan sits up straight in the chair and smiles, and though it is forced—he feels on the verge of crying—he hopes he can convince Father Toibin otherwise.

Thank you, he says and pauses briefly, waits for the emotion filling his throat to pass. Thank you for showing me her letters.

What is it, Duncan? I know this is hard. What is it you're not letting me see?

Duncan stares at the strange, unfamiliar handprint, at her name, which until this moment he has never known, and the place where she once lived, had lived for years without him.

Maggie Bright
34 Divisadero Street
San Francisco, CA 94114

Nothing, he says. He shakes his head, but then has to lower it so that Father Toibin can't see his face and then Father Toibin is at his side and he rests his head against his shoulder and lets the tears come, for somehow now it does feel inevitable and irresolute: He has no power to alter or change the present or the past. His mother left him here for a reason, because she no longer wanted him, and nothing in the world, not prayers—no matter how much he prayed—or hope, would ever change that.

AFTER SATURDAY COLLATION the Brothers direct the children to clear the table and wash and dry their plates in the kitchen sink. There is the clatter of tin cups and plates and the thumping bilge pumping of children submerging hollow vessels in the basin. The children and Brothers move about in seeming bedlam, each driven by the instinct of the ritual and the night to come: the voiding of bowels and bladders, the washing of face and brushing of teeth, the farewell to friends until morning, and the hurdle into cold, dank beds; the preparation of the priests' meals in the refectory, the first bell for the Hours of the Holy Office, and, at last, solitude for divine reading and prayer prior to Vigil in the deep leagues of the night that descend upon the plains. Pretending to be industrious—Duncan scrapes the remains of his apple crisp into a slop bucket to give to the local farmer's sow and her piglets while Julie makes a show of collecting a handful of cutlery—they slowly make their way into the Brothers' lounge, hide behind the couch, and wait for Brother Canice to arrive and turn the television to *The Movie of the Week*.

Julie is drawing in her pad and Duncan is rereading Father Toibin's dog-eared copy of *The Collected Works of Douglas Graham Purdy: Tales of Horror and the Macabre*. Dishes are clattering in the dining hall and from the chapel comes the sound of kneelers banging against the gouged and scarred pew backs. There is sound of glass shattering and sandaled feet running on carpet. A Brother hollers and Duncan hears more breaking glass. Listening, Julie is suddenly breathless, her body rigid. She grasps Duncan's hand, pulls him to his feet.

Quick, Duncan. It's Billy.

In Father Toibin's office chairs lie overturned, and a decapitated bust of Brother Dianmianco rests, as if placed there, against the baseboard. A hole in the wall reveals the plaster lathes, pale as exposed ribs. Burly Brother Brennan and two male nurses have surrounded Billy, who is brandishing a wickedly gleaming candelabra. The candlesticks are scattered across the floor. Above one of the nurses' brows a cut bleeds profusely.

The room is cold. Through a smashed window the wind blows: white lace curtains flutter and flap loudly against the window frame.

Fuckshit, mother fuck you! Billy shouts. I'm not going to St. Paul. I'm not going to fucking St. Paul!

The Brother and the nurses circle Billy, and when they come too close, he swings the candelabra and hollers all the louder and Duncan imagines his voice echoing out into the night and carrying all the way to Stockholdt. Fuck you, Billy says and swings the candelabra at a nurse who steps toward him. Fuck you, Billy says, you asswipe. You pissing asswipe fuck SON OF A BITCH!

The nurse with the cut over his brow is intent on getting Billy now, and the others seem tired and eager to have this over with. Duncan knows they no longer see a small, sick boy before them, and it is just a matter of time before they rush him. If they grab him, they'll disconnect his shoulder, they'll snap his collarbone, they'll fracture his arm, they'll crack his ribs and shatter his spine; the bone shards will pierce his lungs and his heart: He'll implode. They'll break him.

Duncan imagines all the small, fragile, tender bones of which Billy's body is made, shattering into a thousand crystalline pieces and, in the reverse of the glass window, exploding out into the night and scattering upon the snow.

Don't touch him, Duncan screams. You'll hurt him!

Father Toibin holds Duncan tightly as the Brother and two nurses rush Billy. It's all right, Duncan, Father Toibin says. It's all right. They know to be gentle.

Billy swings the candelabra and it slips from his hands and arcs, rotating through the air like a glittering guillotine, gleaming bronze, before striking the Brother, who utters a muffled grunt and wraps Billy up in his arms, and then all four tumble to the floor with such violence that the boards shudder with the impact.

Standing in the shadows beyond Billy's bed, in the Home's hospice, Duncan listens to the furtive noises of the night all around him, the creaks and groans and abrupt muffled cracks as stone and wood rises, settles, and rises once more, as if they are aboard some great galleon tossed upon the sea. The wind sings in the eaves and skitters upon the roof, hurling rain or hail. Trees scrape the glass and tap the leaded panes as if to gain admittance.

At times, Billy cries out in the night, and Duncan goes to his bedside and strokes his brow softly until he sinks into a deeper sleep, and then Duncan returns to a dark angle of the room, and waits and watches.

A young novitiate walks the hallways, and as he makes his rounds—dimming lights, attending to a whimpering boy or girl, scolding perhaps another who refuses to sleep and is disturbing the others—he always stops by Billy's bed, which is the closest to the doors and so is always cast in a meager slant of light. And Duncan watches the silhouette of the novitiate as he stands over Billy, leans an ear to Billy's face and then a hand tenderly upon his belly to make sure that Billy is breathing.

When the novitiate is gone, Duncan sinks against the wall, pulls his blanket about his waist, and watches through the night, counting the bells until dawn. In this way he makes sure that nothing can touch Billy. He does this for nights, then weeks, losing sleep, and gradually he understands the helplessness that parents must feel when they come to the unacceptable yet undeniable realization that they cannot protect their children despite their best efforts. And that in the end, everything is in God's hands. Perhaps some parents realize this at the moment of their child's birth and immediately flee. The overwhelming reality of heartbreak and loss is simply too much to consider yet alone bear.

Tonight Billy has been tossing in his sleep, calling out the names of people, doctors perhaps from St. Paul, or family and friends that he remembers. A nurse comes shortly after Vigil has begun and gives him a sedative. From his corner in the shadows, Duncan listens, and when Billy is calm and his breathing has deepened, Duncan makes his way to the bed. He must tell Billy something that he's been putting off but that he's known he would do ever since Father Toibin showed him his dead mother's letters.

For a moment he sits on the edge of the mattress and looks at him. I'm leaving, he whispers to Billy, who is now snoring slightly. The dim lamp flickers and casts a soft, silvery light along the edge of his pajamas. Duncan touches Billy's shoulder and stares at the back of his head, his small, wrinkled cauliflower ears.

I may be gone a while, but don't worry, I'll come back—I promise. Please tell Julie goodbye for me. And look after her until I get back.

Duncan pauses, trying to think of something else to say. A pleasant heat pulses from the pipes; children sigh and turn contently in their sleep. For a moment he considers crawling back into his bed. His head begins to nod and he closes his eyes, and then a hoarse, cotton-thick sobbing from beneath the blankets startles him awake.

Duncan, please can I come? *Please?*

THERE IS A train depot on the plains of Thule: crumbling red brick, large cracked flagstones, mortar shunted with horsehair and wood shavings. The windows are glassless, boarded with knotted sheets of plywood. The wind moans across the plains, down from the north. In the distance, way up high, an eagle turns in long, slow circles. Nothing moves between the curled wire and pidgeoned posts. The tracks stretch in each direction for vast, indeterminate miles. Squinting, Duncan and Billy look to the left and then to the right. That trains still stop here, that a ticket agent waits or sleeps and dreams in an office here, seems such an oddity they cannot properly conceive of it, so when they see the man, bald-headed, shiny, stooped behind the ticket window, they are momentarily startled.

Duncan asks him how often a passenger train comes through, and the old man lifts his implacable moonbeam of a face and regards him.

Once a day, son, he says. Comes after the Omaha freight, drops a couple of cars, and picks them up on the way back. No need for them, you see. He lifts a scarred, mangled hand as if to illustrate this, and Duncan doesn't know where to look.

How far to Stockholdt, sir? Billy asks, and the ticket clerk jerks a ridiculously large thumb into the air and gestures behind him.

'Bout six miles or so, he says and laughs. You'll need to put your walking shoes on if you plan to walk to Stockholdt. But Duncan is mesmerized by the thumb and stares at it until it disappears beneath the counter, and then Billy nods, thanks the man, and they settle onto a bench and wait.

The freight bound for Omaha comes in an hour or two, over one hundred cars—they both lose count—stretching from the east and passing into the west, thumping the rails one after the other, so hard they should buckle and break, and after a while it seems as if they will. Duncan is lost in their passing, their heavy drumming and grinding and the incessant tap of metal clicking in the gaps.

Then it is gone, the freight tapping into the distance and the air heavy with dust and black cinder and Duncan's clothes stuck to him with sweat. The weight of the afternoon sun bears down. The air is heavy to breathe. Billy keeps his mouth open to it, and watches the sky as the eagle alights over the tree line. The light shimmers on distant, still lakes; bottle flies hop on and off their skin and gather on the empty barrels beneath the gutters. They wave at the bottle flies and wait in the shade for another freight train to pass through and then, after another empty hour, not knowing which way to go, Duncan asks Billy: Do you think you could walk? Billy wrinkles his brow in determination—Duncan has seen this look so many times before— and nods yes and they begin the walk to Stockholdt, their heads bowed and their eyes mere slits against the sun and the unfamiliar land stretching away in simmering nacre waves.

They walk only half aware that they are walking and the hours pass and then twilight comes on quickly and Duncan realizes that he is no longer warm. In the distance the low-peaked mountains are dotted with flitting lights. Gray clouds sweep over flat tracks of land

and small ponds that the bogged land spoons and about which vacant-looking trailer homes sit.

Duncan reaches across to Billy and pulls him gently to him as they walk, and although Billy is no longer sweating, he feels feverish to the touch. Duncan pauses and they take long gulps from his water bottle.

The skin on Billy's face seems stretched and jaundiced and Duncan wonders if he is in pain but refusing to tell him. Are you okay? he asks. It's okay, y'know, if you're not. I don't know if I can walk much more.

I'm okay, Billy says, wiping water from his chin. I promise. Let's keep going. It's harder when I stop.

It is dark when they enter Stockholdt. Everything looks squat and pressed down, even the town: square rows of flat-topped three- and four-story businesses, clapboard tiers, crumbling porches, and derelict row houses in which yellowed signs declaring ROOMS FOR RENT lay at skewed angles on the insides of grimed glass.

A traffic light hangs over the Boulevard, the town's single street that intersects a section of railroad tracks running north to south. To the northeast are vast straits of cold-looking lake and log-sheared forest and the gray nothingness of pastureland let to fallow, broken only now and then by a grain silo or a derelict farmhouse. The single traffic light sways from a fretted cable that stretches across the single intersection. It flashes red, on and off, on and off, throughout the night. And when the wind blows, the traffic lantern rocks back and forth from its cable like a pendulous eye. The 9:15 Northern Pacific, three hundred cars of livestock feed, trundles though, the boxcars metal slivers in the darkness as they catch the lambent light of the town's flickering streetlamps.

Duncan and Billy walk the streets and the dead children from the Festival of Lights Holiday Train follow them. When Duncan glances back, they nod and smile, their skin shining with beatific opalescence, and he is filled with contentment; he senses that he has known them all his life, in the way that he knows Billy and Julie. Perhaps it is the affinity of abandoned children to know nothing other than a singular longing that transfigures all other needs and desires and makes them what they are, and, in this way, makes them kin to one another.

For a moment Duncan almost expects them to break into song and for their song—the song of dead children—to echo and reverberate throughout the empty streets of Stockholdt. Would the sleeping adults hear them? What would their song sound like? Would it be joyous and elegiac or plaintive and soul-wrenching, a caterwaul and baying that would make men and women of the town sit up in their beds with their hearts thrumming in their chests in sudden fear for their young ones. But the dead children's footfalls are silent upon the streets of Stockholdt and their voices are mute. Together, they move without sound from one street to the next.

One of the children, a young girl with wide, bright eyes and thick strawberry blonde hair, which is woven into two braids that swing from each side of her head like whips, points to a glowing light that spins nebulae-like above the town at the black edge of the tracks, the abandoned stockyards, and the plains beyond: the undulations of the aurora borealis, and at its center a fully formed new moon surrounded by a fine nimbus of phosphorescence. In the strange, shifting light, the moon's cratered and shadowed surface seems to move and coalesce until a face takes shape, and Duncan gasps because he knows it is the face of his mother.

An angel, the girl says and smiles, and Duncan smiles also and takes Billy's hand, and the face of Duncan's mother smiles over them as they move on through the streets of Stockholdt, the dead children of the Holiday Train skipping at their heels.

There is a rectangle of four streets surrounding the railroad depot, and six cross-streets intersect these. The street that runs alongside the tracks is lined with wooden row houses from the turn of the century. Most of the steps leading to the front doors are crumbling. The posts are rotted and the foundations cracked and shifting. Each house caves and presses into the other and, in this way, the brick and mortar settles and secures one house to the next and the next all along the street. Duncan imagines that if one house were removed from the center, all the others would topple to their sides. Many of the houses still have Christmas decorations: sun-bleached brown-plastic reindeer and soot-stained potbellied Santas balance precariously on the small, slanted awnings over their porches.

It begins to rain and they move toward a porch, but before they step upon the broken wood slats, Duncan looks up at the plastic Santa peering down and it is as if they have been transported to the Home's chapel and from the apse he is staring toward the altar and the body of Christ. From above Santa and the peak of the roof, the moon briefly pushes its ghostly, milk-white head through a black cloud.

A car's tires hiss through the rainwater close to the curb, its engine motoring slow and heavy, and Billy tugs on Duncan's arm and they begin to walk quickly down the sidewalk. Duncan keeps his attention on the buildings to the left, but there is nothing there but empty, peeling, and withered storefronts and boarded and abandoned textile warehouses. He pulls his hood tight against the rain. His boots are swollen with rainwater. The car keeps pace with them and before the voice calls to him, he knows it belongs to a cop. I'm not going back, Duncan, Billy hisses, his head lowered against the rain. I'm jumping the next train out of here.

Duncan stops as Billy yanks his hand free and the cruiser flashes its light in their eyes. Fuck you, coppers! Billy shouts and is off running down the street with Duncan caught in the cruiser's spotlight and not knowing what to do as the car door opens and Billy is a small, hunched shape scrambling toward the darkness of the rail yards with a cop in a shimmering black slicker chasing after him. Beyond is the blackness of unlit pastureland stretching out toward the plains, and when Duncan looks about him, the dead children are gone.

That night in the Stockholdt County Children's Facility, Duncan and Billy lie in beds next to each other as a storm moves across the country. Duncan listens to the sound of a dozen boys breathing, pulls the blankets about him, and cranes his head to look out at the storm building in the distance and then the wind and rain as it presses against the glass. It is cold. He glances at the sleeping shapes around him, the small bulk of them huddled in the darkness. The top of a head, a tuft of ratty hair, pokes out here and there but faces are mostly covered, hidden. The room collects and holds their mist-breath; it fogs the air and the glass. A boy groans and then farts wetly in his sleep.

We almost made it, Billy says, and when Duncan looks over at him, Billy is grinning, but his voice is thick with phlegm and his breathing sounds shallow. Duncan watches as his chest slowly rises and falls.

He smiles. We almost did.

After a moment: Thanks for taking me with you.

Duncan shrugs. I wouldn't have made it without you.

A flame flickers in the dark; there is a raspy breath followed by a cough and the flame is extinguished. At the far end of the room, at a desk in a small wire cage that separates the room from the hall and the bathrooms beyond, sits a figure smoking. The cigarette flares and dies, its tip glowing amber, and the smell of cigarette smoke carries the length of the room.

Sorry that we have to go back, Duncan says.

Billy closes his eyes and his head nods. It's okay. That's what happens. It's like the astronauts and the moon.

What is?

Getting there, that's what's important even if you can't get back.

They knew that and they went anyway. It's why they went on those other space missions as well, the ones we never hear about. Them and the Russians. If we'd jumped on a train, there's no way we'd be coming back—we'd be just like the astronauts, like Michael Collins and the rest of them.

Billy continues to smile with his eyes closed. Imagine if we had made it, Duncan, he murmurs. Just imagine that.

Duncan watches lightning flashing beyond the wire mesh of the windows and thinks of Michael Collins alone aboard his fiery coffinship hurtling farther out into the dark, forever chasing the curve of the earth and already emerging into daylight upon its far side.

Goodnight, Billy, he says.

Goodnight, Duncan.

Duncan waits until Billy is asleep and then slowly he lowers himself into the bed, lies awake staring at the ceiling and the walls. He listens to the thrum and sigh of boys breathing as the storm lashes at the trees outside, shakes the window grates in their posts, while the lone figure in his cage wheezes and chokes slowly on his cigarettes and holds his vigil through the long hours of the night.

The next day, when the police car pulls up to the monastery gates, Father Toibin is standing there, waiting, his brow deeply furrowed as he squints into the sun, the wind whipping his black pants about his legs. And in this moment he seems to Duncan old but as immutable as the Iron Range beyond, with its hills of hardwoods, conifers, and spruces. Duncan slides down in his seat, wishing to be invisible, and Billy begins to cry softly, now that they are back, so Duncan takes his hand and squeezes it tenderly and tries to smile to comfort him. But when Father Toibin's blue eyes scan the car as it turns sharply in the courtyard, they catch Duncan and hold him with their silent power. And then Father Toibin smiles and nods almost imperceptibly.

Officer Perry opens the door and Duncan and Billy step out,

blinking in the light. Billy wipes at his eyes as Duncan walks toward Father Toibin slowly, and when he reaches out his hand, Duncan feels the weight of the journey home, and he is suddenly exhausted. He stumbles and Father Toibin wraps his arms about him, and holds him close, and then beckons for Billy to come to him as well.

Ah, Duncan, Billy, you're home now. It's all right. Everything will be all right.

When he releases Duncan, he turns and looks at Officer Perry standing by the door of his cruiser. Red clay cakes his long black boots and spots the gray jodhpurs above.

I apologize for the trouble they've caused you, Officer.

Not a concern, Father. Just glad to have helped. Officer Perry tips his hat and stares at Duncan and Billy. He has already told them that he has a three-year-old boy and a girl Duncan's age at home, and if they were ever to do what he and Billy had done, he'd be worried to death until they were safe and sound and home again. Clouds move across the lens of his black sunglasses; he chews on imaginary cud, as if he is weighing a serious problem in his mind.

I know we've already talked about this some, he begins, but it doesn't hurt to put it to you again. Men need to know where they stand with one another. Will I have to come looking for you two again?

No sir! Billy and Duncan say together, and standing straight, push back their shoulders.

Good boys, Officer Perry says, his face pinched in such stoic re-serve that it is hard not to smile. And the next time I see you, make sure you're old enough to pass the police exam in Stockholdt, yeah? We need more men like you.

Officer Perry climbs into his cruiser, speaks briefly into his CB, and then his dusty '69 Chevy Impala, with duel exhausts, rumbles slowly down the rutted road, its police light turning in slow amber-red revolutions on the roof, and Duncan nods toward Billy, who smiles, knowing it is for them. Father Toibin asks Brother Wilhelm to take Billy in for lunch and then to the hospice. We'll talk in a little while, okay, Billy? he says, and Billy nods, glances toward Duncan, and then follows Brother Wilhelm up the path to the gate.

Father Toibin grasps Duncan's shoulders and looks at him. Look at you. You've grown two inches, I swear. Our Lord, Jesus, went into the desert and came back having resisted the temptations of the Devil. What have you done on your journey? What beasts have you seen? What demons have you fought? I gather quite a few, no?

I saw my mother, Duncan says. It was a full moon and I saw my mother in the face of the moon.

Father Toibin nods and smiles.

Do you think that was God's doing? Duncan asks.

I prayed that He would look after you and bring you safely back to us.

But you believe I saw her? You believe God spoke to me when I was born?

Of course. Duncan, wherever you and Billy were and whatever you saw, you can be sure God had a hand in it. Look out there. Father Toibin points toward the range and the valleys and the great hardwoods and firs in the north. Through the gifts of the Holy Spirit we are granted the knowledge, the wisdom to see and understand, to perceive the divine in all things. And it is this ability to see which lifts us from de profundis—out of the depths. *De profundis clamavi ad te, Domine. Quia apud Dominum misericordia, et copiosa apud eum redemptio.*

This, Father Toibin says and opens his palms to the vista before them—a simple gesture, a mere turning of his wrists that stills Duncan's breath and makes him aware of the warm, charged air in this place where they stand. A wind comes down from the hills, clouds moves above the prairies, and something glitters momentarily in the wide swaths of burn upon the distant slopes, like a space ship falling from the stars—and Father Toibin smiles.

De Profundis, Duncan repeats in his head. *De Profundis.* They are words without end.

THEY ARE IN Billy's room in the Home's hospice and Billy is packing his small duffel bag, the one with the picture of Muhammad Ali
on its sides. He seems thinner somehow, and when he places his spe-
cially laundered and folded shirts upon the wax paper in their drawer,
he moves slowly and stiffly, and when he is done, he rubs his hips
tenderly and winces. Their trip to Stockholdt took so much out of
him, Duncan knows, and he cannot but help feel guilty. He glances
out the window at the sound of crunching gravel and sees the small
white Ford Econoline van that has come to take Billy to the Children's Cancer Institute at the University of Minnesota in St. Paul,
two hundred miles away.

It's here, Duncan says, and Billy nods, smiling, watching him.

We almost made it, didn't we? he says.

Just like the astronauts.

Billy reaches toward him and Duncan hugs him, feels his frail
bones trembling against him, then he takes Billy's bag and they

make their way slowly out of the room and down the stairs to where Julie is waiting for them.

It is a clear morning without a cloud in the sky. The monastery is bleached with sun, the light so strong and bright that Duncan's and Billy's eyes can only close to it. There is an odd silence on the flag-stone walk—even their footfalls are muted as they walk to the van. The silence is deepened and magnified by the flickering black shape of an eagle soaring wide-winged above the range and by the sound of its faint distant cry.

In the courtyard the wind ruffles Billy's thin hair, and Duncan sees some of it floating away: little white puffs of flax drifting over the grounds toward the prairie. Duncan stares at the ground, and only at the last moment, when Billy has climbed into the van, does he look up, and it appears as if the fragile bones of Billy's face are bursting out of him and might shatter at any moment: the glowing frontal eminence, the raised sockets about the eyes, the sharply defined zygomatic bones and the tender nose—all pushing against his parchment-thin skin. But Billy smiles reassuringly, and says under his breath to Duncan and Julie conspiratorially: If these bastards think they have me, they've got another thing coming!

Duncan grins and Julie puts her hand to her mouth to stifle a laugh.

They could never stop you, Billy, Duncan says.

Father Canice accompanies him, sitting on Billy's right, while Billy turns in his seat to look out the rear window at Duncan and Julie waving farewell. The sun glares momentarily upon the glass as the van makes its turn, and Billy's face is a white, sun-shocked orb at the window's center, blinking into the light, and searching—desperately it seems—for them.

Duncan and Julie continue to wave goodbye as, spitting gravel and red clay, the van turns in the roadway before the Home. Sun-light shudders on the rear window and Billy is momentarily irradi-ated by its glow so that only the hollow orbits of his eyes and the black line of his mouth are visible. For a moment Duncan sees him as he often does, without disease: His skin is soft and supple, and upon his head a mass of thick blond-white curls, then Billy raises his hand, worsted and speckled and crippled by arthritis, and waves farewell. Duncan knows that even this simple gesture can cause him pain, but that for Billy there is also a certain comfort in this pain—it reminds him that he is still here, waiting in much the same manner as Julie, waiting for someone to return and claim him. The van briefly canters to the left on the rutted track and then straightens and weaves down the monastery's dirt road.

They want to keep him in St. Paul, you know, Julie says. His heart is failing.

Do you think his parents will come for him now?

I don't think they know. Julie shrugs. They gave him up at birth when he looked normal. Just like you. Just like me. Perhaps they didn't know he was sick. Perhaps if they'd known he wouldn't live long, they would have kept him, you know.

Ten years, that isn't too long a time, is it? Even if you're a famous actress or a movie star or a senator or a war hero. That isn't too much time to give up, is it?

Duncan doesn't know if it is or not—he's been lost for ten years and the time since his birth when God spoke to him and his awakening seems vast and without end. He wonders if that is what it feels like for a parent with a child. He tells Julie that he's not sure whether ten years is too long or not long enough. He doesn't know how soon parents tire of their children.

Billy wants to stay here, she says. Father Toibin wants him here, as well.

But why?

This is where Billy's parents brought him. Father Toibin feels it's the Brothers' responsibility to care for him now.

But Billy wants to leave, Duncan says. That's all he wants to do before it's too late. He talks about it all the time. We all want to leave.

No, Duncan. Julie shakes her head; her lips are pursed and determined. The wind throws her hair up in small black tufts about her ears and she presses it back roughly with her hand. We all want to go home, she says.

They stare after Billy's van and out over the valley and beyond, toward Lac qui Parle, where a gleaming sprawl of hastily erected mining shacks, felling cranes, sliders, platforms, and tractors stand derelict and abandoned. From the center of a burn upon distant wooded slopes, an unwavering black line splits the sky in two. There is a flickering high in the eastern sky where the stars will come later, between Cassiopeia and the wide asterism of Cygnus, like a sharp angle of glittering metal, and Duncan sees the disintegrating command module *Columbia* containing Michael Collins falling, tumbling, blazing down from the sky and Billy's van a small speck in all of this as it leaves the winding, rutted monastery road and makes its way north out into the world. *Just like the astronauts.*

August 1981

IT IS THE Feast of the Assumption, and everyone is busy with chores. In the narrow stone halls filigreed with late sunlight there is laughter amidst the bustle. Duncan and Julie are walking the hall from class when Brother Canice gambols toward them, squeezing between the bodies of pressing, pushing children. The bells are oddly silent and Duncan wonders if he should remind Brother Canice that it's time to sound them for prayer. His cheeks are crosshatched with small scratches from shaving. On his neck he's applied small bits of tissue paper to the larger cuts and they're spotted with blood.

Hello, Duncan, he grunts. Hello, Julie.

Hello, Brother Canice, Julie says. How are you?

Oh, good, good, but it's a mad day, he says, absolutely mad! And he glares about the hallway at the children pushing around him. I just don't understand all the fuss, all this rushing about. I mean what on earth is going on?

But isn't it always this way on the Assumption?

The Assumption?

Brother Canice sucks on his teeth and considers this, looks from Julie to Duncan, and then seems to come to some manner of decision. Duncan! he says suddenly, as if just remembering something, and as if Duncan were at the far end of the hallway and not standing directly in front of him.

Yes, Brother?

Father Toibin wants to see you. You can find him in his office. And don't dally, what with all this commotion I forgot he had asked me to find you directly after breakfast this morning.

Aren't you going to ring the bells this morning? Julie asks, and Brother Canice stares at her until they can both see alarm rising slowly in his eyes. The bells, he says softly, like an echo of Julie's voice, and then grasps the hem of his robe and races down the tile toward the campanile.

On a cushion placed upon the high sideboard next to Father Toibin's desk, the cat with the green eyes shudders as if it is dreaming and then stretches languidly. Bits of its hair swirl in the thin feathery light cast by two table lamps.

We are all worried, Father Toibin says, and he opens his hands toward Duncan, a gesture to include, Duncan assumes, all the children in his care.

We are all worried when we feel we might not be as attentive as well as we might. Sometimes we become distracted ourselves and are not always mindful of what it is to be a child and the pressures and forces that they feel. If there is anything bothering you, Duncan? You can tell me.

On the mantel, a clock of black polished ash ticks slowly as if it needs to be wound.

Your mother, I know, loves you and misses you very much, but often parents can be misguided by their own wishes, selfishness which is only brought about by love, really, and they fail to see what is best for their children.

Duncan struggles with Father Toibin's words, and then he struggles to retrieve them. My mother? he thinks, did he say my mother?

We all want what is best for you. Do you understand that?

Father Toibin, my mother?

Father Toibin's voice falters, but even without the words, he attempts to soothe; Duncan is a small boy reflected in shadowy miniature upon his dark pupil: This is your home for as long as you want and for as long as your mother and we think being here is in your best interest. Do you understand that? Do you?

Father, excuse me, but you said my mother?

Yes, yes. Of course, your mother. Father Toibin frowns, pushes a letter across the desk at Duncan, and, momentarily distracted, waves at the window where a red clay road curls into the north—the same road upon which he and Billy returned from Stockholdt.

She's coming to get you.

Duncan holds the letter in his hands as he would the Psalter at Mass, with a sense of the mysterious power of the words on the page before him. He stares at the now-familiar handprint and imagines the letter open upon a table for days before it is sent, and he sees the writer, his mother smelling of guiacol and lily of the valley with her head bowed and her long hair brushing the tabletop, a cigarette smoldering in a glass ashtray, a thin tendril of gray smoke twining toward the ceiling, considering the words over and over again, and wondering if she should send the letter—forever damning herself to him—or tear it up so that no evidence of it or him remains; he imagines that she hesitates, falters, and, finally, succumbing to forces that he may never understand, gives in.

Maggie Bright
34 Divisadero Street
San Francisco, CA 94114

August 3, 1981

Dear Father Toibin,

I have always wanted to do what was best for Duncan and until recently, it seemed in his best interest—and both yourself and Dr. Mathias agreed—that he remain at the monastery in your care. However, given your most recent update, I feel he is ready to come home. I have been separated from my child for too long, and I believe he can and will thrive in the home I provide for him. I am now gainfully employed, have savings in the bank, and close family and friends who are eager to embrace Duncan with love and affection. He will not want for love.

I shall be driving from San Francisco the day after tomorrow, and, after spending some time with friends in Nevada, plan to be at the monastery midday of August the 29th. I would like Duncan to be made aware that I am coming, and that he be prepared to come home with me. I know that, at first, it will not be easy, and that there will be a period of adjustment for both of us, but I am his mother, and however difficult this adjustment might be, it can be nothing compared to what it has been like not to have him here with me all these years. Of course you know something of this from our discussions. There has not been a day or night that I have not thought about my son, and dreamed that he was home with me.

With the blessing of God, I will see you both soon.

Sincerely,
Maggie Bright

Through Father Toibin's office window is everything Duncan knows: harrow-ribbed green pastures, still as a painting, and, at a great distance, ashen smoke plumes along the Iron Range, and men walking on the steeper hillsides beating the furze where blazing stars, goldenrod, and asters bloom, and beyond them the striated ridges of hardwood: red maple and pin cherry. *Everything I know.* And now, his mother coming to get him. Just like in his dream.

Father Toibin is still talking. He's worried about how such a visit might affect him. Would he like to see her? Is he nervous? Excited? Scared? How does he feel about leaving the Home? Has he been sleeping? How are his friendships with the other children? Brother Canice has had nothing but praise for him, but Father Malachy has mentioned his withdrawal, his recent lack of participation in events, and he is worried because—

But Father, my mother, Duncan says. My mother. I thought she was, I mean, isn't she . . . dead?

Julie fiddles with the brilliantly lacquered black wig she has pulled down over her hair, and smiles. This, she says, was from the children's production of *Whose Baby Are You Now?* that the Home put on when she was eight, but of course Duncan wouldn't remember that. She takes Duncan's hand as they walk among the gardens. The smells of late summer come and go with the winds that always seem at twisting motion upon the plains. At a bench they sit down and Julie lays her head against his chest and he stares at the fake tea-colored center part in the hair.

On the far side of the garden, toward the soccer pitch: the sound of children at play. The hoarse coughing of the prefix. They laugh as he shouts, and Duncan imagines his ineffectual attempts to control the children or whatever game they are playing. They listen for the names they know, the usual culprits and offenders.

I have to leave, he says. Julie pulls at a knot in her wig. She sighs.

My mother is coming to get me. You'll get to meet her.

A Brother begins to shout at a boy, and Duncan laughs, expecting Julie to do so also, but she merely stares toward the sound.

I'm the only one who knew you were sleeping, she says. I'm the one that knew you'd woken up from a divine sleep. I'm the one that found you.

I know.

Your mother, she says, is she pretty? Is she a great actress?

I don't know. I don't think so. But Duncan does; in his mind he pictures the woman from his dream standing before the Festival of Lights Holiday Train as it glitters in fractured and failing illumination through the swirling snow, and he sees his mother's bright, damp cheeks, and the fierce blue of her large, almond shaped eyes, and everything—the land, the storm, the train—is lost in her and subsumed by her: In his dream she is the center of the world.

Julie thinks about this for a moment and nods. She says: If your mother is going to leave you, she should be beautiful and rich and fantastic. Those things are important, more important than any child, don't you think?

On the walkway a group of six girls are playing jump rope. On each end a girl swings two ropes, the rope on the left turning clockwise and the one on the right turning in a counterclockwise loop. They pass the two ropes from hand to hand and their arcs are parabolic, shifting orbits crossing and merging, crossing and merging in a hypnotic blur; and as the girls turn the ropes, and as the other girls skip, they sing.

Julie kicks her legs in time to the skipping song. Faintly: the slap and scrape of the jump rope upon the stone, the girls' voices in song, unchanging despite the failing light.

Julie stops her legs and grasps at his shoulder with a thin hand. It doesn't matter anyway, Duncan, she says. She'll leave you again. She will. It's what mothers do.

WAITING, DUNCAN STANDS on the hill and looks out over the valley. The sun is high, and despite a breeze pushing the long grass this way and that, the air is thick. A small herd of cows lazily chews cud, others flick their tails as they drink from the stream. Cicadas thrum loudly in the trees of the arboretum. Upon the pond the heat of the day shimmers; ducks have been attacking one another all day, and their feathers drift through the air like flax.

Upon the far slope a row of wire bales trembles, flashes refracted sunlight in Morse code. He sees the dust cloud first, and then the car as it speeds through the valley and up the winding road toward the Home, the dust cloud behind it growing larger and more violent. As it comes nearer, it takes shape: a black Chevy Impala from the late sixties, a decommissioned police car with the outline of the original star-shaped emblems upon its doors, blacker than the rest of the faded metal, and it buckles and bottoms out on the rutted, potholed road spiraling up to the Home.

After she steps from the car and stretches her long body, she pauses and surveys the land—isolated farmhouses upon yellowed siderite fields, the dark Iron Range stretching like a storm cloud entrenched across the horizon—and then squints up at the sun. Her skin is so white it looks as if it has never seen the sun, and the wind has turned her hair in knots: it's as red and as wild as flame. Something in her shifts, something indecipherable and almost undetectable—he senses it in her posture, in the conflict of softness and tension that comes to her face, and he wonders if it is fear—and then she straightens her skirt, reaches back into the car for a wide-brimmed sun hat, which she places upon her head, and takes a determined step toward the gate of the monastery. And that is when she sees him. She stops and the world seems to tilt about her.

Duncan, she says, and he wonders how she knows it is him.

She crosses the dirt driveway and takes his hand and he searches her face for some truth, some sign of fear or hesitation. Her eyes are the same blue as his own.

I'm your mother, she says. You probably don't remember me— and she laughs as if at the absurdity of it all, and Duncan smiles. From the valley below a wind cock clanging hollow on tin, the far-away thock of axes on wood. Within the monastery's walls children are running and calling to one another and he wonders if Julie can see him from her window.

So, she says slowly, testing the words for the both of them. Shall we go home? Would you like that?

Yes, he nods, yes, wanting to say *Mom* yet knowing that he can't, not just yet, and then she pulls him to her and he holds on tightly, smelling things he will only later be able to identify as her: patchouli, apple-scented shampoo, the pungent red burley of her hand-rolled cigarettes, and strangely, oil and lye-heavy industrial soap of the type men who spend their days working on engines use, as if she had just stepped out of an auto repair shop, and he wonders if this smell comes from the man who might be his father or if her car broke down on the way here and whether it is capable of taking them the vast distance across America to San Francisco and where he imagines home, whatever such a place is, must be.

Beneath the Romanesque arches of the main entrance Brother Canice and Father Toibin are waiting with his bags, a bulging tattered brownish-yellow suitcase held together by old clasps spotted with rust and his army duffel bag. There are some of the boys from his dormitory and other children with whom he has shared classes. Most of them look bored or indifferent and he knows that Father Toibin has arranged this for him. Julie stands slightly to the side as if unsure of what to do or say. The sound of children from the playing field comes to them from over the ivy-covered stone walls.

Today Julie has two red hair clips in her hair, and there is a small beauty spot an inch or so above the far right corner of her lip that he knows was not there before. She pulls him to her, and he can only think of her smell—of glycerin soap and warm, moist skin; of her hair, washed and brushed and shining like lacquer. Finally, smiling, she pushes him roughly away, and he watches the beauty spot rise on the curving edge of her lip. He whispers to Julie that he loves her— and he does—and that he will never forget her.

Brother Canice's eyes are red-rimmed. The thick, untamed orange-red sideburns that run rampant over the sides of his jaws and neck are matted down with oil. He's freshly shaven and so severely his skin looks raw and tender. A breeze bends Father Toibin's pant legs lazily around his ankles and he must constantly mat down the thin hair he lays over his bald crown.

Julie stares defiantly at him as the car pulls away, Julie who every year will never age but remain a little girl, thinking that if she remains a little girl, her mother will finally come back for her and she will be everything her mother has ever desired.

They stand at the gates of the orphanage and wave goodbye and he watches from the back window of the car as they drive away, knowing that he will never see them again. He sits watching from the backseat of the car until he can no longer see them and the Home is nothing but a glinting speck in the divide of two valleys darkened by strip mining. Distantly the bell for Vigil tolls from the campanile and he bends his head toward its plaintive, tremulous sound, imagining Brother Canice heaving heavily upon the ropes.

I'm sorry about your friend, Duncan. Father Toibin told me. His name was Billy, is that right?

The sound of his mother's voice startles him and it takes a moment for him to understand what she's said to him. He nods. Tattered-looking, windswept clouds move quickly across the sky, seeming to follow their car; in the east a large dark front whips the plains with black virga, and he shivers imagining the cold rain that is coming and the trains that he and Billy never took.

Please turn around, Duncan, and sit down, his mother says gently, and he turns back in his seat and sees for the first time the country that they are passing through: gray furrowed hillsides scraped raw from boring the pith. A fine dusty powder of anthracite ash bleached white from the sun lies upon the alkyl hills and plains.

And then they cross into pastureland where men are shadows of black metal in the shimmering fields. They are burning the dead crop: bright flames cutting swathes across the valley, black choking smoke billowing and sweeping across flattened fields and rising, churning, up to the sky. Duncan has seen this only from beyond the walls of the Home and he wonders with not just a little fear at what will become of the two of them, him and his mother, now that they only have each other. He pulls his body inward; the comforting sense of his mother is gone—the physical space between them widening. His hands scrabble for his bag and the hard, reassuring edges of Brother Canice's radio, which he wraps his arms about and pulls to his chest.

If you're tired, she says, and her voice seems very far away, you can lie down. There's some blankets back there on the floor. It's a long trip, and we'll both need to rest.

Thanks, he says, and stretches across the backseat, bunches a blanket beneath his head, pulls another over him. The thrum of the engine and the vibration of the road up through the chassis begin to lull him toward sleep. The partially open windows seem to shudder and bow silently with wind. He hears the clicking of the turn signal as she changes lanes, then the irregular thump of the wipers as they pass through a sudden rainsquall and the interior of the car grows dark. He looks at her in the rearview mirror, watches her glancing back every now and then, until he can no longer hold open his eyes.

Maggie watches him until he is asleep, then allows her eyes to follow the far horizon, its indeterminate distance teasingly close and yet seemingly untouchable, always just beyond them. She turns on the radio, hums softly to an old Western ballad that comes crackling through the speakers, raises her voice slightly and attempts to sing, but her voice falters and breaks and she begins to cough. She reaches across to the glove compartment for the fifth of whiskey that she keeps there, but then pulls her hand back. She doesn't need it, not yet. This is her time to prove to him and to herself that she is a different woman, a better woman than the one she has been all these years.

An hour passes and she considers pulling over but doesn't want him to wake. Heat lightning blurs the top of distant hills. The black shapes of wide-winged birds turn in slow circles way up there and she peers beneath the visor to get a better look at them: buzzards waiting for something on the ground to give up the fight. She punches in the cigarette lighter at the base of the dashboard, and when it pops out, she fumbles with lighting a cigarette, then takes it in long and deep before exhaling out the window, stares blankly at three bowed-backed, dun-colored cows taking water in a grassless pasture, ribs pressed like dark bars against their skin.

When the cigarette is done, she runs her tongue across her teeth and grimaces, checks Duncan in the rearview: asleep and snoring softly. She chews on her lips, is conscious of how dry her mouth feels, heat and dust on back of her throat. Finally she reaches across, careful to hold the car steady, and opens the glove compartment, pulls the fifth from beneath parking tickets and the car registration, does the top with one hand, and takes a swig. It is only for the heat and for her nerves, she convinces herself, and for nothing more. She turns the radio louder over the sound of the car pushing forward toward the horizon and the hot wind pressing in at the open windows, and begins to sing softly. This time her voice does not falter but she knows that this is a temporary thing, that her larynx with its scar tissue will never allow her to sing as fully as she once did. Absently she takes another swig, holds the whiskey in her mouth, and touches her throat as it convulses and the alcohol slides slowly down.

As a child and as a teenager, she'd been classically trained by Madame Buvelle of the Boston and Berkeley conservatories, and in her early twenties had debuted as a coloratura soprano with the Boston Opera. When she sang, she reached notes that had rarely been recorded before—in a bureau drawer, beneath her old stage dresses, programs, and all the yellowed issues of *Opera* with reviews of her performances, she's kept the live recording of her reaching G7, the highest vocal note in the history of recorded opera. And with her remarkable low, which she sang as Amelia in Verdi's *Un ballo in maschera*, her voice ranged over more than five octaves.

People who'd heard her sing likened her to Erna Sack, the German coloratura soprano who was known to reach C4 and nicknamed the "German Nightingale," and Mado Robin, the French coloratura soprano who could hit c7. But it was the Swedish soprano Silva Bröhm, to whom she drew the most comparisons.

She looked like a pale, redheaded sister of Bröhm, the woman she would more and more come to resemble and venerate, the abused soprano who was forced to sing at such heights across such ranges again and again that she destroyed her larynx and committed suicide at the height of her career, threw herself from the forty-seventh floor of the Royal Düsseldorf on Manhattan's Upper East Side in 1927.

Maggie did not kill herself, but then her end took her by surprise. One winter night in 1962, during a performance of Mozart's *Zauberflöte*, which had tested the full breadth of her range and in which her aria as the Queen of the Night brought the crowd to their feet, her voice broke—silently—forever; the folds of her larynx swelled and, in the days that followed, hardened like scar tissue. And all the while she was happily, blissfully, unaware.

It was one note—a B3 perhaps—out of thousands of notes, in a three-hour opera that she had performed dozens of times, but it was the end of her career. After the performance she rushed ecstatically toward the railway station through lightly falling snow—through what was now left of old Scollay Square: the remnants of the Olympia, with its crumbling facade; the Crawford House, famous home of Sally Keith, queen of the tasseled breasts; the Half-Dollar Bar; the famous Crescent Grill; and around the corner from Tremont Row on Howard Street, the peaked roof of the 115-year-old Howard Athenaeum, one of the most famous burlesque theaters in the world. All stood still and empty now. The high-density sodium bulbs that once shone OLYMPIA in an arc across the avenue had been extinguished for years, and in their place all that remained were a few single lamps burning in the windows of derelict brownstones whose last residents refused eviction and awaited the wrecking ball.

A sailor, arm in arm with his girl, both bundled in heavy wools, cross beneath the streetlamps of Cambridge Street, having just come from drinks and hot dogs at Joe and Nemo's on Stoddard Street. At the edge of the square, they pause in a hazy circle of light amidst the slanting snow. They are laughing, and their laughter is bright and clear and resonant as a fine bell chime in the cold air, so attractive a sound that Maggie turns her head for a moment to gaze their way, and she catches the lovers in a kiss. When they part, that kiss—a bright red, full-lipped kiss—floats up, up, up the snowlit night. It rises above the cracked arch of the Olympia, the rusty cable-fretted and pinioned spire of the Athenaeum, high above the Crawford House and Joe and Nemo's, until it is above the rooftops of Tops Hill, where it swells, and all the thousands of caterwauling candy butchers and tasseled strippers and crooning and dying singers and five-piece orchestras—horns and trumpets and drums blasting and grinding—of past burlesques reverberate with that kiss throughout the dimly lit, run-down row houses and huddled tenements of crumbling old Scollay Square.

A tenant on a third floor looks from his lamp to gaze up at that kiss, and for a moment he pauses to wonder at those old ghosts that have haunted his memory so. And all driven white beneath the swirling storm like a magical kingdom within a snow globe, until everything is covered in white, but for that kiss, and Maggie Bright rushing on through it all, rushing to catch a train, the old B&M line from North Station, to meet the man who would become Duncan's father, never thinking that her voice had reached a height it would never again achieve.

As she drives, and as Duncan sleeps lightly in the backseat, covered in an old throw blanket smelling slightly of mildew and oil, she watches him in the rearview mirror and fights to keep back tears, her knuckles turning white upon the wheel, as both joy and fear work upon her and everything from her past—and all her failures, but Duncan—rushes to the fore, and the landscape heading west blurs before her. She wipes at her eyes with the back of a hand, glances again in the mirror, watches as wind from the partially opened windows trembles the hair atop his head. There are shadows beneath his eyes and he is much too pale, but she will make him eat and gain weight and put him to bed at a regular hour as any good mother would. She will make him strong and happy and make up for all that has been lost between them. He swallows and coughs as if his throat is dry, and anxiety momentarily quivers in her stomach until he settles again. She sighs, wants to pull to the side of the road and wake him up, hold him to her, convince them both that this is real. The presence of him within the car fills her senses and she smiles when she thinks of them together—the absurdity and the rightness of it finally—and suddenly she is laughing, laughing with such happiness that it startles her, amazed at where such an all-consuming happiness might come from and how now, after all this time, it could possibly be hers.

Angels, (they say) are often unable to tell whether they move
among living or dead.
The eternal torrent whirls all the ages through either realm for
ever, and sounds above their voices in both.

—RAINER MARIE RILKE

ON A HIGH hill in the middle of the humpbacked city is Ipswich Street, and between a row of once-grand but now-decrepit brick Georgians owned by successful shipmen of the 1800s—the only brick homes in this part of the city—is a gray, asbestos-tiled Victorian where Duncan and Maggie live as tenants-at-will, surviving from one paycheck to the next.

They live in a world above the clouds, where gulls—terns and gannets and cormorants the color of pitch—shriek as they rise and fall and flap madly toward heaven. From his window Duncan can see

the distant orange pitons of the Golden Gate Bridge showing themselves just above the morning fog, like the pointed peaks of some
strange mountain range rising from the roof of the mist-shrouded
world below. And during these moments he can forget that they live
in a city, that its streets and buildings surround and encapsulate them
with noise and the sound of so many people in pain, from the caterwauling drunks making their way from the Barrio down Ipswich toward the Wreck and the Barrows when the bars close at night, to the
men and women who stand on the corner of Columbus and Vine
waiting for the methadone clinic to open each morning. Sometimes
it would be hours before the fog burned away and the cityscape re-
vealed itself, amidst the tolling bells of St. Mary of the Wharves,
and then it was as if a veil had been thrown off, as if he were waking
slowly from a long, still-evolving dream.

From the rented house on Ipswich Street: a long broken street of
buckling sidewalk slabstones, like a bough curved over the hill, and
then descending on either side into the bookends of the Wreck and
the Barrows, from where rail workers, Edison power plant workers,
and tannery workers trudged in the pre-dawn, lunch pails swinging,
cigarettes bursting in silent fiery bloom between their lips, and the
sound of their voices, carrying on the colder days, barking loudly in
greeting to one another.

In the evenings the distant-seeming shouts and hollers of the same
men returning home after the Edison plant whistle has sounded the
changing of shifts, and of barges making their way down into the bay,
moaning like mournful sea creatures through the bruised light, and
the briny smell of fish, of plaice and catfish and shad washed up upon
the oily banks where the old wharves decay and where, during his
walks home from school at twilight, he'd find the fish, left as the
water retreated, half submerged in muck and oil, floundering and
gasping their last.

In the beginning, he hurried to pick up the fish, raced down to
the water's edge and, one by one, hurled them out as far as he could

into the bay, wishing them safe passage back to the sea. But always they found their way back. The next day he'd stare into the eye of a gasping fish, its mouth puckering slowly, and know it was from the day or the week before—he cannot explain how he knows this, only that he does. Perhaps it is the shape of a tattered fin or a corkscrew scar upon the scales, the black dots upon the underbelly, or simply by the large eye that seems to gaze up at him, glassy and slick and filled with some inexpressible and indescribable longing. He'd watch over them and talk to them and sometimes offer up a prayer. Once, an old man in a peaked yellow rain hat and yellow waders stood, tottering, calve deep in the mud at the water's edge, watching him. A rusted clam rake dangled in his hand. Duncan gestured helplessly at him but the man shook his head vigorously and bent back down to his scraping.

And gradually their numbers multiplied, so that soon, of an evening, hundreds of stinking, dying fish lay scattered across the banks of the waterway like silver spars dotted with rot and decay, and only for the occasional slapping and convulsion did they appear like fish at all.

When he asks his mother why they do it, she looks at him and says: Who do what?

The fish. Why do they swim onto the banks and kill themselves like that?

What fish, honey?

Can't you smell it? he says. On my way home from school there's hundreds and hundreds of them every day washed up on the banks. Everything stinks of them. The street, the house stinks of them.

He walks to the open window, puts his nose to the air and inhales. The tide has left the water in the channel at its lowest, and as the sun turns the hollow of the waterway orange and aflame, small black shapes flutter and flap in the mud there, impotent as moths. His nostrils flare with the odor and he gags. He draws his head back in and his mother is laughing.

That look on your face, dear Jesus, Duncan. What on earth is wrong with you?

You can't smell it? he asks, incredulously.

No. She shakes her head. I can't, and I'll have you know that I've got an excellent sense of smell.

There is the park named after Joseph Wood Tyner, the business tycoon and owner of the tannery and steelworks who developed Salt Hill, with forlorn bushes that, ragged as they are, bloom a brilliant fuchsia in the early summer and a rusted swing set and slide and half a dozen crumbling, concrete animals—hippo, elephant, giraffe, rhinoceros, crocodile, and tiger—from the early sixties that no children dare climb anymore. On the days when Duncan chooses not to go to school he wanders here, at times kicking his legs lazily while on the swing, listening to its chains squealing in protest, and watches the trains making their way from the rail yards, the diesel engines thumping rhythmically, the sound reverberating and vibrating off the surrounding houses and, enlarged, sounding like a great heart to his ears.

In Duncan's room there are reminders of the Home—a mildewed, water-stained ceiling, yellowed wallpaper curling at the edges where it meets the painted baseboards—but there is no sense of children here, no haunting quality of their loss or desire or even their sudden, abrupt joyous cries of a day or night. Upon the wall over his dresser are the pictures torn from books and magazines that he brought with him—a smiling, nunlike Olivia de Havilland from *Whose Baby Are You Now?*; the *Times* cover of the '69 Apollo moon landing—and a simple dark-stained wooden cross that Father Toibin said he should keep. Previous tenants left the dresser behind and his mother has painted it blue. In the mornings the sun rises above the waterway, casts its trembling light across the flitting, wave-flecked top of the channel and, as it rises above the dirty leaves of the three speckled and diseased maples, and pokes through his window—a gossamer of sheer lace curtains; a haze of spiderweb—it glows upon this veneer, shimmering waterlike, before reaching his bed.

And then there is the sudden rain that lashes the glass at times, sends the frame shuddering, as surprising and startling violent storms rush in from the bay, or the great shoals of fog that settle oddly for only a few hours at most before being swept away and on those clear nights the brilliant curve of the moon angling bright upon his wall and illuminating Olivia.

Of an evening around twilight, Mother stands beside him at the living room window and they look to the ruins at the bottom of the hill, a valley in which the old factory row houses sit, a jumble of walls and gaps, entryways and alleys out to the channel, with brickwork about the empty windows, and built, seemingly, with granite slate and blue shale sloughed from beneath the waters when they dredged and dug the channel two hundred years before.

You didn't believe I would ever come for you, did you? she says.

And Duncan looks at her, a tall red-haired woman in a black dress, her skin so pale and cold-looking he feels goose bumps rise upon his arms. He shakes his head. No, I didn't.

But here we are, she says and takes his hand and pulls him toward her and squeezes him so tightly, desperately it seems, that he can barely breathe. A record has just ended upon the old Victor phonograph, and Mother begins to sing, her raggedy yet strangely beautiful voice filling the large crumbling Victorian with nineteenth-century ballads, and bluesy tales of woe and loss, and spirituals ripe with redemption, and the smell of rotting fish is wafting in upon a nighttime breeze that stirs the sheer, yellow-bleached curtains before the windows as the earth turns through its meridians and darkness comes slowly down and spins them through the stars. And even with the smell of fish, to Duncan it seems the most wonderful place in the world.

November 1981

ON WEEKENDS, AFTER Maggie's shift at St. Luke's Hospital, they go to the Windsor Tap on Columbus where she sings every Thursday night. Flags and banners of various regiments, divisions, and battalions hang like bunting over the back of the bar. Most prominent are the AAs of Army Airborne and the globe and anchor of the Marines. She buys Duncan a Coke and orders him the one-dollar cheeseburger with fries, and as he sits at the bar and Clay grills the meat, she goes to dance with men on the beer-bleached dance floor. Mostly they are friends of hers whom Duncan recognizes, but sometimes there are other men, strangers who will arrive at their door in a day or two and mother will leave with for the night. He'll hear the key in the lock sometime after midnight, and his mother whispering to this or that man to be quiet and to tread softly on the stairs. Then his mother's door will close, the tabletop Victrola will begin spinning its record softly, and the bedsprings will groan and squeal as their weight settles upon the old mattress.

Tonight Duncan is at the bar, sitting next to Joshua McGreevey, an old friend of his mother's from back east, and together they watch her as she dances by herself on the worn, amber-colored parquet. Charlie Pride plays on the jukebox, and the sound of "Kiss an Angel Good Morning" fills the bar. Maggie drinks her whiskey, Old Mainline 454, straight, and while she dances, she holds the glass tenderly, as if it is something incredibly fragile. When she relinquishes her hold upon it and puts it down on the bar, Clay refills it, as he always does, and because of this Duncan can never be quite sure of how much she has had to drink, but he has often tried to count.

Joshua is singing to himself, so softly and bent so low over the bar that at first Duncan can not make out the words—there is only the melody, a haunting soothing music whose strange familiarity makes Duncan at once feel at peace. Joshua stares into the glass at the back of the bar and only pauses in his singing to drink and wipe beer froth from his mouth. His eyes burn brightly in his gaunt, black face, on his hard-looking cheekbones. *O au o. The lights in Sai Gon are green and red, the lamps in My Tho are bright and dim.* The timbre sounds deep in his chest, much like Duncan's mother's voice when she sings "Roddy McCorley," and yet from Joshua's lips it has a breaking, fragile quality filled with yearning and tenderness. It may have been the only song Joshua knew but still Duncan thinks he has one of the sweetest voices he's ever heard.

Joshua wears what he always seems to be wearing: an old, olive-colored field jacket frayed at the upturned collar and cuffs, but there are no markings on it. The jacket does not even seem as if it belongs to him. A dark blue bandanna pulls the skin tight at his scalp. Joshua works as part of a tunneling crew on the San Padre Tunnel project seventy feet beneath the bay and to Duncan he smells pleasingly of sea silt and shale, of damp and pungent muck and loam, as if he had been dredged from the deep bottom of the world.

Joshua stares down at Duncan, glances at the NASA Apollo patches on Duncan's denim jacket sleeves.

Ahh, Duncan, man, you don't really believe that, do you?

Believe what?

That shit that they landed someone on the moon. That was all done in Hollywood sound studios. It was all a stunt. Joshua gulps his beer and Duncan watches his Adam's apple convulse.

I believed once, kid. I believed in JFK. I believed in doing for my country, never mind what my country did for me. I joined the Special Forces. Ever see John Wayne in *The Green Berets*? What a load of shit.

Here are some facts, kid, and maybe you can tell me what you make of it all. Maybe you can explain it to me. During the moon landing they managed to beam a live TV picture back to Earth, from over 240,000 miles away. That doesn't strike you as odd? You know what television was like in the sixties? And get this, there were no delays in NASA's TV broadcast to the American public—we're talking 240,000 miles here, kiddo, and there's no delay in the transmission? C'mon. Look, we just didn't have the technology. NASA said it in '68 when they gave the odds of completing the moon landings a 0.0012 percent chance of success. They were speaking the truth, man.

Joshua tips back his beer, and bangs the empty on the bar. He stares at Duncan, and Duncan stares back. Joshua sighs. How do you figure top Hollywood execs being on NASA's payroll, including Stanley Kubrick? How do you figure that many of the shots so closely resemble shots from Kubrick's *2001*?

And tell me kid, if landing on the moon was so easy for us twenty odd years ago, how come we haven't done it since? You know why? Because we can't. And the Russians can't. No one can. We failed, kid, and that's the truth.

They landed on the moon, Duncan says, but they never took off. They died up there.

They what?

They died up there. They're still up there. Duncan tilts his head slightly and eyes the ceiling of the bar. He holds his eyes wide as he stares at Joshua.

Up there, yeah? Joshua says like an echo and touches one of Duncan's patches with a finger. Shit, you're on better stuff than the crap they give me down at the VA.

He shakes his head. C'mon kid, don't be like your Daddy.

You knew my Daddy?

Of course I knew your Daddy.

Duncan glances up the bar to see if his mother is within earshot. She's looking back as if she'd already caught him in a wrongdoing, a skill that he marvels at, and that always leaves him frustrated and yet somehow glad. But in this moment he wants her to be elsewhere; he wants to know what Joshua knows about his father.

Joshua, Mother says, and her jaws clench. Do you want me to call Clay and get you kicked out of here? Leave my son alone. He knows nothing about any of your damn conspiracies.

A smile plays on Joshua's lips. He shakes his head. Buy me a beer, Maggie, and let's forget about it. I slipped, that's all. My mistake. I confused your boy with someone else—what's your name, son? Joshua looks at Duncan, feigning confusion, blinking as if seeing Duncan for the first time. He rubs his eyes hard and stares again, opening his eyes wide, and Duncan laughs.

Yeah, I know how it is. Mother gestures toward Clay, and, as she does, she asks Joshua: Do you have your bike with you?

Sure.

If I start buying you drinks, you have to promise me you won't ride.

Joshua holds two fingers to his breast. Scout's honor.

Why don't I believe you? I'm going to put some money in the jukebox. I'll just be gone a minute. Can I trust you with my son?

Sure, Maggie. You got it.

She strides toward the jukebox, and Duncan is aware of men's eyes following her. He glances at the sway of her hips, the straightness of her back. Joshua seems to be the only man not watching. He's staring at Duncan. Suddenly he tugs hard at the patches on Duncan's sleeve, leans his mouth close to Duncan's ear so that Duncan can feel the heat of his breath, the sour smell of cheep beer, and mouths: *Kid, don't be like your Daddy.*

His beer comes and he lifts it to his lips. To America! he shouts. To Neil Armstrong and Buzz Aldrin and Michael Collins! The top of the beer is frothy and the froth spills white down his chin and darkens his T-shirt. From over the rim of the large glass he winks. His Adam's apple works up and down and then he slams the glass down upon the bar.

When he looks up his eyes are red and swollen; his breath comes in deep gulps. Another beer, he says, and Clay looks at him warily. C'mon, Clay. I'm fine. Give us a motherfucking beer, would you.

This time, when the beer comes, Joshua drinks it slow, leans forward on the bar.

Maggie has put in her money and the jukebox begins to play. The sound of Billie Holiday swells around the room. When Maggie returns, she touches Joshua gently on the shoulder and squeezes. Joshua nods, sips his beer, and stares into the bar mirror. They leave before her songs are done playing. When Duncan reminds her that they haven't heard all her songs and that she's lost her money in the jukebox, she looks sad. Finally she says: They weren't for me, Duncan. They were for Joshua.

Every Friday, Duncan and Maggie attend Vespers at St. Mary of the Wharves, and listen to the choir singing *De Profundis*, the psalm of the holy souls in purgatory: *Apud Dominum misericordia, et copiosa apud eum redemptio.* And Duncan sees astronauts, not just Michael Collins, but hundreds and thousands of men adrift throughout the cosmos—faceless men with the sun reflected in their golden, mirrored visors—all dead, all desanguinated and floating through the heavens, flashing through the crystalline, neo-chrome tails of fiery comets a hundred miles long, and always, the star-spangled banner across their left shoulder blinking in the crimson and blue haze of stellar ash a hundred million years old.

He thinks of the astronauts and cosmonauts sent on space missions that the world had never heard of or been told about because of their failures—and of all the astronauts thrust into space upon the pinhead of the great *Saturn V* rockets that were still out there somewhere, lost just like his father and unable to come home. He watches his mother mouth the words, the wet clicking of her mouth like a metronome. She smiles, and reaches for his hand, and when he takes it, and closes his eyes, he hears the longing of all those exiled from Heaven, all that pain and suffering for which prayers, in the absence of God's embrace, Father Toibin always said, offered the only succor.

Later during Mass, when the priest shakes the aspergillum and sprinkles them with holy water, Duncan turns to the back of the church and sees Joshua there, his head lowered on his forearms as if he were at the Windsor Tap and dusk has just fallen outside.

When he and Mother rise, Joshua is still sitting in his pew: head bowed, eyes closed, and looking so peaceful he might have be sleeping. But Duncan knows it's the meds that he takes, that in the evenings he often lines up on the bar and puts back with his beer. Mother sidles down the pew, lowers her head, and whispers to him, asks him to come back to the house with them, but Joshua raises his head groggily and waves her away.

In the transept, Duncan places coins in the prayer box and they clatter loudly in its bottom. He begins lighting as many candles as he can, for suddenly he feels an emptiness so vast he can put no name to it. He thinks of all the souls in purgatory lost to God and he knows that if he and his mother were to die in this very moment, they would need such a powerful intercession of grace to be with Him in His Kingdom that he fears that they might be lost forever as well. *Purgatory* resounds in his head as if his skull were the inner chamber of a bell.

Honey, who are you lighting all those candles for? Mother asks. Leave some for other people, would you?

Duncan ignores her and rests his knees on the padded rest, places his forehead against his entwined knuckles, stares at the flickering flames muted through the blue glass, smells wax and lead wick melting. The lingering odor of incense. Cool air rushing up the nave. He hears an altar boy practicing his swing of the censer for the blessing of the Eucharist, the chain taut through its pendulous stroke, and the slight rattle of the censer at the height of that arc. Mother kneels beside him and begins praying as well, and he takes comfort in this. As they pray, her voice surging beside him, thrumming beneath the bones of his chest as when she sang to him, his fears begin to fade.

On the way out of church she takes his hand in hers and swings her arm. That was nice of you, lighting a candle for Joshua.

Duncan looks at her, and she smiles.

You always light five. I assumed the extra one was for him.

He nods.

It's important that we pray for people, most especially for people who can't help themselves.

Why can't Joshua help himself?

Mother doesn't respond, and when he asks again, she sighs. It was the war. He's not the same as the Joshua I used to know. Sometimes he does things . . . it's not his fault. You would have liked the old Joshua.

I like this Joshua.

I know, honey, I know. She nods and looks toward the rooftops but there is only the dark blue sky with night sinking down through it like ink. The last of the sun has sunk into the bay.

What happened to Joshua in the war? he asks.

I don't really know, honey. He doesn't talk about it. Sometimes, though, I wish he would, just so I could understand him better.

She swings his arm and their footsteps sound on the tile as they skip, but he knows that she is thinking of the Joshua she once knew and the man he was now, and in the space of those years, everything that has been lost between them.

SUNDAYS AFTER MASS Joshua often joins them for dinner. Sometimes he shows up, and other times they don't see him for weeks, but always Duncan waits by the bay window watching for some sight or sound of his bike—a big old Indian Chief from the fifties—coming up the hills. When Joshua is there, the house seems like a different place. The Victor hums in the corner of the room in its mahogany cabinet and Maggie wears one of her fine stage dresses from *Lucia* or *Tristan und Isolde*, which she'd stolen from the opera company before her vocal cords had knotted like wood, and in amusement he watches them play out a romance from when they were teenagers and lived in the same neighborhood, just outside Boston.

She puts out the crystal-cut sherry glasses with dinner even when Joshua and she are only drinking Liberty beer. He has always shaved and washed his hair and put on a clean dress shirt and tie beneath his field jacket, and always he rings the bell and stands at the threshold as if he were a stranger to their house and might be turned away.

And he steps into the foyer in his clean dress shirt and tie as if he were a stranger in his own skin. Lose the tie, Mother always says, and that look on your face—as if someone just died.

But whenever Joshua returns for Sunday dinner he's wearing the tie again, and looking just as awkward and out of place as he looked the first time.

Today when Duncan hears the rumbling of Joshua's Indian from a block away, he rushes from the couch and waits by the door. It's been two weeks since they saw him at the Windsor Tap, and Duncan has missed him, his absence magnified by his mother's keeping company with other men. When Joshua comes to the door, Duncan waves at him through the glass and Joshua nods, his eyes bright in their sockets—when he's been without sleep, the skin beneath his eyes looks bruised and darker than the rest of his face—then smiles and pushes the bell.

Maggie comes running from the kitchen, wiping her hands on a dish towel and shaking her head. You'd think he was crossing the damn enemy's perimeter. For God's sake. Joshua, the door's open— come in!

Duncan smells his sweat, a cloudy tobacco aroma on his shirt, and the faint scent of gasoline and engine oil. He's splashed on Old Spice, something Duncan figures all fathers wear, and when he raises the bottle of Liberty to his mouth as they sit down to dinner, Duncan watches the tendons in his forearm tensing like fine metal cables. He talks about the tunnel, tells them how they have three giant tunnel-boring machines that they've named after Saint Barbara, the patron saint of miners and tunnel builders; Saint Dymphna, the saint of mental illness, because they must be mad to do such work; and the Archangel Gabriel, to ensure should they die he will hold their place with God.

Joshua says: Someone thought about calling one of the TBMs Brooke Shields, but the foreman, Minkivitz, put a stop to that. He asks the guy if he's one of those freaks who likes little girls. Hell, he tells him, I've got a daughter older than her, what's the hell's the matter with you?

When Joshua catches Duncan staring, he nods and smiles, reaches out his hand to touch Duncan's, and his hand stays there tapping, as if to make sure Duncan is truly there or perhaps to reassure him. *My man*, he says, like a chant, *my man*.

February 1982

FROM HIS BEDROOM window Duncan watches old streetwalkers stumbling in their high heels on the broken slabstones before their house as they head down to the Wreck and the Barrows—and he thinks of the different types of men his mother brings home when she's drinking: Bob or Paul or Harry—sometimes Hi kid and a saw-buck or a candy bar or a comic but mostly a look of boredom or disinterest. Some of them can't even fake being interested and he thinks he likes that the best—neither of them have to lie.

For hours after they leave, his mother sits in a chair by the kitchen window looking blankly out at the night, one leg crossed tightly over the other. A Claymore burns slowly down in her hand, a large brown paper shopping bag, twisted and tightly wrung-marked from her worn but strong hands carrying them all the long way up the hill, on the small ash-burnt Formica table before her. A bare lightbulb dangles from the cord and throws something that looks like her face onto the dark glass.

At this time of night there isn't anything to see beyond that square of black but the power lines and the train yards, where engines loudly join with their cars, so loudly it's like thunder amidst the startling screech of brakes. Perhaps she is thinking about where the trains are going and if she possibly might end up on one of them, or perhaps she is thinking about all the trains and all the destinations she had missed in her life. The reverberating echo of a horn and the clanging of the big joining rings, the BA-BOOOM! when they connected, tell of a journey about to begin once again without her, and the *Da dum-dum Da dum-dum* of the wheels striking the metal expansion joints and quickening as the train picked up speed until the sound is almost strung together like the syncopated roll of a snare drum fading into the distance—*Da dum-dum, Da dum-dum*—all these things a constant reminder of places she will never go and of a place she will never leave.

Duncan can't believe they have gotten used to the sound, but they have. Even those familiar strangers to the house, those small tall big fat thin men, all jumped the first time they heard it.

Before dawn Duncan shuffles into the kitchen and finds his mother sitting in there, smoking and staring through the window, watching the trains as they arrive at the rail yard and as they depart, chunting slowly between soot-gray row houses, triple-deckers, and industrial warehouses, and picking up speed as they move out into the open spaces and the east, where the first greasy light is trembling upon the horizon.

When she sees him, she looks up and smiles, says: It's still really early, honey. You should be in bed.

Can I stay up with you for a bit? he asks, and she nods and goes to heat milk on the stove.

He sits and looks through the same window: railway workers in the early morning, sluggish as they cross the rail ties, waiting, glancing dutifully at the rail signals, yet not quite awake, cigarettes flaring as they draw upon them, and the small sparks of light floating and flitting through the darkness like fireflies, lunch pails and thermoses swinging lazily in their hands. Half a dozen men have died crossing the rails in this way in the last two years, the older ones becoming inured to the danger of moving engines and locking cars, the younger ones never cautious enough. Often Duncan and his mother see them sprinting across the network of rails, between the power station's transformers, beneath the high charged cables, and toward the laborers' trailers and shacks, then turning and laughing, taunting the other workers who move from junction to junction, mindful of the signals, waving hello to the signal men, engineers, and security bulls at the end of their graveyard shifts.

Duncan stares at her and knows he needs to speak. Do I have a father? he asks. Joshua said he knew my father.

His mother picks up her smoldering Claymore from the ashtray, ash peppering the Formica, and squints at him as she inhales on it and then exhales slowly. The plume of smoke rises up to the tin ceiling and seems to hang there, churning and dark.

If I have a father, why do you never talk about him? What's so wrong?

His mother grinds the cigarette out in the ashtray. Nothing's wrong, sweetie, except there isn't anything to tell. You had a father—of course you had a father, but he died before you were born. I've told you that.

What did he die of?

She shakes her head. I don't know what he died of. He left us—okay? He left before you were born. I heard later that he'd died back east.

But you never made sure? You never wanted to find out? Perhaps he's still alive somewhere.

He's dead and there's nothing else to say. She picks up the blunted cigarette and then grinds it some more into the rust speckled tin then works at lighting another.

Duncan stares at her. You don't have any pictures of him, nothing at all?

No. If I had pictures, I would show you. We'd only known each other a short while when I became pregnant. I don't think he even knew.

Perhaps if he knew, he'd have come back.

I told you, he's dead.

What was he like?

Like I said, we only knew each other a short while. Okay, he was fine, just fine.

Well, what did he look like?

I don't know how to describe him. He was good-looking, I guess.

Do I look like him?

He has often tried to picture what his father looked like but can only imagine his own face as it stares back at him in the bathroom mirror—the mercury plating worn away so that the glass is pock-mocked with slivers of gray and black—as he brushes his teeth before bed or as he splashes cold water on his face in the mornings before school. The hollow points of large pupils dilating in dark blue irises, strawlike black hair sitting at all angles upon his head no matter how he combs it and no matter how the Spanish barber on Columbus tries to mat it down with sweet smelling pomade and brilliantine.

No. Perhaps. Jesus, I don't know, Duncan. This was over ten years ago. You look a little bit like him. You have his eyes, but then he had eyes like my father, so I suppose your eyes are from my side.

What was he like? You must have liked him to have me, didn't you?

I liked him just fine. Now will you stop with the questions? I'm sorry there isn't more to tell you, but that's just the way it is. I used to be an opera singer, and I never thought things would change, but they did. If it wasn't for the war, Joshua might have made something of himself—he might have been anything he wanted to be. Sometimes things don't work out the way you want them to, and that's all there is to it. Your father died a long time ago, and the only thing I have to remember him by is you, and for that I thank God. She shrugs, and turns away, sucks on her cigarette.

His mother's eyes follow the next engine as it motors out over the trestle bridge above the narrow channel that divides San Listes from Mission Hill, its motor thrumming high and loud before the engineer opens it up, the halogens along the gravel rail cut glinting on the top of the engine's metal canopy and then on each successive rail car, shimmering like water flowing down their dark sides.

When you jump a train, she says suddenly, you must always make sure to move with the speed of the train, to jump and climb in one motion. If you merely reach for a handhold, the train will pull your arm out of its socket. They key is always to keep moving and to match your speed to the train's.

You jumped trains?

Maggie smiles wistfully. No, she says. Never. But I always dreamed of it.

At night Duncan sits by his bedroom window on the third floor with his copy of *The Collected Works of Douglas Graham Purdy: Tales of Horror and the Macabre* open on his lap and looks out at the same rail yard that his mother often does. He stares at the telephone lines that stretch like a jangle of dark snakes writhing toward the horizon, and he imagines the voices from all the surrounding houses and towns and cities that traveled along them and he hears hot water bubbling and gurgling in the pipes and the sounds of his mother's visitors rising with the sound of bursting bubbles—it is like listening undersea. He presses his ears to the pipes until they are too hot to stand

and the underwater voices rise and fall with the bubbles. His mother is usually quiet but sometimes he hears her offering words of comfort, encouragement, or, he guesses, whatever else they want and need to hear. And gradually those voices too meld into the eternal hum in his head, right along with the telephone lines and the electrical conducting towers and the trains thumping and banging in the rail yards beyond.

Nightly, he stares from that window and watches the strangers that pass beneath the streetlights and disappear beneath the awning of their porch; the footsteps on the wooden stairs echoing loudly, abruptly, after the soft hiss, spatter on the rain-washed street, then follows the knock at the door, and his mother's voice in greeting.

He watches them emerge at the far end of the street, these dark amorphous shapes twisting and twining themselves from shadow and molten cement, through the gray rain, rising up from the very fabric of the misty air and the sidewalk like phantasms, and he can tell, even then, by their walk, that they are coming to their house. At first it is a game he plays to pass the time, to see how often he can guess correctly, but in the end, he is always right. These men, even the way they move is predictable. He grows bored and stops counting but he continues to watch and listen, and often he falls asleep, head on his arms, arms folded on the hard surface of the windowsill and the angled surface of the radiator, half his skin cold from the cold night pushing the glass, the other half burning with the heat of the radiator he lies pressed against, and the image of men growing from the pavement and the sound of them below with his mother, and he imagines the distance from his room to the moon and of his body, disintegrated and reduced to subatomic particles, passed along a radio wave and shot out into the cosmos with the speed of a quasar, to where Michael Collins, his father, and all the lost astronauts waited in limbo.

DUNCAN STARES OUT the window onto the avenue. From his mother's room down the hall he hears a man's gravel-rough voice followed by his laughter; the flick of a lighter, once, twice, butane igniting, and the inhale as a cigarette is lit; his mother's tights rasp like snakes coiling across her skin as she removes them, and then the scrape of clothing, the rustle of underthings. SQUEAK SQUEAL the beds springs shudder, BANG BANG the headboard hammers faster and faster and harder and harder, and then JESUS, FUCKING JESUS YEAH.

Water thrums in the pipes and bubbles in the radiators. The window blooms white with Duncan's breath; the cold from outside tightens the skin at the top of his brow. A door opens, closes. Urine splashing in the bathroom, the sound resounding off the porcelain and tiles. A man hacking phlegm and then flushing. Duncan closes his eyes. Footsteps recede, and he imagines they are going down the stairs, out the front door, down the street and the hill to the city,

121

and never coming back. But the front door never opens and then the bed begins to move again, the walls shudder, and his mother's voice calls out as if in pain. The man's voice rises, swearing at his mother, calling her all manner of terrible things, so that Duncan raises the volume on the Vulcanite radio as loud as it will go, places his hands over his ears, buries his head beneath the blankets, and tries to lose himself in the numbing, swirling dark.

110:08:53 COLLINS: Houston, Columbia on the high gain. Over.

110:08:55 MCCANDLESS: Columbia, this is Houston. Reading you loud and clear. Over.

110:09:03 COLLINS: Yeah. Reading you loud and clear. How's it going?

110:09:05 MCCANDLESS: Roger. The EVA is progressing beautifully. I believe they are setting up the flag now.

110:09:14 COLLINS: Great!

110:09:18 MCCANDLESS: I guess you're about the only person around that doesn't have TV coverage of the scene.

110:09:25 COLLINS: That's all right. I don't mind a bit. [Pause] How is the quality of the TV?

110:09:35 MCCANDLESS: Oh, it's beautiful, Mike. It really is.

110:09:39 COLLINS: Oh, gee, that's great! Is the lighting halfway decent?

110:09:43 MCCANDLESS: Yes, indeed. They've got the flag up now and you can see the stars and stripes on the lunar surface.

110:09:50 COLLINS: Beautiful. Just beautiful.

April 1982

MAGGIE SANG ELIZABETHAN madrigals and Catholic hymns and
Baptist choruses and the low blue notes of Muddy Waters from the
bottom of the Mississippi Delta. And in all of this she searched for the
divine, those notes and measures that could hold the soul, make the
heart ache, and break it in two. These songs shared a special grace, for
in them, Duncan knows, she found her way to God and, perhaps, as
she sang, imagined what she was once capable of.

I lost my voice, she says, and had to leave the opera. She runs a
finger along her throat. And after *him*, I lost everything else. I was
ruined.

Duncan cannot tell if she means his father, and, at times, he even
wonders if she might mean him. After all, she's risked so much taking him from the Home and has sacrificed so much for him, including her career. If there is anyone to be blamed for where she is now,
it is him; he is the one who has truly ruined her.

123

La mort his mother calls it, and laughs. Softly she sings the words of the Queen of the Night: *Disowned may you be forever, Abandoned may you be forever, Destroyed be forever.* She shakes her head. I could fail, but not there, not on an opera stage. I'd rather people never knew I ever existed than to hear me sing like that.

She touches her neck again, stretching the skin, flicks cigarette ash absently onto a plate. Now, she says, I can't hold a note to save my life.

She is wrong, she can still sing, and Duncan loves to hear her voice. When he wakes screaming in the night, burning with sudden fever, a great weight pressing upon his chest and so cold he is shaking, she comes to him from her bedroom and soothes him with music. Listen to this, she will say, taking his hand, placing it upon the center of her collarbone and she will sing and he will feel the vibrations of her song humming through the bone. What do you feel?

I feel cold, Mom, he tells her.

Shhhhh, no you're not. Her hand is on his brow, then touching each cheek as if she's blessing him with the sign of the cross: *In the name of the Father and the Son and the Holy Spirit.* It's warm, she says and yanks at the curtains, drawing them back. The night is warm outside, Duncan. See, can you feel it?

It's cold.

Shhhhh, everything's okay. I'm here.

And Duncan will close his eyes and sway with the sound of her voice until gradually her song fills him and there is no clamor or thought or worry in his head and the cold and the pain is only a distant memory. Until he feels completely at peace, until all the monsters are gone.

Monsters, she tells him, is from the Latin word *monstrum,* meaning "omen," meaning "portent." A monster was a messenger, an angel, that in olden days was considered to be a divine messenger. A monster, she says, was something very special and important given to people, it explained that which could not be explained, and only the very blessed received such aid. A monster was not something that could hurt you. Next time you dream or have a nightmare, try to think of it as an angel delivering a message, it is telling you something, if only you can listen and hear what it is that it is trying to tell you. It is not always about bad things, she says, most often it is something good.

Duncan looks at her, and says: Like hearing God speak to you when you're born? Or believing Daddy is really alive, or hearing Elvis singing "Blue Moon," or wishing Joshua peace, and like watching Neil Armstrong take one small step for man and one giant leap for mankind?

More and more Duncan fears greatly for the lives of the Apollo astronauts. In his dreams, he sees Michael Collins aboard the command module *Columbia*, turning in his slow, lonely, vigilant revolutions around the moon, descending again and again in and out of complete darkness, shooting, skimming, sixty-nine miles above its opaque and glittering gray pockmocked surface, spinning without end through the black vacuum, the integrity of his silvery Mylar and Kapton suit compromised, and he an eviscerated corpse within it— yet still he waits. The sad astronaut who can only watch from his small window and imagine what Aldrin and Armstrong are doing in those minutes, those hours after the landing, even as *Columbia* passes into the shadow on the far side of the moon and into radio silence: wondering if he perhaps will ever get the chance to touch the lunar surface himself.

Day after day after week after month after year, waiting for the return of the lunar module *Eagle* while the bodies of Aldrin and Armstrong lie prostrate upon the moon's surface, the American flag held at eternal mast, the powerful sodium bulbs encircling the lunar module slowly extinguishing one by one and blackening into charred oblivion in the black, starless night.

Shhhhh, Maggie says and squeezes his hand harder. Shhhhh. Be quiet, Duncan, and listen to the music.

Later in the night, although he cannot remember having turned it on, Duncan wakes to the yellow glow of the Vulcanite radio upon his bedside table shimmering out of the darkness. Its hum vibrates in the stillness, crackling across empty, vacant wave bands, waiting to receive a signal from somewhere out in the night. And then there comes sound that Duncan at first mistakes as loud, whining static, until he hears garbled words and then, when he reaches out and turns the dial—little more than a touch—there comes momentarily, through the hissing, the distinct beeps and clicks of the Apollo radio transmissions, and then the urgent voices of the astronauts, but he cannot make out what they are saying, and then they are gone.

May 1982

SUNDAYS AFTER MASS when Joshua doesn't show for dinner, Maggie often rolls the old Chevy Impala from the garage, and packed with their sleeping bags and tinned foods, drives them out of the city. From Ipswich Street out along Calistas and then over the Bay Bridge they travel; every weekend driving farther and farther, Maggie moving them southeast in a strange if unconscious parallel with the rail tracks to their left, winding and twisting into the foothills beyond the city and, farther still, the semi-arid desert plains with their small, desolate, single-intersection towns about which the wind seems to constantly swirl fine red sandstone dust. At first Duncan enjoys watching the passing landscape and changing country as Mother shows him the roads she'd traversed as a young woman many years before his birth and the quality of her voice—exuberant and filled with life—as she tells him of a time, smiling as she does so, when it seems she believed everything was possible. But as they move ever farther from the city—perhaps minutes after they've passed the red-winged horse of the Mobil gas station on Route 5 or the Nightstop truckers' motel with its large neon green cactus just after Harlow and perhaps as Mother begins to feel the distance between them and the city widening and only the vast American landscape looming on the horizon and threatening to engulf them—something strange and inexplicable happens to her. She begins to mutter to herself: I can't do this, I can't do this, and swears, Shit, Shit Fuck! and grapples with the steering wheel, and in her fit of cursing, they take the next exit that comes upon them and turn north, his mother in a foul mood until the lights of San Francisco show themselves upon the horizon, shining blearily through a fog as night comes down.

Sometimes they will drive until Maggie realizes they are almost out of gas and they have to refuel, and at other times she simply drives and drives, refueling at one roadside gas station after another until, inexplicably panicked, she turns the car around and heads home or until she seems to wake suddenly—eyes blinking, eyelashes fluttering, tongue licking her lips savagely—from her fugue. And always she stares at Duncan in confusion, as if he is a stranger sitting next to her, and he wonders if she remembers a single thing they spoke of during the many hours of those trips, or if she even thinks of him or of Joshua, in his single room at the Langham Hotel, lying awake listening to men retching, puking, and loosing their bowels into the shat-encrusted toilet at the end of the hall.

And mostly Duncan is too exhausted to care about or to try to understand these seeming fits. Instead he closes his eyes and waits for the smells of the Gravel, the Bends, and the Bottoms, the shift whistle from the Edison plant, the pungent tannic odor from the tannery, the rumble and grind of the diesel engines motoring out of the rail yard, or, hopefully, the sight of Joshua's Indian aslant the curbstone before their house to tell him that they are home again.

C'mon, sweetie, Mother says as she leads him, half-asleep, from the car. We're home, and there is a flatness to her voice as if she has momentarily stepped far outside of herself and her voice is coming from very far away, or as if someone else has taken her place, someone who is merely mimicking her, and he can only think of the disembodied voices of lost astronauts that murmur through Brother Canice's radio late in the night. Soon she retreats to her bedroom with a bottle while Duncan, now suddenly awake, stares at the bare bulb dangling from the ceiling, as it shudders and sways slightly with the thumping bass reverberations from her stereo sounding from down the hall, and wonders where she goes to in these moments, what manner of madness affects her, and, if somehow, he is responsible for it all.

JOSHUA? DUNCAN CALLS into the telephone: *Joshua?* And waits, listening to static; slowly he hears the other sounds on the line from Joshua's netherworld across the bay.

She's drinking again, Joshua. She's drunk.

We miss you, Joshua.

I don't want there to be other men here. I just want you.

Then, from the void: She don't mean anything by it, kid.

I know.

Joshua exhales long and hard and Duncan hears him shifting on his mattress, the click and snap of his butane lighter igniting and the flare as he inhales upon the cigarette, and when he speaks, Duncan pictures him staring at the ceiling just as he is—a parallax view—and his own ghostly astronauts floating there in the empty, long dark unraveling before him.

My father was a no-good, he says softly, so softly he might be whispering but his mouth is directly against the receiver and Duncan can hear his lips shaping the words. He beat my mother. He cheated on her with every skirt that came along. He drove her to drink. All the days until she left us she needed it to get by. She couldn't find comfort in anything else. She was a good woman, and the drinking—it shamed her. Living with us reminded her of that shame, until it was too much to bear. And so she left.

Joshua shifts on his mattress and Duncan hears the clatter of him rummaging on a bedside table.

Joshua?

Yeah.

Will you come by tomorrow?

It's time to go to sleep, my man.

Will you come by?

A freight train's whistle sounds in the distance and Duncan can picture Joshua angling toward that sound, neck craning, eyes lingering on his open window. After a moment Joshua sighs: Sure, kid. I'll come by.

Goodnight then, Duncan says.

Goodnight, kid.

Joshua puts the phone back in its cradle, slowly exhales on his cigarette so that a gray plume of smoke drifts upward in the dark. From the bathroom down the hall there is the sound of puking and of running water. Someone is banging on the door, telling whoever is inside to hurry the fuck up. The torn blinds tap softly against the windowsill; he can smell the oil-thick diesel fumes from the train, the sulfur from its batteries. His eyelids flutter lazily. Cigarette smoke churns slowly out into the night. He thinks of Duncan across the bay and wishes that he could go to him and to Maggie and comfort the both of them, but he is incapable of moving, incapable of rising from his bed to prepare food—even the courage to walk the hall to the toilets fails him and he must piss in the sink in his room like some animal and run the water from the faucet to rid the place of the smell of him. He's been off the tunnel job for a week now, and even though he's called in to the union hall, they'll replace him if he's out much longer.

Another train thumps the rails and the building shudders as it approaches. He turns toward the sound of the train, eyes on his open window and the space beneath the yellowed blinds that offers him a view of the tracks, and in a moment comes the clanging cars, and the engine's mercurial light sweeps across his bed, holds him briefly in its white glare so that he blinks and is awake again with his heart hammering anxiously in his chest. He is surrounded by the thumping of heavy wings, the thrashing disturbance of charged air, the fear of being held as if by manacles and then yanked helplessly upward: the sense of his skin stretched and about to be pulled apart. Trembling, Joshua puts four doxepin and four prazosin in his mouth, washes them down with tepid beer, and waits in the dark for sleep to take him.

ALWAYS JOSHUA AND his men are moving, moving between alternating hues of reddish-brown and green: a misty dusk-land upon which the wind sets the rain at sharp angles across rice paddies against them and everything turns to muck in the dark. Rice paddies and foothills, one burned-out blackened village after another, and mist rising thick from the jungle roof above everything as they approach, and above that mist the mountains rising into her clouds.

It is night when they reach the village of Loc Noi and the land is steaming. Air so thick with moisture that rain drips from bowed leaves. Damp ash smell of extinguished wood smoke from the last of the cooking fires, the murmur of a fitfully sleeping child, a pig grunting softly in a sty of wood and bamboo littered with straw, and *O au o. The lights in Sai Gon are green and red, the lamps in My Tho are bright and dim . . . O au o . . .* the hush of sleep over everything. A laughing thrush sounds in the darkness—a sound so bright with pain and loneliness Joshua will still hear its sound over a decade later.

He turns on his back, resting for a moment. Squares his shoulders against the ground. His breath is mist, his movements ghostlike. He blinks and through the gossamer of a shuddering spiderweb woven across the low canopy above him he can see the stars. The spiderweb glistens with moisture, a drop falls from the canopy and shatters along its silver lines. Shadows are moving through the jungle, the sounds of his men and the company of Montagnard tribesmen, so familiar he can smell them. A rustling in the undergrowth. He can hear the trees breathing. The thick knocking of the earth beneath him. A bale of concertina wire rattles across the muddy track. An old, wizened woman is letting loose her bowels at the edge of a field.

He focuses on the space before him—the foreground of his sight—and then when he looks beyond this: from the complex design, intricacies, and beauty of the spiderweb to the vast expanse of the all-encompassing height of the highland jungle and mountains, and above and far distant, through the veils of mist, farther than the height of the great mountains, pinpricks of stellar light. He is a child again and walking the snowy winter streets of Brighton, the early darkness, the stars blazing in the sky like small flames and dawn still many hours away.

Fresh snow muffles his footsteps, soaks through the bottoms of his jeans, as he walks the empty snow-covered streets, his breath steaming the air. He coughs sharp and loud in the deep stillness. He pauses momentarily to stare at the dark windows, the dusted glass, and then behind him to the footprints in the snow becoming rapidly wiped away. He imagines that if he stands here, not only will his footsteps be gone but so will he.

Steam smokes from his mouth as he listens to the wind, its note and pitch, as it sounds off glass and stone, sighing then moaning in the crooks and valleys of streets and buildings, of boulevard and avenue, as gentle as a soft breath through a flute and then gentler still—no more than a tremor of air vibrating an octave. A trash can bangs in a covered alley suddenly startling him and rolls on cement untouched by snow.

Before him remain all manner of possibilities: He is still a boy and in this wondrous moment the world seems to revolve around him; he is capable of anything. Joshua smiles and holds his face up to the snowfall, stretches wide his arms to receive the snowflakes in hands and hold them in his fists.

A large city plow rumbles down the main avenue with the force of a locomotive, pushing the snow from its canted plow to the side of the road—a great arc of snow from which the spray is taken by the wind and churned into a billowing smoke. A bright red Chevy Nova rumbles slowly down the street, its rear end slipping and fishtailing slightly whenever the driver guns the engine, snow spraying from its racing widewalls.

Hey, lookit the little nigger playing in the snow. Hey, nigger! Don't you know there's a fawkin blizzard? Get home to your momma, you monkey, before you get run over by a plow!

The driver and his passengers have rolled down their fogged windows to stare at him but Joshua sees only their eyes, blazing it seems from their deep-set sockets, the indistinguishable white faces, and the hovering O of their mouths.

And perhaps it is the falling snow, the gusting wind roaring in his ear like the sea, and the encroaching darkness or the numbness that has taken him, but he has an impression of everything blurring, as if wipers had moved across the men's features, smearing them, turning them into grotesques, and the car rumbling slowly past. Its taillights burning through the white. The deep-set threads of its tires filled with wide ridges of snow. Its dual exhaust shivering with steam. And then the car with its passengers seems to boil into a wispy nothingness. The end of the street is gone and only the closest houses emerge gray and hazy through the rising gusts with the suggestion of architecture: a meager and frantic outline of stolidity, of brick and mortar.

Joshua stares at his legs and boots frozen with snow and at the drifts between buildings, at the scalloped slopes, which have quickly risen to first-floor window lintels. He is wet and cold and can only see a foot or two before him and he thinks of his mother at home waiting anxiously for him. In awe and dawning fear he suddenly understands the power and the ferocity of the storm as he stands briefly at the center of everything, and is obliterated.

He stares at the spider silk spun so unerringly and with such precision from its spinnerets, night dew trembling upon its latticework, and it offers him such a calm that he cannot put words to it—for a moment he closes his eyes in contentment, but only briefly. He looks for the web's maker, hiding secretly at the edge of the web perhaps, with one foot on a signal line from the hub, waiting for the vibrations of prey caught in its web, and finally sees it there, large and unmoving in the low leaves.

Beautiful, he says softly, and the web shudders slightly with his breath, bowing back and forth as if with a breeze. As a child he once saw a 110-million-year-old web preserved in amber. He and his mother had taken the train together from Medford to Boston to see the exhibit on fossils and millennia-old preservations at the Museum of Science. He remembers that she had taken the day off from work as a bookkeeper for the Old Colony Abattoir in Dorchester for their trip together. It's one of the last few memories he has of her before she left them, before she jumped off the Elevated Orange Line train platform at Northampton Street and was electrified by the third rail.

The smoke of mist twirls up through the green jungletop and up the misty mountainside, shadowed and bent by movement as if figures are moving within its cover, like ghosts. Years later, walking through the downtown alleys of the city, along Townsend and Beckman, Windsor and Marlboro, late at night he will observe steam rising from manhole covers and hear the rumbling of the subway below and imagine men—fellow soldiers, phantasm creatures, eviscerated and delimbed, black-scorched flesh hanging from red sinew, bones protruding from severed limb ends, climbing and crawling from the manholes. He will think of villages in the highland and of the jungle breathing about him, the strange beauty of the ancient silent mountains looming over them, over it all.

And he will experience this later again, on those nights that he emerges from the tunnel beneath the bay through the temporary air vent shafts, up eighty flights of stairs in darkness, his footfalls echoing, his breath loud and magnified in the narrow concrete column— the ballast of a hundred lungs pumping, beating in the dark alongside him, beneath him, around him: a hundred footfalls following him up the stairs, and out onto the street, a bedraggled, partially limbed squad of Special Forces. Emerging from beneath the ground as he had a decade before, only he was crawling in that darkness and unsure if he would ever walk again, let alone upon a city street. And the ghosts of men are with him here also, as elsewhere; always they are with him.

July 1982

THEY ARE SITTING at the kitchen table, Maggie in her too-tight nurse's uniform smoking a cigarette, and Duncan eating a bowl of cereal. Sunlight spills through the yellow-stained kitchen curtains turning everything sallow. The curtains are used, bought at a Salvation Army thrift Store. Maggie has scrubbed and bleached them, trying to make them white again. For a while she had become almost obsessed with it, as if by doing so she would be able to make other things right in her life as well, make them pure, but her efforts have merely thinned the material, not its dog-piss color.

Duncan watches light dance on the top of her head, highlight the red there like sparks, and shimmer amber along her bare, pale neck. When she exhales, her mouth is a fuchsia O; it floats in the air with the smoke and rises to the ceiling, and then, as it settles, returns to the filter of the cigarette, where it marks its tip, bright pink and wet with the shape of a kiss.

Sometimes he will catch his mother staring at him, tears forming in her eyes, and it will take her a moment to realize he is staring back before she looks away. Duncan sees himself reflected in her eyes, and he wonders what she thinks of him and whether she is thinking she made a mistake in coming to the Home to get him.

Maggie looks up from a magazine on muscle cars that Joshua took from the barbershop and Duncan says: Does it upset you when I look at you?

It makes me sad—she pauses as she takes a drag on her Claymore and her eyes squint through the smoke of her exhale—only because I know why you look at me the way you sometimes do.

Why?

You're trying to figure out if I'll leave you again.

He shrugs. He couldn't explain why he looked at her the way he did. Sometimes he felt invisible and assumed that she couldn't see him even if he willed her to. He stares at her now.

Never, sugar, she says and shakes her head. Trust me. Never again. It's just you and me, together. Always.

Only slowly does Duncan realize that he is still staring; his eyes drift to some point beyond his mother. If he focuses on that point, soon he will be gone, and there will be nothing left, not even a reflected image: he will disappear.

Honey, that's why there's not a line on your beautiful face, Maggie says and laughs. You never smiled as a child. She comes to him then and squeezes the sides of his face tenderly, but there is a flicker of remembrance there too that she quickly pushes away.

Why did you leave me in the Home? he asks again, and even to his ears it sounds like a brittle, grating echo—the sound of the stylus scratching and hissing upon the phonograph late at night, when she's staggered drunkenly to bed and fallen into an impenetrable stupor from which nothing will awake her—something that he has asked so many times and to which she gives no proper answer and the question continues to reverberate empty and vacant and unanswered.

Maggie continues to smoke, puts back her chair and paces the kitchen. It's not the question that bothers her; it's the place where the question brings her, someplace many years before, and neither of them knows why it is so important, but it is.

You were shy, incredibly introverted, so much so that you never socialized with other children your own age. I was worried about you, you wouldn't speak, you wouldn't tell me what was wrong—if I'd only known what was wrong then, I would have tried to fix it, but . . .

She shakes her head. You were my special child and so I brought you to them. She grits her teeth and exhales, quickly tears the plastic from another pack of Claymores. Opens the pack. Shakes her hand violently to remove the plastic that sticks to the edge of her palm, but in her agitation it seems to cling all the more. Duncan reaches over and peels it off and she is like static electricity to the touch.

The middle of nowhere, she says. Bumfuck America. I hated it, going back there. Not in the beginning though, only later. You never did catch sight of the town, did you? That's where I had to stay when I came to visit. Let me tell you something, honey: You didn't miss a thing. The place was a complete shithole. Those fuckers.

Don't swear, he says softly, and with pursed lips she nods, closes her eyes and inhales deeply on her cigarette.

Duncan rolls the Claymore wrapping in his hands. He wants to tell her that he and Billy saw the town with the dead children from the Festival of Lights train and that he imagined seeing her face in the moon, that in a way he could never explain all these things were leading him to her, to the day when she would come back for him. The day stretches long and far away beyond the curtain blinds. Through the open window comes the sound of children playing on the rusted iron and crumbling stone animals in Joseph Wood Tyner Park, squeezed in between the abandoned warehouse, the Edison plant, and the train yards. Clang of metal and then laughter. Scrape-scrabble of sneakers on rock dust. Gulls shriek harshly as they swirl over the bay.

They had a good reputation, back then, Maggie says. They said they had a wonderful place for special children, an environment where they would flourish, interact, develop, grow. She waves at the air, makes big looping circles with her cigarette. A place where children like you would shine.

She sighs, leans against the countertop, crosses her ankles, and folds her arms beneath the swell of her breasts. She's holding her cigarette loosely, almost even with her mouth, as if it is a talisman, something that can protect her from the truth, a stake that she might drive into the heart of the demon thing fluttering its wings darkly before her. Duncan stares at the hard roundness of her belly that he knows she clutches at night while she sleeps.

It was hard enough to support myself, let alone the two of us. You needed special attention, constant attention. She looks at him. C'mon, honey, look at what I do for a living. This is it. This is all I could have given you.

But this is all I need, Duncan says, his voice cracking suddenly.

Her eyes glisten and she coughs harshly, breaking phlegm in her throat, stamps her cigarette out briskly in the sink and lights another as if to keep her hands busy.

Now it is, honey, but not then. Then you needed more. I'm sorry, it wasn't supposed to happen the way it did. How did I know you would get worse in there, and them telling me everything was fine, would be fine, that it was all adjustment.

She nods her head as if remembering agreeing with them all those years ago. They said it would take time and we all had to be patient. But you didn't get better; you got worse. And they restricted my visits but I was there. Damn their restrictions—who are they to tell me I can't see my own child? I was there every two weeks and every time hoping things would be different, that this time you would look up and recognize me, and see me and smile, but—she shrugs sadly—you never did.

Maggie's shoulders sag. She says: You were in a place that seemed untouchable. You would look at me and look right through me. I was so scared. I thought I was being punished for something I had done. That somehow I deserved this—a child who doesn't even recognize his own mother. But you didn't recognize anyone, sugar. You didn't speak, you didn't smile, and you didn't cry.

She laughs but she is no longer here; she is somewhere far away, and it seems as if she is on the verge of tears although she is laughing.

I wanted to take you out of there so many times, get you real medical care, but they wrangled me with legalities and what I'd committed to with the papers I'd signed all those years before, and they fought me, fought me so hard I didn't understand it. I saw you less and less . . . Her voice trails away, and when she begins again, her voice is subdued. She stares at the glowing tip of her cigarette: Four years before I got you out of there, baby, four long years.

But they told me you came during the winter storm. That you left me on the monastery's doorstep when I was just a few days old. Flea-bitten and howling with the hunger, Brother Canice liked to say.

But that's not true, sweetie. Who told you that?

The Brothers, the other children.

I didn't bring you to that place until you were six. That's what I'm trying to tell you. We had a life before you went into the Home. We had a life together. Don't you remember any of it?

I remember being born and—

Stop, Duncan, she says, suddenly angry. Not again. I don't want to hear it.

Maggie turns to the sink, and though she has barely smoked her cigarette, she stamps it out, banging it against the tin, her back trembling.

The day has darkened and Duncan is aware for the first time of the shadows in the normally bright hallway and the shifting gray beyond the kitchen windows. The children from the park have gone home. Gulls shriek as they swoop down across the street, skimming the parked cars, and a distant clap of thunder is quickly followed by rain tapping the glass, a soft, soothing sound that seems to resound in the silent room, rain-shadow through the diffuse light shuddering upon the walls, and then the shift siren from the Edison plant sounds, startling the both of them.

IN HER BEDROOM, Maggie pours herself a drink, sets it upon the dresser, and sits upon the bed, stares blankly for a moment at the vanity mirror atop the bureau, where she has taped pictures of her and Duncan, squeezed their edges into the space where the glass meets the tin frame, the old black-and-whites she has stared at all these years, the ones she has forced herself to think are real. Late sunlight comes down the hill, shimmers in the glass tumbler.

She pulls out her drawer, rummages through her clothes, takes the pictures from under its cloth-covered bottom, lays them on the bed, spreads them with her hands, and stares at them: a woman and a young boy hand in hand, an abject-looking young boy by himself standing in the center of the frame, a blurred background of three-story buildings beyond wrought iron railings, perhaps where they once lived, stark and dissolved in black and white and something she can almost believe in, and she hopes that Duncan will as well. She is his mother, after all—that is all she's ever been and hoped to be.

Here she laughs bitterly and shakes her head, for amongst the photographs there are also his letters, crossbound by two faded ribbons, letters that speak of his love for her—oh, how eloquently and, at turns, graphically, and crudely he spoke of his love!—and of their future together.

And now on the bed with these photographs of someone else's life and decade-old letters from a man who had promised her so much—who'd been so much like father, had his strengths and his weaknesses too, and she'd wanted to make him love her, love her so greatly he would never want for anything more, but in the end, he'd left her just as her father had and after everything had already been taken from her so that what she regrets most is the sacrifices she'd made for him: her voice, her child, her sweet, strange, beautiful Duncan, who managed to believe in angels and God and all manner of goodness in the world with such faith that it made her heart ache to experience it and yet not believe in it and know that sooner or later the world would crush him also.

Sighing, she pulls a record from its sleeve, drops it onto the phonograph, and, suddenly fatigued, sits heavily upon the edge of the bed. Through the sheer lace curtains she can see gulls wheeling silently above the street. A mother with her child walking hand in hand toward the park. The distant pitons of the Golden Gate Bridge rising above shoals of fog like the walls to some distant, impenetrable fortress in one's dreams.

Mom? Duncan calls hesitatingly from the hallway, and she feels the uncertainty in those words, and she wants to go to him but in this moment right now she doesn't have the strength or the courage and she is very much afraid. She closes her eyes and sips from her glass and calls out: Yes, my sweet, what is it? I'll be right there. Don't worry. I'll be right there.

She reaches for the bottle of Old Mainline upon the weathered bureau and considers it: the only comfort in her isolation, in this daily giving up. And how much can one give up in one's life before there is nothing more? The stylus has slipped into the groove and she turns away as a young woman's voice spills through the old speaker, haunting amidst the popping static and hiss, then rising, resplendent and disorientating in its power. How proud he'd have been if only he could have seen her on the stage, if only he could have heard her like this. How proud he'd have been of her, his only daughter. If only he'd known, he never would have left her while her mother lay in state, gawked at by family and old acquaintances, caked in mortician's makeup and smelling of the disease Maggie still smells as she makes her rounds through the terminal ward. Slowly she raises the bottle to her lips and drinks deeply, nodding to herself bitterly. And if he could only see the woman, the mother she'd become. *Oh, how proud.*

It wasn't until half a decade of trying and of touring with poor production companies all across the country that Maggie knew her opera career was over. On the night she realizes that she can no longer sing, the truth comes to her in a dream in a motel room on the Arizona-Utah border. It is a sweltering midsummer night, and hours after what will be her final performance, Maggie lies in a semiconscious stupor, inebriated and drenched and tossing upon the bed. The lights in the room have been turned off and the curtains pulled back; the black glass that looks out upon a second-floor landing above a motor court shimmers with heat lightning pulsing through slow-moving darkness in the north. An ancient air conditioner, alternately clicking on and off, thrums and rattles in its brackets, and a gust of fetid air billows weakly across the bed, lightly rippling the bedsheet. When its motor dies and there is silence, you can hear the tap, tap, tapping of dank water dripping slowly upon the red shag carpet.

In her dream, Maggie Bright is sitting with Silva Bröhm in a bleak, empty opera house. There are black velvet chairs, shadowy ribbed walls, a dark glittering proscenium. They seemed to wait forever, sitting together in silence, until finally the red curtains part to reveal the stage, and there stands Maria Callas, and she begins to sing, only it is with Silva Bröhm's and Maggie Bright's former voices that she sings, stolen as it were, or incorporated, into the vast *spiritus mundi* of which they are no longer a part and from which they can draw no sound.

Together they watch Maria Callas with such fierce longing their chests ache. How could their voices be lost to them forever. How could they?

As Maria's song reaches its height, the two woman rise in silence and their voices follow them from the hall and into the vast hallways of the opera house, where Maggie and Silva fade and depart like pale phantasms to Callas's rendition of Lakmé's "Bell Song," softly reverberating and resounding in the high domed eaves and falling empty in all the caverns of the hall.

Maggie wakes, sobbing but quite still. From the open window just above her head she hears the thrum of locusts in the desert night, at first such a soft and distant sound that it seems to magnify her isolation, and then, as she wakes more fully and her ears attune themselves to that sound, she realizes that there are thousands and thousands of them out there, rasping their legs and wings together, a frantic, violent vibration without voice conducting thunderheads and lightning in the dark.

Maggie raises her head off the pillow, hair matted and stuck to her neck and shoulders and wrapped to her face. She looks through the glass and gasps. In the desert night beyond she can see the shape of them, millions of them writhing and undulating: a single swarm, perhaps two hundred miles wide and four hundred miles long, stretching farther than the eye can see and so high and dense that it obscures all light and darkens the distant desert mesas. She watches as they writhe and crack, their shells splintering as they climb over one another, as they pulverize one another to death with their wings, and she continues watching, her mouth working soundlessly, her voice hardening in her throat, until she can no longer tell whether she is awake or still dreaming, or, in that dark, terrible writhing, where she begins and the locusts end.

She could never go back, and she would never sing as the phenomena she had been ever again. In that moment, for all intents and purposes, she becomes a different woman altogether: She begins to make herself into someone other. A year passes and then another, and soon so many years lie between what she was and what she has become she no longer recognizes the difference.

AT TIMES WHEN the company generators in the tunnel fail, Joshua and the other men are cast into darkness, and as they wait for the light to return, wait for the first faint flickering from the safety bulbs at the bend of the tunnel five hundred feet away that will signal that the generators are working again and that more light will soon illuminate the space between them, Joshua quotes Dante's *Purgatario* aloud to himself in the dark.

It's a book his mother had him read to him as a child, in both translation and Italian, and although he did not know the language, gradually, as he poured over the words, with their strange sounds and constructions, and spoke the words aloud, they began to make a strange and mystical sense to him. Later, in Vietnam, he came to understand the book in other ways, in those places where words had no meaning or articulation but merely hummed in his head, thrummed beneath his skin, and ached in that place his mother might have called a soul, the place where the center of all good things lay; it was an understanding so quick and terribly complete that he felt as if he was no longer reading but in the slick, sloshing belly of It, as he believed Dante must have been, and with this reality came a certain peace with and even acceptance of his condition, the war, and his part in all things that not only ruined other men but also, fundamentally, irrevocably ruined himself.

When his recon party passed through the sites of day-old firefights deep in the jungle, and he slowed at the sight of their fellow soldiers' bodies or what remained of their bodies turned pulpy in the heat and black with flies, so that the bodies seemed to shudder as the flies moved in waves across them, it might have been Dante rather than Sergeant O'Neil at his side, uttering a cadence that would become so familiar to him that it would soon come to mean how far he and the other soldiers could distance themselves from the death about them and how long before they became strong in the ability to survive here by coming to feel almost nothing at all: *Ain't nothin but dead meat, Greenie. Ain't nothin. But dead meat. Keep walking.*

Now, as the men wait for light to return to the tunnel beneath the bay, they listen to one another's breathing and, perhaps for the first time since their shift began, become aware of the smell and the physical presence of one another and of their world around them: the drip and ceaseless stream of water pushing up through cracks and fault lines in the pit; the cooling tick of extinguished filaments and motors of the jackhammers and pneumatic shovels; the swamp of old, bilious, tepid, green-colored water upon the floor of the tunnel; the muck and paste of the thirty-foot-thick chalk marl they are boring through; and the smell of the sea pushing in on them and down on them, just feet from their faces. In the darkness the tunnel boring machines have stilled. The slurry tubes and conveyors are quiet.

From the section of the tunnel where he waits, foot resting upon the pneumatic press, Joshua forces himself to inhale and exhale, to calm and relax his tired muscles, which every so often spasm uncontrollably. He leans his head against the damp shale, sweat dripping into his eyes, and speaks softly, as if to himself, letting the words shape his breathing, slow his pulse, but all the men hear him, and listen:

Toiling in tight quarters and breathing sulfurous fumes, slaves and prisoners of war, we were forced to work amidst the screams of our wounded and dying fellows.

Shut your trap, McGreevey! Charlie Minkivitz, the foreman, snaps at him, the angry breath of him close and heavy as if he'd just materialized out of the dark, and then turns back to the tunnel wall, stares blankly at the seams of water running in small rivulets there, visible now in the darkness as fluttering movement, his eyes seeming to float in the darkness, reflecting the small glints of droplets, and despite the anger, even hatred, in his voice, Joshua realizes that he is scared.

The men's breathing continues to thump the darkness, even and measured yet deeply drawn and exhaled with the anxiety of waiting. Leg muscles clench and cramp, acid churns and sours in the muscles, as if they are animals and all waiting to lunge, to flee, and to rush forward, screaming, as they each imagine that the rear wall has collapsed behind them, trapping them, and that in a moment the waters of the bay will come rushing in to crush them. *Que Dios nos ayude*, Javier Lopes says softly in the dark, his voice trembling. He hears the muted bickering of P.J. Rollins and John Chang and the other team: Joe "Sully" Sullivan and Billy Gillespie. The distant sound of Charlie's younger brother, Jamie Minkivitz, retching echoes in the cavern, and then of his vomit splattering onto the watery floor.

Sully? someone calls but the voice is moist and phlemgy and Joshua cannot recognize it.

What are they saying? Any word from up above? What's the delay?

No word, Jimmy. We're waiting for the engineers. All of you sit tight.

This is the world of our ancestors, Joshua says aloud suddenly. It don't matter if we die. He spits into the blackness. At the far end of the tunnel a man coughs wetly.

Shut up, McGreevey, Minkivitz says again, but this time his voice is subdued, tired-sounding, defeated. This is the third time this week the lights have failed and each time the men have waited in the darkness as if it is their End, and the constant anxiety, fear, and anticipation of impending disaster has taken its toll upon them.

Eternity, Minkivitz, Joshua calls. Eternity! What do you think about spending eternity together? They'll find our bones in two hundred years. They'll dig us up and our bones will have come together, a black man and a white man clinging to each other as they die, as if they needed each other to survive. Maybe we crawl the last ten feet to each other as the air runs out. Maybe you whisper sweet nothings in my ear.

Fuck you, McGreevey.

You're as black as me down here, brother.

Oh for Christsake, will someone shut him up.

August 1982

HOLDING HANDS, MAGGIE and Duncan walk the rooms of the
Museum of the College of Physicians and Surgeons of San Francisco,
their footfalls reverberating on the stone tiles. For a while it has been
one of her favorite places to visit; she'll be waiting for him after
school, standing on the corner of the street, squinting into the sun,
looking slightly lost, and when Duncan emerges from between the
double doors with the throng of squirming, hollering children, she
will seem both surprised and strangely elated, as if she's convinced
herself that she's only imagined him into existence, as if with the sight
of him she is always waking from a dream. They'll jump a trolley
with the tourists and head downtown, perhaps get dim sum in Chinatown or fish chowder in the Mission, catch the second matinee at
the Viceroy and then stroll over to Humboldt Street.

Today they enter the high-ceilinged gallery that houses the collec-
tion, two floors of stately dark-wood-trimmed display cases backlit by

soft warm light, their footfalls sounding upon the tiled floors. Hanging from the wall on wires are two eviscerated children and an adult. Their chest and bellies have been cut open and the skin pinned back to reveal the internal organs. There is the skeleton of a man whose muscle turned to bone and who died in the pain of rigor. The limbs are so horribly and fantastically contorted that for a moment Duncan can't believe that he could ever have been a real man.

Young doctors, aspiring surgeons, move about the room smiling. Two men laugh and their laughter follows them down the wide stairwell. Shivering Duncan stares at the brains of murderers and epileptics as if he can understand them, as if they share something in common, a hereditary closeness perhaps, like brothers.

And then in the last room there is the sad body of the nameless Soap Woman, who died of yellow fever sometime in the nineteenth century. Buried deep in warm, damp ground her corpse turned to soapy adipocere. An accompanying display shows an X-ray cross-section and tells her brief story. All that's left of her is bone, a little bit of hair, and the soaplike substance, which preserves her.

Mother is at his side. She stares down at the Soap Woman and her face visibly softens—there is a release of tension and of pain perhaps but in this there is also incredible sadness. I used to bring you here, when you were little, she says, as if she is speaking from a dream. This is what she always says to him when she picks him up at school and on the trolley ride here. Her eyes open and close slowly. She stares at the Soap Woman's face and says to her, It's not right that you don't have a name. It's not right that they took it away from you. She whispers reverently, evoking a past only she can see, her fingers lightly, frenetically touching the mahogany cabinet, like spiders scuttling across wood, as if she is unable to help herself from touching it. Duncan looks at the contorted face beneath the glass and tries to feel something, tries to remember the past she speaks of.

Have you seen enough? she asks, and Duncan nods and touches the glass and although he hasn't spoken, mother seems to understand this and rests her hand over his, and they stay that way together for a long time until a security guard comes over and tells them to take their hands off the exhibit.

Later at home, after they've stopped off at the Windsor Tap, where Mother bought him a burger and fries and herself a highball, she leads him to her bedroom, telling him she has something she wants to show him. There is a look of gleeful anticipation upon her face; her eyes shine blearily.

Look, she says and sweeps her arm back like a magician to reveal the photographs—hundreds upon hundreds of them—she has spread upon her bed.

What are they?

Pictures of us, of you, Duncan—before the Home. I've gone through all my old boxes to find them for you.

Duncan stares at the photographs, feels his mother watching him. Most of the pictures have been taken with an old camera and are blurred and indistinct, but clearly, there is a young boy holding his mother's hand and another where the mother is pushing the boy upon a swing in a park, and another of them hugging each other outside the doors of a church that mother tells him is on Divisadero. And here's one of you on your birthday, Mother says and points to a photograph of a young boy bent over a birthday cake, caught in the moment before he attempts to blow out its candles, his face aglow in their shimmering light. Duncan turns the photograph over and sees the Fotomat date stamped, SEPTEMBER, 1974.

They're really us?

Mother nods and smiles. What's wrong, Duncan?

At the center of the pile there is a black-and-white picture of a young boy, and Duncan reaches for it and holds it to his face. The boy is walking away but looking back over his right shoulder and staring into the camera, as if someone had called his name. *What is your name?* Duncan asks of the picture. *What is your name?* The boy's right hand is clutched by a man's hand, whose arm, angled upward to the shoulder, is cut by the borders of the photograph, and bodiless. Duncan can tell it is a man's hand by its size, the thick-boned wrist, the heavily veined backhand, the large wristwatch. He can even make out the time by the sharp-looking black hour and minute hands upon the dial face: It's three A.M. The boy's gaze is oddly vacant, and his mouth is parted slightly, as if he is calling to the photographer, asking perhaps why the photographer is not going with them. It is a strange, questioning expression, but the eyes are merely white pinpricks of the camera's flashbulb. And if this eyeless boy is him, then it must be his mother who is holding the camera and watching him leave with this strange man—could this be the priest Mother entrusted him to when he was six? He can make out the texture of the man's dark jacket sleeve—heavy-looking, like the wool jacket a priest wears over his clerical shirt, of the type Father Toibin wore in the cooler months. Or could this be his father?

Duncan?

I don't know. Duncan shrugs.

You don't know what?

It's like looking at ghosts.

That's only because you don't remember, sweetie, but you will, you will.

October 1982

DUNCAN OFTEN IMAGINES that he sees Billy and Julie standing on various street corners, watching him from a distance. When he turns, he sees them briefly, an accusatory flickering of light at the corner of his eyes: Julie's black brilliantine wig from the Home's production of *Whose Baby Are You Now?* and her pouting mouth; Billy's large, blue eyes burning fiercely in their ever-prominent sockets, the fragile, pale dome of his oversize skull—and then they are gone. At other times Duncan has the sense that they are following him, but if they are, they never make a sound, never call out his name. He doesn't mention their presence to mother—they seem to move too quickly for others to see—and after a time he thinks they might merely be ghosts, materialized into being by the power of his longing. And though they never show themselves fully, he remains convinced that they are there.

It's a Friday evening that has turned chill. Leaves rustle and scrape along the street and Duncan lies on the couch watching *Creature Double Feature* on the television, glad for the heat thumping from the radiator. Outside it's already dark and his mother has closed the outer storm windows against the cold. The narrow windows continue to rattle in their wide frames; the wind bangs and bows the glass. Every now and then a car makes its way slowly up or down the hill, and its lights sweep briefly across the porch and up the far wall, and for a moment it is as if the images upon the television had come writhing alive and his breath momentarily stills. The door buzzer sounds, startling him, for he's heard no footsteps on the porch, and he rolls off the couch and crawls slowly to the door in the way that he imagines a deformed half-man, half-mutant fly might.

He opens the door and Julie is standing there, pale-faced and grim. Finally, after all this time, one of them has shown themselves! She's tracked him down, and at any moment, Billy will appear. Duncan's mouth has already shaped Julie's name, but then he closes his mouth. This girl's hair is glistening and long and pulled back tightly from her scalp so that he can see the roots and her eyebrows are much fuller and dark, arched as if in constant thoughtfulness over large, puzzled eyes. And then he realizes that her mouth is fuller also and there is a fine wisp of hair above her lip and at each side of her long neck. He stares at her long forehead, pale and unblemished, so like Julie's, and back to her eyes, and her mouth, to the lips that are chapped and cracked from biting. There is an odd smell off her, a pungency like old cheese or damp clothes molding in a pile before a laundry basket.

Duncan! Mother says sharply. Stop staring at the poor girl. Mother steps around him and, apologetically, waves the girl forward.

Come in, Magdalene. Don't let his bad manners stop you. You know, I really do try my best.

The girl steps into the hallway, adjusting a heavy satchel on her shoulder. From its depths she pulls a plastic soup bowl, fogged by heat, and hands it to Mother. That's okay, Mrs. Bright.

She glances at Duncan, frowning. I go to school with you, she says. I'm in your class.

Duncan nods. I know. I know who you are. I'm sorry. It was dark. I thought you were someone else.

He's seen this girl on the streets, at the bus stop and on the opposite side of the street as he walks home from school. Sometimes she will be just ahead of him, walking slowly, following the cracks of the sidewalk, and he'll match his pace to hers so that he can continue watching at a distance. At other times he catches her behind him, seemingly unaware of his presence, her eyes never straying from the broken and fractured concrete.

Every autumn, to make extra money, Magdalene Kopak goes from door to door asking if anyone wants to buy her elderly aunt's homemade Polish soup and chili for $2.50 a bowl. Magdalene's parents died in a car wreck on Big Sur Coast Highway when she was eight, and so most seem to buy her soups more out of pity and a sense of obligation than anything else. When the neighbors are finished, they're expected to leave the plastic Tupperware containers outside their doors so that Magdalene can retrieve them—in much the same way that his mother leaves her empty bottles of Old Mainline 454 on the front porch so that the homeless man can collect them and cash them in for the deposit down at Bradford Avenue Liquors.

I thought you were someone else, Duncan says again, as Magdalene clasps her satchel shut and steps out onto the porch. She's pretty, he stammers, like you. Magdalene pauses and stares back unsmiling, dark eyes reflecting twilight like nail heads. Lying is a sin, she says, and thumps gracelessly down the porch stairs, her frowzy overcoat billowing about her.

ON RAINY DAYS that mist the glass and turn everything gray beyond the window and the bay is covered in fog, Maggie and Duncan sit in the living room before the big bay window and listen to the horns moaning beyond the wharves. There are no men in Maggie's life but Duncan and Joshua now and she knows Duncan is grateful for this as she spends more time with him reading and talking, and she begins to feel like the girl, the young woman she was—had once been: inquisitive, daring, adventurous, humorous, easy to laugh and smile, and impassioned and pleased by the simple things around her.

She plays music on the old Victor phonograph: arias, operas, madrigals, and in the evenings before night comes down these become spirituals, then Paul Robeson. She'll imitate his full baritone singing "Old Man River" or "Roddy McCorley," and she and Duncan will laugh together as she shapes her face to reach the notes deep down in her belly, then Billie Holiday, Nina Simone, and, often at the end of the night, before Duncan sleeps, Elvis.

Her voice fills up all the spaces of their house, the narrow corridors she swept, the cold kitchen she mopped, the mildewed bathroom she scrubbed, and Duncan no longer notices the peeling paint, the dripping faucets, the cracked plaster and tile, the dark-water-stained ceilings, the pictures and markings and odors left by other people in the place that they call home but that can never rightly be theirs. It is only later that Duncan realizes how hard his mother has worked at making it a home, or at least, keeping him believing that it is, and how hard she has worked at maintaining the safety this allowed him.

Gray mist comes in off the bay and climbs the narrow side streets. Duncan is in the front room doing his homework on the shag carpet, which, although Maggie has cleaned it countless times, still smells of dog piss, especially on the damp rainy days. Maggie is in her bedroom upstairs and her door is open so that as she sings he feels she is somewhere close by and this makes him feel safe. He sits upon the reading chair by the bay window and looks out over the cloud-shrouded city. Birds wheel carelessly in the street, their wings as sharp and white as bone. Masses of gulls coming in from the bay, huge thrashing clouds of them trailing the fishing boats into port as dusk falls before the window. The image of the birds holds him in silence, and, Duncan feels, that moments upon moments like this must be what make up a life.

Maggie moves back and forth in her room, the floorboards creaking slightly beneath her feet. She is singing the Magnificat, the Virgin Mary's joyous prayer in response to her cousin, Elizabeth, who recognizes that Mary will become the mother of the Son of God. She sings in Latin plainchant, and then sings it high and sweet in English. Later he knows that she will play Bach's rendition of the Magnificat on the old Victor, perhaps as she prepares dinner. But he finds nothing in that joyous, resplendently overwrought version that compares to her spoken word-song.

The first time he tells her how lovely it is and asks her what it is, she looks at him in amazement. You never heard the Magnificat in the Home?

He shakes his head, and his mother frowns, kneels to pick a book from the floor. Never? she asks. She seems perplexed, and more than that, she appears stricken.

No, he says. I never heard it until you sang it to me. The Capuchins only prayed; they rarely sang.

Mother bares her teeth and chews on her lower lip as she reaches for her cigarettes.

Slowly, she unwinds the cellophane; a breeze rustles the drapes, and white light shimmers on the tabletop. Suddenly she laughs. Those damned Franciscans. I knew I should have taken you to the Jesuits.

March 1983

NEAR MIDNIGHT BENEATH the blue lights of the Windsor Tap, Maggie, dressed as a torch singer from the 1930s, is singing the last slow ballads of her set. As she sways slightly to the subtle backbeat from the band, the stage lights sparkle and shine and coalesce upon her form-fitting, blue sequined dress, creating the illusion of sinewy, slick movement. She's been singing since nine under the hot stage lights, with fifteen-minute breaks every half hour, and her face is covered in a fine sheen of sweat. Sweat beads her upper lip and her red hair clings damply to the sides of her pale face and to her neck and shoulders, like a wick soaked dark with oil. Duncan can hear Joshua on the bar stool beside him breathing deeply. Maggie's eyes are stretched dark and seductive with kohl, but rarely does she look up at her audience as she sings and only once does she look in Duncan's direction, smiling briefly.

As Duncan watches her, it seems as if she is experiencing exquisite pain, sadness, and pleasure, and the vacillation between these states has left her exhausted. With the last note, she strikes a pose that he's seen in old posters and movie stills for singers of that era—she bends her knees, arches her back and raises her gloved arm high, following, chasing, trying to catch up to that elusive note perhaps, as it rises from her throat and drifts up into the steamy air above the lights where tobacco smoke spirals in narrow winding tapers, and she remains in that pose until the note recedes and then dies and the lights go down and the stage is in darkness. It's as if the room wakes from a dream and only slowly a smattering of applause begins, and then lengthens as Maggie makes her way to the bar.

Sweat shines in the space between her breasts, pressed and bunched by the tight dress, and Duncan is suddenly aware of the physicality of her, of her breath burning so hot he thinks she must have a fever, of the large pores of her face, the kohl streaked about her large eyes, the dampness of her skin, of her breasts and hips, across which the dress stretches, wrinkles, and clings as she moves.

Can I get a hug from my biggest fan?

Duncan leans toward her and she wraps her arms about him and he feels the strength of her, the muscles of her shoulders and back, the damp of her sweat, and a sense of her tension as it is released through the act of hugging him.

Oh my. Sometimes I forget how tiring this can be, she says, plopping herself down on the stool and reaching for a glass of water, and then the bottle of Old Mainline and the shot glass that Clay has left on the bar for her.

What did you think of the show?

I loved it.

Maggie harrumphs, then nods. Well, it's not the Palais Garnier, but I suppose it'll do. She raises her glass, the umber liquid sloshing, and Duncan raises his Coke bottle. Smiling, Mother ruffles his hair and then they drink and Duncan watches from over the rim of his bottle as she empties her glass.

She eyes Joshua. Cat got your tongue?

Maggie, Joshua says and smiles serenely. I'm still six thousand miles away. I'm in the war, only it's 1943, and I'm sitting on the left bank. I'm the only black boy in a mishmash unit that has set up in the burned-out Continental with a platoon full of New Hampshire farm boys who spend half the night crying for their mama and the other half whispering in the dark: Nigger, nigger, nigger, tomorrow Jerry gets you. But y'know, it don't matter. It don't mean a thing, because I'm sitting on the left bank in Paris, drinking Pernod and listening to you sing, and when you sing like that, it just don't matter.

That's what you're thinking while I'm singing?

Sure. I imagined it just like you sang it.

Damn. Remind me to sing some sad numbers next time.

No. It was good. It was real fine.

What was your favorite?

You know what my favorite was.

Take my hand, Maggie says. Dance with me.

You know I can't dance, Maggie.

Come dance with me.

There's no music, Joshua says, and Maggie tugs playfully at his arms. His body leans from the stool.

Dance with me. C'mon, we'll make our own music. Listen to that. I can hear it—can't you?

Maggie woos Joshua until, with a roll of his eyes, he half-slides off the stool and, taking her hand, follows her to the dance floor, the eyes of the other men in the room upon them, blinking vacantly, longingly, desperately. At first they move slowly, with Joshua stumbling slightly, and then, with Mother leading, they move with more assurance. When Joshua looks down at his feet, Maggie whispers something to him and Joshua throws back his head laughing, and

Duncan smiles but then sees the scars there, crisscrossing Joshua's Adam's apple in a ragged X.

In the kitchen before the sink, Maggie and Joshua stand in darkness holding each other. Maggie strokes his hair, a soft *Shhhh, Joshua, Shhhh* hissing from between her lips. After a moment, in which it seems as if both of them have fallen asleep, chests rising and falling deeply, their eyes flutter and they press against each other, stumble to the wall, and begin kissing desperately, their mouths grasping and searching for the other's just as their hands reach for the other's face, the other's body, as if with a great and frightening hunger and each with such pained sounds they might have been wounded animals.

From the shadows of the hallway Duncan watches as the gray shimmering light cast from the streetlights turns their skin ashen and blue. Joshua holds his mother by her hips as they kiss and she takes his bruised face in her hands so tenderly you would think he were capable of breaking. They move against each other in the gloom, as if trying to find a way into the other's skin, and hold each other so tightly it's as if they fear losing each other. Duncan understands this fear, holds it close at night in his thoughts and in his heart as he listens to his mother breathing down the hall, the clatter of her whiskey bottle upon the floor, as his senses seek out the minor permutations, imperceptible psychic shifts in the air, those signals that might tell him of her intensions to leave and abandon him again as she had so long ago.

Joshua's open belt buckle bangs the countertop as their feet scuffle on the tile, and they stumble, breathless, legs and arms entwined, toward the doorway. Duncan's hand trails against the peeling wainscoting of the hallway in which the haunted light flickers as he slowly retreats to the stairs and to his bedroom. In the morning Joshua will be here and Duncan will wait in the kitchen for him to awaken and see him and reach across the kitchen table, place his large broken hand over Duncan's and say, *My man, Duncan. My man.*

In his bedroom Duncan turns away from the sounds from the radiator pipes and hears the wind whistling across the snowy plains of Thule, bending its notes in the drifts and rills of snow and the Home rising darkly from between the divide of two mining valleys and the stars above blazing in their cold, divine glory. In the dark kitchen Brother Canice is placing more wood in the stove, and the light from the open grate, glowing orange-red embers crackling, bends warmly upon his plump face and upon the peeling wainscoting. Snow taps softly upon the windows. The Vulcanite radio glows amber upon the shelf of tinned goods, humming its vacant, searching sound, which Brother Canice listens to with his head cocked like an old dog, his mouth spitting sunflower seeds into the fire. In a moment he will begin a story and tell Duncan what comes next.

A person is disposed to an act of choice by an angel . . . in two ways. Some-times, a man's understanding is enlightened by an angel to know what is good, but it is not instructed as to the reason why . . . But sometimes he is instructed by angelic illumination, both that this act is good and as to the reason why it is good.

—ST. THOMAS AQUINAS

EVERY MORNING JOSHUA rises at four A.M., and Duncan, listening to the dark, is waiting for him: the creak of the bedsprings, the shifting of the mattress as he begins to stir, rising toward waking, his body and mind so attuned to this schedule that he will wake each morning five to ten minutes before the alarm he has set whether he wants to or not—it's as if the dark, labyrinthine reaches of the tunnel and the sea are calling to him. Just as the memories of Vietnam are—the two entwined and now inseparable from each other—one reflecting, paralleling, and so powerfully echoing the other that Joshua cannot forget those memories that he has tried all these years and with incredible difficulty to press into darkness, memories that now, as they emerge from darkness, emerge stronger, more powerful and crystalline than ever.

Duncan knows that Joshua is staring at the ceiling in this moment, just as he is. The anxiety of this time in the morning, when—despite the quiet, the stillness—the weight of the day seems to press heavily, burgeoning upon the nerves, a day when so many things can go wrong and this hour when all he has is the time and space to think of them. Joshua sighs in the darkness and Duncan knows he wishes he could sleep until it is time to rise, less time to think and contemplate, but every morning it is like this. The darkness pressed against the windows, the coldness of the room, and the gray of half-forgotten dreams and memories swirling as fragments in their heads.

Joshua always prepares his breakfast and his lunch pail the night before and showers before bed. All there is left to do is to rise and dress. All there is left to do is wait for the alarm. But these minutes are the longest. Often he will simply rise and turn off the alarm long before it sounds. A few times he has left the house so early in advance that he has forgotten to turn it off and Duncan will hear it ringing, growing louder and more incessant as it continues, and he will rush into his mother's bedroom, where she is snoring loudly, the air stale with her breath and the sickly sweet smell of alcohol, and turn it off before she awakens. Only then, will Duncan return to his bedroom and sometimes drift back to sleep.

Duncan leaves his door partially open in the hope that Joshua might glance in, see him awake, and that he might wave farewell. Duncan has thought about rising and fixing himself breakfast in the kitchen these mornings so that he can be with Joshua, but he senses that this time is a time when Joshua most wishes to be alone, that he is still finding his way through the fog, and if Duncan were to surprise him at the breakfast table, he might not even recognize who he is. Instead, Duncan wakes with Joshua and waits with him from his bedroom and slowly in this way comes to know him better.

UPON DUNCAN'S BEDROOM ceiling his mother has painted a sky: varying shades of blue, white clouds, and a 1,021 silver stars—with each paint stroke, mother had counted them—all arranged in distinct constellations. And in the center of this is the skylight through which the true sky is visible. It reminds him of the ceiling in the Home's charnel house through which he and Billy and Julie often watched the day fade to night.

Duncan and Maggie lie side by side upon his narrow bed, watching the ceiling and the manner in which it changes as the light outside falls toward dusk. Maggie is drinking; every so often she raises her tumbler from the floor and ice rattles loudly in the glass.

How is your friend, Magdalene? She asks, her voice loud in the stillness between them. On the ceiling, Mother's Cassiopeia and Virgo, at the darkest corners of the room, begin to glow.

Poor child. She's such a tragic little thing. You must invite her over more often. Think about how alone she must be.

She pats his arm. You have me, Duncan, and you always will. She has no one but that crazy aunt who only knows she's there because her damn soup bowls get returned to her.

Maggie raises her legs and scratches absently; her nails rasp against nylon. She kicks off her heels and with a clatter they bang against the baseboard. She stretches her feet, curls her long toes until they crack.

How do they treat her at school?

At school? How would I know? I rarely go to school.

Oh, Duncan. You know that's not true. You go to school all the time. You were in school just over a week ago. Maggie waves her tumbler glass in the air, remonstrating.

I thought we were having a nice time. If you're going to be so sour and difficult, I see no need for us to talk. Let's just be quiet then, shall we? We don't need to say anything at all. We can just be quiet. Look at the stars. My!

Maggie lifts the tumbler of amber liquor to her lips but it takes a moment for them to grasp the rim. She sucks hungrily and then there is only air, and the pop and rattle of the fully formed ice cubes that remain. She sighs, realizing the glass is empty.

Feebly, she reaches for his hand. Do you remember the Soap Woman, honey? she mutters. That woman we saw in the museum? Her body left like that for strangers to gawk at and with no family or friends to claim her for their own. That's what happens when you're alone in the world. You would never let that happen to me, would you?

In the Home, the children played a game where they pretended that they were dying from some exotic, rare, incurable disease and that at the End their parents rushed to their deathbeds, to tell them how much they loved them. The children wanted to believe that their parents, no matter their flaws, would come for them when they had no time left and that they would always be there waiting for them—their sons and daughters—when it mattered most.

Maggie's glass tumbler slips to the floor, and moments later she begins to snore softly: a warm and pleasant sound like an old, spring-wound, wood clock ticking slowly and imprecisely.

That poor, poor, unfortunate child, Maggie slurs suddenly into the dark, as if she were speaking from within some terribly sad, prophetic dream, in which only she and Magdalene had a part, and Duncan follows her voice upward toward the ceiling, where the major constellations have emerged, luminescent as fireflies. Maggie rolls onto her side, away from him, and, hugging her arms and legs, curls into a ball, until she seems no larger than a child herself. And Duncan wants to touch her but something holds him back—he feels as he had when he first stared at the Soap Woman through her coffin-glass at the museum.

Such a tragedy, Maggie murmurs in her dreamsleep. It's such a tragedy.

He stares at the clouds turning black on the ceiling and the stars shimmering distantly through the glass skylights and the room becomes cold and he turns inward against Maggie and imagines her as a young girl—not much younger than Magdalene—even as her drunken snores fill the room with their familiar, discordant warmth.

April 1983

AT THE TUNNEL site great excavators and cranes with hydraulic hammers prepare the way for the tunnel crews, and while they shore slurry and silt, set piles for cement and iron forms that will hold back the sea, the tunnelers are allowed a reprieve. It is a warm day in early spring, two weeks after the latest blackout, and the men sit on the slope of President's Hill, overlooking the construction, dozing or eating their lunches, smoking and talking with one another. A cool breeze blows in off the water, pushing at the grass, bringing goose bumps up on their skin, and with it the pungent low-tide smell of the excavations and further the black bilge and sulfur from the old tanneries across the bay in Oakland.

Joshua sits, smoking a cigarette, beside Sully, John Chang, Javier, Minkivitz, and Minkivitz's younger brother, Jamie; he focuses on the physical sensation of inhaling and exhaling and the burn of the cigarette in his throat, the smoke streaming through his mouth and nostrils. The insides of his eyelids are turned red by the sun and crazy, elliptical shapes bounce and tremble there and in their center, small static dots like the snow upon a television screen when programming has ended. The sound of the heavy cranes dropping their hammers into the piles booms across the bay. Like the footfalls of the colossal prehistoric beasts of the Cretaceous, whose remains they had found buried in the shale and silt at the bottom of the sea.

You know, we build on major fault in the earth here, Javier says. Right on the very top of it! Through the ground Joshua feels the slight tremors from Javier's agitation, and he opens his eyes. Javier is rabidly chewing on his sandwich, his cheeks bulging and his Adam's apple working up and down, and as soon as his mouth is clear he begins speaking rapidly again, wags a finger at the bay: Right here, man. Right fucking here.

Jamie stares at Javier. Jamie is as pale as porcelain, with small ears, like those of a young boy's, protruding from the sides of his oval face. Blue veins show beneath the skin below his eyes. His brother, Charlie Minkivitz, the foreman on the job, slurps loudly from a plastic bowl of soup. Every few moments he pauses and glances at his younger brother.

Javy, man, Joshua says, there's major faults everywhere in San Francisco. Calm down.

Yes, yes, of course, but—and now Javier is nodding his head passionately—but no one builds directly over them like we do!

Listen. If there's a quake, we're in the safest spot in the city.

This is true?

Sure, that's why we're building the tunnel beneath the water. It's safer down there and stronger than any bridge. When the next one hits, I either want to be down there with you or else on the Transbay.

Minkivitz looks up from his soup again, thick lips pursed and wet. He wipes his mouth with the back of his hand and then chortles. Whoo, boy, that's a good one. We have the chance to die a hundred times a hundred different ways before this dig is ever complete and he's telling you it's safe being underground. What you think he knows, Javy? You think he went to goddamn Stanford or something?

Harvard, Joshua says, and draws from his cigarette. He rolls his shoulders and stretches into the sun. His back creaks loudly and something—a tendon or ligament—sounds in his neck. The muscles spasm and then relax and Joshua winces.

Wha?

I went to Harvard, Minkie.

Bullshit. Can you believe this guy? Can you believe him? Went to Harvard, he says. A nigger in Harvard! Bullshit, I say. You're a fucking liar.

And Joshua, looking at Minkivitz's puckered face, begins to laugh, a belly laugh that shakes his whole body, that leaves him weak, muscles trembling and jittery. He wipes at his eyes, and when he is done, he looks toward Minkivitz, shrugs at Javier, and then stares out over the bay with a serene wide smile on his face.

Jamie clambers awkwardly to his feet, as if he has suddenly lost his equilibrium, as if he is walking the bow of a ship cresting a great swell at sea. He moves farther down the hill and, after a moment, they hear the sound of retching. Joshua, Javier, and Minkivitz stare after him: the silhouette of a tall narrow figure doubled over upon the scaffolded embankment, swaying uneasily as he stands, and then bending to retch again.

What's the matter with your brother, *che*?

Minkivitz continues to stare after him—they all do. Finally: He doesn't like the work, he says. The tunnel—he's not cut out for it. Says he keeps hearing and seeing things in the dark. I should never have brought him on; he's too young.

Maybe it's the bends? Javier says. Site managers from Bextel and Sonoyama International have been rushing the men through the compression chambers more and more often as the tunnel falls behind schedule—in the last week alone the superintendent has cut the time at each stage by five minutes. He says: I know a man once who had the bends and he used talk to his dead mother. Always puking too. He bleed from the eyes and think he's Jesus. He went crazy, y'know? I think we all go crazy down there.

What types of things is Jamie seeing? Joshua asks.

I don't know. I don't ask. Why the hell would I? You listen to too much of that kind of crap and it'll drive you nuts. He shrugs angrily.

A moment passes and Minkivitz shakes his head and swears: Fuck! Angels. That's what he says. He's seeing fucking angels everywhere. Minkivitz exhales loudly through his nostrils, as if he is trying to contain some great, inexpressible frustration and sadness. Joshua is aware of his chest rising and falling and the silence that has fallen over the three of them and over the hill upon which they're sitting.

Our father passed away when Jamie was young, Minkivitz says. I asked the super to make him go get a medical, y'know, see a shrink.

Joshua and Javier nod. Everyone in Local 223 knows that the Minkivitzes' father committed suicide by jumping from the Golden Gate Bridge when they were boys.

Above, gray, swirling clouds move in a twisting gyre over the middle of the water, seeming to turn in co-centric circles and then, at the bottommost turn of the screw, seeming to turn fully in upon themselves, and then to churn backward, as the gyre rises once more, moving upward into the dense thunderheads, which seem to have suddenly swept in from the sea, and above these, so high they must crane their necks, an icy white cloud has expanded and spread, pressed against the bottom of the stratosphere until it has flattened into an anvil.

Well, friend, Javier mutters, glancing up at the clouds nervously and putting out a tentative hand as small chunks of hail begin to fall. The boy not seem well, that for sure.

May 1983

JOSHUA AND DUNCAN ride beyond Oakland through a strange dusken light, pink-tinged clouds feathering the sky above them, not speaking but quietly enjoying the sensations of the ride: the sound of the Indian's heavy engine, the weight of speed pressing upon them, and the world changing so quickly, weaving through the fragmented light seeping down beyond the tree line flickering and blinding as a strobe and then the sudden and comforting reprieve of the nether light before dark. Evening birds—doves and whip-poor-wills— sounding and challenging in the gray, ashy bracken, and barely visible through the high firs, a feathery skein of stars.

They motor though the ashen twilight, Duncan holding tight to Joshua's field jacket, along twisting roads soured by the odor of strange tamarind trees and through the high-roofed tunnels of giant Douglas firs, the evergreen smell of them sharp in their nostrils, the loud rumbling sound of the bike's exhaust cast back at them from the thick surrounding growth, muted and strangely echoed, altering all sense of space and of the distance over which they travel to Admiral's Point.

The night comes fully then and a cold breeze with it so that Duncan clings tighter to Joshua's waist, his eyes watering in the chill, moist air. The Indian's headlight a narrow white light trembling on the road before them and sweeping across the firs that press out at them from the darkness at the sudden sharp angles of the road, which Joshua handles effortlessly, as if without thought, merely leaning this way and that and slanting the bike so steeply at times that Duncan thinks gravity will pull them down and smash them upon the road, send them spinning like a sparking, gasoline-spewing whirligig hurtling out into the dark.

Finally they reach Admiral's Point, cindered gravel crunching beneath the tires, and Duncan climbs, shivering, from the bike. Beyond the wide grass expanse of Soldier's Park the distant city shimmers.

Joshua walks toward the flagstone walkway and Duncan instinctively reaches for his hand even though he knows he is too old for this gesture and Joshua takes it in his calloused grip. Duncan wonders about the nights mother rode with Joshua on his bike, which was rare, and to the places they traveled. What did they talk about? Was he ever a part of their discussions? Did he have a place in their plans for the future?

Do you take mom up here? Duncan asks.

No. Only you.

Why?

Joshua seems to think about this and then shrugs. Some things a man just has to show another man, yeah? Some things that don't need explaining, some things that you don't want to explain even if you could. It's like those trips you take with your momma, just between the two of you. So, this is just between us. I mean, what do *you* two do when you're together?

Nothing. We just drive. And sometimes Mom gets sad or tired and she cries and then we come home again.

Joshua purses his lips, considering this. Is that all right with you? he says. The driving, I mean. If you don't want to go, you can tell her, y'know?

No, it's okay. I don't mind.

Far, far away a tugboat blows its horn. Duncan thinks of the things that fathers say only to their sons and the words that never need to be spoken, uttered aloud. For no reason at all, his heart begins to hammer; it feels tight and squeezed and sore in his chest.

Joshua, will you tell me about my father? And although this is what Duncan asks, for the first time he is no longer interested in discussing him, who he was or what became of him, he merely wants Joshua to speak and to hear Joshua's voice.

Joshua fills his mouth with air and then holds it so that his cheeks balloon. He stares out at the water, lets go of Duncan's hand, making Duncan wish that he hadn't spoken at all, and presses hard at his eyes. Finally he exhales. Nope, he says. I can't do that. I promised your mother. Why do you care so much about this anyway? What has he ever done for you? Here you got your mother who loves you. And she's struggling, and it's hard.

I don't know why. He's my father.

Joshua thinks about this for a moment. Yeah, I know. My father's out there too.

Joshua laughs, and Duncan smiles, glances toward the stars.

No, I mean right out there—he lives in Oakland, I haven't seen him in fifteen years. Joshua's smile widens momentarily, teeth flashing, and then as he looks out over the bay, his expression hardens.

One time, he says, my father took me to a basketball game, to the Celtics. That's back when your mother and I lived in Boston. She never tell you things about when she was a little girl?

Joshua looks at Duncan and Duncan shakes his head. I was so

damn excited, man, I must have been talking about it for weeks. It drove my mother crazy. I thought if I kept talking about it then there was no way my father could change his mind, but I also worried that if I talked too much, he would change his mind, but I couldn't help myself. See, my father never did stuff like that, never did anything with us.

The C's were playing Cleveland, I remember that. And I remember that at some point in the game my father stood up, just for a moment, to cheer. Someone scored a basket, I don't remember who, and someone shouts from behind us: Sit the fuck down, you fucking nigger, and my father paused, turned around to see who had shouted at him. He stood there and looked back at the crowd. And then a whole group of voices cry out: Hey, nigger, sit the fuck down! And my father did, but first he turned back to the game and stood there for a moment as if he were still cheering and wouldn't give them the satisfaction. Then, real slow like, he sat down.

He didn't watch the rest of the game and neither did I. We just stared straight ahead without saying a word to each other. When the game was over, my father sat there, and finally, when the Garden was empty, he stood up and we left. We didn't talk the whole ride home and he never took me to another game again. We never did anything together again.

And it may sound stupid, I was only ten, but I knew that my father was a broken man, that he no longer had any pride left. When he beat my mother, deep down I think I knew he was trying to beat the pride out of her too. And I hated him for that. I've always hated him for that. He thought he was strong, but for him to do that to my mother, to me and my little sister . . . Joshua shakes his head. I promised myself I'd never be weak like that.

You have a sister?

Had. I had a sister. Long time ago.

Joshua rolls a cigarette with his battered fingers, hands Duncan his pouch of tobacco as he lights it, breathes it in deep and then exhales. The familiar sweet smell of Mother's Burley hangs there between them. He nods toward Oakland.

My father came out here after my mother left, after Boston. Back east we'd lived in West Medford near my mother's aunts and brothers, me and my little sister, my mother and my father. It was hard then, but my mother's family were all educated, had good jobs. My mother had gone to Tufts and my father never could stand that. Very proud he was. Always angry at my mother for showing him up. That's what he'd say, she was always showing him up, with her book smarts. He couldn't stand that she was better than him—it shamed him.

Joshua turns to look at Duncan now and his face is rigid, set like stone.

Don't you ever touch a woman, okay? A man that touches a woman ain't no man. Look at me. Do you hear me?

Duncan stares at Joshua unblinking, and nods.

Duncan, there's going to be a time when I won't be here and you'll need to protect your mother and yourself. And I don't want you to think about it, okay? Just act. Do whatever it takes to protect the both of you. When you hit someone, don't just hit them once. Hit them so many times they'll never be able to lift a finger to you again. You got it? Are you listening?

I'm listening. I just don't know if I can ever hit someone.

Well, then, my man, you're going to have to learn, because in the end no one can protect you but you. And your mother needs you, Duncan. She'll never say it, but she does. Will you promise me you'll be strong for her?

I'll try, I promise.

Joshua nods. My man, I know you will. You're a good kid.

He stares out at the bay; cigarette smoke steams from his nostrils.

I shouldn't be telling you this, but I think you should hear it, you so stuck on your father. When I was sixteen, my father almost beat my mother to death with a wrench and the only thing that stopped him was me getting in the way. I hit him and I didn't stop hitting him. He crawled out of our house on his belly while I was still hitting him. I broke his nose and his cheekbone. I fractured his eye socket. I doubt the man ever saw properly again. I wanted to kill him, and perhaps I should have. If he'd been around when I came back from Nam, I would have killed him, and he knew it.

Joshua shrugs. But my mother was already dead by then, so it didn't matter any more. He quiets as if he is suddenly aware that he's been talking too much. The sound of him seems to fill up the night; it seeps into the air about Duncan like the fog snaking up the wide banks of the bay.

Duncan looks at him. How did she die?

Jesus, I shouldn't be telling you these things.

His jaws clench and the hollows of his cheeks deepen with shadow so that he appears even more gaunt. He says: She fell on subway tracks, the El in Boston—two years after she left us. It was the rush hour commute and the platform was crowded so maybe she was pushed, or maybe it was an accident, who knows? Anyway, she touched the third rail and she died.

I'm sorry.

Yeah, me too.

He draws on his cigarette and after a moment it steams from his nostrils. He says: I always thought I'd get a chance to see her again.

Below them, and perhaps a quarter of a mile away, at a short distance from the coastline stands a large derrick, two hundred feet high, and on either side within a floating caisson, two cranes. At their height small amber and red lights flash on and off. Out at the center of the bay another derrick tower emerges darkly from the water, its metal and iron skelature like the eviscerated remains of some prehistoric serpent held and frozen aloft in ice, and that remained when the glaciers retreated. Fog swirls and trickles through its vast ribs and spine and they watch—Duncan is aware of Joshua breathing close to him—as the fog slowly engulfs the derrick entirely, until only the lights remain visible, blinking dully through the ghostly banks of white. The tugboat horns come again, muted and seemingly even farther away.

Right there beneath the water, under the bay, is where we're digging the tunnel, Joshua says. By next Christmastime we should be done.

Joshua points to the center of the strait where the water shudders with sudden movement and turns round and black. Damn, my man! Will you look at that!

A geyser of water shoots into the air in a mushrooming spray. Two massive rudders slap the surface of the water, and then a colossal tail arcs from the whitecaps. Duncan sees a mouth of tufted baleen, a gleaming back and side encrusted with barnacle and scar.

A whale, he says in disbelief.

They watch as it makes its slow way down the bay, a green phosphorescent wake shimmering two hundred feet behind, beneath the fog-entrenched Golden Gate, mist swirling about it like smoke. And its moan a deep, low foghorn sounding the lonely depths of the vast Pacific before it, responding and calling to others of its kind, perhaps a thousand miles away, each sailing its own shadowy and vast corner of the increasingly empty dark spaces of the sea. With one final plumed exhale, it begins to sink beneath the water. Its wide flukes show, and then it rolls and spins into the deep.

October 1983

MAGDALENE KOPAK AND her aunt don't have a television—they survive on the aunt's monthly social security checks and that's barely enough to pay for rent and heat—and on the weekends Duncan becomes accustomed to hearing Magdalene's footfalls upon the front stairs and then a knock upon their door, which, on Saturdays, his mother always answers in the simple, black faux-silk dress she wears to the Windsor Tap. He imagines the sight of her as she swings the door wide and stands in the brightly lit vestibule before Magdalene, her coils of red hair coifed in an intricate and elegant French bun atop her head, the short black dress shifting slightly, its diaphanous weight clinging to her lower belly, her thighs and hips, the length of her long legs and muscular calves towering atop three-inch black heels.

Bonjour, Mademoiselle Magdalene, Maggie will say, and then, if Magdalene hesitates, as she often does, Maggie will take her by the hand and escort her the rest of the way into the living room. With bowls of badly burnt popcorn that mother has prepared for them in a frenetic and excited stir of emotion as she readies herself for work, they sit wrapped in a blanket thick with old animal hair on the long threadbare couch, through which the springs poke and press maddeningly.

Together Magdalene and Duncan wait as the television Maggie and he bought at the St. Vincent de Paul in Chinatown hums to life, its slowly warming transistors clicking, and then the flickering, grainy black-and-white images of NBC's *Saturday Night at the Movies* or ABC's *The Movie of the Week* shuddering in rippling horizontal waves on the bowed screen, in much the same way as it did on the television in the Home, and, always, briefly, Duncan thinks of how he, Julie, and Billy used to crouch behind the couch in the Brothers' lounge, and of Brother Wilhelm snoring and trembling softly in his sleep before the ancient Zenith.

Magdalene's eyes widen when Joshua walks into the room, greets her, and then walks the hall to the bathroom.

Is that's your mother's boyfriend?

Duncan shrugs. I guess.

He seems nice.

He is.

He's older than I thought.

Is he? I hadn't noticed. He was in Vietnam.

Oh, I guess that's it.

They stare at the television but Duncan is aware of Magdalene peeking at his mother, following her movements about the apartment—a darting shape at the edge of their sight—and when she and Joshua have left, Magdalene says: I don't think my aunt likes your mother much.

Duncan looks at her.

I heard my aunt talking to Mrs. Polati. She says your mother is a stripper in a bar down on Columbus.

She isn't a stripper. She sings, Magdalene. She doesn't dance. She sings.

Magdalene shrugs. My mother used to sing, she says. But she wasn't as pretty as your mother. Your mother's beautiful.

I bet she had a nice voice, Mags, Duncan says, and imagines Magdalene on her bed at night, listening to water shunting and hissing through the close radiator pipes, and laying her head toward that sound, perhaps hearing her mother's distant voice, just as he often heard his mother's voice through the pipes, straining to catch those quarter notes and elusive C7. *What might she say to her?*

Magdalene considers this. No, she says. Not really. She didn't have a nice voice at all, but I miss it. I miss her.

She shrugs as if to shake herself from the dream, the memory. You ever think what it would be like to have Mr. McGreevey as your father?

Duncan pauses—he doesn't know how to answer. He wants to say, But I have a father! How could he think of someone other than his father being his father, but he can't answer the question because he has wondered about it at times, even wished for it, but the thought of saying it aloud frightens him.

I don't know, he says. I hadn't really thought about it.

November 1983

WHEN JOSHUA COMES home from work, he smells of deep sea silt and shale, of damp and pungent muck and loam, as if he had been dredged from the bottom of the bay, as if it is a part of him now and oozing, seeping from his pores. And his breath is always slightly sour and metallic, something that Duncan imagines occurs like a physical reaction during the stages of decompression in the air locks, that the men slightly change, become something other as they leave the watery world, the world of darkness and weight, for the world above. Or perhaps it is the dream and the fear fantasy of the sea rushing in on them that keeps him and the other men constantly coursing with adrenaline, which long after their shifts are over, turns to acid in their muscle and tendon, makes them feel as if they'd hefted and carried the tunnel itself, much like the hydraulic jacks that push the concrete partitions centimeter by centimeter beneath the seabed.

It is no wonder Joshua sleeps before dinner and then almost immediately after. He tells Duncan's mother that it will not always be this way, that he must take the work when he can, for within the year the tunnel will be completed and there will be no more work other than the odd welding job that comes along. Later Duncan will hear the shower running, and steam will seep beneath the door, making the plaster and paper of the hallway moist—an hour will pass and beads of condensation will slowly trickle down their surface, as Joshua tries to ease the pain from his joints. The corners of the ceiling are already dark with mildew and each night these dark stains grow further, slowly stretching out toward the center. Duncan's mother complains about them, says that she needs to bleach the paint, but they don't have a stepladder and the stains are too high to reach without one. At breakfast Joshua will barely eat because, he complains, his teeth ache, and when Maggie tries to kiss him, he smiles but gives her his cheek as if that, too, causes him pain.

Each crew can work at the tunnel face for only two hours at a time and then they must exit the tunnel as they entered it, through a network of interconnected air locks, going into the lock, the doors sealing after them, waiting for the air pipe to hiss, the men's ears popping as the air pressure climbs. When it has equaled the adjoining lock, the connecting door automatically unlocks and they move into the next chamber. Mostly they do not mind this process, even though it occupies hours of their work shift; when someone becomes restless—a shifting of feet, the rolling of eyes, a deep and pronounced sigh, a grumbling at the back of the throat and then the hacking of phlegm or snot upon the metal floor runner—the shop steward or second man will retell one of the countless stories from the early tunneling days or perhaps a story of the men who died from the bends, in horrible pain as nitrogen bubbles exploded in their bloodstream, bleeding from their eyes and from their bowels, during the building of the Thames tunnel, and the men will nod or joke and shake their heads, but the eye rolling and restless shifting will stop.

When Joshua is standing in the locks, he is never in the lock itself but outside, rising violently through a bubbling stream of turbulent and violent water as a sudden air breech splits the lock in two and sucks the men from the chamber, hurls them up and then down. Some will never surface and the others will be thrust to the surface so suddenly they will explode upon reaching it, bits of flesh and bone and blood spraying the tops of the waves in a bloody spume. Joshua has imagined being crushed by the sea, of it sweeping in and taking them all, pressing them back down into the primeval slime or hurtling them toward God. There is an immense and spiritual beauty in the sea taking them, he imagines, although he cannot make sense of this nor explain why this should be so as compared with any other type of death. Yet he is not alone—many of the other men also fantasize about death in the tunnel. At night they lie awake next to their girlfriends or wives and upon the black ceiling of their bedroom see the sea rushing in and down upon them, sweeping them up in her arms and dashing them to the bedrock, obliterating them into bone fragments at the bottom of the bay. This manner of death they understand is a type of calling, a spiritual vocation.

At the dinner table Joshua seems sedate and at peace. He breaks bread from the loaf Maggie has placed upon the table, butters it, and, as he chews, tells Duncan of the tunnel that will one day stretch beneath the San Francisco Bay across the northern point of Calisto County. He speaks of the men who work with him in the caisson, of the air locks and the three giant TBMs that they call Barbara, Dymphna, and Gabriel, and of the cutterhead that burrows through the muck and silt. He talks of water breaking through the cavern. Of men detonating on the insides from the force of decompression, of hydrogen bubbles exploding in their veins, of men rising too quickly to the surface and dying horrifying, agonizing deaths. He speaks of them all being swept away by the sea and his eyes are lit with the passion of a penitent in prayer. He cuts into his steak and says: Today as I was working I dreamed I saw Jamie's angel. It came down into the tunnel, reached beneath my arms and lifted me up through the water, up through the sea and the waves. Up, he laughs, all the way up. He carried me clear across the sky.

Maggie pauses in chewing her food and eyes him warily, as if he might be high, strung out on his meds, or if it's the side effects of Prazosin. You're tired, honey, she says. You work too hard. It's not right that they make men work so hard, that they've been cutting your times in the air locks. There's going to be an accident if they keep pushing all of you this way. Someone's going to get hurt.

But Joshua isn't listening. He sips from his beer and continues talking about angels.

Joshua, she begins and taps upon the table with the bottom of her knife to get his attention. Joshua, remember when we were kids and your mother would drag you around Medford Square on Saturday while the rest of us would be at Carlano's sharing an Italian ice or coming from watching a movie at the 1&2? Remember, they had an old theater organ that they'd play between the double bills?

All the way up where? Duncan asks, and smiles.

To heaven, man, all the way up to heaven.

Duncan blinks and then asks him: Are you sure you were dreaming?

December 1983

FROM HIS ST. PAUL hospital, Billy sends Duncan a postcard and a letter in an envelope. The post card shows an ice breaker on the Mississippi River and the St. Paul towers dusted with snow in the background. A Christmas setting with snow on the streets and rooftops and blue and green lights frozen and alight in every storefront window. The card says *Seasons Greetings* and on the back Billy has written in his poor penmanship:

> **Happy Holidays from the most livable city in America.**
> **Just makes you want to come live here, don't it?**
> **They haven't broken me yet, Duncan!**

> **Yours,**
> **Billy**

In the letter Billy has drawn a small map of his ward, and he writes about what he eats and where he sleeps and the room that contains the dyna-chamber where he receives monthly isotope bombardments. The final spot on his map seems to be in one of the southern hallways on the sixteenth floor, at a window looking out upon the wide Minnesota plains beyond stretching into an indeterminable distance. Duncan assumes that this must point toward the Home, and he imagines Billy late at night—while the other children sleep and nurses quietly pad the tiled hallways and distant monitors beep and muted, garbled voices tremor from the ward's intercoms—sitting alone before his snow-frosted window, the city lights cast upon the glass and his wide-eyed old face reflected back to him, searching the darkness for the distant flicker of lightning spidering across the vast Iron Range beyond the Home, and perhaps he hears the soft brass peal of church bells from the minaret resounding outward into the far towns across Thule's frozen valleys, and as Duncan stares at the card, he wishes he was sitting in the dark with him and watching over him so that he might sleep.

Later that evening during Mass at St. Mary of the Wharves, Mother takes his hand.

I know you miss your friends, she says. Would it help if we called the Home and spoke to them, to see how they are?

She seems surprised when he shakes his head and says no.

Why not, sweetie?

I don't want to know that they're still there and that their parents haven't come back for them like me. And I don't want to remind them of that. I already said goodbye once. If their parents come for them, they'll call me.

Are you waiting for that?

I don't know. Sometimes.

Honey, I'm sure they're very happy for you and that they'd love to hear from you.

Duncan shakes his head again. The priest raises the Eucharist in his hands, *Agnus Dei, qui tollis peccata mundi, dona nobis pacem*, and the altar boy rings the bell.

No, they're not happy for me, he says and blesses himself. But that's all right. If I was them, I wouldn't be happy for me either.

In the rectory, as Mother waits outside, he requests a pair of Mass cards for the dead, and when the old priest who is no longer capable of performing Mass asks him who the cards are for, he tells him that they're for Billy and Julie and under *The Departed* he writes their full names:

Billy Bowen, Julie Connors

He does this every Friday after the Stations of the Cross, and on Sunday he sits in a rear pew of the church and listens to the priest calling out Billy's and Julie's names and the congregation bowing their heads and offering up their prayers, and the sound of their names spoken in a low, sorrowful timbre by a hundred voices trembling in his belly and then rising higher with all the names of the other faithful departed and reverberating off the polished stone balusters and columns in the nave like a great clanging of bells that reminds him of Brother Canice swinging from the ropes of the bell tower in the late hours of the night, and he wonders who Brother Canice tells his story to now that he is no longer there or if perhaps he speaks it to himself before the pulsating embers of the woodstove in the dark kitchen and if his story is any less real without anyone to hear it.

Christmas Eve 1983

SNOW FALLING SLOWLY down over the humpbacked city and the soft hiss of car tires churning on the street outside. Christmas lights blinking from porches, the front of houses, along glistening rooftops. Plastic Christmas trees decorated and blazing in living room windows up and down the street. On lots with small front yards: rotund snow-men, Santa Claus and his reindeer, the Virgin Mary, Joseph, and the baby Jesus in their manger surrounded by cows and sheep and the Three Wise Men, the glow of their interior bulbs shining through the plastic where the paint has been worn away.

In the corner of the living room, a pine tree, brought that morn-ing by Joshua from a plot down on Divisadero, sparkles and glitters with multicolored miniature lights that Duncan and Magdalene placed in staggered rows; it fills the room with the scent of pine sap. On the television a video of the 1968 Apollo 8 live Christmas Eve lunar orbit broadcast that Duncan has pleaded to put on with the promise that he would keep the sound low.

Joshua wears a full apron as he brings out the turkey and lays it on the table to Duncan's and Magdalene's applause. He turns off the lights so they can watch the snow drifting softly down through the dark upon the electric-lit street, spinning in whorls between parked cars and the spaces between houses, brushing the windows and sticking to the glass with a strange, almost angelic geometry.

The table is covered with a red and green tablecloth and at its center blazes Maggie's giant, ornate candelabra, surrounded by holly and containing a dozen wax-encrusted gilded stems upon which white tapers flicker, casting an incandescent light in the dark room. Maggie says it was given to her as a gift from an Italian set director on Verdi's *Requiem* at La Scala, but winks as she says it.

Damn, Maggie, Joshua says. I never knew you were such a thief. Looks like you bled those poor suckers dry. He nods to the heavy red velvet drapes with intricate gold scrollwork that she's hung on either side of the window. I suppose those were a gift too?

Maggie grins. Oh yes, all gifts. You see, I was a special talent and they knew I deserved these things. They couldn't bear for me to leave and not give me something!

Yeah, after the lights were out and the doors were locked. What did you do? Smuggle them out under your dress?

Now, now. Magdalene doesn't need to hear any more of your sordid suggestions. Instead of blabbing why don't you do something useful and cut the turkey, you turkey.

She pats Magdalene upon her hand, and squeezes. I'm sorry your aunt couldn't make it, Magdalene.

That's okay, Mrs. Bright. She's at the community center with her friends. She goes every Christmas—I think she was glad that I had somewhere else to go this year. We're going to open presents together later.

Good. We can drive you over to pick her up, if you like.

Yes, thank you.

Would you do us the honor of a blessing, Magdalene?

Sure, Mrs. Bright.

They hold hands and Duncan watches Magdalene, feels her hand sweaty in his. Magdalene closes her eyes and whispers hoarsely: Thank you, God, for everything you give us. Thank you for this meal and for us all being together.

Amen, he says softly and his mother looks over and smiles and he stares at all their faces—Maggie, Joshua, and Magdalene—brightly lit by candlelight.

Magdalene opens her eyes and blushes when she sees Duncan staring at her.

Thank you, Magdalene, Maggie says. That was wonderful.

She scoops some mashed potatoes and squash onto her plate and passes the bowl to Joshua, and for a moment, there is only the sound of bowls upon wood and cutlery and knives scraping plates.

Outside, revelers and carolers are singing "Silent Night" and ringing bells as they walk the street and cars honk their horns and Duncan thinks of a Christmastime when the astronauts recited Genesis as they crossed over the meridians of the earth turning below them and thanked God for all their blessings.

After dinner they pull crackers and don colored paper hats, and Maggie refills their glass—wine for her and Joshua; apple cider for Duncan and Magdalene. In the living room, beside the tree, they open small presents. For Duncan, the entire set of NASA Apollo patches and a small box of vintage train schedules of the Midwestern lines, the Union Pacific, the Missouri Pacific, and the Grand.

For Magdalene a small boom box. And here, Maggie says and hands Magdalene a green bankbook. Joshua and I opened an account in your name and put fifty dollars in it—you have to go down and give them some of the personal info I didn't have so that only you have access to it. It's not much, but it's a start.

Thank you, thank you! Magdalene says and stands and gives both Joshua and Maggie a hug.

You're welcome, sweetie.

Joshua laughs. Don't spend it all in one place, okay?

Mother pulls Duncan to her and squeezes him against her side; he wraps his arms about her, feels the hard bulge of her belly, as if a child made of stone slept curled in her womb. He opens his arms to Magdalene and she grasps him and suddenly kisses him on the lips. She parts the hair that has fallen before her face and he stares into her dark, unblinking eyes. Her lips are wet and her breath is hot and Duncan can feel the taste and sensation of her upon his mouth, and he touches his mouth and holds his fingers there. Magdalene looks at him wide-eyed, surprised it seems, and then Joshua and Maggie pulls them both to them in a hug and Maggie begins to sing "O Little Town of Bethlehem" and they reach out to hold each other's hands and Duncan laughs and tries to hold this moment in his thoughts and in his heart before it is gone.

He begins to sing and looks to Mother. She's mouthing the words but not singing, and when he pauses, she smiles at him and nods and moves her mouth, and Duncan knows that she wants to hear them singing instead and to take joy in their voices. Her face, cast brightly in the glow of candlelight, is the way he remembers her from his dreams in the Home, when he struggled through the snow toward the Festival of Lights Holiday Train, or perhaps after all these years he has transplanted her image upon that dream so that it was always this woman before him who he waited for even as he thought her dead.

Through the falling snow outside the night shows itself in an il-lusory manner, with the city seemingly so far off and distant and unreal that time here seems to pause. From the wharves bells sound for Christmas Mass. The television flickers with images of the 1968 Christmas Eve broadcast from lunar orbit and they all look toward it: the swirling, cloud-covered Earth as seen from the command module and then turning slowly to show the bright, empty face of the moon. The astronauts each take turns reciting the opening passages from Genesis, and at its end the voice of Apollo 8 commander Frank Borman filled with emotion even through the static: "From the crew of Apollo 8, we close with good night, good luck, a Merry Christmas, and God bless all of you—all of you on the good Earth."

February 1984

NIGHTTIME AND THE second shift in the oncology terminal ward at
St. Luke's, where the dying count the minutes and hours listening to
the meager span of their heartbeats: a single wail of pain from a patient's room, the soft shuffling of slippers upon tile, the muted sound
of prayer from Mrs. Polaski's bedside, where the family priest is performing the last rites, a telephone ringing at the empty nurse's station.
From partially open doorways that look in upon dark rooms comes
the sound of monitors and IV pumps clicking and beeping softly, methodically. Maggie sits in the dark and stares at Deirdre Malone asleep
on her bed, breathing raggedly through a respirator. On the railing of
the bed a PCEA pump, which allows her to self-administer morphine
at the push of a button. From a radio on the nightstand comes the soft
sound of big band music from World War II. She recognizes "A
Sleepy Lagoon" and then Jo Stafford's "Long Ago and Far Away"
and then perhaps Benny Goodman or Harry James.

Earlier in the day, Maggie had sat with Deirdre after her latest biopsy; she'd cried herself to sleep and now her cheeks are streaked and sullied. Tenderly, Maggie wipes them with a warm, damp cloth, lifts the mouthpiece of the respirator, and wipes it clean, softly sings the Latin from the Requiem Mass, for she can never be sure that Deirdre can't hear her, and hopes that it provides some small measure of comfort: *In paradisum deducant te Angeli; in tuo adventu suscipiant te martyres, et perducant te in civitatem sanctam Ierusalem.*

She takes Deirdre's vitals, records them on the patient log at the bottom of the bed, stares at her face so that she can memorize it for when she's gone; she tries to do this with all of her patients, especially those who have died alone without family or loved ones, as if this small act can somehow allow them to live in the world after they're gone, and by doing so she is promising that she will never let go, that she will never leave them. Her head is filled with the faces of hundreds of dead and she often feels so powerless and sad it is as if a great weight were placed upon her heart that she feels will never lift; but if she can keep their memory alive, then they will not be alone, no matter where they are, where they have gone on to. And when she and Duncan attend Mass at St. Mary of the Wharves, she will imagine their faces and light a candle for them and pray for an end to their suffering.

She pulls a chair up to the bed and takes Deirdre's hand now: She will be here when she wakes and here with her when she receives news of the biopsy—she will not leave her. Maggie closes her eyes, lets the dim pulse in Deirdre's hand inform her breathing. Deirdre's monitor clicks and beeps softly. From the hallway comes the sound of slippered feet, the loose clattering wheel of a gurney, a page for a doctor from the nurse's station reverberating forlornly through the empty halls, and then the silence of the night, which somehow seems worse, capturing as it does in the absence of noise and hectic industry the solemn weight of pain and suffering and loss. So much loss.

Maggie rubs at her eyes. She is eight again and staring up at the adults passing about her, their footsteps continually thumping up the back stairs from the landing to the third floor of the apartment on Bartlett Street just outside Boston's Dudley Square. The sullen heat of late summer and even the birds silent in the trees outside the window.

Tar-streaked ceilings still smelling of other people's smoke, the broken latch hook by the back screen door that jangles soft and metallic as people come and go, the smell of boiled foods, and a fan turning impotently in the window of her mother's bedroom, where Mother was lying with closed eyes and dressed in her pastel blue floral summer dress, the spit that glistened her lips in the final rictus of pain now dried, and those same lips that had kissed her goodnight a mere night ago already seeming shriveled and pale despite the recently applied lipstick, like two slivers of worm left upon the sidewalk in the hot sun, and no breeze at the window—the lace curtains flat as a board—to push the strange smell of her out. But where was her father?

Men, holding bottles of beer or glasses of spirits, attired in their mourning wear: black pants and jackets, crumpled white shirts, and thin black ties—she smelled their aftershave and cologne, cigarettes and sweat, a sense of her father in all that, as if many of them had just come from their daily labors. Pushing in and about them she desperately searched for him, an unexplainable panic rising in her chest, first in the kitchen, then the crowded small living room overlooking the street, the bathroom, and finally her mother's bedroom, where she stood looking at her mother, and then to her aunts and female cousins sitting on chairs arranged about the bed, red-eyed and crying softly.

She expected to feel his heavy hand on her shoulder and for him to pull him to her, to hear his voice in song, some manner of lullaby, soothing and yet heartbreaking, filled with the loss of past generations of his people—hundreds upon hundreds of years of it, and that loss came to life with his voice at night as he crooned her to sleep when he and her mother came in from the Dudley Street Opera House or the

Rose Croix, and his breath warm with stout and whiskey. The comfort and shelter of her father's songs, which captured such tragedy and yet were so filled with passion it trilled beneath her skin, reassured her that as long as he was near, nothing could harm her, and if he were here to sing now, surely her mother would awaken. Why wasn't he here? Why wasn't he by her mother's bed?

Where's Daddy? she asked Aunt Una, the one with the lantern jaw and the sharp nose and the sweat beading above her upper lip and the red hair like Maggie and her mother.

I looked all about the place, Maggie said, but I can't find him anywhere—did he go down to the square? And the women in the room stared at her with such pity that she felt she couldn't breathe and Aunt Margaret reached out her hand and then pulled her onto her lap, held Maggie's head against her shoulder and began to cry, her great bosom heaving, but this brought Maggie no comfort—she only wanted to pull away from this woman and demand that they all tell her where he was; she wanted to scream: Where's my father! I need my father! And as if she knew this, Aunt Margaret's words came to her slowly, hiccupping with grief: He's left dear child, sure his heart is broke with your mother's death. He left this morning before dawn. I'm so sorry, my dear. I'm so very sorry.

It's near two A.M. when Maggie leaves the hospital via the emergency room. A young man with long, disheveled hair and high on PCP is bleeding out onto the floor and hollering about angels. He's fallen from a second-floor balcony onto a wrought iron railing, impaling his eye socket, stomach, and leg, and yet somehow he is upright, talking and walking, searching the room with his one blazing eye and clutching his guts spilling from the cavity in his abdomen. She stares at the purple intestine, the deep red of muscle, the strings of tendon and white bone as two nurses and a surgeon frantically work to hold him down upon a table and stop the hemorrhaging.

At home Maggie heats up leftovers in the kitchen, pours herself a whiskey. She pads the hallway, looks in on Duncan, sleeping, turned away toward the wall, the light from the hall casting slivers of refracted light upon his ceiling of stars and constellations. Static pops and bursts from the old Vulcanite radio glowing amber at his bedside, like an eye in the dark, and from which comes the sudden, brief sound of someone talking. She waits, listens to Duncan's breathing, and then, satisfied, goes to change. In the bedroom the television is on, casting shadows upon the wall, and Joshua is on his back, arms stretched wide, and at first she thinks he's asleep. She leans over the bed, kisses him on the cheek. He's looking at her in the dark; she can see his eyes glistening with the light cast from the television.

Florence Nightingale, he says, and she smiles. How was your night, baby?

It was fine. I'm fine, just tired.

How's Deirdre?

Still alive.

She has the sense that he nods in the dark.

You should be asleep, she says. You've got to be up in less than three hours.

I know, baby. I already slept a bit, once Duncan went to bed.

She knows he's lying, and that if he's awake now, he'll probably stay awake until the alarm sounds. She asks: Did you take your meds?

Joshua sighs, rolls his shoulders. She can hear tendons and ligaments crack. Nah, you know I don't like how they make me feel. I can only do so many days and my head gets messed up.

You're not supposed to start and stop, she says. It'll make you manic. No wonder you can't sleep.

I promise I'll go back on them tomorrow. Don't look at me like that, baby.

Howabout you take them now?

Okay. Sure. They're on the dresser.

Maggie brings him the pill bottles and he takes them from her and she can see that his hands are trembling. He pops three of each in his mouth, washes them down with water from a glass on the side table.

That the right amount?

It's whatever works.

By the way, thanks for dinner.

No problem. Duncan and me, we made it together. Was it good?

Best lasagna I ever had.

Liar.

Maggie grins. Maybe just a little bit.

How is he?

He's fine. Wanted me to listen to that radio of his when he went to bed. So, I did.

And?

And what? The damn thing doesn't work, yet he still listens to it.

Maybe it comforts him to have something from the orphanage with him. I think he gets scared in the night.

We all get scared in the night. I get scared in the night, especially without you. Why don't you come to bed?

In a little bit, I need to unwind first, decompress.

I'll help you unwind.

Shhhhhh. You'll sleep, that's what you'll do. Should I turn the TV off?

No, no, I like it on. It helps me sleep.

Okay. Close your eyes.

Joshua laughs and closes his eyes. Goodnight, Baby.

Goodnight.

Maggie pulls the bedroom door closed, leaving it slightly ajar in case Duncan calls out in the night, and glances back at Joshua, bathed in blue light, still staring blankly at the flickering black-and-white images on the screen. She wonders if he's even aware of what he's watching. She thinks of Deirdre not because Joshua is dying but because he is never at rest and his soul, she knows, like hers, is a damaged, fragile thing, and she wonders if two people such as herself and Joshua can, together, make the other one strong, and with Duncan, if they can make a life.

May angels lead you into Paradise; may the martyrs receive you at your coming and lead you to the holy city of Jerusalem and O sweet Lord Jesus, grant them rest; grant them everlasting rest.

March 1984

AN HOUR AFTER Joshua's night shift on the tunnel has ended, he and Duncan sit at the counter of a greasy spoon over on Kirkland, where the bay washes up against the old forgotten docks and the skeletal remains of wharves, timbers and spars pitched and oilblack sprouting from the sea. The wastes of a once-thriving dockland with cobbled motorways running parallel to empty canning and fishery warehouses stretch as far as the eye can see.

There is the clatter of plates and cutlery, the hoarse voices of railworkers and dockworkers sitting in ripped and torn vinyl booths. The sound of spitting grease warms the small space even as the rain and cold hisses and presses at the grimy glass. From the windows of the diner Duncan can see the gray waters of the bay and the ragged, frothy tufted heads of decayed piers and pylons first thrusting then disappearing in the small swells as wind and angry dark rain squalls press down from the north.

Behind the counter the single employee of the place, a fry cook in a soiled vest, stokes the grill, breaks open eggs, spills their innards upon the hot metal, shovels potatoes, bacon, sausage back and forth across the charred surface. He's a tall, gangly, olive-skinned man who seems to suffer from lack of sleep, and has the look of anemia that comes from working in enclosed, sunless places. When he takes their order, Duncan notices the bruise-colored semicircles beneath his eyes, the ashen pallor of his skin.

When the workers are done, boots banging and scraping on the wood, he takes their bills and rings them up on the cash register. Soon the booths are all empty and his shoulders hunch and he moves slowly from counter to grill to clearing the tables to the windowed door, where he stands for a long moment staring out at the empty street and the rain. Beneath his feet the runoff from customers' shoes has collected, forming a ring as black as an oil slick. The fry cook offers up a forlorn sigh to the glass.

I was an angel once, he says suddenly aloud, to no one it seems, but then he looks, pleadingly, in Duncan's direction, and Duncan turns his attention quickly back to his food.

Shit, Joshua mutters beneath his breath, and the fry cook sighs again, deeper this time. He turns his head slightly as if listening to something, something other than the grill or the radio or the wind and rain banging against the walls.

I clipped my wings and I can't go back.

Damn, man, Joshua says, and begins cutting into his egg.

The fry cook shrugs and stares at the blackened lumps of meat slough curling at the edges of the grill. Every so often they start to grow back and I have to cut them again, he says. They come in all wrong. The feathers don't fold, they're twisted and bent hard as nails. They hurt.

Joshua sips his coffee and nods.

And when it rains—weather like this—they itch like hell.

I know how you feel, man.

You got wings?

No, just some old scar tissue.

What did they do to you?

It's nothing.

Jesus, man, the fry-cook says, his voice rising with sudden and surprising desperation, his eyes shining feverishly. What did they do to you?

Duncan stops eating and looks at the two of them, Joshua and the fry cook staring at each other. Joshua has yet to take a shower and chalk marl, throw-off from the tunnel's muck cars and conveyors, streaks his skin, turning him pale. The fry cook breathes deeply, his mouth partly agape, and then he nods. I know it, man. Don't I know it, and he touches Joshua briefly upon the hand in which Joshua holds his egg-smeared knife, so that Joshua looks down at his hand as if something had been burnt upon it, and then the fry cook turns back to the grill. From his shoulder blades Duncan sees two stumps pressed against his soiled vest. At the neck of his vest and on the backs of his arms, whitish gray feathers pressed flat quiver as he turns meat with a spatula and then scrapes at the blackened slivers stuck to the grill, and curl slowly into themselves like dark, loam-black worms.

Joshua stirs sugar into his third cup of coffee and says: Didn't you like it there?

Where? says the fry cook.

With the heavenly chorus, man. Close to God.

Of course I did.

Then why did you clip your wings? Why stay here?

Duncan stares at the cook's back as he scrapes the grill, as he pushes hash and home fries across the metal surface and through the grease and at those bulging stumps, which jerk and flex with his movements—the amputated nubs of musculature and tendon straining to push through his undershirt.

I had to, he says. Every day here brings me closer to Him. Soon . . . soon I'll be able to go back.

Duncan swallows a forkful of omelet and washes it down with milk. What if your wings never grow back right? he asks.

The fry cook looks at him and then slowly turns back to the grill and goes to work vigorously scraping at the hardened meat bits with his spatula.

Go back, Joshua says. Go back, man. Shit, what are you waiting for?

The fry cook bangs the spatula down upon the grill. Dammit, don't you think I'd go back if I could? Do you think I want to be here? I'm sick of this shithole!

He stares at them, goggle-eyed, fevered and pale as a fish strewn upon a beach, its undersides bared and steaming in the hot sun, then at the rain sweeping relentlessly across the glass, the wind seeming to bow the glass inward; the window frames groaning as if they might shatter. He takes a deep breath and exhales. After a moment: How are your eggs?

I've had worse, Joshua says.

Overcooked?

Overcooked.

The fry cook nods sadly. I'm sorry about that. And about the toast and bacon.

A gust of wind rattles the glass. From beyond the sunken piers, a bell buoy clangs. A long groan as the old wharf sways back and forth on the swells, followed by a wet popping sound as old wood collapses.

Joshua rummages in his jean pockets and pulls out a fistful of singles. He places a five on the counter but the fry cook shakes his head. It's on the house, he says.

Joshua takes back the five and leaves a single instead. At least let us leave a tip then, he says, and the fry cook watches them wistfully as they climb off their stools. Duncan is slow getting off his seat and Joshua's hand hovers by his shoulder.

Y'know, the fry cook says, our hearts beat faster than any other animal. We breathe faster, we move faster. Our bones our hollow. We weren't made for staying still in one place, y'know.

Angels?

Birds.

Joshua nods sympathetically and then they head to the door. When Duncan looks back, the fry cook is staring toward the windows over the tables and booths, staring out at the bay and scratching his back vigorously with the spatula. Duncan watches as it moves up and down beneath his vest, back and forth across his shoulder blades, and imagines the stumps of his severed wings and the ragged tufts of nail-hard soot-colored plumage. From the fry cook's shirt a single feather falls and drifts slowly to the floor, followed by another and then another; yanked from their follicles, they begin to collect on the floor about his boots in a drift, their hollow, pointed calamus, translucent as a filament, bloodied and raw.

C'mon, Joshua says and urges him outside. Slowly, heads turned aslant the wind and rain, they cross the cobbled alley to Joshua's bike, draped with a tarp lashed down with cord.

Do you believe in angels? Duncan asks him.

Joshua glances at him, squinting against the raindrops as his fingers work to untie the tarp.

All the time, my man. I have the feeling they're all around us— good and bad—doing their thing, y'know?

But what do they do?

Protect us, I guess. Isn't that what angels do?

You said good and bad.

Good and bad, sure. I didn't always think that, but now? Joshua considers this as he folds the tarp and thinks about Jamie Minkivitz and about the way the men pray to St. Barbara, of the various forms of madness that affect the men in the tunnel and of his own dreams of the in-rushing sea.

Duncan's jacket is soaked through and he's shivering, but right now he doesn't care. Yeah, now I do, he says. They do their thing, and it doesn't really matter what we want or don't want.

You mean they don't always protect us or keep us from harm?

I suppose most of the time they do—I don't know. Mostly I don't think they give a crap whether we live or die.

Do you think there are angels who would want to hurt us?

Joshua smiles. Kid, imagine if you were stuck here and couldn't get back. I wouldn't be too happy, would you? I think I'd be mighty pissed.

But you don't think he's an angel, do you? Not like the angel you dreamt of?

I think he's full of shit. But hell, the man believes he's an angel. Who are we to argue with him or tell him otherwise? But then Joshua laughs—he closes his eyes and leans against the bike for support as tears come to the corners of his eyes. Oh man, he says and wipes at his cheeks. That angel has his vaccinations. Joshua claps the top of his bicep. The vaccination shots that left big old circles for scars. They did away with them in the sixties. Your mom and me, we got them. Most people who were born before 1970 did. But tell me, man, what's an angel doing with one?

Joshua shakes his head and laughs some more. Damn, he says. An angel working at a diner down by the old docks. Maybe he stopped being an angel once he'd been here too long. Maybe you just can't go back. Seems to work that way in the real world too.

And then he nods. Well, I guess that's about right. He's the last one left. All the old whores and gangsters are gone. So where the hell else would an angel be?

FATHER MAGNUSSON SITS looking out the plate glass at the snow falling heavily through the darkness, his down-like hair resting back upon his pillow. Wind shudders beneath the Pullman, ripples against the stamped metal of its sides, and whistles in the spaces of empty rivet holes as if it were stroking the skin of a beast succumbing to sleep. The carriage begins to grow cold, and Duncan shivers.

Father Magnusson sighs. Quite a sight, isn't it, Duncan?

Duncan is wide-eyed and silent because, after all, this is a dead man who is talking to him, and when the dead speak, he's come to learn, it is important to listen to them. Yet it seems like the most natural thing in the world that Father Magnusson is talking to him; it's almost as if he's been waiting for this from the first moment he dreamt of his mother in the snow and she showed him the Festival of Lights Holiday Train frozen to its rails and imbedded by drifts of snow fifteen feet high. It is necessary that he be with these people at the end and during the final hours of their lives.

213

Finally Duncan speaks: Are you scared that you'll die soon, Father? And he is shocked that he has said such a thing—where have these words come from?—and if he could, he would clamp his hands to his mouth, but his hands remain motionless at his sides despite his urging. Father Magnusson merely looks at him and then laughs at his expression.

No, son. I'm not scared. None of us are. You are not seeing us as we were but as we are. We are no longer scared.

You mean you're already dead?

Yes. And it is no longer important.

But if you're dead, why are you here? What are you waiting for?

Father Magnusson leans his head away from Duncan. The worst storm in seventy years, isn't it? They ever say it's worse than the storm of 1901. I lost an older sister and my grandmother in that one.

We lost most of our livestock and our holding too. Our father had to work the iron range afterwards, and it destroyed his lungs. He contracted mesothelioma from breathing taconite dust, and the arc flare of welding torches ruined his eyes so that he was almost blind.

I was the youngest child and I don't even think he even knew what I looked like, but I always watched him of an evening when he came in from work and the way he moved about the house, doubled over with the effort to breathe. Often he'd walk into a room and I'd stay very still until he passed through. Sometimes he'd sit and listen to one of his favorite shows on the radio after supper. I don't think he ever knew I was there watching him, sharing the same space.

They'll bury you in the spring when the thaw comes, Duncan says.

In the cherry blossom grove beyond the charnel house?

Duncan nods and Father Magnusson smiles as if the idea pleases him immensely. That will be nice, he says. I suppose they will give me an enviable spot. I'm an old man and I've spent most of my life here.

The roof creaks and groans with the weight of snow and then settles once more.

214

I suppose they will say the Requiem Mass in Latin. I do so like the Latin. If only I could remind them not to sing *De Profundis* at the anniversary. I wish someone would mention that to young Toibin. Ahh, well, but I suppose there are others to think of. There are so many of us lost and in need of help, even here.

The lamps of the carriage suddenly tremor and dim, and then go out. Father Magnusson's hair seems to glow in the dark. When the wind recedes, Duncan hears a child crying.

What about the woman in the snow—my mother—do you know her?

Oh, yes. She'll be coming also. Have you heard her sing? It's beautiful, absolutely beautiful. I've never heard anything like it in my life.

She's here on the Holiday Train?

Father Magnusson turns back to the window, about which the glow of Christmas lights shimmer and flicker incandescently from the dark and casts a slight, pulsing glow into the carriage.

She's always with us, he says. Didn't you know? She's an angel.

Duncan? a voice calls into the darkness, and it is as if he is floating and unraveling and spiraling down. It's snowing, cold and sharp on his face. The clouds are parting briefly, and in the space that remains he can see stars, small and distant, and then growing brighter and falling, blazing from the sky.

I heard you calling, Duncan. Are you all right?

Upon the wall over his dresser the familiar pictures: a smiling, nunlike Olivia de Havilland from *Whose Baby Are You Now?* staring down at him, her full breasts pressing against her robe; and the *Times* cover of the 1969 lunar landing. Instinctively he pulls the covers up beneath his chin, listens for the bells of Lauds, of Brothers shuffling and chuffing in the frozen stairwells, stumbling toward morning prayer. He imagines the water in his basin upon the nightstand with its skin of ice, of it splintering beneath his fingertips and the chill of water as he washes his face in the predawn. Then there are the eight footsteps it will take him upon the cold timber floor to reach the door and another twenty to the toilets along the hall and by other rooms in which children he knows only by face moan and snore and toss and dream and for whom there are still hours of sleep.

But the room is not cold and the radiators are silent. From down the hall, a record spins softly upon a phonograph. A moist cough sounds outside his door. Feet move restlessly upon the creaking floorboards. Duncan? the voice calls again, slurred and urgent now.

Yes, Mom, Duncan says, and he wonders if he is still dreaming. Yes. I'm okay. Please go back to sleep.

And he waits and listens to her pad back down the hallway, to the volume of her phonograph rising as she opens the door and then diminishing, to old bed springs creaking in distress as she settles upon the mattress. The phonograph's tone arm swings out and then back and her song begins again and he recognizes it as "The Bell Jar" from mother's *Last Rose of Summer* album and the only recording of her startling five-octave range, years before her voice broke. He hears the sound of her whiskey tumbler sliding upon wood, of glass tinkling as she lifts the bottle of Old Mainline to the tumbler, and knows that Joshua must be working the graveyard shift again, for he isn't home yet. He stares into the darkness long enough and his eyes adjust to the light.

From a pair of tall windows on which the blinds are rolled up comes the sounds of the street and the diffuse, blue ashen light in the hour before dawn. He lifts his arms above the bedclothes, turns them this way and that in the strange moon water as if they are ghostly, translucent limbs belonging to somebody else. He imagines that this is what Joshua sometimes does as he works in the tunnel, as he sits in the compression chamber before sinking down the shaft with the other men and then later as he rises to street level, always surprised by the quality of light that greets him and the strangeness of his feet upon sidewalk absent the pressure of the sea.

Sitting on the edge of his bed, his toes curled from brief contact with the floor, he peers out the window. The tops of cars shine dark with dew. A dog squats on the sidewalk, empties its bowels, and moans as if it is in pain. Yesterday he saw a homeless man in an alley crying out in much the same way. In the gloom a bus idles on the street corner bathed in the light of a sodium streetlamp. Its doors close and then, with a belch of exhaust, a hydraulic groan and a hiss of air-brakes, it humps up dark Divisadero: gray, faceless, seated figures shuddering behind its windows like small, hungry children waiting at a cold breakfast table.

I will love the light for it shows me the way; yet I will love the darkness for it shows me the stars.

—AUGUSTINE "OG" MANDINO

May 1984

AT THE WINDSOR Tap, Duncan sits on a stool beside Joshua, waiting for Maggie to finish her shift at St. Luke's. Joshua buys him a second Coke after he promises that he'll make it last, and Clay tells him to go easy on the bowls of nuts: They're for paying customers, son. I can't keep replacing them. Don't your mother feed you?

Joshua is humming to himself and tying a red cocktail straw into knots. In the backroom, a shouting and hollering begins and a body thumps the floor. Joshua pauses in his knot tying.

My man, it's time to go. Charlie's everywhere.

Duncan nods. *Charlie,* he knows, refers to the Viet Cong, to the enemy, to anything that poses a threat or is, as Joshua often says, just a pain in the fucking ass.

They climb off their stools and Duncan eyes Clay at the rear of the room with his Louisville. A man lies on the floor by the pool tables, clutching his arms to his body and sobbing. A dark stain spreads across the crotch of his pants and then a rivulet of urine trickles from his pant leg across the wood. Joshua moves Duncan toward the door, his hands pressed gently on the backs of his shoulders.

Joshua's bike looks as if it has been left out in all manner of weather: The leather is torn and the chrome pipes oxidized, the metal of the gas tank stamped as if by a ball-peen hammer. Duncan sits on the saddle behind Joshua and holds on tight to his field jacket as they speed through the streets with Joshua leaning the bike at right angles as they take the curves. My man, will you relax, he says. You want to take us both off the bike? Just enjoy the ride. Chill. Be cool.

They cross an old rusted trellis bridge, tires thumping the dividers in trainlike cadence, and Duncan peers down: wind in his face and a slow-moving gray channel streaked with iridescent oil smears passing into the bay. Joshua parks the bike down by an empty lot that abuts the water, knocks down the kickstand with a shudder that trembles through the frame, and jockeys the bike slowly backward until the rear tire bumps the curbstone. A rusted metal guardrail lines the wall. Behind them: Industrial buildings and tenements waiting for the wrecking ball. Two large stacks blowing white smoke into the sky. The twenty-four-hour diner across the narrow cobbled street where the fry cook believes he's an angel, and a bar. Paint-peeling facades. Adverts in the window from another generation. A faded poster for Chesterfield cigarettes. Kohl's beer. A handwritten sign: PRESCRIPTIONS FILLED.

Joshua climbs from the bike and sits upon the creosote timbers at the water's edge. Before them the water heaves out to the bay and there is the bridge with traffic moving like small Matchbox cars across it. Duncan sits next to Joshua, waiting for him to speak. Joshua pulls a cigarette from his shirt pocket and lights up. It's pungent and smoky and better smelling than Duncan's mother's Claymores. Joshua purses his lips and glares at the horizon. When he looks at Duncan, his brow remains furrowed, gnarled like a knot of scar tissue. His skin shines like resin. His eyes are yellow-tinged and cracked by blood vessels.

Are you okay? Duncan asks. You don't stay around much. You're always taking off.

I know, I'm sorry about that.

It's all right.

Joshua puts his hand on Duncan's shoulder briefly, and then sighs long and slow. No, it's not, he says, but thanks for saying it is. Sometimes it's just hard for me to be around people, no matter how much I want to. Sometimes I forget things, I lose track of the days. I forget that a lot of things have changed and that a lot of things haven't changed at all. I get all mixed up—the things I think are important, that everyone should remember, they don't. And the things people talk about—well, it's all so much crap.

I had a dream last night and in it I was talking to my best friend but I couldn't even remember his name. We were waiting in the tunnel, and he had no face—it was like there was a veil or a caul over it, something those old sailors used to say they'd been born with so that they could see the future, or the stars, or the weather or some such fuck. Anyway, he started walking down the tunnel away from me and I tried to call out, tell him to come back, but I couldn't remember his name—you believe that? My best friend and I couldn't remember his name—I just kept shouting: Hey! Hey!

Duncan nods. It's the war.

Is that what your mother says?

Yeah.

What else does she say?

Duncan shrugs. That you're not the same person you used to be.

Joshua holds his smoke, then exhales slowly, nodding. He laughs then and slaps Duncan's shoulder. He keeps his hand there, and the weight of it feels good and reassuring. On the water a dredge turns in the fading sunlight and it is as if it is rolling, belly up, its underside squaring the last of the sun at their faces, and Duncan squints against it.

What's your mother cooking tonight?

Meatloaf.

Goddamn. I love your mother to death but her meatloaf is enough to make a man wish he'd never come home.

I know, I tried to tell her. She thinks it's her best dish.

Joshua tosses his cigarette onto the walkway and, for a moment, as they rise, Duncan hesitates, wondering if he should pick it up. The light has gone down and Joshua stares across the water, his face lost in shadow: faceless. Duncan is suddenly seized by the impulse that Joshua might tell him something real if only he were to ask him in this moment. Joshua, he says, what was the war like? Is that where you knew my daddy from?

War? Joshua bares his teeth and they flash in the gloom. He seems to be staring at something beyond the bridge and out past the bay. But it's already dark and there's nothing to see but Venus shining in the east.

I don't find much use in talking about the war, Duncan. You know that. The people that can't seem to shut up about what they did and what they saw, I can never understand. Seems like if they saw so much when they were over there, they'd have enough of it by now, y'know? You never forget what you've seen. No need to talk about it, make it real, more than it is. It's already too real. Sometimes I feel as if I'm watching a movie and it's my life, exactly the way it is—was— and I can't do a thing to change it. It's just a film reel playing over and over again, and I can't take back the good or the bad and I can't switch it off. And so I just have to live with it.

He stares above the rooftops as night comes slowly down and points to a meteor that flares briefly across the horizon. He says: I guess that's what war is, never forgetting even when you want to.

221

But then there are some things you never want to forget no matter how hard it is, like watching your friends die and not being able to do a thing about it. You're nineteen, a fucking wise-ass punk that can't stop fooling around thinking you're so cool, that you're invincible and then—Poof! a Viet Cong bullet blows your face apart and you're gone.

Your friend? The one whose name you couldn't remember?

Joshua slides flakes of tobacco across his teeth with his tongue.

Yeah. Company medic.

Duncan waits but Joshua is silent. And my daddy?

Your daddy? He never did a tour. Joshua shakes his head. No, that's not where I met him.

The streetlights are broken and slowly the stars come into view as the clouds clear—the Big Dipper and the Six Sisters and most of the autumn constellations, all glittering in slow winking cadence.

Damn, Joshua says and sighs deep and long, will you look at that beautiful sky.

And Duncan is sure that Joshua is not seeing the sky at all. He points to the top of the sky where day and night meet. I sometimes think of my daddy up there, he says, with the astronauts and the angels.

And he expects Joshua to grunt dismissively or laugh at him but Joshua says, as if he is truly considering this: Well, that's as good a place as any. Better than here for sure.

And perhaps he is thinking of his friend—a young man laughing, joking, singing exuberantly on a trail with the ash-gray loam light of dusk filtering through the jungle canopy—up there with Duncan's daddy, the astronauts, and all the angels. And Duncan smiles with the thought that they are looking down upon Joshua and Duncan and holding them in their care, for that is what the dead do, just as much as we pray for them and ask for God's divine intercession, the dead who have been left behind and are not yet at God's side remain like angels to look after their loved ones, to guide and watch

222

over them and keep them from harm until they are all reunited at the End. And this is what he tells Joshua.

Jesus, kid, Joshua says, Jesus. You have a way of getting into a man's head.

When they pull up on the bike, Duncan's mother stands at the curb, arms folded stiffly across her chest. Her face is set and stern, yet with the flicker of shadow and light she is disarming in her beauty. Even Duncan recognizes this. Joshua's back stiffens and he gives a low whistle of admiration. For added affect, he guns the engine as they coast toward her.

Joshua, I don't want my son riding motorcycles.

Joshua pushes out the kickstand, turns to look at Duncan, and then grins and shrugs.

You, she points. Get off that bike now. I don't want to see you on it again.

Maggie, Joshua says softly, reassuringly.

Get in the house.

Maggie.

What?

It won't kill him, you know.

Since when did you become his parent?

I'm just saying, it's all cool. Let him be a kid.

Duncan stands in the alcove watching and listening to them. Joshua blows mother a kiss and begins to back the bike away from the curb. Above him Orion and Ursa Major blink into life, and somewhere up there the astronauts and his father are looking down.

Where the hell are you going? she says.

Joshua looks at her in surprise—it is one of those rare expressions of his: a veil is lifted and in that brief glimpse Duncan sees no pain or rage or loss or confusion, and perhaps something of the Joshua that was there before. What? he says.

223

I've got meatloaf on, and I was counting on feeding three mouths. Park that thing and get your ass in here. And for a moment Duncan thinks Joshua will merely gun the bike and careen off down the hill, but instead Joshua smiles, relieved it seems, bumps the curb stone with his tire, swings out the kickstand, and shuts off the engine.

On one condition, he says.

Yeah? Mother plants her weight firmly on a hip. What's that?

Let my man Duncan on the bike.

From the alcove Duncan grins. Sitting on his black motorcycle amidst shimmering vapors from the steaming exhaust, Joshua is an angel and a messenger, a divine portent of things to come: He is an intercession of grace.

September 1984

THE END OF summer and the beginning of school. Raining after-
noons, suspended in gray dusky light, and the sense that the day will
never end. In class, sitting amidst the hubbub and throb of other children, with their whispering, their groaning and gurgling bellies, their
kicking and tapping feet, and the chairs and desks creaking with the
barely restrained tension of their movements. The walls are softly
dripping with condensation and the radiators pinging and clanging
and then sighing their warm exhales, and he stares out at the playground and off toward the distant rail yard and the towers of the
Edison plant. Clouds are staggered in rows, as if they'd toppled end
to end upon each other and lie there, still and foreboding over the
horizon. Every once in a while a sudden squall comes up, pushes a
spattering of rain against the window and sends the partially drawn,
unfurled slats of the wooden blinds clattering, and then the wind
subsides and everything is gray and still again. The glass shudders

and clears, and then the wind and the rain pull back, birds flee their roosts, the yellow lights burning in the windows of three- and four-story clapboard houses shimmer blearily through the gloom. Seagulls settle in groups upon the playground tarmac and then, like a blast from God's bellows, the wind sweeps them up and they are tossed, thrashing and crying, into the churning gyre over the city.

His teacher Mr. Hotchkiss suffers from a rare pathology that prevents him from controlling his tears. It comes from a head injury sustained during the war, he says, when he was blown from the top of an LV carrier by an RPG round. Part of his frontal lobe was damaged and now he no longer has the inhibitors for certain emotional faculties and so he cries whenever his emotions are stirred. He cries when he is sad and when he is angry. He cries when he is happy and immensely pleased by something. He cries when he looks out at the playground and sees light glancing in a particular way through the clouds or a figure of birds streaking in the northern sky or rain drifting in from the bay bent aslant through the yellow streetlights. He cries when he watches smoke belching from the Edison plant's stacks. And he cries when a student admits to not having done his homework or when it is apparent he has not done the required reading. Duncan wonders what it would be like to cry all the time. He wonders how you would ever get anything done. He wonders at the manner of injury that would cause such a condition and he wonders if Mr. Hotchkiss knows Joshua from his visits to the V.A.

Mr. Hotchkiss is writing something upon the board and the deep timbre of his voice vibrates nasally on certain words and is as calming as a distant foghorn out at sea. On these long, gray days, Duncan is content to merely listen to it. Magdalene is at the front of the class, listening attentively. Her black hair is pulled into a tight, gleaming bun, and he imagines her aunt taking the hair and, from her wheelchair, yanking it back with such force that Magdalene staggers and cries out.

When the bell sounds, Duncan is glad for the escape but waits for the other kids to leave first until only he and Magdalene remain. But she walks to the front of the class to talk to Mr. Hotchkiss, and Duncan leaves alone.

In the school playground he stands in the farthest corner, facing east, looking through the chain link toward the rail yards and, beyond, the squat towers of the Edison plant, ash gray columns upon which white and red lights alternately flash as a warning to low-flying planes. White smoke pumps in steady funnels up from the stacks and melds into the low clouds covering the city. Rain spatters the ground and brings up the smell of warm concrete. It begins to fall harder, and soon it is dripping and shimmering upon the chain link. Duncan stares at the towers of the power plant and the giant transformers, ribbed ceramic pylons arranged like rows of giant sparkplugs.

A teacher clangs the bell and the other children race from the school yard, whooping and hollering, rushing to the lockers to gather their belongings to take home, and to the buses waiting at the front of the school or for their parents waiting in warm, idling cars. The lights upon the smokestacks revolve through their alternating flashing cycle. The dark shape of a jet bound for San Francisco International descends through the clouds silently and passes, trembling, over the city spread out before it, and only after it has passed does Duncan hear the backroar of its turbines, a startling whine pressing out against the clouds.

After a moment there are footsteps through the rain, long and determined, and the sharp strike of high heels upon stone.

You're easy to find, you know, his mother says. You're always the one standing on your own, staring off into space. Didn't you hear the bell? It's time to go. Purgatory's over for another day.

She reaches for his hand, shakes the sleeve of his jacket.

Duncan, you're all wet.

So are you, he says, without looking. He can smell the heat of whiskey off her breath.

No I'm not. I've got an umbrella.

Duncan turns and Maggie grins. Rainwater rushes down her long face and spills into her open mouth.

C'mon, I've got a surprise for you.

What is it?

It wouldn't be a surprise if I told you.

At the car she reaches into the backseat and from a bag pulls a package, meticulously wrapped in sparkling blue paper that details the moons and planets of the solar system.

Duncan smiles and rips at the wrapping paper. It's a miniature replica of the *Saturn V*, a Makemark C series, with fuel propellant and a remote control firing switch. When he pulls it from the box, raindrops bead upon its red paint and trickle down its sides.

They don't come painted, Duncan says, turning the rocket it his hands, marveling at the glistening sheen of the latex.

I copied it from the pictures in your magazines, Maggie says as she carefully collects the wrapping paper, folds it, and places it back in her bag. Looks pretty good, doesn't it? Joshua helped.

Duncan nods. It looks just like the real thing, he says.

He pokes at the lunar module affixed to the top, with its miniature convex windows, plastic portals though through which the small plastic shapes of Buzz, Armstrong, and Collins are visible. Of course their features are indistinguishable, but he tilts the rocket from side to side anyway to get a better glimpse of them in their chairs and he suddenly has the suffocating, claustrophobic sense of them trapped, and of Collins circling the moon, spiraling alone through the dark.

You've even painted the LM the right color, he says. It must have taken you forever.

Happy birthday, she says and grins.

This cost a lot of money.

She shrugs. It's not every day you turn fourteen, and like I said, Joshua helped. And so did Magdalene. There she is now!

The rain has finally stopped and Magdalene is treading across the waterlogged pavement toward them, stomping through the puddles. She waves and rushes forward, breathless. Happy birthday, she says. I wanted to give you and your mother a moment alone. Besides, Mr. Hotchkiss had made a mistake on our biology exam.

You knew and you didn't tell me.

Magdalene raises an eyebrow, conspiratorially. I'm good at keeping secrets.

Duncan laughs, hefts the rocket in his hands.

Maggie is looking at him, smiling. Well, aren't you going to try it out?

I can try it?

Of course.

Duncan chooses the empty railway cut as their test site, where shale and cinder piles, gleaming black and mercurial in the gray light, and dark creosote soaked track timbers lay stacked one atop the other. Beyond the switching signals and engineer shack, enclosed by a barbed wire fence, a grid of transformers adjust and pre-amp the flow of electricity from the power plant, and beyond that the lights of the Edison plant blinking red and white. Standing a dozen feet back from the launch site, Duncan, baring his teeth, flicks the switch on the remote and Maggie and Magdalene cheer as the rocket's thruster ignites and the rocket surges upward upon a white-gray plume of combusting fuel.

About two hundred feet up the rocket's nose dips as it adjusts its telemetry just as the real *Saturn V* would to propel itself out of Earth's orbit. And then the C series rocket dips lower, the lunar module seeming to tremble and vibrate at its tip.

Uh-oh, Duncan says, hoping it might right itself, but then it rolls, inverts, and shoots in mad, looping circles down, streaming circles of white smoke behind it.

Uh-oh, Maggie and Magdalene echo, and they watch as it arcs in crazy parabolas toward the distant power station's transformers.

Turn it off, Duncan! Turn it off! Maggie shouts—her hands

cupped around her mouth like a bullhorn—but it's too late. The propellant has already extinguished itself and the rocket continues on its spiral downward.

Duncan drops the remote and the three of them run across the rail yards, stumbling and falling down the empty rail bed amongst the wet coal and tinder and then splashing through the muddy pools that fill the length of the cut. They're a hundred feet away when the rocket strikes the transformers and the first generator blows. There's a muted explosion, a dull thump and a shower of sparks, and then another explosion, louder than the first, and then a third: rising concussive blasts that suck the wind from Duncan's lungs, and from the center of this black cloud, a fireball emerges, blazing orange and red. Blue silvery light snakes up the towers and across the conduits and cables between the generators. The lights pulse and throb, convulse and tremor like writhing bands of water, and then, beneath this umbrella of electricity, the generators begin to blow, one after the other.

A great firework of electrical sparks showers into the air and floats down around them. Duncan's toes and fingertips go numb with the charge. His heart seems to have suddenly been jump-started. He feels the currents of electricity passing over him, wave after wave, and he fears for a moment that more will come, and that when the last wave buffets them, they'll be burnt to a crisp like the life-size mannequins posed amidst the prefabricated plywood houses he's seen in the films of the 1955 Operation Cue A-bomb tests at the Nevada test site. But the sensation remains the same and he, Maggie, and Magdalene stare, entranced, at the electrical umbrella of showering sparks a hundred feet high, its strands of charged particles, crackling blue wisps and tendrils, falling and dissipating ghostlike in the air about them.

Maggie reaches out and takes Duncan's and Magdalene's hands as the city begins to darken, whole neighborhoods suddenly falling into blackness, and then it continues, each section of lit homes becoming dark, street after street, as if a wave is passing over the rooftops and obliterating the light, as overloaded street boxes and transformers blow. Only the lights upon the plant's smoke stacks continue to flash, blinking off and on, a strange beacon belching in the dark. Car horns begin to sound.

Mom, how come we're not electrocuted?

I don't know, Maggie says, shaking her head.

She puts her hands out as if it is still raining and they are merely catching raindrops. And then Duncan and Magdalene do the same. The sound of arcing hisses in the air about them. Orange and white and blue slivers of discharge snake back and forth above them and at their sides, and only slowly does it dissipate, dissolve, and then disappear. It begins to drizzle again and the raindrops hiss and sizzle upon the metal, white smoke steaming from the charred remains of the generators. The burnt smell of the electrical charge comes with the rain, and Maggie searches his body and his clothes and then does the same to Magdalene to make sure neither one of them have been scorched. She takes hold of Duncan and turns him back to front and then back again. They smell of sulfur and magnesium and of something oddly metallic. For a moment Duncan imagines they shine phosphorescent blue.

You're both all right, she says, and he nods.

I thought we were dead. Are we dead?

The sounds of police cars and fire engines come from the Bottoms, and Duncan can see their lights as they descend the hill and motor along the San Cordono riverway and over the Cantabery Street trestle bridge. We've got to go, Maggie says, and she takes his and Magdalene's hands again and they race to the derelict warehouses along Montgomery and the Tannery, Maggie stumbling in her heels. As they run, she lets go of their hands so that in mid-stride she can slip off her heels, cursing as one splinters loudly. Thank you, Mom, Duncan shouts as they run. That was the best present ever.

Maggie laughs breathlessly. Good, she says. Because that's the last rocket I'm ever getting you.

In the electric charged air above them, clouds of arcing blue spiderwebs pulse and throb and it is as if a million pairs of eyes are looking down upon them, watching them as they race and stumble along the muddy rail cut to the car, their shadows cast in startling black against the background of phosphorescent flames.

Duncan! Magdalene says at his ear. Your mother's crazy!

And Duncan, laughing, turns to look at her. I know! he hollers. I know!

Three days later Duncan and Maggie return to look at the remains of the transformers. The center of the facility looks as if a fireball had raged at its heart for hours. The chain link and barbed wire fence surrounding the generators to the east and west are melted. Only the blackened tops of the rooted stanchions remain, half-torn from the ground and canting away from the center of the explosion. The sun is angling toward the roofs of the city, and the shadows create stark, moonlike craters before the crumbling buildings and abandoned warehouses along the rail cut.

Thirty feet before them the ground is fused and turned glasslike. They walk and gaze in awe at the destruction before them and, as they move, Duncan is keenly aware of his body performing its functions, his legs lifting, fingers sensing, eyes peering upon the wreckage, of his breath coming from his mouth, lungs working like efficient bellows, and of his heart thumping softly, anxiously beneath his thin breastplate. He feels a strange, exhilarating aching there and the sense of being alive suddenly overjoys him. Maggie pales. Her eyes are wide and unblinking. They stare at each other and color slowly returns to her face. Jesus, she mouths. Jesus, Duncan, and then slowly they begin to grin.

There is nothing left of the rocket and only the melted remains of empty metal containers, their torn edges thrust outward in dangerous-looking shards, but there, glinting in the fulgurite, lies the unscathed gray lunar command module. Duncan steps forward, stomping on the glittering ground cautiously, picks it up, and peers through the plastic windows into the interior, where the miniature figures of Aldrin, Armstrong, and Collins sit strapped into their seats, tipped at a forty-five degree angle, waiting for liftoff and the thrust of the rocket upward.

It survived, Duncan says. They survived. He turns the command module in his hands, unbelieving.

How did we not die, Duncan? Maggie wonders aloud again. How come we're not dead?

On their walk home Duncan considers the manner in which they survived the electrical storm, caught as if they were beneath the sheltering, invisible hand of God and his angels, and he is convinced that he saw them peering down upon him and his mother—their gaze implacable yet obviously tender and benevolent—as they fled from the explosion and as the Bottoms fell into darkness. The entire time God was with them, he was everywhere around them, they were in His care—he hadn't forsaken or abandoned Duncan any more than his mother had, and Duncan holds Him in his heart now and his heart seems to swell with the sense of Him. Maggie squeezes his hand and looks at him. Are you okay, Duncan? she asks, and he nods, smiling widely.

A few stars twinkle dully near the roof of the world in the dark blue that is the end of the day. Night will soon sink down like ink through a sieve, and suddenly the sky holds numerous unforeseen, unconsidered wonders—he now knew that beyond the astronauts and Apollo rockets, beyond the moon and the stars, there lay something far greater. God had been with him all this time and now he had a clear sign of his presence. He had called out to him, just as he had at his birth.

IN THE EARTH the men find strange things: the fossilized bones of ancient cows and horses, the curving swanlike neck of some strange feathered raptor impressed into the frozen chalk and clay, half a wing section of a WWII hellcat, and a giant billboard for Regal Pale beer. No one can explain how such a thing came to be, three hundred feet below San Francisco. At times such as these, they feel as if they have been blessed, deigned to witness such sights, chosen from millions of others for this special task, and they think of the men and women upon the city streets above them, the throng and press of bodies, the blaring of car horns and screeching of brakes. Working in the tunnel they realize they have been granted a special dispensation, a divination promise of brotherhood and illumination as long as they continue to strike and chisel and hammer and drill and pull and cart and drag the earth of the ocean bed.

While the cutterhead on St. Dymphna is being replaced and Gabriel is moved ahead in the shaft, there is a pause in their work and Joshua stares at the whorls of gravel and mica upon the tunnel wall. Gradually, a woman's face, the length of her body, and an up-raised hand emerge. She seems to be stretching, yearning out of the rock face at him, and he stands transfixed as she comes more fully to life the more he stares: She is smiling at him.

When they lived in Boston, when he was young, and it rained, all manner of things would come to the surface, in the basement and in the yard: old bikes, prams, pushchairs, even bedposts from the turn of the century. His father said it was because the houses had been built upon landfill. That most of Boston was landfill. And that's where the poor people used to live. Their houses flooded in the rain and the sewage came up out of the ground so that they were living in it, and it made them sick, spread cholera and tuberculosis through the im-migrant and black tenements. The rain always pushed up the past so that you couldn't forget it. In that place nothing could stay buried.

Shit, get a load of that, someone says from behind him, and the men converge about him. They set to wiping the grime and silt from the image emerging in the rock and then dig into the earth to pry it free. A billboard from the 1930s of a housewife: wide gleaming smile, apron stretched taut by the rocketlike thrust of her pointed cone bra beneath her red cotton cardigan, holding a loaf of Byer's home-style white: Just Like Your Mother Made!

P.J. Rollins shakes his head. How the hell did something like that get way down here? But no one can answer him properly, although they all have theories:

I'd heard they began building a subway down here in the thirties but the quakes of '42 destroyed it. Didn't believe it till I saw this.

It must be part of the old wharf that gradually collapsed and sank into the bay. The current has just kept pushing it deeper and deeper.

It came off the junk barges that ferry the trash from Santa Clarista to San Mucal.

The men plant the billboard near the mouth of the tunnel and, to a man, touch it when they come and go in the manner that they touch the statue of St. Barbara, for good luck, for a blessing of sorts, although none can explain why they believe that it is a good omen and that it will keep them safe. For most of them it becomes a holy article imbued with the power of the Holy Spirit in the various and distinct ways each man perceives his god. It draws them together and forges a sense of community, of alien brotherhood in the murky, Silurian dark.

In the evening Joshua brings home some of things he has discovered and lays them upon the table before Maggie serves dinner: the narrow whalebone of a woman's corset, an arrowhead, the fossil of an ancient worm, a bent pewter fork, a civil war musket ball, a rag doll from perhaps two hundred years ago, pressed flat by the earth, with small holes where its eyes once were. Duncan lays the plates and cutlery on the table and sits next to him, listens as Joshua narrates the possible history of each object or as he pauses, fascinated by another, with an origin as unexpected and startling as the one that came before.

These things, Joshua says pensively, they remind me of other things. He holds up the musket ball and pulls something from his pocket, something small that he rolls in his fingertips, and then places it upon the table: a misshapen lump of gray metal, rubbed to a bright tarnish.

Once, he says and moistens his lips, when I was a kid and we'd first moved to the house in Brighton, someone shot into the house. We never found out who it was and my daddy wouldn't let my mother call the cops. Said it was probably cops who'd done it, and even if they hadn't, if we called, they wouldn't come anyway. I was young, so young I never really thought about the danger of it. All I remember is finding the bullet in my mother's drawer the next morning. I followed the path of it, through my wall all the way into my parents' bedroom.

I kept it with me, he says. I took it out of my mother's drawer and

I've had it all this time. Kept it through Vietnam, could always feel it burning through my pant leg as if it was made of heat, as if it was imbedded in me. I don't know what the hell I've kept it for. Perhaps to remind me. He shakes his head. This was before we moved to West Medford, before I knew your mother.

Duncan has rarely heard him talk so much, and he listens enthralled, watching Joshua's face as these memories work upon him.

Joshua rolls the bullet between his fingers, finally places it carefully upon the table and stares at it. His lips pucker. He doesn't tell Duncan that he remembers one other thing about that night, one thing he's never forgotten. When his mother told his daddy to call the cops, he told her to shut up. Shut the fuck up, he said to her. Shut the fuck up, you stupid bitch.

He tells Duncan: I was little still but I had my own bedroom, so it must have been in the fifties, and my mother slept next to me that night, her legs curled up beneath her so that she could fit on the bed. She was frightened, I could feel how frightened she was, and it had nothing to do with any bullet.

Joshua takes Duncan's hand in his own, presses the bullet into Duncan's palm so that he can feel the smooth ridges and divets upon its surface, and looks guardedly to the kitchen where Maggie is preparing a roast.

BREATHING IS THE life of your voice, Maggie says as she applies kohl eyeliner, stares at her work in the mirror. It's Thursday evening and she and Duncan are in the room behind the bar, waiting for Ray Cooper and the Hi-Fidelity Blu-Tones to set up onstage. Maggie's blue sequined dress catches the meager lamplight in the room and seems to sparkle with small glints of flame. From the bar comes the sound of Clay shouting at a customer, a chair being overturned, and something hard slamming against the floor.

Any singer will tell you that. Common sense, isn't it? she says and laughs. We breathe to live, and we imbue life into our voice and our songs by breathing!

You let the breath come slowly. Your vocal cords, your larynx should never be pressing. It's the breath that does the work.

Always, she says, the voice is striving to reach the heavens. And as you sing, you strive for each note to remain pure, in pitch and tone, for each vowel to remain rounded as the notes rise in scale.

238

And if you can learn to sing on a minimum of breath, you can do all these things without harm to your vocal cords. You can sing . . . Maggie pauses: Forever.

Forever?

She laughs. Well, not forever, but for a long time. It's the type of breathing that allows you to last as a singer.

Duncan thinks about this, and about his mother's meteoric rise and her vertiginous fall, as if she were plummeting, blazing from the heavens.

But this isn't how you sang?

No. She shakes her head, and in this gesture Duncan senses her defiance and her pride but also a great sadness. I sang like Silva Bröhm, she says.

What did your teacher say to do?

She thinks about this for a moment, stares into the mirror before them, her face fragmented in the splotches of gray-black mercury showing through from the undersides of the plate, reaches across the bureau, pulls a tumbler glass from behind her perfume bottles, and sucks greedily from it.

When he listened to the range I was capable of, he told me that I would be a star. He said To sing until my heart burst, to sing until my voice screamed. To sing as if every night was the End, and if I did, that there would never be anyone else like me. And he was right. There never was anyone like me. And there won't be. When I'm gone, that's it, kiddo. Done. Kaput. Kapow!

Maggie mouths a giant O, opens her hands wide mimicking an explosion and Duncan laughs. Maggie studies her face in the mirror, opens wide her Kohl eyes and asks him how she looks.

You look great, Duncan says, although even with the makeup her skin appears sallow and stretched thin.

Her lips curl and flex and then her face calms. She opens her mouth and a deep bass sound emerges. She begins singing the end of the duet between Rigoletto and Sparafucile and then, rising raggedly up the scale, into the Angelic Voice from Don Carlos, comforting the heretics, who are preparing to be burned alive, that their souls will find peace and that they will join Him in His Kingdom.

When she is done, sweat shimmers upon her upper lip and at her hairline. She coughs violently and then hacks phlegm into a plastic cup filled with cigarette butts sitting on the bureau. As she attempts to regain her breath, she wheezes, You recognize any of that? When Duncan nods, she leans over, spits some more, and takes another lungful of air. The tendons in her hands show white through the skin as she clutches at the desk.

Good, she says, wiping at her mouth. Living with me has taught you something then.

She purses her lips, folds her bottom lip over her top, moistening them, as if she were applying lipstick, then reaches for her tumbler glass, but it's empty. God, she sighs, I need a drink. She begins rummaging in the bureau drawers, lifting and slamming things upon its top, and Duncan shakes his head, rises slowly, and leaves through the rear exit. In the alley he lifts the lid off a trash can and drops the whiskey bottle into it. In the room behind him there is the clatter of things being overturned and Mother's voice bellowing in weak-trilled anguish: Dammit, Duncan! You've taken my bottle again, haven't you? Duncan! I need that to sing!

ON THE LAST hot day of the season, a day the native Ohlone Indians traditionally celebrated their harvest in the Bay Area, Duncan and Magdalene walk home from school together, trudge sluggishly along the streets. A strange silver sun simmers above the rooftops and casts its mercurial light down into the shadowy alleyways where drunks lie sleeping. When Magdalene spots an empty soda can or beer bottle poking from an alley or storefront trash can, they pause as she picks it up or rummages through the bin and pushes the bottles and cans down into her backpack. Soon her backpack is bulging and its underside dark and ripe-smelling. And then they begin to fill Duncan's.

Jesus, he says, frowning, we're going to smell like a brewery, Magdalene.

Yeah, but between us we collected twenty cans and bottles.

That's only a dollar.

She shrugs. A dollar more than we had when we started.

As they make their way up Ipswich Street, Duncan hears the

sound of the Magnificat from Mother's Victrola, humming and crackling in the muggy afternoon heat—you can hear it for blocks. The threadbare, overbleached lace over the windows lays so straight and rigid it appears to have been pressed by an iron. Duncan looks at the porch and at the windows and at the strange flickering shadows that move amidst the peeling columns and ivy-wrapped trellises, and there is his mother swaying in one of her ermine-collared and black-beribboned robes from *Zauberflöte* and singing the Magnificat.

Oh, Magdalene says weakly.

Duncan pauses on the pavement—he's never heard her sing so loudly. Neighbors have come out on their stoops to listen. He stares at the porches, driveways, and sidewalks: Mrs. Uribe sweeping her porch; Mulligan in his greasy tank top rattles open his lawn chair and settles onto the meager patch of grass between their houses; Mrs. Scotelli lugs her week's washing up from her basement in her large green hamper and begins stretching her laundry onto the clothesline; Jacko Bilty sits on his step smiling sedately, his elbows resting on his knees and his small head cupped within his large hands; L.J. the Loon has brought a sixty-four-ounce bottle of Private Stock, whose rim pokes from the top of a brown paper bag, and he leans against a lamppost, and faces the Bottoms; dog walkers rest against a wall at the intersection while their dogs circle and sniff one another, urinate against the dying, speckled maples. All of them bend toward the voice of his mother and Duncan feels a sudden tenderness and an intimacy for them—suddenly he understands that his mother's voice captures each of their separate longings, longings that they can put no name to.

When Mother stops, the listeners remain suspended in that pause, the last note holding the air, and they are held in that finite moment. Mother hacks like a cat with a hairball lodged in its throat, and a bottle of Old Mainline 454 appears almost magically from the folds of her robe. She sways slightly as she lifts the bottle to her mouth and looks out over the bay. Her jaws clench and unclench and her throat works soundlessly. The bottle falls from her hands and clatters hollow on the stone, and then mother fills her diaphragm with air and begins to sing again.

And she keeps singing, even when the notes strangle in her throat and become a screech rising over the rooftops. She stands as straight as a lightning rod, her legs planted apart on the stone steps before the porch, her torso straight, her head arched slightly, and her mouth spread open in a ghastly yawning O. The veins in her neck bulge with blood. Her face turns crimson and then slightly purple—she is reaching for that single note that could reach the ears of God, she is reaching for a G7, and Duncan imagines this is what she looked like giving birth to him.

The tortured sound of her rises up over the rooftops and shatters the sky out over the bay. Duncan senses that the cars out on the bridge speeding to and from Oakland have stopped, that the boats in the harbor are still. That workers pause in their labors upon the high buttresses and cables, and even the hiss of their acetylene torches are muted before his mother's wail—the pale blue flames jetting in impotent flickering shudders the only movement in the entire city.

The neighbors stare at her and then quickly turn away. Packing up their lawn chairs and blankets, pulling the leashes of their dogs, their features caught in a strange asphyxiation—a mixture of pity and revulsion—upon witnessing such a grotesque. A green laundry basket rolls across the grass like a tumbleweed. Doors close. Footsteps fade. A bicycle whirs over the hill. And his mother's voice continues to press violently at the air, her whole body shaking with the effort of it, her arms tensed and her fists clenched at her sides. From Mother's right nostril a bubble of blood suddenly blooms and then bursts and trickles slowly down to her mouth.

Then mother stops, and there is silence. Not even a seagull sounds. Her scream reverberates in his ears for a moment longer, and then that too is done. The Victrola's stylus hisses in the record's run-off, and Duncan listens as the vinyl spins without music.

Mother wipes at her nose and looks at the blood there, flicks her hand so that the blood splatters the porch.

Fuck Maria Callas. *I* was the Queen of the Night, she says and stumbles into the house.

Duncan picks up the empty bottle of Old Mainline 454 from the steps and stands for a moment in the hallway as the shuddering sound of deep, belly-empty retching comes from upstairs. He looks toward Magdalene and she is staring at him with something like pity in her eyes. Softly, he closes the door behind them.

Later, Duncan stands at her bedroom door and listens to her moving about the room, pulling open drawers, the bedsprings creaking under her weight.

Mom? Duncan calls through the door, as she had once called to him, and he imagines her lost and unraveling and spiraling down through darkness.

The days pass and nothing changes. He leaves a tray at her door three times a day, but she never touches any food. The only time she leaves her room is to replenish the bottle of spirits she's polished off with another and then another, leaving the empty bottles neatly arranged in a row outside her door, which he picks up and throws in the trash.

Lying on his bed Duncan stares at the haphazard arrangement of constellations painted on the ceiling plaster. He stares at the stars until the streetlights come on and the stars glow and then blur. He wonders if at his birth his mother might have offered up her own Magnificat in joyous celebration, or if, as she sometimes says when drunk, she cursed his father and was determined to forget all and any part of it. He likes to think that love and resentment and prayer were commingled, and that whatever his mother refused or was unwilling to acknowledge was in part due to the pain it caused her and, like her songs, called out the loss of something far greater than words could ever convey.

From his drawer he pulls the lunar landing schedule for the Apollo missions 1 through 20 from *American Aeronautics and Aviation*, the NASA transcripts of the communications between the astronauts and Houston command center, William Safire's heartbreaking letter that the president read to the nation after the tragedy of Apollo 11, the NASA patches that mother gave to him at Christmas, and, at their center, the Apollo 17 crew patch.

The gold face of Apollo stares across the blackness of space, and behind his head the blue outline of an American eagle containing within it four red bars and three silver stars, and beyond this, the moon, about which a ringed planet and a galaxy appear to revolve. Duncan's fingers trace the raised stitching in silver detail along the blue-gray edge of the emblem and the names of the astronauts: Cernan, Evans, Schmitt, who traveled 240,000 miles and walked upon the moon for the last time shortly after he was born and then abandoned to the Home.

Across the top of the bureau he spreads the other crew patches emblazoned with the names of long-dead astronauts. From Apollo 11: Commander Neil Armstrong, Command Module Pilot Michael Collins, Lunar Module Pilot Buzz Aldrin; from Apollo 18: Commander Richard Gordon, Command Module Pilot Vance Brand, Lunar Module Pilot Harrison Schmitt; from Apollo 19: Commander Fred Haise, Command Module Pilot William Pogue, Lunar Module Pilot Gerald Carr; and from Apollo 20: Commander Charles Conrad, Command Module Pilot Paul Weitz, Lunar Module Pilot Jack Lousma. All of them still spiraling somewhere up there in the darkness.

From his mother's room comes the sound of her retching again and then her toilet flushing. Duncan places the Apollo patches back beneath his T-shirts on the wax paper, and slides the drawer shut.

He lies back on his bed and stares out the window at the night sky; fog has rolled in and climbed the hills: there isn't a thing to see but he tries to imagine the stars anyway and the place where he was conceived.

It's not yet five o'clock, and a dense drizzly fog lies low upon the city. Even the horns of the bay seem very far away. Down the wharves, where bells are softly tolling and boats' lanyards are jangling, the streetlamps shine with a diffused amber light through the mist. A yellow glare from basement walk-ups streams out into the steamy air and throws a murky, shifting radiance across the streets and on each passerby who walks, ghostlike, before their window. Maggie places the dinner plates upon the table before them. She's been crying and her eyes look swollen and tired. Slowly, she spoons mashed potatoes and peas from serving bowls onto their plates, her shoulders trembling slightly.

Hush, Maggie, Joshua says. It's okay, baby, it's okay. Don't fret so. C'mon, Sit down and let me do that. He pushes back his chair, puts on the oven mitts, bangs open the oven door, and checks on the roast.

She looks at Duncan, stares at him with her red-rimmed and bloodshot eyes. She sees an image of her mother in her blue-flowered summer frock with eyes as blank as pennies and the white glare of the bleached sheer curtains blinding and the smell of her parents' bedroom high in her nostrils and all the things she'd wanted to say to her forever left unsaid.

I love you, she says now to Duncan and reaches for his hand. You're my special Duncan. And then, when he doesn't respond: You're so special, she says and stares at him as if her look can convince him that this is so.

Yeah, that's what they called me in the Home.

Forget about what they called you there, she says angrily. You *are* special, my special Duncan, and don't you ever forget it. She leans forward and takes his face in her hands. Her nails are long and chipped, and without meaning to, she scratches him.

Her eyes widen, her brows lined in expectation. And I'm so lucky to have you as my child, she says. She almost impresses him with her faith, or perhaps it is her determination.

Sure, he says, and shrugs. After a moment his mother relaxes, lets go of his face, and reaches for her cigarettes. Damn right you're special, she mutters as she fumbles with her lighter.

Just hush now, Joshua says. Let all that old stuff go. Let's just enjoy our meal. He lays the roast at the center of the table, pulls off the oven mitts.

After dinner Duncan and me will do the dishes, he says, eyeing Duncan knowingly, and then you and me can head down to the Windsor. That'll pick you up, baby. You'll see.

Fuck, fuck, fuck, Maggie says suddenly and slams the lighter down upon the table. She raises her head back, and looks as if she might cry but doesn't. She stares at some point at the top of the wall and speaks softly, as if to herself: Why does everything have to be so hard, kiddo, hmmm? Why?

And Duncan might have answered her then for he feels sure he knows the answer.

Later, when she and Joshua have gone down to the Windsor Tap, Duncan treads the carpet of her bedroom, slowly parts the clothes in her closet, runs his hands along its top shelf, opens and then closes shoeboxes, stares at the box of black-and-white photographs sitting in a box on the floor. Finally, he sits on the edge of her bed listening to the familiar creaking of its springs and watches the fading light wavering upon the lace curtains as it spills through the trees. Amongst his mother's belongings, in the third drawer of her bureau, beneath frayed and faded underthings and tattered copies of *Opera* magazine describing her meteoric rise as a young soprano phenomena and a scathing and heartbreaking review of her final performance, he discovers a photo that she has never shown him: an image in black and white before he was born. It is a picture taken by the front-seat passenger in a car. His mother at the wheel of a convertible, her hair held back with a kerchief, and she's looking toward the lens—looking toward the man whom Duncan imagines is taking the picture—and smiling, a length of hair pulled free from her kerchief and lashed in a blur across her face. She has on the large oval sunglasses that were in vogue at the time and she might have been a movie starlet or a Jackie O impersonator.

There are more pictures in this sequence, and when he looks at them, one after the other, he has the sense of movement, of her turning back to the road, and the car pushing ahead, moving farther and farther down the glittering desert road. It becomes a running silent film in black and white, her turning to the passenger and talking to him, laughing, nudging the wheel from left to right. But always Duncan sees only her, sees what the photograph has already given him, and the perspective the picture projects into some near future, but nothing more. He wishes he could make the leap and imagine the lens from her eyes, and see what she sees—the sweeping landscape, hundreds of miles of flat plain or incomprehensibly vast peaks stretching to the far edges of the distant horizon and the towns and cities through which she passes, and the man with whom she shares this all, his father, he assumes—but he cannot. Perhaps this is due to a flaw within him, and the absence of something fundamental. Dr. Mathias might be interested in that.

October 1984

HOURS AFTER HER shift at the hospital has started Maggie is still sprawled upon her mattress, face turned into the pillow, spittle caking the side of her mouth, eyelashes fluttering in the dark hollows of smeared mascara. A record spins hissing on her turntable. Mid-morning sunlight traps the room in frowzy light through which clouds of dust motes spin and tumble, the windows shuttered and the sickly reek of stale alcohol and sweat lifting warmly from the sheets when Duncan pulls them back.

Mom, he calls. It's time to wake up. He sits on the edge of her bed and shakes her shoulder, calls her again. He shakes harder and still nothing. Mom, you need to get up for work.

Eyes opening slightly and then rolling back in her head, Maggie slurs: Fuck 'em.

C'mon, he says and urges her up, wraps her arms about his neck and, staggering, drags her to the bathroom.

Let me go, she says.

Yes, Mom.

Shifting his weight from hip to hip for balance, he bangs them against the hallway walls, knocking a framed picture from the wall, which falls and the glass shatters.

Where's Joshua? I want Joshua.

Duncan clenches his jaws in anger as her feet give out and the full weight of her comes down upon him. Where is he ever? he says. How should I know. He's wherever Joshua goes.

They make it to the bathroom and he yanks the shower curtain wide and, slipping on the tile, drops her awkwardly into the tub.

You're ruining everything, he hollers, and turns the shower full and cold upon her face, making her sputter and thrash her head violently from the side to side, as if the water were causing her pain. Finally she manages: Duncan, stop it—Stop it! Turn off the fucking water!

Instead, he leaves her struggling, with the water continuing to beat down upon her and splashing onto the linoleum, and stomps to his room to change his clothes.

Maggie stares at the green army duffel bag at Duncan's side, the one she says she bought him years ago, the one in which he carried all his belongings from the Home. She is in her white bathrobe and curled up on the couch with her legs beneath her. Her hair hangs wet and limp on her head and her face is still flushed from the shock of the cold shower. She smells of cold cream and cigarettes. On the television the closing credits to *Three's Company* scroll down the screen.

Why do you drink so much? he says, but it's more an accusation than a question.

Maggie lights her cigarette and stares out the window. I like to drink, she says. There's nothing wrong with that. You should mind your own business. I've done just fine all these years without you counting what I drink, you know.

You're not doing fine.

And you're not my nursemaid.

Well, it feels like it. I don't know how Joshua—

Duncan, you're really pushing me, okay?

Duncan shrugs, shifts the bag to his shoulder.

Where are you going?

I'm going to look for my father, Duncan says. He's convinced that he'll find him too. He'll hop a train in the yards and, using her postcards, he'll visit every place his father has been. Duncan imagines that his father might return to the places he once visited and that he might find him there. He might even still live in one of those far-off destinations captured in mother's photographs, the Kodak prints of azure and Technicolor desert skies.

He has the train schedules that mother gave to him for Christmas listing every train running out of San Francisco on the Midwestern lines, and more besides. The Union Pacific timetables and schedules are on blue-colored paper, the Missouri Pacific on yellow, the Grand on green, and he even has some copies of the B&R on orange paper, but he knows he won't be going that far east to look for him. That's not the way someone like his father would have gone. This he knows. He imagines that he will jump a train in the rail yards before the waterfront and do what his mother could never do—he would leave, and in a matter of hours he would be closer to his father.

Well good, his mother says. She continues staring out the window. For a moment he thinks he sees anger or perhaps pain in her eyes—and then he realizes it is hurt.

Color rises to her cheeks. She draws slowly on her cigarette and exhales. Good, she nods. When you find him, would you give him our address so he can send the back child support he's never sent. I guess it's about ten grand by now. He can make it up to you with trips to Disneyland, I suppose. If you find him, that is. And if he's not really dead like I said he was.

Duncan stares at the floor; it seems a safe place to look. He can't look at the hurt in her eyes. Finally she says: Where will you go, to look for him, I mean?

I don't know yet. I'll figure it out.

Mother groans. Duncan, she says. Please, honey, will you just listen to me, for once and for all: You don't have a father. He died a long time ago, before you were even born. And I got the best parts of him in you. All the parts I ever wanted.

I don't believe you.

Fine, don't believe me. What else can I say? We all want things we can't have, but that doesn't make it so just because we want to believe in them so badly.

Jesus, Duncan, Maggie says and pushes the hair roughly from her forehead. You drive me to drink, do you know that?

Duncan clenches his jaws, mutters: You don't need any help from me for that. He stares at her, daring her to contradict him.

You think if you look hard enough you'll find him? she asks.

Yes.

Is that what you really, really believe? It's not just something you'd like to be real?

No. I really believe.

The way you believe God spoke to you when you were born. The way you remember being born. The way you remember all kinds of crazy things and yet you can't remember any goddamn thing before the age of ten. But because you believe your father is out there just waiting for you to find him even though I've told you he is dead, that makes sense does it?

Yes.

All right, Duncan, have it your way. His mother's oft-rigid shoulders noticeably sag. She brings her knees up to her chest and curls in further upon the couch, turns slightly away from him. I'm just a liar then, she says and continues smoking. Outside the light is changing, the air growing cooler, and it brings her smoke his way. Children, their bright voices swelling in the dark, are still in the playground. Rain begins to patter the windows. The sill darkens with rain but mother refuses to move.

God did speak to me, he says and runs from the room. He slams the door behind him and flees up the stairs. From his window overlooking the city and the bay he watches great thunderheads roll in. Smoky shafts of amber split the clouds, and it seems as if a thick writhing gray rain is falling over everything as far the eye can see. Everything is the colour of gray metal and in that metal dark writhing shapes move, falling down from the sky, and the hills and mountains beyond are wreathed in white smoke like mist and then are gone from sight. The ground trembles, the glass panes beneath his fingers vibrate. Thunderous hoofs beat at the air. Ash and smoke are falling through the sky. The ground is boiling up, thrust up into the high clouds and then spent, raining back down to earth. Everything darkens. The city is gone and with it the bay and the sea beyond. Cars screech and horns wail. People are screaming. *God*, Duncan thinks, and then calls aloud: *God*; and his window overlooking the bay suddenly bursts wide and shards of glass shower down upon him.

He feels the splinters falling through the air, and when he opens his eyes, the glass lies in crystalline shards about him; a fire is igniting the sky and its bellows is a wind that shakes one corner of the world to the other. God, he says again, and he is terrified by the reply when a boom shakes the building and an electrical generator blows down the street and a heavy, charred utility pole falls blackened into the road. A fire hydrant blows its plug and a shower of rain arcs like silver over the parked cars.

He is on the floor moaning, his eyes closed, hands covering his ears as everything trembles and cracks and breaks around him. Mother is at his side, It's okay, honey, it's okay. It's an earthquake. We have to move somewhere safer. It'll be over soon. She picks him up and carries him to the bathroom. She lays him curled in the porcelain bathtub and crawls in next to him, covers him with her body and sings to him as the building shudders and shakes about them and they hear glass crashing and tinned goods tumbling from the cupboards in the kitchen.

Later, he is amazed by her strength, how he felt himself moved and lifted through the air by her strong arms. How gently she had eased him into the tub. The world around them shakes, the ceiling above them splinters, and though he feels and sees all this, it is in fragments. He hears his mother's soft breathing, the reedy whistle from her lungs, and the varying soft pitches of her melody, the words of which seem to be another language, for their meaning is lost on him and he wonders briefly if they are real words at all or merely made up in the moment to match some half-remembered, half-forgotten melody she'd known as a child and from a time and place when her own mother sang to comfort her.

When it's over, she lifts him from the tub. Plaster flours her hair white. There's a gash on her right cheek and bright blood streams from it. She is pale and her eyes red-rimmed. Just when he thinks she will say something to comfort him, something of her love for him, something of how they were okay—everything was okay because they were both still together and would always be together, for nothing could separate them—she says: You don't have a father, and then, He's dead, as if she dares him to argue with her, as if in this moment there can only be this one great truth and it cannot be questioned or challenged or denied. Tears stream silently from her eyes.

Your father is dead, Duncan, and he isn't coming back.

And then she says no more, and he stands there as the last of the tremors subside. Everything is still but the shaking of his body. He sits again, curls himself up by the porcelain bowl and lays his cheek against its coolness, listening as night comes on and the room and the city, absent of electric light, darkens, as mother sobs from her room down the hall and sirens wail through the night: a great caterwauling that seems to sound and respond to the aftershocks, the last echoing booms reverberating through the hills as damaged buildings finally collapse in upon themselves.

Later he wakes and he is in his bed and his mother is curled next to him, a blanket wrapped about them. It is still dark and the streetlights are out and, for a moment, blind and panicked, he does not know where he is and he feels his heart pressing in his chest.

Shhhh, Duncan, she says, I'm here, and her breath is warm and close and slightly sweet, so he knows that she's been drinking. She kisses his forehead and then pulls back. Her eyes are open, large glistening ovals in the darkness, watching him.

And he must have nodded or smiled or spoken somehow because she kisses his brow, like the seal to some arcane pact, and then the comforting, reassuring heat of her closeness, his head pressed into the pillow and the sense of his heart thumping slowly in his ears like loud footfalls, like Brother Canice's voice of God.

He mumbles something then, with the weight of the bed pulling him down and a semi-paralysis seeping down his body, a black ink being poured through him and through the bottom of him, the sense of it dripping through the sieve of his toes and fingers and the emptiness that comes with that: *You miss him.*

What's that, sweetie?

I know you miss him too, he says, clearer this time. Just like me. You've always missed him.

Mother strokes his hair and after a moment whispers, as if she is talking to herself in the dark, and perhaps thinking that he is already asleep. No, sweetie, you're wrong. I don't miss him. I don't miss him at all. Not anymore.

IN THE MORNING Mother is waiting by the Chevy Impala, determinedly wringing her long red hair into a ponytail. When she sees him, she pulls the wide-brimmed sun hat, the one she wore the day she took him from the Home, down upon her head. *Duncan*, she says, and the world, just as it did all those years ago, seems to tilt about him. The buildings and the bay and the sky above are stretching backward, and she fills the space that remains. Toward the Bottoms men are working on downed power lines. From the breakwater a tow truck pulls a crushed car onto its flatbed, chains groaning and flashing sunlight as the lines grows taut. After the quake steam billows up through cracks in the road from dozens of underground ruptures and a breeze pushes each fissure as if it were a fog. Gannets and shearwaters are a smoky haze out over the distant water, following the small seiners and trawlers in the bay.

She crosses the driveway and wraps him in her arms, then pulls back and stares into his eyes.

Mom, he mouths.

Do you forgive me?

No, he says and smiles.

Mother throws her head back and laughs. No, I didn't expect you to.

Come, she says, smiling, and tells him what she always tells him of a weekend: I'll show you what it was like before you ruined my life.

The land changes dramatically as they drive southeast from San Francisco along winding Route 58: above them, lush green overhanging boughs of maple and oak like the arches of wild cathedrals buttressed by ancient redwoods and pine dwindling as the landscape becomes rocky and acrid and dry. Within hours burnt-looking scrub huddle meekly against the side of the road and the hills have turned brown and dun.

Where are we going this time? he asks, and Mother turns to him with her red hair whipping madly about her face. She smiles and even her smile seems mad, distorted and held in its strange rictus so that in looking at her he thinks of animals stuffed and mounted by a taxidermist, dead eyes and mouths and postures holding the illusion of movement and life.

Nowhere, she grins. We're just driving!

They pass a pig farm sitting upon a rise on the otherwise flat, black plain, its corrugated metal silo flashing and blinding. The smell of offal, of silage and pig runoff comes to them suddenly, forcing Duncan to pull the neck of his T-shirt up to his nose. He reaches over, as Maggie drives, and pulls her headscarf down about her nose and mouth. When the farm has disappeared behind them, she takes the scarf from her mouth, turns her head, and spits into the wind. Thanks, she says, and they glance at each other and grin.

They drive until an hour or so before sunset, with the sun

shimmering above distant sandstone peaks to the northwest, and it seems to pause there like the curved bow of a great upended ship, ablaze, with the last of its ballast holding it just above the surface of the sea and the darkness sucking at it hungrily, pulling it slowly down. Its light burns in the rock and buttes, glowing amber—a vast sliver of glowing red flames stretching from east to west—and, as Mother takes an exit and pulls up a deep-rutted dirt road, the great ship of the sun slips over the crest of the horizon and a cobalt-blue, cloudless sky descends with a blacker darkness spilling through its center and from which the first stars begin to show.

Duncan's head rocks as the car bottoms out in the ruts, the undercarriage scraping and shuddering against the bowed ridge of sun-hardened dirt at the center of the trail. Far away a train whistle, the sound moving in rings through the darkness and falling on the wide, flat land. The car's headlights push back the dark desert on either side of them and the sand stretching beyond the guardrails seems to be whispering, as if something or someone was moving stealthily in that vastness, just beyond their senses. At intervals a strange wind comes up and buffets the car, sends sand whirling against the rocker panels, scattering it like hail in the wheel wells and in ghostly, swirling sand funnels across the highway before them. Heat lightning flashes and shimmers in the spaces between the dark hills, and the heat seems to hover in the air just above their heads, sliding like a dense weight over the car. When he turns to follow the path of the lightning, like small explosions blooming in the hills and moving northeast of them, his shirt sticks to the car's seat, sweat trickles down the channel of his spine, and he pulls at his collar angrily, but then they come over a rise and Mother slows the car as the desert spreads vast below them.

Sand drifts press against the shale and rock, the highway posts and guardrails, as if the desert is reaching out to reclaim everything, including the road, but mother turns on the stereo and music blares out into the creeping, haunting desert night, and the car accelerates.

She looks at him and smiles, the wind whipping her long hair, plastering it across her damp face and neck, and reaches out a hand to touch his. He takes her hand and their knuckles entwine fiercely and Mother begins to shout-sing the song: unintelligible words collapsing out into the desert and lost in the night. She clenches his hand all the tighter until it seems she might break the bones with the excitement she feels, and it's contagious. Duncan hollers out into the night as well and the desert takes his words and her smile widens and they drive on.

A hundred yards farther on, Mother swings the car before a rock outcrop so that the headlights show its scarred surface and then, surprisingly, emerging from the dark a chain link fence upon which a rusted sign reads:

UNAUTHORIZED PERSONS WHO PASS INSIDE THE LIMITS OF THE
LAS VEGAS BOMBING AND GUNNERY RANGE MAY BE SUBJECT
TO INJURY FROM OR AS A RESULT OF THE
ATOMIC ENERGY COMMISSION'S TEST ACTIVITIES.

He looks toward mother and she shakes her head, smiling, and says: They stopped testing in the seventies.

Duncan raises his eyes doubtfully, says: Okay. I guess.

Mother grins. We do have to watch out for radioactive snakes though. She puts the car in gear and the headlights tremble against the rock. All right, she says. Take your penknife and cut as much scrub as you can for a fire. Looks like there's plenty just beyond those rocks. Stomp your feet—okay? Make as much noise as you can.

Why?

To shoo out those radioactive rattlesnakes. Don't worry though, you'll see them before they see you; they glow in the dark.

Beyond the enclosure of boulders there is little sound but for a wind moving across the sand and moaning softly in the sandstone outcrops that burst from the desert here and there. Duncan steps out between the rocks toward the plain. A tuft of ragweed rolls lazily across his shoe and then the wind sucks it out into darkness. Across the striated ridges of sand the surface of the desert seems unbroken, until he kneels and looks closer and tunnels with his finger the zig-zag hollows made by snakes and the small marking of things for which he has no name.

Don't go too far, Mother hollers from their campsite, and he pauses and looks out at the desert. It's moaning and shifting with a strange, unnatural life. The wind seems to spiral about and turn back upon itself, rising to a scream—sand blasting his face so that he lowers his head—and then subsiding to a moan, and he cannot be sure where it originates nor through what it moves to create such a sound.

When they get a fire going, his mother heats some chili over the small flames and Duncan makes a bed for them with their blankets. They pause and listen to coyotes wailing across a far ridge and his mother smiles at him. She lights one of Joshua's rolled cigarettes and absently curls and uncurls her bare toes before the fire. She inhales on the cigarette and, after a moment, lets the smoke out, long and slow.

They closed the last of the firing ranges just a few years ago, she says. All the newspapers were saying how through the fifties, sixties, and seventies the army had been conducting secret radiation testing while soldiers trained on the desert flats. They'd been repeatedly bombarded with lethal doses of radiation during routine training missions. No one knows exactly how many men died; there's no record of them. It's as if hundreds of men and their families simply disappeared.

The tip of Maggie's cigarette turns molten as she inhales. I slept out here once, she sighs, just like we're doing now, a long time ago. When I left the opera and knew I couldn't sing any longer, I got on the road and just started driving. I had no idea where I was heading, no thought of where I'd go.

I was alone then but a lot braver than I am these days. Lit myself a fire and watched the night come down, but I couldn't sleep. It was a strange thing, being here. At twilight you might see soldiers in the shadows that lengthened across the plains and all the desert stretched before you filled with them. At night, you might imagine them moaning with the desert wind.

Maggie shivers and places a log of deadwood on the fire. The flames hiss and roar, sending up a shower of sparks into the night.

You really saw that?

The mind, she says and taps her head, it can play tricks on you. And I was young, she says, the flames sending shadows flickering across her face. That night—she holds her cigarette smoke and then exhales—I also saw Silva Bröhm.

The singer who killed herself?

Maggie nods, points with her cigarette toward the darkness beyond their fire. Walking right out of the desert toward me, the black and garnet gown she'd made famous in her scenes from *Die Zauberflöte* flapping madly about her.

Maggie flails her arms in the air and moans: a comic ghost; and Duncan laughs.

Silva, she says, was telling me that I should continue to sing.

But your throat, Duncan says, and his mother smiles, touches her neck. He imagines the scarred cartilage from the last concert she'd ever performed thickening in her throat. She nods. I know, Duncan, I know.

But why? he persists.

Because that is what we do. We do what we are made to do. If we didn't, we'd die as well. No matter how bad it gets, when I stop singing, that's when I'll die.

So, what are we doing here now? Duncan says. We've never actually stopped before, we've never—and he mouths the words slowly, emphatically—*actually camped.*

He looks at her seriously, eyes wide and questioning.

Mother grins, hugs her knees to her chest, and rocks slowly back and forth. She shrugs. Okay, okay, I get it—I do! We've never *actually*

263

camped, despite all my driving us around, is that it? Jesus, you're a hard one.

Well?

Well then, it's about time that we did! After all, this is the road I took, and she hesitates, a long time ago, before . . . when you were born.

Duncan stares at the sparks from their fire rising into the black sky, and higher, where they seem to merge with the sparks of stars that revolve up there, and in the vastness: a glove lost by astronaut Ed White on the first American space walk, Michael Collins's camera lost near *Gemini 10*, garbage bags, a wrench and a toothbrush, struts, orbital dampers, empty fuel cells, fragments of rocket thrusters, fuel recyclers, filters, piping, tubing, a fuselage, floating in space and decaying and crumbling in their failing apogee about the moon, flaring as embers themselves as they break apart and disintegrate in the outer reaches of the atmosphere. Night and day the various pieces of rockets and satellites and men falling from the sky and a million more pieces still that would continue to circle the earth for a century or more.

Duncan looks at her and smiles. I think you're meant to do something special too, he says.

Maggie reaches forward and takes his face in her hands. Her eyes are black and wide and unblinking. Firelight reflects in them, and there are two small burning embers at the center of each pupil. Perhaps we're meant to do something special together, she says, perhaps we're meant to be here, right now, just the way it is.

She pulls him close and sighs, shuddering deep and long, and Duncan cannot tell whether it is due to profound contentment or merely resignation, an acceptance of defeat and giving in to the insurmountable obstacles that she believes await her, or perhaps it is simply the desperate need for a drink.

Oh my Duncan, she says. I think the one special thing I may have done in my life was to have you, and in this brief moment, he believes her.

Above them the stars spin lazily across the curving plane of the earth and with them the blinking fuselage lights of airplanes, jets from the Nevada airbases, and the low trajectories of half a dozen satellites. Duncan has never seen a sky so black and so full of light, so full of artificial movement and yet seemingly so far away. In San Francisco the sky pushed down upon them as it seemed to swell and rise, curl like the crest of a wave coming in off the bay and them caught in its trough. The stars so low at night sometimes that it seemed you could reach up and touch them.

Mother cranes her neck up at the sky; again, he is taken by the paleness of her neck, all the more startling in the dim light. He follows her eyes as they search the night. Her eyelashes are speckled with sand. He waits for her to speak, and when minutes pass and she doesn't, he points with his stick.

It's Michael Collins and the *Columbia* command module, just by Cassiopeia, in Orion's belt. The hunter. See that star—the bright one in that group of stars? See how it's moving?

Mother frowns and Duncan strokes the sky with his stick again, as if he is writing upon a sheet of glass.

Do you see it?

Slowly she nods. Yes, she says and smiles. And perhaps it is the drifting smoke from the fire, the fluctuations of visibility in the atmosphere, but the star appears to shimmer and flicker and then burn ever more brightly.

It might very well be, she says. It might very well be. The fire crackles and spits as it burns down, the scrub sending small gasps of pungent, acrid smoke up before them, burning their eyes and making them weep even as they smile. Mother laughs and Duncan feels he might laugh as well, and then she holds her hand to her mouth as tears comes suddenly, surprising her.

Duncan pokes at the embers of the fire with his stick, watches the wood smolder and blacken. Out on Route 95, a tractor-trailer speeds past, its engine thumping loudly against the night and the loneliness of the desert, headlights floating across the tops of the surrounding stone, and then when it is almost gone, its sound and light fading, the driver downshifts and its engine gives one last combustive roar, like a distant howl down through a long, winding tunnel, out into the trembling darkness.

He watches the stars falling across the wide sky and he even imagines he hears the crackling, fizzling hiss of their tails burning brightly out. The fireworks above them gradually die down, and when they are done, the stars seem even brighter than before. Now and then beyond the sandstone boulders a lone car passes out on the desert highway, honky-tonk or threads of a revivalist's radio show drifting by on the warm air, the car's halogens arrows of light barely breaking the night, trembling on the tops of spindle and acacia and merging with the horizon until they too become like stars themselves and the night seems like a giant cocoon on the verge of sleep and waking.

Duncan looks over at his mother, asleep, and snoring lightly. Beneath the blankets he can make out the shape of her arms wrapped about her stomach. Sparks from the fire spiral heavenward. He follows their spinning gyre, leans his head back, and watches the stars stagger across the dark roof of the world.

THE CAR BREAKS down two hours after they leave the Valley of Fire. At first it is merely a slight bucking on the hills but then the engine begins to whine, as if it is slipping its gears.

I don't need this, Mother groans, and holds a hand to her temple. Jesus, my head feels as if I went on a bender.

It's because you're not drinking, Duncan says, and when she glares at him, he looks back at the road before them.

Mother turns on the heat and opens the vents all the way. Duncan smells rubber and burning plastic, and from deep in the cloth and leather, the vinyl and metal and all the crevices of the car, the smell of fish: a thousand fish swarming and slapping and slowly putrefying in the muck along the banks of the waterway before their house after the tide has gone down. He gags. Mother's eyes flicker from the road to the dash.

What is it? he asks.

The damn radiator. We've been at the top of the red for the last ten miles. I've been mostly coasting, hoping to cool the engine down. Dammit, I checked everything before we left.

A small explosion sounds beneath the hood and steam begins to billow from the front of the car. Waving one hand at the cloud of steam, Mother steers them to the side of the road and brings the car to a stop. She steps out and strides to the front of the car. The radiator lets go and steaming water gushes about her feet.

Oh you bitch, she says.

They lock their belongings in the car and begin walking, and soon the car is a black shape on the road behind them. When Duncan looks next, it is gone. The road before and beyond them stretches into an indeterminable distance with withered shrub grass, dry willow, and yellow tamarisk. The breadth of the plains trembles and shudders at either side of them from a breeze that Duncan cannot feel. His duffel bag bangs against his back and the straps pinch and chafe his shoulder. Sweat soaks his sides.

How far have we gone? he asks.

Mother glances at him and then at the road before them. Oh, only about a few miles, Duncan.

It feels much longer than that.

You should have left the bag behind, she says. We'll get the car towed once we get to where we're going.

He wants to ask where that might be when she looks at his bag and asks what's in it. He's brought clothes, underwear, a bottle of water, two tins of baked beans, and a tin of Labrador herrings, but when he tells her Brother Canice's radio and his rail maps and timetables, she rolls her eyes and stares back to the road. You should have left the bag behind, she says again.

Upon a distant low hill a plume of black diesel smoke bends in the wind and Mother pauses, cocks her head listening. Her legs tense as if they have become conducting rods to every vibration in the earth. It's a train, she says slowly, and then perhaps a mile distant or so its whistle sounds across the fields. *It's a train.*

Mother searches about them, and he watches as her eyes seem to grasp a telephone pole and follow it east, and his heart begins to hammer when he thinks of what she is contemplating. She begins walking quickly, striding through the wild grass, following the direction of the pole. Come on, she says. We're going to jump this train, and her legs begin to move faster, and Duncan races to keep up, his duffel bag bouncing against his back. Wait, Mom, he calls, Wait.

The cars bang and rattle upon the rails as they pass, coal soot and grain flax smoking the air, sunlight glinting off the cars and making them squint. A hundred cars pass, and Mother searches for an opening, seems about to rush the rails and grasp one of the cars by its front pinion and wrestle it from the tracks. Duncan's throat is dry and his T-shirt drenched to his skin. The dry grass upon the slopes of the rail cut sways and shimmers dreamlike and it is suddenly difficult to breathe. He sits heavily upon the crumbling wood and watches as his mother stalks back and forth as another hundred cars pound their way east.

Goddamn it! Mother hollers, and they watch as the engine and its cars snake slowly into the distance.

They walk a cinder embankment, following the train tracks, with their heads down against the sun. The sun glints off the hot-looking rails, the gleaming track of steel that train wheels have scraped and worn to a luster. Cicadas vibrate and thrum in weeds and bushes that line the gravel furrows. The heat of the sun presses on the back of Duncan's neck, and he feels himself stooping lower and lower before it, although when he looks at his mother, she is walking straight as a chisel. Only her head, her large hat flapping and billowing softly with the hot wind, is lowered upon her neck—she could be sleeping and yet moving forever resolutely forward, one foot up, one foot down, one foot up, one foot down. The wind billows and presses her dress about her legs, and Duncan can see the muscles in her hips quivering under the light material.

Blisters begin to burn at the sides of his toes and upon their bottoms, and then, after they've walked another mile or two, he feels them burst, and his toes become so raw he can only hobble on the edges of his feet and heels.

Mom? he says, and then again: Mom?

Maggie's head jerks slightly but she doesn't look back. Yes, hon? What is it?

It's my feet, he says. I don't think I can walk much farther. He licks his dry lips, watches her back with growing desperation. Mom, he wants to scream: Look at me! Listen to me!

Hmmmmm.

Hobbling, he drops the duffel bag to the ground.

A wail sounds startling close, and the rail ties are thrumming between the tracks. Duncan blinks and yellow and orange sunbursts float before his eyes. *Mom?* he calls weakly, and mother turns and grins.

This time, Duncan, we'll do it. We really will.

Maggie hops the rails to the embankment and Duncan stumbles after her and the train is quickly upon them, its metal dump cars and flatbeds flashing by and rattling and banging the rails so hard it is deafening. Flying cinders bring up welts on his arms, on the skin beneath his shirt and jeans, and he cries out. Mother is shouting but he cannot hear her. She has begun to run and, looking back, waves for him to reach for a handhold. And he thinks what type of mother allows their child to jump a speeding train.

He sees his lower legs torn from his knees, so that when he looks down there are only the bloodied white stumps of his kneecaps, shining white through the glistening gore, and there on the tracks, ten yards or so away, where they've been dragged by the car's wheels, the bottom parts of his jeans, with his sneakers twisted aslant the tracks, his legs twitching as they spurt blood from their hollows.

Mother looks back at him and blinks, as if she suddenly sees him and is envisioning the same thing. They are moving up an incline and the train begins to slow and mother runs to him, takes his hand so that they are running together.

Duncan, she says. You can do this. Now, we will only jump a train when it has almost come to a stop.

At the top of the rise they are still keeping pace with the train and Mother guides him toward the ladder of a dump car, takes his duffel bag from him, and screams at him to grab hold. The metal is burning to the touch and he clenches his teeth as the skin blisters. Hold on! Mother says, don't let go, and she grabs his shirt and pushes him up. His heels grasp the bottom of the rail and, with Mother pushing from behind, he begins to climb. Hurry up! she hollers. Get over the top!

And then suddenly there is a face of a man above Duncan, peering down, floating like a pale balloon in the blue sky, and an arm reaches down and grasps his hands and with a grunt hauls him up and over the top of the dump car. He's hurled against the side of the car and lies there breathing heavily, clutching his side and waiting for the stabbing pain there to subside.

The man squats on his haunches and stares at him, long arms dangling between his legs. Hello, he says and grins, flashes the most astonishingly white teeth Duncan has ever seen.

Never seen a bum with teeth like these, have you?

Duncan shakes his head, and the man leans close, so close that Duncan can smell him: ripe as day-old meat spoiling in the sun. His eyes shine pale and sick looking.

And you never will, kid, he says. You never will. He laughs and claps his hands, and then glances up as Mother makes her way overthe lip of the car. Her hair and dress billow in the wind as she momentarily saddles the lip and then swings her legs over and drops to the bottom, coughing raggedly and gasping for breath. She looks to the man and then to Duncan.

Duncan, are you all right? she finally manages, and Duncan nods, but she keeps her eyes on the man. His long, sun-darkened face bobs up and down as he looks at her.

Folks call me Spider, he says.

Mother nods, still sucking in air, but Duncan asks: Why Spider?

I don't know, perhaps because I'm tall and lanky and I can climb anything.

Why not a monkey?

Spider bares his teeth. Do I look like a monkey to you?

Mother bunches her dress between her legs and sits against the wall beside Duncan, reaches over and pulls him close. He looks up at the sky passing above them, blue and absent of cloud. There is the sweet, cloying smell of tamarisk, the rusk of limber pine and piñon, and narrow-leaf cottonwood, its fluffy white catkins floating above them like small clouds a mile distant and falling as if in a dream and then a glaze of heat settles upon the dump car and Duncan's throat is suddenly raw and dry.

What's the matter with him? Spider asks and gestures at Duncan, his hands dangling weakly from his wrists. Why's he making so many faces?

Nothing. Nothing's wrong with him.

Spider snorts and shuffles forward. Mother's hand squeezes Duncan's shoulder firmly, and Duncan knows she's trying to be reassuring.

He looks into Duncan's eyes. There's something wrong with you, all right. He taps his head. It's up here, isn't it? Something not quite right. I can always tell.

His gaze flickers to Mother. He stares her up and down, eyes moving slowly across her body. After a moment, he hisses: You two don't know ANYTHING. You be good to Spider and he'll show you.

I've been on every train in the West. I've been all through California. I know where to get food and who to talk to and who to avoid.
I get things done and nobody messes with me. There ain't a person
riding these rails who don't know the name Spider.

Okay, Spider, Mother says very slowly. We'll all be good.

THE HOURS PASS in the dull daze of heat, the click-clacking of the wheels, and the slow, metal groan of the cars as they move across the plain. From half a mile ahead the engine sounds its horn as they pass through signals, empty transfer stations, and water depots. Duncan leans his head against his mother's shoulder and dozes. When he opens his eyes, Spider, sitting just beyond the edge of the tarp yet engulfed in its shadow, is looking at them.

What do you want? Mother asks but she sounds bored and closes her eyes again. Spider sips slowly from a silver flask bound in bands of old leather wrap, tarnished a blackened brown. But it isn't Spider's. Duncan knows this just as he knows that Spider will hurt them if he can, and he shudders at the thought of who it had once belonged to and how Spider had made it his own. Duncan sees a body in a ditch just off an abandoned rail cut and flies crawling upon a pulpy, indistinguishable face, turning it black.

Spider stretches his long, emaciated arms forward, the sun-darkened skin loose and sagging against the bone. On his left bicep a dulled tattoo of the 23rd Infantry Division, which Duncan recognizes from the flags at the Windsor Tap, shows itself. And below that a cheap blue-ink caricature of a Vietnamese wearing a *nón lá* with a dagger piercing the far eye and emerging through the cheek, and the slogan Dead Cong, Good Cong!

You were in Vietnam? Duncan asks.

Oh yeah. Spider nods vehemently and spittle flies from his mouth. Did a tour in '68 and '70. He chews on his tongue and looks thoughtfully at Duncan. Hey, you like my tatts? I got some more too.

Spider pulls back the short sleeve on his right arm and shows an ace of spades tattoo and above that an American soldier spearing a bayonet between the spread legs of a naked Vietnamese girl.

Spider stares at Duncan and licks his cracked lips. You like that one, Huh? Got it done special in Saigon.

Duncan, mother says, and gestures for him to come by her side.

Those gook whores loved us Americans.

Duncan, come over here.

Yeah, I was in Vietnam all right. Killed me a lot of gooks, killed anything that moved.

He grins. As many gooks as I could, I killed them. I killed women and children. It didn't matter if they were civilians. I shot so many civilians I lost count. If they weren't supposed to be in an area, I shot them. If they didn't understand fear, I taught it to them. There's this time when we'd pulled this family out of a hooch—

We don't need to hear any of your stories, mother says.

Spider pauses and grabs violently at his crotch. I got more tattoos, pretty lady. You want to see 'em?

We don't want to hear your stories, Duncan echoes, and Spider lets go of himself and rolls his eyes.

So anyway, this gook was trying to hide her baby and the thing wouldn't shut up, so, Second Lieutenant Calley, joking around, fires his 45 at it, and he misses. He's not really trying to hit it, but the mother and child are both roaring now, and we're all laughing. So Calley, he gets closer now and fires again, and damn, he still misses. And this makes us laugh even harder, but it's getting old, y'know? So while everyone's laughing, I go right up on top of the thing and plug it and suddenly everyone is real quiet.

Duncan thinks of Joshua's few words about the war, his long silences, his staring off through the kitchen window and out into the night when Duncan knew that the war was all he was thinking about, and of how, in the end, there is no salvation and no redemption from the past, and about the type of men who talked about such things, the things they did, as if they took pleasure from it, and he wonders how much of what Spider is saying is true.

Spider shakes his head. Nobody who hasn't been in a war understands what fear is. The way to live is to kill, because you don't have to worry about anybody who's dead. Over there you get a medal for it. Here they put you away. And that's why Spider rides the rails where no one can tell him what to do.

He unscrews the flask and puts it to his lips. He tips back his head and Duncan listens to him, drinking long and slow, watches his Adam's apple moving up and down.

Spider shuffles forward on all fours, presses the flask to Mother's face. You want a drink?

Mother opens her eyes and looks at him.

No. I don't.

Spider withdraws the flask, leans in and loudly sniffs the air about her like an aggressive dog, then stares at her and smiles. Sure you do, he says. Sure you do.

In the heat of the sun Duncan begins to doze, but he can feel Spider looking at them still.

You ain't got no daddy, son?

Mother tenses beside him.

Shame. Your mother's too pretty not to have a man in her life. She's just sooooo pretty, ain't she? But I bet all the guys tell you that.

My father was in Vietnam, Duncan says. Just like you.

Spider's eyes narrow. He killed over there?

Duncan considers this for a moment; tears come to his eyes and his chin trembles and he hopes Spider will mistake his fear for grief.

He nods.

Mother is working at something in her hand and when Duncan glances down he sees she's pulled a nail file from her bag, concealed it in the flat of her palm. Spider stares at Duncan and then at her for a moment longer and then returns to his spot beyond the edge of the tarp. Mother exhales long and slow, so slow and long the tension it contains is almost undetectable. She relaxes her fingers on her nail file and lays its curved and soft hook against her thigh.

I don't like you, she says finally, and Spider looks at her blearily and then flashes his pearly white teeth.

He nods. That's good. That's real good.

AT A PLACE called Brandon, incorporated 1912, the engine stops for water. Duncan listens to the metal hiss and tick as it cools, as the engineer and rail workers shout over the din of the diesel. Giant dragonflies swoop over the tops of the cars. Spider climbs the side of the car and looks out across the yard toward the small town. His shirt pulls up and Duncan can see the knobbed ridge of his spine, curved like a snake.

He looks back and grins at them. Need supplies, he says. Going to show you two how it's done, and then he is clambering over the top and they hear him dropping down onto the tracks.

Duncan and his mother climb up onto the rim and watch Spider zigzagging his way toward the far shape of squat, flat-roofed buildings, obscure and shimmering in the haze of heat.

I don't trust that man, Mother says. We can't let him back on the train.

.   .   .

At a little past two in the afternoon the engineer hollers and big die-sel engine thrums and Duncan and his mother hold on to each other as the cars suddenly jolt forward and then bang against each other and they begin moving. The few clouds in the sky race above them and a sluggish breeze pushes at their hair, and then they hear Spider hollering and they climb to the ledge at the top of the dump car. He's twenty or thirty yards down the track, breathing hard to keep pace with the train. He throws something from his hand and a knotted plastic bag sails into the car. It bangs against the side and slides along the hot metal. Finally, Spider covers the distance between them and, catching hold of the ladder, swings himself up onto the bottom rung. He begins hauling himself up the ladder as the ground blurs beneath him.

Mother stands at the top of the dump car looking down at him. You're not coming up here, she says. Jump before the train picks up any more speed.

Spider stares up the ladder, blinking. Oil smears the creases above his eyes. His nostrils flare. You fucking crazy?

He hacks phlegm, turns his head into the wind and spits. The engine is moving faster now and Duncan watches as his spit flies down the tracks behind them. The wind whips the hot air against his face.

Bitch! I ain't jumping from no train, he hollers and begins to climb again.

He reaches up to the top rung and Mother slashes at his hands with her nail file, stabbing the sharp nub again and again into his hands so that blood flows from the puncture wounds and streams into the air, drips down upon Spider's upturned face. Spider howls and then with surprising strength lunges and catches both of moth-er's arms in his own.

Maggie screams as the weight of Spider yanks her forward. Dun-can tries to pry Spider's hands off of her but her arms are streaked with blood and he can't get a grip on Spider's fingers. Spider looks up at him, laughing, his grimy neck stretching as it convulses, and Duncan punches him full in his Adam's apple, feels his fist driving the bulbous flesh back into his throat. Spider's eyes widen and his mouth opens and he gurgles loudly, and then Duncan punches him again and again. Spider's hands reach for his throat and then he is falling backward through space, Spider strikes the rails hard and fast, his legs crumpling beneath him, and then, arms outstretched, rolls and bounces, upon the ties.

In a cloud of dust and gravel he smacks the wood, one tie after another, perhaps twenty in all. His straw cowboy hat is tumbling and lifted by the warm air into the silver sky. And then he is still. Only his hat continues to rise and float and then gradually, as the dust cloud collapses, it, too, settles, a hundred or so feet beyond him.

The sun sinks lower in the sky, blinding Duncan and his mother and turning the rails and hillsides black. They are almost at the top of the ridge when they see the black shape of Spider moving between the divides, struggling to slowly pull himself up. He stands, weaves for a bit, and then his legs seem to go out from beneath him and he sits again.

Do you think he's all right? Duncan asks, and as they stare, they see him look in their direction. Duncan has only the sense of his face—a pale, barely distinguishable oval—and then his hands begin to wave and a skew of curses come to them on the air.

Mother says, I think he'll be fine.

What's he saying? Duncan asks, and, looking back, Mother shakes her head, purses her lips. I can't make out a damn word.

Above, momentarily, a single telephone line dissects the sky and then there is only the wide expanse of blue, which, Duncan imagines, must parallel the wide expanse of desert stretching out on all sides of them with nothing in between for hundreds and hundreds of miles, and Spider fading into that expanse.

After a moment Mother turns to him, squeezes his shoulder. Shall we see what's in that bag?

There are hamburger buns, hot dog rolls, tins of pork and beans, and tuna fish, two tins of tomato soup, and a fifth of Jack Daniel's. Duncan stares at his mother as she contemplates it. She takes it up in her hand, pauses, and then pats the bottle. We'll save this for when it gets cold, she says and pushes it back to the bottom of the bag.

What if it doesn't get cold?

Why then, Duncan, she says primly, we won't drink it.

Soon a breeze comes across the plains, whistling across the tops of the cars. Duncan and Mother stand for a while in the center of the car and watch the passing landscape, the warm wind drying their sweat and plastering their clothes to them. The rails seem to thump and tremor beneath them, as if the landscape itself is undulating with the train's rhythmic pounding, and as if each stretch of land, field, pasture, and prairie is being tamped into shape by their passing.

Beneath the tarp they lather themselves in sunscreen, and mother double checks to make sure Duncan has covered the tips of his ears, the back and side of his neck. She rummages in her bag for her kerchief, and Duncan slowly ties Joshua's bandanna about his head.

Where did you get that? Mother asks.

It's Joshua's. He gave it to me for when I'm riding on his bike.

She leans forward on her knees and pours water from his bottle onto the bandanna until Duncan's head is soaked and water trickles down his face and into his mouth. Then she moves close and touches her face to the cloth. She closes her eyes, and after a moment says: It smells like him.

Later, after the sun has set and the stars come out over the plains and a pleasant wind has cooled the car, they open two tins of pork and beans with Duncan's penknife and scoop out the beans with bread, mother begin to speak of Spider again, but then a laughing fit takes her so that tears come to her eyes and soon Duncan is laughing as well. They both let the laughter take them, and when they are done, they lean their backs against each other and watch the sky.

Long after mother is done, Duncan can feel her laughing still, deep in her belly, the vibrations trembling in his backbone. Finally she sighs long and hard: Oh, my Duncan. What shall we do?

The wheels bang the rails beneath them in a slow, sleepy cadence. Warm air sighs above. The fluttering tarp shows black and then cloudless, high blue sky.

Duncan, I didn't want to really hurt that man. You know that, right?

He is hungry. Saliva rises up in his mouth, wet anticipation. Between bites of bread and beans he looks at her.

Mother nods. Okay. You're right, I did want to hurt him. Damn right I did. That man was just waiting to hurt us. I'd like to say that I'm thankful that he's all right, but you know, sweetie, I'm not thankful and I am glad I hurt him. I only wish the bastard wasn't getting back off the ground.

There are some people in this world that will hurt you without blinking an eye. You have to look out for these kinds of people, and when you see them, you have to hurt them before they can hurt you. Do you understand?

This is what Joshua has told him, but he doesn't tell her this. Mother chews her bread, the rails clatters beneath them, and Duncan lays his head back upon his duffel bag, listens to the sound of her. Above them, the rippling black cables of telephone lines stretch, an undulating merging and intersecting that seems to vibrate and hum with her voice.

With some one like that, you can't take any chances.

I'm sorry I got us into this. I just wanted us to have an adventure together.

I can't believe I let us jump a train. What the hell was I thinking?

If Joshua had been here, he would have known what to do.

I almost killed a man.

Goddamn hobo.

And then she shakes her head in disbelief and laughs: Did you see

282

the way he hit those rails and jumped up like a goddamn jack-in-the-box?

And then she sighs.

My. God certainly does work in mysterious ways.

By the time they arrive back in San Francisco the night has lengthened and become cold, and when it begins to rain, large hail-like drops bouncing loudly on the metal, they huddle against each other. And Duncan is glad that mother, distracted by her efforts to get warm, has forgotten all about Spider's fifth of Jack.

The rail cars slow as they pass through the center of the city, and together they look over the rim of the dump car at the houses along Main Street. Mother's breath is warm and comforting against the side of his face. Trucks and flatbeds and rusted cars bump and bang and hiss through the rain up and down Belmont. A traffic light thumps and clicks, flickers red at intervals and the traffic waits and then moves on again. No one seems in a hurry and the frequency of the light's changing might be the same as it was two decades before. An old pharmacy sign glows blue in a white-framed win-dow. Duncan can see men sitting on stools and drinking coffee, smoking cigarettes, reading newspapers, and staring out at the strange fogged-steamed night. Through the mist their figures look numb and vague, as if they are merely the memory, the afterprint or shade of old men who have long since passed. A barge sounds out in the bay, and farther north, toward Calistas, a horn bellows deep and low in response.

Mother's face is bright and wet, scoured young by the rain. We made it, she says, and takes Duncan's hand, and squeezes hard.

It's a little after eight thirty and the large oval clock over the pharmacist's shuttered counter knocks loudly, even over the sound of Charlie Pride. Maggie drinks cup after cup of coffee and stares out through the plate glass, her face caught in the glow of neon blue. Every once in a while she purses her lips and wipes at the condensation that has formed there, squints out onto the black, gleaming street. Duncan has read most of the comics in the magazine rack when she stirs, her mouth opening and then spreading into a smile.

C'mon, she says. Joshua's here.

Outside, across the street, is an idling wrecker with the words *Joe's Auto and Tow* painted in elaborate but faded script across the rusted metal. Sitting in the cab, Joshua is waiting for them, his steam fogging the windows. Wipers clack back and forth across a cracked windshield. Cigarette smoke curls white and lazy from the half-opened window. Music sounds softly from the truck's radio, and then is broken by a DJ's animated voice.

Joshua! Maggie says as she opens the door and then slides across the bench seat to hug him, lays her head against him for a moment, and then is sitting up and wiping at her eyes.

Maggie, Joshua says, and then: Duncan. You okay, kid?

Duncan looks to Joshua and nods, and Joshua throws his cigarette butt out into the night. He glares balefully through the steamed glass to the fog-swirling street.

You can't keep doing this to him, Maggie, he says softly, and he might have been referring to anything. You know that. It's got to stop.

He keeps his eyes on the road, lets the words sink in. Maggie's jaws grind in the shadows of the cab; Duncan can feel her tension, like something simmering, and then before it boils over, she sighs and all the tension is suddenly gone.

Yes. I know, she says. I'm sorry. I—I guess don't know what I'm doing.

It's okay, baby. It's okay. You're home and you're both safe now.

We are?

Of course you are.

Joshua mashes the clutch, wrestles with the gearshift, and then they are moving again.

Maggie stares at Joshua as he drives, rain shadow passing crookedly down his rigid face, and finally seems to risk speaking: Do you have anything, honey? A little something in the glove compartment to take the edge off? You wouldn't believe what we've been through.

Shit, Maggie.

She rummages in her bag and laughs victoriously when she pulls out Spider's fifth. Joshua glances at her as she unscrews the top.

Where'd you get that?

Some hobo on the train, nasty piece of work, but Duncan and I showed him, didn't we, sweetie?

Duncan remains silent, stares at the streets passing blurred before them.

Joshua reaches out a hand. Can I see it?

Sure, honey, one minute. She swigs deeply from the bottle and sighs as she hands it to him.

Joshua rolls down his window, takes the bottle, and throws it out into the night. A moment later they hear it smashing upon the road. He shakes his head. You drinking from the same bottle as a goddamn hobo? How low can you get, woman?

Maggie opens her mouth and then closes it again, stares blankly through the windshield. *A goddamn hobo.*

I'm a good mother, Maggie says. I've always tried to be a good mother.

Of course you are, baby. Everyone knows that. I'm just saying you've got to watch the other stuff.

The truck's wipers wheeze back and forth and the headlights shudder and the truck bounces and rattles along, the tow chain banging and the swing arm groaning from the rear. Joshua fiddles with the radio but all that comes is static and eventually he switches it off, lights another cigarette, and shares it with Mother. Duncan stares at the headlights floating misshapen in the black like two oyster shells. He can barely make out the streets through the rain. A mile passes and then two, and although Mother is silent, he can feel the tension of her, or perhaps it is anxiety or fear, building, and he tries to gauge her expression but her face is lost in the shadows of the cab.

Est evacuatio timoris propter confirniationem liberi arbitrii, qua deinceps scit se peccare non posse. Fear is cast out because of the strengthening of the will by which the soul knows it can no longer sin.

—ST. BONAVENTURE, ON FEAR IN PURGATORY

March 1985

MEN'S FACES GREASY with condensation shimmer in the pitch-black of the tunnel. Beneath his hard hat Joshua's hair is slick and wet. Sweat trickles down the men's backs, in the folds between clothes and their rain gear. Mold grows in the creases of their skin, in the warmth of their armpits, between fingers and toes, in their crotches, in the tender places about their ears, and their skin begins to rot. But Joshua has experienced this before many thousands of miles away. And this is not the only thing that reminds him of other places.

From cross-sections and secondary tunnels—ventilation shafts and sluice breaks—men appear suddenly, faces peering out of the dripping darkness, and he cannot tell who they are until they mutter their name: Javier, Sully, John Chang, P.J. Rollins, Billy Gillespie. And the hollow, eternal sound of water droplets falling and reverberating through the tunnel as if they are at the bottom of some abyssal well.

Eyes glisten from pale and gaunt washed-out faces like hard gems in the gloom, like the backs of darkling beetles. And some eyes bleed from their whites, as nitrogen-starved corpuscles explode. Or stepping from pillars of steam: black, shifting figures like the soldiers that move through the misty jungles of his dreams, moving seemingly without end, much like the workers of this tunnel—and always they are following him, always searching for a way to move up, up into the light.

And always the deep, falling, cavernous sound of raindrops, dropping from the walls into holes and cracks and pools about them and echoing like minor concussions enlarging and then diminishing, settling back into the earth and creating the suggestion of vastness, of a free-falling dark without end. And in this dark, faintly, Joshua hears Jamie Minkivitz crying and his brother telling him to stop, pleading with him for the love of God to just shut the fuck up.

EVERY NIGHT FROM the Vulcanite radio the same message repeats itself like a looped recorded broadcast from some indeterminable source: the moment of the lunar landing and then the tragic hours before the *Eagle*'s scheduled return to orbit with the command module and before its ill-fated abort. But tonight is different. Duncan turns the radio's knob past Radio Luxembourg to a point on the dial where the needle goes no farther, a channel of static from which, when he listens in the dark, a faint sound begins to emerge, at times a ghostly jumble of voices and at others a crisp enunciation punctuating the charged ether. He hears the voice of Michael Collins, ghostly and insubstantial yet filled with urgency:

Collins to Eagle. Over.
Collins to Eagle. Over.
Buzz. Neil. Come back, over.

Collins to Eagle. Over.

Houston, are you picking this up on the LVL? I think there's a problem with telemetry between the CM and the LM, over. I can't tell what's happening down there. I'm changing frequency to NasCom, over.

Now operating on NasCom. Houston? Eagle? Can you hear me?

CM to Houston, do you copy?

Passing into lunar shadow in forty seconds, and counting.

CM to Houston. Hope to return to radio transmission in two hours, over. Houston, do you copy?

Forty seconds.

Be great if you guys could get the RCT up and running by the time I've made sequential orbit. It's getting pretty lonely up here without any human voices for company. Over.

Twenty seconds.

I'll look for Neil and Buzz on my next pass. Buzz brought his baseball bat. Wanted to see how far in he could hit a baseball in space. [laughs]

Ten seconds.

I think . . . [garbled].

Out of the dark . . . [garbled]. Over.

Collins to control. If you have a moment, say a prayer for all of us, would you? We need everything we can get up here.

The Hyginus Rille is in sight. Beginning transmission blackout. If you make contact with Neil and Buzz, tell them I was asking for them. Am eager for rendezvous and excited for their return. What a job they've done! See you on the . . . [garbled].

And then it ends and there is only a vacant electrical hum and soft bursts of static as power surges down the line. Duncan reaches out and turns off the radio and the room is dark once more, but when he lies back in bed, pulls the sheets and blanket to his chin and stares at the ceiling, the deep night of space swirls above him and there are no stars and for the astronauts and his father no promise of dawn and only the never-ever of returning home again.

April 1985

JAMIE MINKIVITZ AND the angel climb higher and higher, the moon rises vast and colossal before them, and they are held momentarily in its lambent light, with the darkness of space stretching all about them, and the angel lifts his face and smiles and his eyes are the color of basalt.

Jamie stares into that face, which appears so beatific and strangely illuminescent and charged with the best and most human of qualities—benevolence, empathy, kindness—that he is entranced and captivated by it, held in its divine light as if he were glimpsing some small part of the face of God, and then the face is suddenly transformed.

Now the thing that looks down upon him, even as it pulls him ever skyward, higher and higher so that the wind is ripping the air from his lungs and he can feel the cold knotting his muscles, a cold paralysis seeping down through him like ink, seems absent of anything human. It stares at him and nothing is reflected in its blank eyes, and then it lets loose its hold and he wonders how he could have mistaken what he'd seen. And even in that moment before it lets go of him and he falls into the darkness, Jamie Minkivitz stares at the fine avian bones of its knuckles and wrists shining white as it squeezes him tighter and tighter so that for one fleeting moment he thinks that his fear is misplaced and that something wondrous is about to happen.

He is six miles up and alone, falling at 120 miles per hour, and in three minutes he will strike the surface of the bay. From pain, cold, and lack of oxygen he is buffeted into unconsciousness. He falls incredibly fast for the first fifteen seconds or so then the air thickens about him—atmospheric drag resisting gravity's acceleration—and his plummet begins to slow. With every foot, he slows even more. He wakes, sputtering into consciousness, at about twenty thousand feet, and vomits. This is the final part of his descent, which will last about two minutes.

He knows that he is going to die but does not feel peace in this, no strange comfort calms him, rather he feels rage and incredible fear, and the longer he must wait to die and see the bay emerging fully before him, the more this fear increases, and he begins to wail and cry. Tears force their way from his eyes and freeze on his cheeks. Snowflakes swirl in brief, random orbits down from the sky and he raises his face to them as he falls, feels them melting slowly on his skin. The air is sharp and crystalline and the moon so bright that he is momentarily blinded.

For a moment it feels as if he has slowed again, and things come much clearly into focus; everything appears incredibly sharp and distinct, as if a veil had been lifted from his eyes. Below him now the lights of San Francisco, in dazzling, wind-blurred heliographic quadrants, the flashing red warning beacons atop the Golden Gate Bridge, to the cars, minute streamers of white and amber lights, and the water, a serrated silver and gray, which when he strikes will be as hard as concrete.

There is so little time, he knows, and he wants to hold on to something, something that he can hold to his heart, some happy memory, of his life, of his family, of his loved ones, but all he can think of is the fear that very soon he will be dead and he is powerless to prevent it.

The water looks like fractured glass, hard and sharp and unforgiving. Once he strikes it, whatever is left of him will be swallowed up and carried out to sea on the wake of the barges humping slowly through the sound. But there will probably be very little of him left. Small whitecaps stir the tops of waves as freighters and tugs pass beneath the bridge's massive pylons and cables.

He stopped struggling long ago and gave himself over to the talonlike hands that had carried him ever upward, and when they were rising through the clouds and he was looking into its wind-sheared face, he knew that it was hopeless to argue, or plead, or fight any longer. Now he opens his mouth to say something, a prayer perhaps, or to call out to his mother or father or brother—perhaps it is a name—and his lungs fill up with rich, briny air so cold and clear it is as if he is drinking it, gulping it down, and then he strikes the water and explodes.

San Francisco Chronicle

TUESDAY, APRIL 12, 1985

SAN FRANCISCO—COAST GUARD ID
BODY FOUND IN SF BAY

At about 7:30 a.m., the U.S. Coast Guard recovered the body of James Minkivitz, a worker on the San Padre underwater tunnel project, off Brooks Island. An autopsy conducted Monday found that Minkivitz died from multiple blunt-force injuries, a county deputy coroner said, most likely, from a high fall onto the rocks. Speculation as to where Minkivitz's fall occurred remains but there is no suspicion of foul play and the cause of death has been pronounced accidental.

Brooks Island Regional Preserve, a 373-acre island off the Richmond inner harbor, is a nesting ground for terns, herons, and egrets. It is also the site of an ancient Indian burial ground, with shell mounds as old as 2,500 years, and lies approximately six miles north of the San Padre underwater tunnel project currently underway and scheduled to be completed in four years.

At the Windsor Tap, Duncan and Joshua play Texas hold 'em, with Clay placing the blind, slapping down another card at their request as he passes back and forth behind the bar. Because they must wait for Clay, it is a slow-moving game and Joshua seems distracted and keeps glancing at the crumpled pages of the *Chronicle* spread upon the bar. Duncan knows he is bored, but, to Duncan, this movement—sluggish and melancholy through the shifting hues, fragments of the day passing outside and filtered through the cubed windows—is immensely pleasing: They are outside time and Duncan can pretend that Joshua's presence is not merely a temporal and transient thing, but something that will last. When these games end, and Duncan cannot explain why, he is often filled with sadness.

As Clay thrumps back and forth behind the bar, Duncan changes his mind repeatedly, and if he pauses in deliberation when Clay returns, Clay does not wait but continues on behind the bar. Duncan is about to say something and then catches himself and Clay shrugs and is past them, and from somewhere in Joshua's throat comes a raspy, almost undetectable moan. He takes a swig of his beer and glances down the bar toward what's left of the day simmering and coalescing and then fading in the glass. Duncan looks down at his cards.

Jamie, Minkie's brother, Joshua calls to Clay, but Clay has his back to him and doesn't appear to be listening and Joshua continues anyway. They think he committed suicide just like his father.

They say he died jumping off the Golden Gate Bridge, that his body floated upriver to fucking Brook's Island—can you fucking believe that? But he didn't hit no rocks. Minkie told me Jamie's insides imploded when he hit water. Means he dropped a long way. A long, long way. Much higher than any bridge.

Duncan considers his cards and what lies beneath Clay's blind. He's not really thinking about what Joshua is saying. There is the tinkling of glass as Clay empties the dishwasher and places the glasses behind the bar.

I mean that's motherfucking bullshit, man. Bullshit!

Duncan looks up. Clay gestures with his hand for Joshua to lower his voice.

That's all right, that's all right, Joshua says and nods. I know what's going on. Fucking bullshit, that's what. He lifts his beer bottle again, and when he's done, his chin glistens wetly.

Angels, he says and laughs emptily. An angel lifted Jamie up miles above the bay and then let him go. That's what happened.

Joshua makes his hands into wings, the touching fingertips of each hand like the apex of two muscled foramen, and, pouting his lips, creates a whooshing sound like bellows as he flaps the wings slowly and raises his arms up, up, up, high above his head, and then holds them there for a moment. A wall-eyed drunk at the far end of the bar holds his cigarette before his mouth and watches mesmerized; Duncan holds his breath and glances at Clay, who seems to be doing the same. And then Joshua lets his hand go. One rigid, calloused finger

298

drops in a straight line to the bar and slaps the wood violently: a plummeting Jamie Minkivitz turned to pulp upon the surface of the bay.

That's enough! Clay hollers and shakes his head when Joshua stares him down.

Duncan looks at Joshua questioningly. As he waits, there is only the sound of the fan revolving above them and sloughing the smoky air, thrumming so loudly in his ears it is as if hands were squeezing his head. Joshua leans close to him, puts his arm about his shoulders.

I used to think they were good, my man, he says hoarsely. I believed in their goodness. Just like God and Jesus and doing what's right for your country, no questions asked. Don't you see, my man? They're no fucking good—they ain't never been good. It's all shit. They need us for our pain. They fucking thrive on it. It's what keeps them here.

Who, Joshua? Duncan asks, alarmed; he can feel the weight of Joshua's arm tightening across his back. What are you talking about?

When Joshua speaks it is in an urgent whisper: Angels, my man. I'm talking about fucking angels.

IN THE TUNNEL beneath the sea Joshua tries to find some manner of peace, peace like he once knew in the jungles of Vietnam, in those rare moments in-country before and sometimes during a nighttime mission when he listened to the jungle breathing about him, felt it moving beneath his skin, his fingertips, vibrating like a tine through his body as he lay prostrate in the dark or as he lay upon his back, staring up at the jungle canopy and the mist through which a scattering of stars sometimes glimmered.

As he labors, his mind becomes vast and empty and the great centrifuge, which so often spins there, whooshing and thumping like a never-ending press, like the giant cranes with their drop hammers bludgeoning the piles into the bay, is suddenly silent. There is only the grunt of physical exertion: the digging, the drilling, the hammering, the shoveling, the excavation of chalk and marl spoil, the hooking and unhooking of electric tow carts, the clearing of the bore face when the giant TBMs go off track or the cutterheads seize, the realignment of the hydraulic jacks, and the meager interactions with the men who surround him through almost imperceptible nods, glances, and reflexive gestures and movements, an intricate and complex orchestration as one man fills the space of another, changing his role as each new job requires.

This, too, is familiar to him, to the way he worked with the other soldiers in his unit, who although he could rarely see them in the dark, were there with him, waiting and then moving quickly but silently into action, each fulfilling his necessary role. It is the moments before these actions that Joshua tries to hold on to, those moments of peace and the comforting silence he feels in that peace, a peace he must eventually turn toward the great emptiness that spirals inside him, growing ever larger and larger like an abyss into which he is always on the verge of falling.

Above him, above the jungle top, a meteor flares briefly as it arcs the sky and he thinks suddenly of Jamie Minkivitz—it covers the breadth of the world in seconds, hurtling on its journey across the black of space, and he blinks: This is the trajectory and the space that he feels within himself growing ever larger and expansive so that the longer he remains here, the more lost he becomes. It begins to rain, tapping the fat leaves above his head, pooling in their center and then spilling to the ground. He turns on his stomach and slithers deeper into the undergrowth, burying himself in the pulsations of the warm, heaving darkness.

In the darkness it is always Vietnam with its atrocities again, always the past, his father's brutality, his mother's leaving and her death; the way she looked at him once as his father struck her and called out his name and he turned away in fear—the darkness created in the space of her absence, of all the absences that now seems to fill him; a darkness that not even the depth of the tunnel, nor all his digging and labor, nor his love for Maggie and Duncan can affect. And gradually, even with his meds, this small manner of peace is no longer enough. He thinks of Jamie Minkivitz and his brother trying to look after him and keep him safe all the years since their father's death and knows that no matter how much he would want to, he cannot keep Maggie and Duncan safe in this world.

Gradually Joshua loses his sense of temporality: space, distance, and time come to mean nothing. His sense of the world above changes as well, so that in certain moments, when he has passed through the air locks and is ascending from the tunnel, climbing the stairs of the massive ventilation shafts, it feels as if he will never reach the surface, but merely some destination in between, and he pauses in the semi-darkness, peering up and waiting, his breath thumping loudly, amplified in the concrete chamber. He begins to dream of the sky far above him, high above the city: blue sky and startling white cloud; the slow, wide thump of a gull's hover, and in the background, almost a mile distant, up at what seems to be the farthest edge of the sky, the white jet stream of an airplane, its fuselage blinking in the sun, and beyond that, such a vast, impossible emptiness. And silence.

IT'S LATE AFTERNOON and the light in the Windsor Tap is smoky, the color of gun metal and ash, filled with hours upon hours of cigarette smoke; Duncan's eyes sting and it's as if a hazy, sheer gauze has been pulled across them—the men in the room sit on their stools or move from the pool tables to the toilets as trembling, gray chimeras moving in and out of darkness, oblivious, it seems, to the smoke.

At the farthest corner of the bar Joshua is licking the edge of a rolling paper, and when Mother sees him, she smiles. Clay waves and, laying his towel on the wood, reaches up to the shelf for Maggie's whiskey. In the dim light it takes Duncan a moment to see Joshua properly as he turns toward them and as his dark face emerges from darker shadow, but the shadows remain and Joshua suddenly seems deformed. One eye is a blood-encrusted slit, the lids swollen and enlarged. Beneath the closed eyelid his eyeball moves back and forth blindly; his long eyelashes flutter.

His good eye stares at them, bright and fierce from shimmering

303

dark skin. His cheek and the side of his neck look as if he has been struck repeatedly by a mallet, black and purple where the blood has congealed just beneath the skin. Joshua tries to smile but only one side of his mouth seems to be working.

It looks worse than it is, he says slowly, tenderly shaping his lips as if even this small movement hurts. Looking at him, Duncan is amazed that he can talk at all.

Joshua, Maggie begins, but can say no more. She stares at his face, her eyes following the damage along his cheekbones and jaw, the swollen tissue above the ridge of his brow, the splice of skin at the bridge of his nose that exposes the pink and raw skin beneath, and the edge of his mouth where his lips have been torn. Her hands reach out for him, trembling tentatively at either side of his head, wanting to touch him and afraid to—his face looks bloated and swollen with blood—and then her hands fall back to her sides.

Really, Maggie. The VA patched me up. I've got cotton in my mouth. It makes it look much worse.

Joshua reaches into his mouth and pulls out, one after the other, four dark, blood-soaked cotton balls, and throws them into the trash barrel behind the bar: The cotton matting slaps the plastic bag wetly, and leaves behind black smears at the top of the barrel's insides.

He runs his tongue about the insides of his mouth, spits brown, rust-colored saliva into an empty glass at his side, and takes a large swig from his beer bottle. The lacquered bar top glows faintly. At the back of the bar, above the cash register where the flies congregate, the motor of a yellowed and greasy electric sign for Dockyard Ale drones as it unfolds and loops a rolling holographic picture of a waterfall cascading down a mountaintop into a shimmering blue pool. Joshua's rolled cigarette sits wrinkled and fat on the wood, twitching slightly from the tapping of his fingertips to some melody sounding in his head.

Who did this to you?

It's nothing Maggie. No one did anything to me.

Who did this? Is it someone from this bar? Is it because of you and me? Is that why?

Maggie. I'm a grown man. I can take care of myself. He laughs—a bright, forced sound. You should see the other cat. Man! I fucked him up!

Mother looks to Clay as he slides the glass of Old Mainline across the bar. Who did this, Clay? Who did this to him?

Clay steps against the back of the bar, his round stomach distended, and raises his hands in an expression of utter helplessness. He shakes his head. Beats me, Mags. I know nothing about it and this shit-for-brains won't tell me. I'm as angry as you are.

Well, doesn't anyone care? Has anyone called the police?

Maggie, Maggie, Maggie, Joshua says softly, and it is the voice Duncan hears when he sings. Please, sit down. You and Duncan, sit down. I'm too tired to get into it right now. I just want to have a quiet drink and be with my two favorite people. Please, just sit down.

Mother refuses to look at him and instead stares hard at Clay and, after a moment, something seems to pass between them.

He's good, isn't he, Clay? He has all the answers in the world.

Clay nods. All the answers, Mags. All the answers.

And what do you do with a man like that?

Clay takes his bar towel and throws it over his shoulder, raises his hands helplessly again, and shakes his head as he makes his way down the bar to a customer at the far end who is tapping his bottle aggressively against the countertop. Beats me, Mags, he says and looks back toward Joshua, who is sitting clench-lipped and sweating even though the room is cold. I'm just a freaking bartender. What the fuck do I know?

BEFORE MAGGIE'S SHIFT at St. Luke's, she drags Duncan to Mass at St. Mary of the Wharves, and they sit for Vespers in the dark pews smelling of linseed and wood soap and the stale sweat of old women, and they pray. Duncan closes his eyes and tries to offer up words to God but can only see Joshua's mangled face, swollen and purple and bloodied. Beside him Mother's mouth moves fervently, almost desperately in prayer. Unable to sit any longer, he stands, upsetting the kneeler, which bangs loudly against the pew, and walks to the rear of the church, where he begins the Stations of the Cross. After Vespers, Maggie blesses herself and, when she sees Duncan standing at the font watching, she comes and kneels before him and softly touches his brow, heart, his left shoulder and then his right, with something like desperation. Before she stands, she places her hand back upon his heart and closes her eyes, and her hand rests there in recognition of His sacrifice.

You're scared for Joshua, Duncan says.

His mother stares into his eyes as if she is attempting to see what he sees. Her first impulse is to lie, but they are in a church and she has just prayed. He thinks that she'll begin to cry but she doesn't. Her lips press firmly together; her jaws bunch as she grinds her back teeth. Yes, she finally says, I'm scared for him.

As they exit the church, she looks back at the portrait of the Savior in the clerestory, at the artist's rendition of the Lord nobly displaying his pierced and bleeding heart. Duncan wonders what his mother sees in it, if she sees the pain and suffering, the pain and humiliation, some manner of salvation and blessed protection for Joshua, some promise of illumination or reward in His Kingdom or simply the hope of better things to come.

At home Joshua is sitting at the kitchen table with the *Chronicle* spread open to the article about Jamie Minkiwitz and the mangled bullet from his childhood rolling slowly in and out of his callused fingers, twining over and under, seen and unseen. A cigarette smolders at the edge of the page, burning the Formica.

Joshua, Duncan asks. Are you okay?

Okay? Joshua says, as if he has never been asked this question, and stares at the bullet. Duncan has seen him do this before, when he's overmedicated or when the meds have simply stopped working, and Duncan fears that he is losing him again.

Joshua's mouth works and the words come hoarse and as soft as a whisper: They say it was a suicide. It wasn't any fucking suicide.

Duncan nods and sits down beside him. Minutes pass, and because Joshua says nothing more and darkness is pressing against the windows and in the amber glow of the kitchen's single lamp they cannot see their reflections in the dark glass and everything beyond seems to be pressing in at them and Duncan feels the need to hear his voice, he asks him again: Joshua, are you sure you're okay?

Okay? Joshua says and shakes his head and stares at the mangled bullet he is rolling over and over in his callused hands, its copper and zinc gilding sparking like a tinder flint in the dim light of the kitchen and he begins to rub his thumb along its foreshortened shank, burnished umber by years of such friction, and Duncan reaches for his hands and holds them until the bullet is still and Joshua is here with him again.

Joshua's eyes flutter as if he is waking and he looks at Duncan. I have to go, he says suddenly, urgently. My man, I have to go. And he rises, clambers from the table, which shudders violently, and stomps toward the door. A moment later Duncan hears the engine of the Indian turning over, rumbling into loud life, and then Joshua roaring down the hill toward the Bottoms.

May 1985

TONIGHT, HIS MOTHER'S face is the moon, as he remembers her above Stockholdt, the night he ran away from the Home with Billy: shining beatifically, casting her white light into his room so brightly that he cannot sleep. The trees outside his window stretch and bend black upon the wall—dark shapes of men running crouched through tall whispering grass—and he thinks of Joshua, who has yet to come home and who, he knows, has returned to the boardinghouse in Oakland.

In his room across the bay, Joshua is dreaming again of angels lifting him up through the wreckage of the tunnel as it collapses a quarter of a mile beneath the sea, lifting him up through the black, rushing waters crashing so hard down upon him that they are like iron beams shattering his bones, and finally bursting into the dark skies over San Francisco, dangling exhausted and broken, and very near death, but such a welcome death, with the angel's wide wings beating the air above him as they rise higher and higher still.

Below them a derrick tower collapses in a grinding scream of twisted metal into the churning waters, and Joshua's sodden clothing clinging in tatters to him is suddenly engulfed in heat as flames burst and billow in orange blossoms upon the oil-black sea.

It's a miracle, Joshua says, eyes fluttering now and clouding in pain, and there is the face of the fry cook looking down at him, pale and shimmering wetly between the dark V of outspread wings.

Didn't believe I was an angel, did you? He shakes his head. I told you it would hurt, didn't I?

Up they sweep into the churning strata of clouds above the bay, Joshua glancing wearily back at the city, its blinking lights growing dim and farther and farther distant below them until he is engulfed in cloud. Joshua's head lolls upon his chest as merciful darkness takes him and the fry cook carries him higher and higher into the ether and to the place of his dreams, where he has so often prayed that nothing be allowed to harm him and his loved ones ever again.

From Duncan's mother's room the startling loud clatter of an empty bottle of Old Mainline 454 striking the floor and then rolling upon the wood. He sees her outstretched hand and her mouth parting in sleep. There is a mumbled accusation or prayer and then her snores and Duncan stares at the moonlit walls searching for and trying to retrieve some tender image of her face.

HIGH ON A four-day binge at the Windsor Tap, Joshua grabs Duncan by his jacket sleeve and pulls him close, tells him that he loves him and Maggie. His gaunt face is bruised. Swollen flesh and broken blood vessels pool darkly beneath his skin.

Your face, Duncan says, but Joshua shakes his head and takes Duncan's hands in his and tells him that there isn't another woman in the world like Maggie Bright and he's going to ask her to marry him. His eyes blaze with passion; his forehead gleams with sweat. Duncan looks down and sees the raw pink, blood-encrusted skin upon Joshua's knuckles.

Do you believe it, my man? he asks, and Duncan nods, does his best bug eyes, stretching them as wide and as incredulously as Joshua's, even though he is on the verge of crying—What has Joshua done to himself? Who has done this to him? Duncan fights against the tears and the fear that threatens to overwhelm him, and Joshua looks at the clock over the bar, puts back his beer, and slams the empty upon the table. Goddamn it! I've got to get to work, he says. I've got to get to work.

And then he is gone, stumbling out the back door of the bar and into the dark alley, as if Duncan were not there, and Duncan supposes that now he will not see him for a week or more. On the table before Duncan sit two empty tequila glasses, lime rinds folded in their centers, a glass of frothy beer and a bottle of Oakland Depot, the gin that Clay sold to the down-and-outs, mostly homeless vets who moved from one shelter or hospice to another.

When Duncan looks up, Clay has placed a cheeseburger before him and is taking the glasses from the table. You all right, Duncan? You want me to call Maggie?

Duncan shakes his head, wipes at his eyes with the back of his jacket, and begins to shovel the burger into his mouth so that he will not have to talk.

Clay looks at the bottle of Oakland Depot in his hand and grunts. No one else will buy this stuff, he says. I've got crates and crates of it in the basement stacked against the wall of the old coal chute bunker. It came with the place when I bought it after the war. Must've been there for at least a decade before that, because the distillery from across the bay closed in the early sixties, when I was fourteen. Something else.

What's wrong with Joshua? Duncan finally manages through a mouthful of bun.

I don't know, Duncan. I wish I did, but even if I did, I doubt I could make it right.

Clay's words trouble Duncan. Was Joshua so damaged that he was incapable of being saved? And if he couldn't be saved, redeemed, what did that mean for Mother and him?

But what about my mom? Duncan says. What about Joshua saying he's going to marry her?

Clay purses his lips, wrings the bar towel in his hands. Color seeps into his thick, benevolent face, and he swallows. Son, that's just what it takes with these guys. A good woman, and your mother is the best. He nods as if he can convince the both of them. If anyone can turn Joshua around, it's your mother. Don't you worry about that.

Clay looks about the room, at the brick walls, the greasy, smoke-stained wallpaper and paneling, the few grizzled men in the booths and on stools, a drunk stumbling, sliding from his stool at the far end of the bar where two men are loudly swearing at each other, and another tottering to the toilets.

The bar is no fucking place for a kid, he says softly. I should call goddamn social services.

He blinks as if taking it all in—the sight and the stink of it, and pushes out his lips as if to rid himself of something foul-tasting. He wipes at his eyes and sighs. I'll call Maggie, he says. It's time you were home.

THERE IS A full moon and Duncan climbs to the rooftop to see it better. Back in the Home he would merely have to look from his window and the open plain would lay the whole sky before him. This time of year the farmers of the pasture country would have laid rills of silage upon their fields. The scent of it would come to the children in the mornings, when they stepped from the main house and walked the courtyard to the chapel. Perhaps snow has fallen during the night, and the wind pushes it in now in drifts among the alleys between the buildings as their footfalls clatter on stone swept clean by one of the novitiates at dawn; the snow covers the plough ridge and hangs in heavy frozen lumps from the tops of the pine and yellow rod, and if he could see the distant Iron Range through the low, churning storm clouds, he would see snow on its top as well.

From this height upon Ipswich Hill, the moon's bright reflected light illuminates the city's skyscape, throwing other roofs, with their chimneys, exhausts and fans, pigeon coops and transplanted garden sheds and rainwater barrels, into stark black, sharply outlined relief. Planes coming in from the west emerge from the darkness over the bay like suddenly materializing stars, blinking into shimmering, unsure life. A satellite, flashing from a mile above, curves over the arc of the world in its lonely trajectory and Duncan thinks of Michael Collins in his lonely vigil aboard the command module, circling the moon and, as his orbit decays, falling slowly through space, and though his mouth is opening and closing, he is falling without sound. He thinks of angels lifting Jamie Minkivitz high above the bay and then dropping him only, it is no longer Jamie but Joshua instead, for he can put no other face to the man falling from the sky.

He hears the screen door creak open behind him, soft footsteps upon wood and then upon tar, and mother's voice: Are you counting the stars, Duncan?

She carries two blankets and she lays one over his shoulders, squeezes him tight, and steps away to look out over the city.

My, it's beautiful, she says. No wonder you come up here.

I couldn't sleep, he says, but his heart tightens with sudden anxiety that he cannot explain and a strange hollowness like a vacuum of air hardens in his gut as if he, too, is falling and he doesn't trust that his mother will catch him. He searches the air about them for the scent of liquor, for the heat of it on her breath.

As if reading his thoughts, she says: I'm trying.

I know.

Well? I've been good, haven't I?

Yes, he says, and then adds grudgingly and because she's waiting to hear him say it: You've been good. He wants to smile, wants to let her know that he believes in her, but in this moment he can't, even though he knows it is such a simple thing and perhaps what she most needs to hear.

His mother nods and stares at the houses and apartment buildings teetering upon the hill, at the lit windows through which the figures of people, crouched and bent or talking into phones or to one another, are still visible, even at this late hour. Some with the curtains pulled and others black shapes moving restlessly behind their vinyl shades, through which the pale yellow light from interior lamps spills.

Ahh, Maggie says. Half the people in this city can't sleep. Look at all those windows and imagine the people within, staring from the darkness, just like you. They're looking up at the stars and feeling nothing but their own emptiness and their own fear of being alone. I feel it all the time, but I feel it a little less knowing that I have you here with me.

That's true?

Of course it's true. You don't believe me?

I thought God wanted me to do something special. I thought that was why he'd spoken to me when I was born. I thought that was why I was here with you. I dreamed of you and you came. I thought I was special.

You don't hear God speaking to you now?

Duncan shakes his head.

Sweetie, she says as she takes his hands, places them between her own and blows on them. He hasn't gone anywhere. And neither have I. Why are you so far away tonight?

I can't hear him, he says.

His mother's eyes widen in sympathy, eyebrows arching. Perhaps he is talking to you, my Duncan, but perhaps you're just not listening.

Duncan nods but he knows his mother doesn't understand. He thinks of her loneliness and her fear of being alone and the bottle of Old Mainline that she often brings to bed with her and the songs and photographs and memories and ghosts that occupy those nights long after he is asleep. He wonders if his being here perhaps reminds her of everything that is lost to her.

He imagines his mother dying alone and her body being found days later. It will be winter and cold, because the gas company will have shut off the heat, and she will be perfectly preserved, as beautiful and frozen as she appeared in his dreams, emerging through the white gales of a blizzard and standing before the wreck of the Festival of Lights Holiday Train. She will be wearing her finest gown, the one in which she performed before thousands at the Boston's Symphony Hall. He imagines that he will have forsaken her—although he doesn't know why this would be—and that, like the Soap Woman, she will be abandoned at the End, tragically alone and with no one to share or evoke her life, carrying a mute undistinguished history of loss and grief to the grave.

A seizure of some kind they might say after, and he can hear Father Toibin explaining it: A blood vessel burst high up near her eye, Duncan. So small it was almost undetectable. Such a little thing, Duncan. No one could have known or have done anything about it. Or: Poison in her blood. It was the drink, you see. And your mother did like to drink, didn't she? Her liver stopped working and, well, her belly filled up with poison and made everything hard as stone. It's the disease of alcoholics. When they cut her swollen belly open, they found her liver enlarged and speckled and pockmarked by cirrhosis.

Truly, Father Toibin will say, it reminds us of the fragility of the human body—no matter how beautiful and strong this shell is, it is a fragile thing, a transient thing—and the power and permanence and perfection of the soul. Your mother is with God in His Kingdom now.

And Duncan will think of how strong his mother was. He won't believe that there was one weak spot in her. He will tell Father Toibin that he doesn't believe mother's blood leaked slowly away because something could no longer hold or that her stomach bloated with poison and that her drinking killed her. If she died, it was because her heart wouldn't quit. It burst from pumping so hard for so long. It could do nothing else. Duncan will tell him that she was strong before she ever came to the Home to claim him, that he's the one who made her fragile, who made her weak. And that he's the type of son that would leave his mother to die alone.

His mother laughs suddenly, surprising him, and then laughs even harder, and pulls the blanket more tightly about them. Jutting her chin out toward the night like some determined and obstinate astronomer checking the readings of her astrolabe with the celestial, it's as if she, too, can now almost see what lies above and before them and as if she is determined to discover it, to see beyond her ability to see. And Duncan watches her eyes, the manner in which various sources of meager light from the surroundings buildings and streets refract and spark in the dark of her large pupils like a devastating collision of stars.

Remember, Duncan . . .

Remember what?

You dreamed I came for you.

Yes.

And then I did come, didn't I?

IN THE TUNNEL Joshua turns to find Buzz Aldrin and Neil Armstrong working next to him, having taken the place of his co-workers. Shambling awkwardly in their thick Mylar suits. Faces glistening with sweat. Mist steaming along the floor of the drill. Ahead, St. Dymphna is seized in the rock.

Joshua blinks sweat from his eyelashes. It was all a sham, he says to them. None of it was real.

That's what you think, Aldrin says, grunting, shoveling sludge and rubble onto a black dump truck last used in the days of the gold rush. We sent men up on missions no one has even heard about. They're still out there. They never came back. If it was all fake, why would this be secret?

Go fuck yourself!

Aldrin squints at mica in the rock, pokes at it with a gloved finger. Tell that to Collins. He's still up there.

Armstrong seems intent at prying something from the far wall with an ancient forty-niners pickax, and Joshua momentarily considers asking him where he found such a thing. When the hole is large enough, Armstrong drops the ax with a clang onto the rail ties and prods at the hole with his geospectrum analyzer. Its frenetic ticking charges the air with tension, as if a flame had suddenly burst from the device and alighted upon rills of oil. Joshua wants to ask him what the hell's he's doing. Armstrong reads the instrument's gauge, looks toward Aldrin, and nods grimly. He switches the machine off and the three of them stare at one another in the silence.

I don't believe it, Joshua says. You and the fucking angels. I don't believe any of it. In his head he sees Jamie Minkivitz struggling and fighting even as he is pulled by emaciated yet incredibly strong, sinuous arms high above the clouds.

Aldrin purses his lips and shakes his head; Armstrong sighs, deep and mournful. We hear them every night, Armstrong says. Tune your radio in. You'll hear them too.

Hear who? Who the fuck do you hear?

Them. Michael and the others. Listen for yourself if you don't believe us. Jamie heard them, and so will you. You'll see.

June 1985

THE CLOCK OVER the bar seems frozen, its hour hand trembling yet never advancing forward, even as its ticking resounds in the almost-empty room. Outside it is near dusk; a bright red sun sinking into the bay has set the alleys alight with flame and sharpened the black outlines of rooftops and cars parked along the street. Absent of a record, the turntable within the jukebox spins silently and vacantly. There is the sound of pool cues striking balls, of the clatter of beer glasses, of men hacking phlegm in the bathroom, and of flushing toilets and water splashing loudly upon porcelain.

Joshua stumbles from his stool as he goes to stand and when Clay eyes him, Joshua reaches down to massage his thigh, places on arm on Duncan's shoulder for balance, and swings the leg back and forth, wincing as he does so, showing Clay the manner it which the leg has failed him and that he is not inebriated, but Duncan knows better.

You taking the bike, tonight? Clay asks without looking up. He

321

squints into the glass he has just wiped with the bar towel. But Joshua ignores him.

I have to go now, he says to Duncan, and Duncan feels the sour heat of his breath on his face. Your mother gets off her shift in half an hour. Do you want me to give you a ride home or do you want to wait for her here?

Where are you going?

I have a meeting over at the VA.

Clay glances at the clock upon the wall. At this time?

Duncan shrugs and looks away. I can wait, he says.

All right, my man. Later then.

Once Joshua is out the door, Duncan steps down from the bar.

You leaving too? Clay says. I thought you were waiting for your mom.

Nah. I'll head home.

Suit yourself, kid.

Duncan reaches his Raleigh and is pedaling hard down the avenue when Joshua's Indian rumbles past, and Duncan follows as close as he can, praying that the lights at each intersection will be against them. Farther and farther they travel, with Duncan pedaling as fast as he can, down through Potrero Hill and the Mission, and the back of Joshua's green field jacket at the farthest edges of his sight, and always in danger of disappearing entirely. Duncan watches it bobbing and diminishing as the Indian rumbles ahead, weaves in and out of honking and screeching traffic, darkening twilit shapes of flashing metal from within which the shadowed faces of drivers emerge, glaring intently or open-mouthed, and spewing curses with sudden and startling violence, and then Joshua is gone. Duncan pauses on his bike, gasping for breath, sweat soaking through his shirt and turning his skin cold. He is aware of the traffic lights changing from green to red and back again and the last of the sun flickering red and molten in the spaces between buildings but stares toward the distant, shimmering, ghostlike impression of Joshua that remains before his eyes with only the vaguest suggestion of where he has disappeared to.

He pulls his bike to the curb, lets it clatter on the concrete. He considers the long ride back to the Windsor Tap and, farther, to Ipswich Street and the Bottoms, and everything is suddenly pulling at him so that he has to struggle not to give in to it and cry. A door bangs open and a man, squinting like a burrowing animal breaking through the earth into sunlight, steps out from a bar, a narrow black railcar of a room visible at his back. The door closes slowly and the man makes his way up the street and Duncan is left staring after him.

He feels the dull, heavy thump of his heart in his chest, the wet suck of his lungs, and tiny electric currents coursing along his arms, just as he felt the day he, Magdalene, and Mother stood beneath the exploding transformers of the Edison plant, protected as they were beneath the cusp of some great hand; and when he looked above Stockholdt and saw his mother's face swimming in the moon and when Father Toibin informed him that she was coming for him and would finally take him from the Home; and on that fateful day when the television screen showed the black-and-white images of the long-dead astronauts walking upon the lunar surface. *De profundis clamavi ad te, Domine,* he whispers. *Apud Dominum misericordia, et copiosa apud eum redemptio.*

Pedestrians pause momentarily on the street as they pass him, perplexed or strangely fascinated by him perhaps, this slack-jawed, gape-mouthed boy staring so fixedly at the curbstones, the alleyway walls, and the storefronts, and even gawking now and then at the throngs pressing and pushing about him. The air feels charged about him; it grasps at him as he moves forward, and through it, and as he clambers onto his bike and out into the stream of traffic once more.

The spokes of Duncan's wheels tick loudly amongst the abandoned canneries and warehouses along Oakland's decrepit waterfront. It is a vast, labyrinthine corridor of dead and vacant industry: sawmills, tanneries, slaughterhouses, stockyards, dairies, a jute mill, a flour mill, dry docks, and a brewery with the original company names faded upon their weather-beaten exteriors: California Cotton, Joseph Rusk Canning Factory, Lowell Manufacturing, Triton Carriage Works. From an ancient, crumbling loading dock, a rail tie stretches to the black water and then disappears, and Duncan pauses as he looks at it.

In the gloom, at an angle of the dock, Joshua's Indian sits upon its kickstand, and there, parked away from the road and hidden in the shadows of the warehouse, late-model cars, and rusted pickups, is a gleaming blue Continental.

A fluttering of wings and Duncan looks up. From a window at the top of the building, pigeons crowd and press, cooing quietly as the sun sinks into the bay, turns the surface of the oily black water orange, burns red on the buildings' white corrugated tin, and bathes the birds in a soft fiery warmth.

He clambers up a rusted fire escape to the top floor of the building, the metal flaking away in his hands, and then, with the pigeons parting on either side of him, unbothered by his presence, climbs through a small window covered by shattered boards black with rot and hardened bird shit to a catwalk girder that stretches the length of the building. The sound of men shouting comes to him, reverberating off the tin. The room below is a wide wooden barn, perhaps used to store linens or wools at the turn of the century. There are marks upon the concrete where ancient wide looms once lay bolted to the floor. Large roof fans, their cases encrusted with stalactites of pigeon shit, turn slowly over his head. The heat at the top of the building makes him feel light-headed; the odor of dried shit mugs his head and he has difficulty breathing.

Below him a crowd of men arranged in a loose circle are shouting and pushing and he moves farther out onto the catwalk to get a better view. The dock's doors are open and late sunlight spills in across the floor of the warehouse and, beyond, he can see it dazzling and flickering upon the rippling water of the bay. Flax and wool dust spirals in heavy umber clouds in the shaft of light and then the doors are suddenly closed, a man hollers, and the warehouse is immersed in gray nether light and a furnace heat.

Industrial lights mounted atop tripods flicker into buzzing life and Duncan can see more clearly. There is a rippling movement among the throng of men, the edge of the circle parts, and Joshua is sitting there, stripped to his vest. He looks small. His long, sinewy arms are heavily veined and emaciated, the biceps clinging tight to the bone.

Breathing hard, Joshua stands, muscles quivering and body trembling with adrenaline, and though he should feel fear, he feels nothing at all. In his head the great thump of the compressors and the rumbling thrum of the TBMs, the muted roar of the cutter face shearing rock, the pistoning of hand and arm as he and Jamie bolt the connecting rings, and all this sound filling the silent, dead space within him.

He holds his face up to the rafters and for a moment Duncan is convinced that he can see him, but his eyes are closed as if he is praying. Sweat trickles down his gaunt face. The scar across his neck shines black against his dark skin.

The far edge of the circle parts and another man steps forward and with sudden movement he and Joshua are on each other. In the greasy, smoky light they seem to move as wraiths, hazy vapors swirling about each other and then suddenly and startlingly through which muscle and sinew seems to suddenly thrust, pummeling and bludgeoning each other as if their fists were sledgehammers as they move back and forth across the floor and into the center, where the industrial lights catch them in their harsh glare.

As the crowd shouts and swarms and pushes, Joshua and the other man grapple and punch and drive each other onto the dirt floor, and then rise and do it again. There is struggling movement, flailing arms, and then only Joshua rises. He sways and waits. The other man is helped up and taken off the floor and someone hollers: Five minutes! and Joshua staggers toward the wall where a chair waits, the crowd stepping back and allowing him a wide passage. He sits, drapes his field jacket over his shoulders, and lowers his head.

On the concrete, blood and dirt pool together. Two more men are taken off the floor. Fists shatter against jawbones and skulls and men stumble and fall, clutching themselves. They mewl and howl like wounded animals or scream and sob like children, and then there is Joshua, who, bloodied and damaged, seems more dead than alive and, aside from his grunts of exertion, utters no sound at all. And outside night has come down.

When Joshua's name is called, he stands slowly, places the jacket over the back of the chair, and walks to the center of the room. This time the crowd has already parted for him and is momentarily silent. The second man is shirtless and pale and young with long, lank orange hair. When Joshua knocks him to the ground, the hair fans the ground about his head and Duncan doesn't think that he'll get up again, but he does briefly. When he crawls blindly on his hands and knees toward the circle, Joshua waves him away, stumbles to his stool, and waits for his next fight.

In the rafters pigeons coo and thrum, sometimes stirring their wings, seemingly unbothered by the violence below, the grunts and squeals, the wet-smack of fists sliding off slick, bloodied skin, the crunch when a fighter breaks his hand or a nose, a jaw, or when a man's entire face seems to disintegrate beneath another man's fist, buckling inward for a moment and then shattering about the cheekbone, nose, and eye, blood spouting from his nostrils in two thin jets.

It is Joshua's turn again and he rises shakily from his chair, moves slowly into the center of the room. Sweat glistens on his arms, soaks his vest. Blood has hardened on his nose and mouth. The men part again and another man steps forward. He is bald, his brow deeply furrowed with ridges of scar. Military tattoos ink his two shoulders like shields and encase his large biceps and forearms in a complex scrollwork. Joshua seems incredibly small before him, and Duncan thinks: *Please God, let this be the last one, let this be the last one. Joshua's going to die.*

His stomach roils and he closes his eyes to the sound of Joshua and the man striking each other. When he looks again, Joshua lies sprawled upon his back, his face and chest drenched in blood. The muscled, bald man strides toward him and the shouts and hollers of the men grow. The man reaches down, grasps Joshua by his ears, pulls his bloodied face toward him, regards him as if he is about to ask a question, as if he is looking for something in his expression that he might recognize, and then he drives his fist like a pile driver once, twice, three, four times into his face—Joshua's head rocks back and forth and then the man lets him go and Joshua's head falls back to the floor.

The other man waits at the edge of the crowd, hands on his knees, doubled over and breathing deeply. When he sees Joshua attempt to move, he comes forward and kicks him squarely in the face, as if he's punting a football, and Joshua feels his jaw dislodge and teeth splinter and come free of his gums.

He lies there gasping for air, feeling the warmth of blood seeping out of him, from his mouth, his nose, his eye socket, and out of his ear cavity and the ruined flap of his ear. His body seems to scream when he tries to move; he breathes in slowly and knows that his ribs are busted. He reaches down to cradle his swollen testicles and with the touch pain and light flicker in his head and he thinks he will pass out.

He hears Duncan's shouting, calling for him over the din of the other men, and at first he thinks he must be imagining it. Sound is dimming and with it the heart of his rage. And in a moment he is too tired to care; he is cradled by the strange comfort that is pain.

To Duncan the crowd is a great mass of squealing and crying, of retching and swearing. The sound rises up and fills the warehouse as if it is a bowl of sound, each squeal and scream and retch and curse

327

and slur caught like a visceral echo of history amongst and within its metal clapping, wooden joists, iron beams, and studded sheet metal; and the great fans, revolving slowly above Duncan's head, pull up these sounds and emotions and the terrible pain within them, turn them in the tumid, charged air above their heads, hold them there for one great inexpressible moment so that the din of suffering is an indescribable and uncontainable sonic thrum. Duncan clamps his hands upon his ears and falls to the ground, and then with a great thrush of rushing movement, he feels it all cast out into the night above Oakland and the bay and farther above San Francisco, where the stars glitter bright and low and a satellite circling the earth blinks at the farthest edges of the night.

AT HOME MAGGIE insists that Joshua empty out his pockets and then asks what meds he is currently on. Joshua sags against the table, sips from his mug, and then slowly tries to light a cigarette, but his fingers seem incapable of doing the work. Duncan stares at the knots of swollen tissue on Joshua's knuckles and at the hardened blood there and reaches over to help him, and Joshua laughs suddenly when they succeed in lighting the cigarette together. After he exhales, he picks tobacco pulp from his lip and says: Doxepin, prazosin, topiramate, propranolol, and lithium, Maggie.

Nothing else? Mother asks, and when Joshua says no, she nods. From her time at St. Luke's, Duncan knows she's seen plenty of her friends and patients OD or slip into comas after taking otherwise harmless drugs in lethal combinations. As she often tells him: If ever I die, it won't be because I'm a fool. But of course she never says this when she is drinking. He listens to her rummaging through the medicine cabinet in the bathroom, and then she returns with gauze, tape, antiseptic, Neosporin, and a brown pill container, which she places on the table. She takes Joshua's vials and, after studying the labels, hands one back.

I'll give you these two back after you've slept, she says. Tonight's it's Percocet and propranolol for you. Mother undoes the tops of the vials and pushes four pills across the table. Asks Duncan to run the sink faucet and pour Joshua a glass of water. Together Duncan and she watch as Joshua takes the pills. He lays his head back, and his dark, hairless Adam's apple bobs as the glass empties, and Duncan has to look away from the narrow loop of scar tissue that stretches from ear to ear and that seems to stretch wider, baring itself, as Joshua swallows. Duncan glances toward his mother but she refuses to look at him.

When Joshua is done, Mother heats some water and begins to clean Joshua's hands and face. Duncan watches as Joshua closes his eyes and she moves the washcloth tenderly over his skin, wincing as she feels the swollen tissue and as she dislodges hardened blood. Under her breath she begins to sing, and it takes Duncan a moment to realize that it is the same song she sings to him during his nightmares, when she holds her hand upon his heart in an effort to calm him and to remind him of the physical world of which he is a part, that they both share together, and that nothing of the world outside this can harm him.

She kneels by Joshua's chair, reaches up and takes his face in her hands, holds the sides of his face tenderly as if she might hurt him here too, as if this is the only place she can touch him without pain.

Please, J. Don't do this anymore. Don't do this. Promise me that you won't. If not for yourself, then for me and for Duncan. And then Mother surprises Duncan by what she says next: I need you. I need you to be here for me. I love you.

Joshua lowers his head. The black whorl of hair there reminds Duncan of a child's and only the full, splayed ears, one mushroomed and slightly swollen, its top split in two and raw-looking, suggests that a man is sitting before them.

Please, Mother continues. Promise me you won't do this. But Joshua doesn't answer and finally she rises from her knees and Duncan stares at the pink, patterned designs the linoleum has shaped upon the skin there.

Good, she says. I'm holding you to it. And don't you dare forget. She looks to Duncan, tries to smile but fails, and comes to him, kisses the top of his head. You need to go to bed, she whispers. It's been a long night. Don't worry about Joshua. He'll be fine, okay?

He sees the doubt in her eyes but he nods, watches her take Joshua's hand and lead him to the bathroom. Joshua sits on the toilet, head bowed, eyes flickering open and closed, head snapping back every few moments as if he is struggling to stay awake, his shirt open as mother washes his chest and the thin, sharp angles of his stomach with a warm, soapy washcloth. In the weak yellow glow of the bare lightbulb dangling over their heads, Duncan watches how she attends to his wounds, patting him dry and then applying a salve from the medicine cabinet. He watches for a moment from the door and then treads to his bedroom softly so as not to disturb them.

Mother puts Joshua to bed and through the night Duncan looks in on him, moonlight temporarily washing his swollen face clean of pain. Discolored lumps make his face look misshapen and strangely disfigured—beneath the white sheets he might have been laid in state—but then he sighs and his mouth parts slightly as if he is about to speak and then closes again. The room grows bright with moonlight so that even in the dark Duncan can see him, hear his breathing at times rattling and gasping in his throat as if some unseen damage has been done to the insides of him, damage to his heart and lungs, to his liver and spleen. Anxiously Duncan treads the landing to his mother's bedroom throughout the night, fearful that each time he will no longer hear Joshua breathing, that something within him will burst and spill silently through him. That he will die in his sleep unaware that people who loved him are at his side. That he is not alone. That he has only to call out and they will be there. For a while Duncan crouches in the hallway, squats on the cold linoleum with his back against the wall, watching over Joshua in the way that he had with Billy all those nights when he was in the most pain or distress.

Yet every time Duncan checks in on Joshua, from the doorway, he still looks strong and the beating to his face doesn't change this—it makes him look even stronger, as if, despite the brutal violence and damage, the outward sign of such violence reveals how little could actually affect him. That other men could never really touch him or hurt him—the place where pain remained was a place so deep no one could reach it—and that he needed nothing and nobody.

Duncan thinks of the way Joshua had led him though the throng of men in the warehouse and the way they'd parted for them, and how they'd sped home on his motorcycle through the derelict neighborhood and along the waterfront and over the bridge and home to Mother as if Duncan's life depended upon it, as if Duncan mattered and as if he cared about what happened to him. How Joshua had protected him and kept him from harm. Now, staring at him asleep in Mother's bed, Duncan suddenly wishes that he were the man he might call Father and that in the morning he would search Duncan out, look for him, and pull him to him, and that come evening, another night would pass with him beneath their roof and this is the way it would continue until they no longer knew anything else or remembered anything other.

Joshua sleeps through that night, and through the next day. Around dusk he stirs on Mother's bed and Duncan listens as the bedsprings creak and he knows that Joshua is taking in his surroundings, staring at the walls, the ceiling, at the strange light coming in over the bay. Duncan wonders if Joshua knows where he is—he is motionless for a long time—and then Duncan hears him sitting upright and swinging his long legs over the edge of the mattress. He listens to his bare feet padding the wood and the slow, struggling stream of urine as it sputters in the porcelain and then the flush of the toilet tank beyond the bathroom door.

It's a little after dusk and St. Mary of the Wharves is tolling her bells for evening service. Joshua has come down to the kitchen and sits, bewildered and groggy, at the table sipping his coffee.

We made it, he says wearily, but it seems more a question, and Duncan nods.

Do you remember last night? Duncan asks. Do you remember bringing me home?

Joshua laughs, but it comes up through his throat like a painful bark and he winces as he swallows. Did you steer?

ON THE MIDNIGHT tunnel shift, amidst the grind and bore of the TBMs and the pumping of the compressors and hydraulic jacks and the clatter of the conveyers carrying shale and spoil through the tunnel to the surface, comes a frantic hissing sound, and the men pause in their labors, listening to the escape of compressed air. A moment later a section of the south tunnel collapses and the sea rushes in. It comes with such force and speed that the men are swept along by it. P.J. Rollins and John Chang are shattered against the tunnel walls, Joe "Sully" Sullivan and Billy Gillepsie are hurled like human darts and pinioned misshapenly into small crevices and air ducts, and others are sucked into impossible shapes back through the breach and upward into the mud at the bottom of the bay.

The bodies are found slowly. At first twelve men and then no more after a week of digging and dredging. Another body, in an advanced state of decomposition and absent its head, is recovered on June 20.

The last five workers, Minkivitz and Jimmy Paterniti among them, are finally found huddled together in the north tunnel on June 23. Their clothes are mostly rotted away and their bones gleam as if some solvent had been rubbed across them—where Minkivitz's left eye had been a decaying fish hung limply, as if it had been caught there, wriggling out of the eye socket, when the water receded.

On June 27 the final human remains are recovered: It is the missing head, submerged in silt and slurry, and like the artifacts the tunnelers have, over time, pulled from the floor of the bay, it remains strangely preserved, so they are finally able to give one man his name: Javier Lopes.

Joshua is not among the dead. He is at home in bed, bathed in morning sunlight, with Duncan sitting upon the edge of the mattress spooning cereal in a bowl, when they receive the news, the damp washcloth that moments before he'd held to his bloodied eyes lying upon the sheets and wrung tightly in his hand, as he watches the television replay images from the semi-darkness before dawn, of helicopters hovering above the water, divers emerging and submerging like glistening seals in the wide oval wakes created by the helicopters' propeller, and flashing harbor rescue craft cutting wider and wider silver swathes upon the surface. Duncan looks at the screen and then to Joshua and then Maggie comes and quickly ushers Duncan from the room.

From Maggie's bedroom Joshua stares out toward the bay's perfectly flat surface, glittering with reflected sunlight, its calm undisturbed by the churning violence of the night before. Who would know that thirty men had lost their lives two hundred feet below its gray water? Cars are passing as ever over the bridge; pedestrians are laughing, their voices sounding all the more distinct on the late-summer air; workers are making their way from the Edison plant and the rail yards; and his mind rails against the sickeningly strange normalcy of it all, as in the days when he first returned from Vietnam and, he realizes, all the days since. He is floating, flying numbly above it all. He gazes down at the destruction below him as strong, talonlike hands carry him upward, and he thinks of Javier, Sully, Chang, P.J., Gillepsie, and their foreman, Charlie Minkivitz. He closes his eyes as he imagines how Jamie Minkivitz must have felt at the end, and there is a tightness in his shoulders and chest more painful than the many beatings he has taken or the wounds he received in the war, and he is powerless before it. He opens his eyes and stares desperately at everything about him, and attempts to see, to really see for the first time in over a decade, and to make sense of it all. Yet the act of it engulfs him and overwhelms him. Tears come to his eyes as he remains silent, unmoving, and stares at the heaving view of the sea beyond the bedroom window where nothing and everything has utterly changed, and he can smell the smell of it upon him still, stuck to him, a skin-deep, mucky putrescent sea smell that when he inhales makes his stomach roil. He begins to gag and retch and puts a hand to his mouth to stop the vomit from spilling onto the floor.

July 1985

IT'S SUNDAY, A pleasantly mild day, and Joshua and Duncan sit outside on the steps as the light fades. Joshua smokes a cigarette, throws it on the stone, and then lights another. He hardly touched his dinner, and even Maggie's singing couldn't soothe him. Duncan thinks that he will jump upon his bike at any moment with the need, the urge to be gone, but something seems to prevent him—perhaps it is Duncan or his mother keeping him here imprisoned, as it were, and against his will.

There is something frenetic and strangled-seeming in the way he rolls his cigarettes and in the way he looks at them, and Duncan wonders if he needs a fix, the violent physical brutality of the warehouses or the oblivion of pills. Mother has him on a more rigid schedule with his meds and hands them to him one by one at breakfast and then again at suppertime.

337

Now he is staring so hard that Duncan looks away. Why are you still wearing that crap? he says. I told you, it's all a lie.

Duncan hugs his jacket and his patches tightly and looks up at the marble sky. In his head he recites a litany: The moon is 240,000 miles away. Apollo 11 Mission Commander: Neil Armstrong. Lunar Module Pilot: Edwin "Buzz" Aldrin. Command Module Pilot: Michael Collins. Apollo 11 was carried into space by a *Saturn V* booster rocket, the most powerful rocket ever built. Reaching speeds of 24,000 miles per hour, Apollo 11 took four days to reach the moon. After thirteen lunar orbits, the lunar module *Eagle* separated from the command and service module *Columbia*. On July 20, 1969, lunar module *Eagle* touched down upon the moon's surface, and Neil Armstrong took one small step for man and one giant leap for mankind. But they never lifted off the moon and died up there. And there are other astronauts up there and his father too, and someday they would all come back—once their orbits decayed they'd blaze up in the outer atmosphere and come hurtling down like fiery angels, that is unless God wanted them at His side.

How old are you?

Almost fifteen.

Shit, you were barely born. Joshua shakes his head, frustrated. After a moment he rises and gestures for Duncan to follow him to the curb, where his Indian angles its weight against the kickstand. Look, he says, forget that crap and come here. He sits on the seat, moves the bike with his legs so it is upright, and motions for Duncan to sit before him. When Duncan struggles to get a leg over the gas tank, Joshua grabs a handful of jacket, and hoists him up. Duncan's legs kick at the air.

C'mon, get your feet over. Now rest your feet flat on the ground, jump up and down. Move from left to right, get a feel for its center of gravity.

The bike leans to the right, and Duncan feels the immense weight of it falling.

He turns to look at Joshua.

I'm here, he says, it's not going anywhere. He places Duncan's hands on the handlebars. Good. That'll do. Now watch.

He turns the key, pumps the kick start with his boot three times. Can you hear that? he says, and Duncan listens: like the sound of a small bellows wheezing. Compression, he says, not too much now, just enough to turn her over. He jumps on the kick start, the bike shudders, and the engine rumbles into loud, syncopated life.

Eighty-cubic-inch V-twin, he says, the last they made. She needs a lot of choke in cool weather, but if you're good to her, she'll treat you right. Duncan cranes his neck at him, and Joshua smiles but there are tears in his eyes. His breath shudders against Duncan's back. Duncan holds tight to the handlebars, and Joshua holds tight to Duncan's shoulders.

He places his hands over Duncan's, squeezes them until his knuckles are white, and though Duncan winces, he doesn't say a word, and Joshua revs the engine louder, and the motor turns faster and faster until it whines. Mother is coming down the stairs and she pauses and looks at Joshua warily. She carries a pot of coffee, and two ceramic mugs clutched in her hand. Joshua takes his hands from Duncan's, and the blood rushes back into Duncan's fingers; the motor settles into a choppy rumble. He tugs at Duncan's jacket, and Duncan climbs from the bike.

An Indian, my man, Joshua says, the best-built American bike ever. He strokes the black enameled gas tank then thumps the metal with his fist again and again until the metal is dented. Ye*sss*, my man. Made the last of them in the fifties, this same line, fucking Springfield, Massa-chu-setts!

Maggie places the coffeepot and cups on the stone sidewall. J, you're drunk, again. My son's not getting on that thing if you've been drinking.

Joshua shuts off the motor and continues to stare at Duncan. He climbs from the bike and pulls Duncan tight against him, and

Duncan listens to the manifolds ticking as they cool, smells Joshua's sweat, the Brilliantine in his hair, the burnt-oil smell of his clothes, and still the sea, always the sea.

Duncan, Joshua says. You trust me, don't you? Don't you? Of course you do. So don't worry, it's all cool. It's all going to be okay, my man. I promise. Then he looks at Maggie for a moment. His jaws clench and unclench. A bubble of rheum bursts from his nose. Quickly he wipes his eyes with the back of his bloodied hand and shakes his head. Mother hands him a cup of coffee.

I'm not drunk, Maggie, he says. And I haven't taken my meds in weeks. I've been flushing them down the toilet. I'm fucking alive is what I am. Fucking alive again, and it's killing me.

We wake at the self-same point of the dream—
All is here begun, and finished elsewhere.
—VICTOR HUGO

HE CONSIDERS SUICIDE, the ending of it, that simple passage to silence. Not as a giving up but as a passing on, in the way of his mother perhaps stepping off the train platform at Northampton Street of the El Orange Line in Boston on a summer evening twenty years before. From where she stood, she would have been able to see into the third-floor windows of the factories, tenements, and apartments that abutted the elevated tracks. Perhaps she stared briefly at the families who lived there—a woman smiling as she watched a child moving a fire engine–red car across a shag carpet in the center of the room—and perhaps his mother briefly considered him and his sister before she stepped forward. A passing on in the way of that angel lifting him up somewhere that he can't yet envision, but perhaps that "seeing" is part of the journey. He thinks of Javier and Minkie and John Chang and of water rushing into the tunnel and of loam and shale and marl filling their mouths and he thinks of the others drowned beneath the bay and wonders where all their souls are now, whether they are looking down on him or not, and he longs to have been with them when they died.

Jo Stafford's "There's a Kind of Hush (All Over the World)" plays through the bar's radio and Clay turns it up, so it becomes loud and tinny, the words and vocals stretching and distorting across the wide space of the empty bar flickering with Christmas lights: *There's a kind of hush all over the world tonight, all over the world you can hear the sounds of lovers in love. You know what I mean. Just the two of us and nobody else in sight, there's nobody else and I'm feeling good just holding you tight.* It's the USO performers station that Clay closes the night with. Tonight it's being broadcast from East Germany. Soon the show will end and they'll play the "Star-Spangled Banner," but the soldiers in the bar will already be gone.

Maggie leans her head on Joshua's shoulder and each seems to take the weight of the other and they lean and rock to the music, but the tempo is much too fast, the horns punchy and upbeat, and Duncan imagines the bandleader snapping his fingers, and keeping pace with the song seems to exhaust his mother and Joshua, until finally they give up and adopt their own rhythm, turning slowly, decrepitly, on the dance floor. Mother's eyes are closed. Mascara stains her eyelids and upper cheeks black. When she opens her eyes—the shocking whites of them gleaming out of those streaks of black—she stares at him and through him and he knows that she is crying.

The bar is empty now but for them and Clay pulls the mop and wash bucket from the closet and wheels it to the toilets, the plastic cast rollers squeaking across the burnished parquet. He props the bathroom door open and Duncan hears him stop, then curse—Dirty fuckers!—and begin banging with the mop around the urinals and against the stalls of the toilets, and the smell of ammonia seeps from the bathroom and out into the bar and fills Duncan's mouth and the back of his throat. He strains to hear Jo Stafford's voice, *So listen very carefully, closer now, and you will see what I mean it isn't a dream. The only sound that you will hear is when I whisper in your ear, I love you, I love you forever and ever,* and he sips from his bottle of Coke and forces himself to smile as Mother and Joshua continue to turn around and around and around and the night's cigarette smoke floats down from the ceiling now that Clay has turned off the fans and like a thin greasy haze settles upon the bar and the branches of the armed forces flags.

Clay swears and bangs his mop in a frenzy, against the stall walls and pipes, around the urinals and toilets, pushing the piss and puke spilled onto the floor into the gutters and drains, as if it is a job with no end, and the radio continues to play amidst the bar's flickering, pulsing Christmas lights, *There's a kind of hush all over the world tonight, all over the world you can hear the sounds of people in love. The swinging sounds of people in love,* and Clay hollering all the while: Goddamn, you dirty fuckers, God damn you!

August 1985

ON THE LAST night that Duncan will ever see Joshua, they leave the Windsor Tap and Joshua rides them down to the wharves and the empty lot overlooking the bay. It's a full moon and the waters seem to be lit up all the way to the bridge. In the dark places beneath the abutments, a shoal of fish spirals in shining phosphorescence. Joshua slowly smokes a cigarette, silently considers the traffic upon the bridge, the soft murmur of the waves slapping against its distant pylons and coming to them seconds later on the breeze.

Joshua shudders, then undoes his field jacket, empties the pockets into his bandanna, folds it, and places it on the seat of his bike. He drops his jeans, removes his socks, and stands there in his grayed underwear. Duncan looks at him, waiting for him to say what he's doing.

How long do you think before he comes down, Joshua says, and gestures with his head to the sky and the stars there that have seemed to suddenly emerge one by one.

Collins?

Yeah. Collins, your daddy, all the angels.

Duncan looks instinctively toward the horizon, searching for Cygnus and Andromeda at the height of the autumn sky, the next conjunction of *Columbia*'s erratic rendezvous with Earth, but the stars all seem a blur tonight and he rubs at his eyes and thinks: A hundred years, it might be a hundred years before the spaceship decays and Collins's Mylar-encased body falls like a star from its orbit.

I don't know.

Joshua nods. I keep thinking about Jamie Minkivitz, he says. I keep thinking about Javier and the others . . . my friends . . . I can't seem to stop thinking these days. He sighs, throws his cigarette butt out to the water, puts his long arms wide and something in his back cracks. He rolls his shoulders, stretches his head upon his neck. Too many thoughts, my man. A man isn't made to think so much.

He sighs. I need to go on a little recon, he says, and when he grins, his teeth flash. I won't be long. Keep the home fires burning, kiddo. His face looks lean and taut in the gray light, the skin pulled tight over his brow.

What are you doing? Duncan asks, and Joshua pauses and something comes across his face—fear? Confusion? Sadness?—and he reaches for Duncan's hand and pulls him close. My man, he says, my man. You're going to be a better man than me, a better man than your father. In a while this will all make sense to you. Just don't be angry with me, okay? You'll know that this is what I had to do, you'll know that. He squeezes Duncan hard and then lets go.

When Joshua turns, shadows play upon his back, and as he walks toward the guardrail, Duncan's throat tightens: Below large, rounded shoulders his back is scar tissue, the color of blackened meat. Joshua pads down the stones as if they are hard on the soles of his feet, and he might have been a child at the beach about to take a midsummer dip but for the arcs of the halogens, the cars humming over the metal dividers, the empty beer cans lining the wall, the smell of butane and gasoline exhaust, and his wound from the war.

Joshua eases himself over the edge and slips slowly down into the murky black. He begins stroking his way out into the bay: strong, fluid strokes that seem effortless. His skin glistens in the dark waters and then he is almost lost in it. He turns, and for a while floats on his back. He raises a hand and waves and the current carries him farther and farther out. Sound comes on the air, Joshua singing *O au o. The lights in Sai Gon are green and red, the lamps in My Tho are bright and dim. O au o.* High up and out over the bay cars hiss over the bridge; high-density sodium bulbs glitter along its length. Upon its towers airway beacons flash on and off. A foghorn blows out in the bay and the top of the water bends with shuddering parabolas of silver.

Duncan cups his hands together and shouts his name—*Joshua!*—once, twice, and a third time, but there is no reply. He climbs over the guardrail, races up and down the embankment, stumbling and slipping on the slick shale, hollering Joshua, Joshua, Joshua, and tears of panic come streaming down his cheeks and still Joshua does not call back to him. The waters lie unbroken but for the sharp black edges of the towers emerging from the strait, as beneath the far bridge everything churns relentlessly toward the Pacific.

On Joshua's bike seat, wrapped in the center folds of his greasy bandanna, he has left behind the mangled bullet that had been shot through his family's home in Brighton and six medals. Beneath the halogens, the tarnished metal gleams dully. Only later will Duncan learn that one is the Medal of Honor, one the Distinguished Service Cross, and another the Silver Star, the highest commendations a soldier can be awarded: all for uncommon valor. Another is the Purple Heart. Duncan folds them back into the cloth and holds them tightly in his hands. In Joshua's field jacket pocket vials of doxepin, prazosin, librium, and diazepam, their seals closed, and the date on the prescription from a month before. When it grows cold, Duncan slides his arms into the jacket and zippers it to his neck so that he is lost in the size of it. He smells engine oil and Brilliantine and Old Spice; he smells Joshua's tannic sweat.

The constellations turn slowly in their orbits: a satellite flickers at the close edge of space. It's a full moon and Duncan can see its craters and its rippled hills, almost see where Neil Armstrong's boot prints remain perfectly preserved, just the same as when he'd first touched its inviolate surface two decades before. On the moon nothing changes. Neil Armstrong is sitting at the bar of the Windsor Tap in his spacesuit, drinking a Budweiser, and Duncan's father sits next to him, great wings draped over his bowed and bent shoulders and spread on the bar before them and tremoring impotently upon the scarred and burnt wood. Joshua strides barefoot on the moon, and Michael Collins waves from the window of the command module as he passes above the Sea of Tranquility at the perigee of his orbit, but Joshua pays him no mind: He is all alone and far from God. Duncan's mother, locked in her bedroom, listens to the Magnificat on their Victrola, finishes her bottle of Old Mainline 454, and dreams of a time when she sang like Maria Callas, and somewhere out in the dark, like a spark of dimming light, Elvis sings a halting version of "Blue Moon," and angels are falling with hundreds of dead astronauts through space and no matter their struggles never any closer to God.

Duncan sits on the bike and watches the moon track across the sky and the light bruise in the east. And still he stares out at the water, waiting. But there is nothing there. Joshua is gone. Dawn comes slowly up over the rooftops of the factory, and when the lights on the bridge wink out, one by one, Duncan walks to the twenty-four-hour diner and calls his mother to come get him and take him home.

DAYS AND THEN weeks pass and there is no word of Joshua. After work each day Mother is too drained to eat and merely wants to collapse upon the sofa bed in the living room but Duncan heats some lasagne that Magdalene left at their door earlier in the day, tinned vegetables or chicken soup and perhaps makes pasta or rice—dishes he'd learned from Joshua on those nights when mother worked the second shift at St. Luke's or was singing at the Windsor. The gas has been cut off for the last month and he cooks on a small Primus stove, oil from the butane cylinders flickering small and blue in the dark of the room. When the food is ready, he sits with her at the table in the kitchen, watching her eat—masticating a small mouthful of food until it is mush—and urging her to eat more.

Swallow, Mom, he says, and take another bite.

She puts her knife and fork down on the table. I can't, she says. I'm full. Look how much I've eaten.

You've barely touched it. C'mon, another four bites. You can do it.

He scans the channels on Brother Canice's radio for music, but nothing comes except a low hum and brief static. He listens for the beep and squeak frequency of passing satellites, for the voices of the astronauts, for Michael Collins, but although he knows they are up there somewhere a hundred thousand miles distant, tumbling and cold and lost in their numb revolving halfsleep, the San Francisco night sky is empty, and when he peers from the greasy front window, even the stars seem to have collapsed into the void.

When he can no longer urge her to eat more, Maggie pushes back her plate and climbs onto the fold-out bed, the thin mattress sinking and the frame groaning beneath her, and Duncan turns on the black-and-white to *Dallas*, the sound of it somehow comforting, reverberating off the faux-wood paneled walls, and Maggie leans toward the picture, watching until her eyes grow heavy. On the table by the bed, like a bottle of medication, sits her whiskey, its umber liquid half finished.

After a moment, he looks to the fold-out. Mother lies there, staring at the ceiling, hands crossed over the hard stone of her swollen belly. Every so often the Primus stove gives off small belches of liquid fuel, startling him.

He turns down the volume on the television set and watches her. She's as still as a corpse. What does she see on the ceiling, on the tin? Angels perhaps. Bearing her up to that place where Joshua has already gone. Perhaps Joshua, now with the wings of an angel, is carrying her. The black-and-white images flash silently on the screen. He listens for the sound of her breathing.

Mom? he says, and she turns briefly in his direction, her eyes glassy and unseeing.

Are you okay?

Her face contorts in silent, anguished pain. Wind trembles the room, like some small boat pitching upon a sea; a soft rain patters upon the windows.

No, she groans. I don't feel so well.

Mom, you need a doctor.

Finally: I'm okay. But then, as pain grips her gut, she grimaces, turns onto her side.

Mom, I think you need a doctor.

No, she shakes her head. No, Duncan. I'll be fine in the morning. I just need to sleep.

And then more softly: I'll be fine.

Mom?

Mom?

But she is asleep again, and after a moment, Duncan looks back to the television, stares vacantly at is flickering black-and-white images, turns the volume loud so that he doesn't have to hear the empty silence and his own fear churning in his head and belly. He climbs onto the mattress next to his mother, places his arms about her and his ear against her heart, listens to it thumping meekly in her chest.

AFTER TWENTY-NINE days the harbor patrol and police finally give up their search for Joshua and declare his death a drowning: body unrecovered. Once he's pronounced dead, Maggie arranges a funeral service, and the Veterans Administration sends a group of three army riflemen to Joshua's funeral at the St. Mary of the Wharves grave-yard, which sits on the small, grass-covered hill overlooking the Bar-rows and from which Duncan, Maggie, Magdalene, and the other mourners can see the narrow channel of water undulating as dark and sinuous as muscle on this gray, overcast morning.

The soldiers lift their guns and, at the command, fire, then again, three times in all. A group of young, clean-shaven Rangers, in their field colors, stand at rigorous attention, saluting. In various straggling groups about the grave stand Vietnam vets. Magdalene, holding a small bouquet of wildflowers, keeps her head lowered; her mouth moves silently in prayer. Maggie grasps Duncan's hand and stares blankly at Joshua's coffin, plain particleboard painted brown, all that she could afford, although it so pained and shamed her to give Joshua so little that Duncan could hear her weeping after she got off the phone with the funeral home.

When the soldiers are done, the sergeant withdraws the American flag from the coffin and, folding it into a triangle, hands it to Maggie, who moves to the bottom of the grave, where Duncan imagines Joshua's feet lie, or would have lain had the coffin not been empty. Magdalene lays her bouquet on the wood and Maggie mouths, Thank you. A recording of "Taps" plays from a tape recorder that the soldiers have brought, sounding tinny and slow, as if the batteries are dying, and then it ends and the tape recorder loudly clicks off.

At the Winsdor Tap the bar and dance floor are thronged with people, laborers from the second and third tunnel crews, a shop steward and BA from the union hall, veterans, their girlfriends and wives, and workers from the VA. There are also dockworkers and stevedores, local shopkeepers from along Divisadero, and auto mechanics Joshua had, at various times, worked for. Duncan watches Father Brennan from St. Mary of the Wharves moving amongst the crowd, shaking hands.

Clay has left tin buckets on the bar, at the entrance, and by the toilets for donations to help pay for Joshua's burial fees, and within a short time these are brimming with five- and ten-dollar bills. After a petition by Clay and the San Francisco Veterans of Vietnam Community, the VA had provided five hundred dollars toward his burial, and Clay holds up the check so that everyone can mock and laugh at it.

The jukebox is playing but around dusk, when a pale yellow light seeps in through the thick glass cubes that pass for windows and twilight takes hold of everyone's mood, a type of sluggishness comes into the room, the heady and often loud talk of a few hours before has died and now the words spoken are subdued and muted by the clinking of glasses and the clatter of beer bottles. Some friends of Joshua's are drinking shots of tequila at the bar, lining them up and turning them on their ends as they empty them, shouting together in Spanish and nodding passionately with each shot and as the empty glasses tumble across the wood. Duncan watches as one begins to cry and reaches out to hug another. The smell of backup from the toilets seeps through the room and mingles with the heavy, eye-burning clouds of cigarette smoke. Mother's band, Ray Cooper and the Hi-Fidelity Blu-Tones, begin to assemble their gear upon the stage. And amidst all of this, his mother sits at the bar wearing her blue sequined stage dress. Joshua's field jacket is draped about her shoulders and she keeps tugging at it as if she is cold.

You know, Mags, you don't need to sing tonight, Clay says. He reaches across the bar to hold her hand, takes it between his, and rubs briskly. Thanks, she says. You know, Clay, I don't think that I can. Not right now. If it's all right with you, tonight perhaps I'll just let the band do their thing. Tomorrow night I'll sing, tomorrow night or the next night I'll sing for Joshua.

Sure, Mags, sure. Whatever you want. Just let me turn up the heat in here before you freeze to death.

But the room is already warm. Duncan sways, suddenly light-headed, the heat of so many people pressed against him that he has to focus on breathing deeply through his nostrils. The smell of grease from the grill as Clay cooks some burgers puts his stomach roiling. His mother drains the whiskey in her glass but Clay doesn't refill it. She stares, eyes red-shot and unblinking, into the mirror behind the bar and quietly taps the empty glass upon the wood. Duncan looks at her reflection in the mirror, searching for her eyes. He puts his arm about her shoulder, and when she looks at his face in the glass, he mouths the words: It's okay, Mom. Her eyes blink and look through him and she continues to tap the bar sharply with her glass until Clay brings her a bottle of Old Main-line 454.

Late that night they stagger home, with Duncan holding tight to Maggie's waist and Maggie seeming to lean her full weight upon his shoulder, as they lurch stumbling up Ipswich Hill from the Bottoms with a quarter moon glinting like a scythe suspended above them.

He leads Maggie into her bedroom, lays her upon her bed, unconscious and snoring, it seems, from the moment he lets loose her hands and she drops to the mattress. After he pulls off her shoes and spreads the comforter over her, he sits at the kitchen table beneath the yellow glare of the bare bulb and stares at the black windows. Hours pass like this, time in which he is not conscious of sound or thought or physical discomfort. But then slowly he becomes aware of the room about him; it is a sensation he has experienced once before—when he'd first woken in the Home and heard the sound of Elvis Presley. The washer on the faucet over the sink needs replacing and water drips methodically upon the tin basin. As he becomes aware of it, the sound seems to grow—a singular loud, incessant hammering—and only as he becomes aware of other sounds and sensations about him does this sound decrease and fade to the background.

He rises from his chair and begins to open the kitchen cupboards, slamming and banging open the doors, finding one of his mother's bottles almost immediately, and then another and another, and slamming and banging the doors with more and more vehemence with each bottle he discovers. He looks beneath the sink and under the trash can lining and then moves to the St. Vincent de Paul sofa bed, where amber-colored bottles lie between the rows of rusted springs, and when he looks up, he sees Maggie standing in the doorway, swaying.

I'm sorry, she says, hiccuping and holding a hand to her mouth. I don't feel so well.

She goes to wash but halfway across the room she clutches her stomach, doubles over, and upon her knees vomits onto the bright blue shag carpet. She vomits until there is nothing left to vomit, her mouth agape over the floor, gagging and retching painfully, a thick thread of mucus hanging from her nose and mouth.

Oh, Duncan, I'll clean that up as soon as I'm able. Don't touch it, sweetie. I'll get to it in a moment. Just give me a moment. And then rocking on her heels, gagging some more, and finally rising to her feet, she makes her way to the bathroom, closes and then locks the door behind her.

The faucet runs and he listens as she splashes water upon her face, rinses her mouth, then lowers the toilet seat and sits down. Duncan stretches back on his bed and stares at the ceiling. Stares through it, up through the plaster and Sheetrock, through nails and joists, up through the crawl space and ventilation shafts between the headers, up through the roof joists and the plywood and shingles to the night beyond with Michael Collins and all the angels and astronauts and perhaps Joshua up there with them, and then he is simply gone, gone from his bed and the room and the house and everything it contains.

THE BOWED ACETATE revolves slowly on the Victrola's turntable, its warped black surface creating the illusion that it is made of liquid, that if Duncan attempts to pick it up, it will merely slip through his fingers. He winds the motor and sets the tone arm upon the record. Maggie sits in the chair by the window, looking out onto the street.

What's this? she calls at the ceiling.

This, Duncan says, is the only recording we have of you.

The Victrola's stylus rasps in the grooves, and gradually, rising in volume, Duncan's mother's laugh, startling and bright, emerges from the speaker, followed by her talking, it seems, to a technician, her voice fading now and echoing ghostlike as if it were traversing some vast hallway and moving farther and farther away: *You gotta pay the dues if you wanna sing the blues, Harry.*

The phonograph's spring-powered motor clicks as its worn tumblers rotate and the old acetate sighs and hisses against the stylus. When his mother's voice comes, Duncan holds his breath, just as he

357

always does, for on this recording, where she emulates the velvety vibrato of Sissieretta Jones, her voice seems suddenly such a fragile and tenuous thing, momentarily suspended between this world and some other and filled not with the desperation and longing of a latter-day, ruined Silva Bröhm, but with a singular, plaintive joy:

'Tis the last rose of summer,
Left blooming alone;
All her lovely companions
Are faded and gone;
No flower of her kindred
No rosebud is nigh,
To reflect back her blushes,
Or give sigh for sigh!

I haven't listened to this in so long, Maggie whispers. Her mouth is open and her breath comes deep and loud, almost as if she is snoring, sounding the way she does when she's been drinking, or after a night of singing at the Windsor Tap, when her adenoids and cartilage tightened and became like bark in her throat.

So soon may I follow,
When friendships decay,
And from love's shining circle
The gems drop away!
When true hearts lie wither'd,
And fond ones are flown,
Oh! Who would inhabit
This bleak world alone?

Sunlight fades from the room and the darker hues upon the ceiling take prominence and Maggie and Duncan watch, stilled by the music, as the room turns to night. His mother seems to be daydreaming, jaundiced skin pulled tight at the edges of her mouth. Beneath half-closed eyelids her eyes remain fixed on some distant point upon the ceiling. She sighs, opens her eyes wide. After a moment she says, with something that sounds like envy and sadness: This young girl, she's a great singer. I don't think I could ever sound like that.

His mother's song is fading. The record ends. The stylus hisses and spits in the groove, and Duncan picks it up, listening to the whirr of the motor, and lowers it again. He kneels beside her as her voice blooms young and strong through the speakers, and takes her hand, squeezes so hard that she flinches and looks at him with something like recognition. This is you, Mom, he says. This is you, and this is what you're meant to do.

She shakes her head, eyes wide in fear. But I can't, she says. I can't Duncan, and I so wanted to make him proud. I wanted to be—I wanted to be better than this.

You can sing. You need to sing.

He stares at her until she looks away, and then she hears him pulling out the bureau drawers in her bedroom. Duncan, she says softly, what are you doing?

When he returns, he's holding an issue of *Opera* and rustling through the yellowed pages. Please, Duncan, she murmurs, don't. I don't need to hear you read what they said about me.

But Duncan ignores her. Mom, they call you extraordinary, they compared you to Callas and Bröhm . . . They say that no previous singer in history excelled to such an extent in both the Verdi Requiem and the Mozart C Minor Mass . . . That your Vespers was in a class with the fabled recorded versions by Ursula van Diemen and Jennifer Vyvyan . . . They say your voice was angelic, that it was immaculate and as close to God as possible and that it brought them to tears . . . One reviewer says—

Duncan, please stop. You didn't read the final ones. They spoke the truth. I was an embarrassment not fit to be on the stage.

You're wrong, I've heard you. You need to sing.

Maggie sighs and wipes the back of her hand across her mouth. Why?

Because you'll die otherwise. That's what you said. Remember?

Mother shakes her head, waves weakly at the air. Duncan, maybe that's not enough of a reason.

September 1985

THE SAN PADRE Tunnel beneath the bay is never completed. With the price tag twenty million overbudget and a multitude of OSHA infractions, fines, and forced work stoppages, the federal government steps in and shuts Bextal and Sonoyama International down. California governor Jason Pettite decries the abysmal failure of the major contractors and subcontractors and the lack of federal supervision to oversee the tunnel management and how all have combined to fail San Francisco and the Bay Area and all the men who have died. This is a sad day, he says on the Channel 7 evening news, as Duncan and his mother, chewing stale popcorn, watch from the sofa. Governor Jason Pettite is a tall, dour man shimmering in black and white and ripples of static upon their old television. *A sad day for our great city.*

Two hundred feet beneath the Golden Gate Bridge, one hundred and fifty feet to the floor of the bay, and seventy-five feet beneath its

361

shale and silt sits a dark, cavernous tunnel extending three fourths of a mile out into the bay—fully formed and shaped upon bedrock, its slurried walls partially reinforced with cement pylons, and within its tub the floors leveled to receive the hydraulic drill and the t-jacks. The boot prints of Joshua and the other men remain hardened and compressed in the cavern's floor, reminders if one were to look for them that men had indeed been here, had struggled and labored, and had even died. For now it is like the surface of the moon: An inviolate space undisturbed by wind or motion.

Through the string of construction lights electricity still flows and a meager light continues to glow—the bulbs stretching into the tunnel's depths, breaking the darkness at intervals, and occasionally shuddering and trembling in some unseen wind, until even their light, staggered farther and farther apart, disappears in the darkness.

In another month the electricity will be turned off, the light will be extinguished, and the tunnel will return to darkness. Gradually the pressure of the bay will begin to exert itself in fractures here and there in the partially formed structure, along its seams, crumbling cement and warping metal. Within eight months water will trickle and stream and flood the chamber and then the once celebrated San Padre Tunnel will be gone.

From Admiral's Point, Duncan and Maggie watch with other spectators as they detonate what is left of the tunnel, its underwater caissons, transepts, sluice tunnels, and derricks. A rumble sounds deep below the water and the water churns and steams. The concussive shock of the explosions echo off and reverberate about the shoreline and the tunnel's labyrinthine corridors and secret walkways to the surface collapse beneath a hundred pounds of explosive charges staged at two-hundred-foot intervals along its three-quarter-mile length. Three large circles ringed with white waves appear upon the surface of the water. The rings rise up briefly and then collapse and the surface seems to collapse with them and into them, spiraling downward into the empty space they've created. The vortex lasts only a moment and then the surface is as it had been before, with the wind stirring up whitecaps. In his mind Duncan sees all the parts of the blasted tunnel turning and falling through the deep and with it everything Joshua has told him: the fuselage and wing section of a WWII Hellcat, the giant tattered face of the housewife on the Byer's bread billboard comes gleaming, the bones of a cow and the wings of some prehistoric avian. And he imagines he hears whales, a vast school of them far, far out, moaning, crying in cadence to one another in the deep and to others still waiting across the vast breadth of the ocean half a world away and that they might never see.

Maybe that's where Joshua was going, Maggie says, staring out at the water and the headlands. Maybe he was swimming out there to be back with the men of the tunnel, to be back with his friends.

One day maybe we'll put some of his things together, put them in a metal box and seal it up. We'll row out there—my father taught me to row when I was a little girl—right to the place where they finished tunneling and we'll drop it down, down to the deepest part of the bay. I think Joshua would like that.

They sit there long after the crowds upon the banks have gone. Duncan looks at Maggie and asks: Should we go, Mom? and she continues to stare off toward the bridge and the distant horizon and everything Joshua left them for and finally says: Go where, honey? Where are we gonna go?

THROUGH THE SCREEN door Duncan can sense the man's tension filling the space like electricity, in the way you can feel the resistance coursing through a charged fence without even touching it. The man leaves the porch light off, and the only light cast is from a lamp in the living room and the television flickering blue behind him and which burns softly at the edges of his clothes, as if he is caught and held in amber. The man leans closer to the screen door and the liquid of his eyes glistens from the streetlamps as he searches the darkness, and Duncan can make out their shape and then he knows that he is Joshua's father.

What do you want? he asks.

Down the street a couple of kids play stickball and a group of teenagers lean against an Oldsmobile sitting on cinder blocks, smoking and swearing loudly and calling out to some girl moving on the other side of the street and in the darkness. From one of the backyards comes the smell of a barbecue and there is the splash as someone jumps into a pool. It's almost ten o'clock and yet the air is still and muggy, and pushing a hundred degrees. From the streetlights, telephone poles, and apartment buildings comes the cicada thrum of electricity—that dulled and numbing sound that only seems to exist on the hottest days of the year in the city. Air conditioners click on and off, hissing and dripping into life. Up and down the street, window fans burr like hornets and above them the cables thrum in a numb, bruising way.

Finally, Duncan speaks: Are you Joshua McGreevy's father? He gave me something I thought you should have. Duncan holds out the bandanna, wrapped and tied in a loose ball, toward the screen door.

Huh, the man grunts. Joshua left a lot behind but that was a long time ago. I haven't seen Joshua in years. He's my son all right, but I bet he hasn't thought of me as family in a long time. How did you find me?

He told me you lived in Oakland.

I'm not the only McGreevey in Oakland.

I looked in the yellow pages. There's a hundred. I called them. I called you too but no one answered the phone.

They cut it off a while back. He nods to Duncan's hand.

What is it?

His medals.

Medals? Medals for what?

For bravery in the war. For uncommon valor. Joshua was a hero.

Hero? The man smiles in the darkness, his teeth flashing. And then he laughs but it is a sad, defeated sound. Shit. My Joshua was no hero, boy. Did he tell you that?

No, sir. But these are his medals. He left them behind. When he left.

Duncan stares at the screen door, searching the man's eyes. The street grows darker, and when more and more streetlamps come on, everything beyond their glare—the sidewalk, parked cars, and front yards—disappears into blackness. Duncan squints into the light and then turns back to the door, losing his hold upon the man in the doorway and his sense of him. He has returned to an amorphous, barely formed shape. For a moment Duncan cannot even be sure that he is still there. His arm begins to tremble and he lets it drop to his side and then he hears the man's breathing, the sickly sweet warmth of cheap beer, the sound of his lips as they come together. He swallows hard.

Where did he go, my Joshua? Where did he go?

Duncan thinks of Joshua swimming across the bay, beneath the bridge and out to the Pacific, and he sees him, his strong stokes churning him through the water and farther and farther from everything he has known. Duncan hears his voice singing still in his mind, reverberating and echoing in the high, hollow metal spaces of the bridge's iron balustrades and stanchions and the cars tires' hissing on the cross-sections four hundred feet above his head, moving back and forth in their endless journey through the night from Oakland to the city and back again. When he imagines this, he imagines that Joshua is still swimming and that he has made it all the way to the Pacific and he hears his voice singing out at the stars and this is what he want to tell this man who is his father.

I watched him swim out into the bay, he wants to say. I waited but he didn't come back.

But instead he shrugs. I don't know, sir, he says. He just went away.

Duncan reaches out his hand to the door again. He left these behind, he says. They're for you.

Large winged insects throw themselves at the dim glow beyond the screen door; they tap the screen like heavy drops of rain and then fall to the concrete, dazed.

The screen door opens with a groan and the man calls out to him: Jesus, boy, get in here then. And with Joshua's father shaking his head, muttering to himself, There must be something the matter with you, Duncan steps into the hall and follows him to the living room.

He watches the man's bowed back swaying from side to side, shoulders brushing the plaster walls, the pain evident in every movement. In the living room he can see him more clearly. His brown skin is sallow and stretched-looking. His legs and arms are thin, the muscles clinging tightly, feverishly to the bone. Only his stomach protrudes, a large belly that, when he brushes past Duncan, feels as hard as cement and makes Duncan touch his arm with surprise, unsure of what he has felt.

He eases himself onto a couch before a coffee table stained with white rings from the bottoms of beer cans and upon which tattered, dog-eared paperbacks and a few framed photographs sit, and points impatiently for Duncan to do the same.

On the television the Oakland A's are playing: a pitcher in his windup and the runner on first breaking for second. The muted banter of announcers talking to one another about their weekend plans and the oppressive heat of the city and how difficult this must be on the Oakland batters tonight.

With a sigh Joshua's father reaches for his beer, puts it to his lips, and tilts his head back. When he's done, he looks at Duncan, pulls the tab on another can.

How you know my Joshua?

Eyes narrowed to slits, he looks at Duncan over the rim of his beer can and drinks. And then he closes his eyes, his throat convulsing, the Adam's apple bobbing up and down. Necrosis, he says, and his eyes remain closed. The long-term effects of tunneling in a compressed environment.

You worked in a tunnel?

I worked on the Midway tunnel. Was one of the first men up the other side. When I was a boy they called it caisson's disease, he says and slows the round, aspirated syllables of both words as if it is some alien contaminant, as if even in pronunciation it has to be handled carefully: Cay-sss-on dis-eee-ease. He crushes the empty can in his hand and opens his eyes: corpuscles bright and enlarged from the rush of blood and alcohol and, at the edges of his eyes, the pinched sallow-brown skin. Duncan can see the damage that Joshua did to the eye socket, the way one eye seems to be glazed and the lid partly paralyzed.

Over time it destroyed my bones. Shit, everyone thought they knew everything back in the sixties. Now people just seem confused. And at least there seems to be some God-respecting humility to that.

Most people think the excavations were all done by machine and that the sections were lowered into place by machines, and that was that. Hell, machines and engineers are blind without men. We had to dig the first conduits, and then the trench lines and exhaust shafts. We had to work in sections two hundred feet down, moving from one conduit to another all across the bed of the bay. We had air locks and decompression chambers—they told us we were safe. We thought that it didn't matter how long we stayed down there, that the chambers would flush everything bad out of our systems, y'know, like a goddamn sonafabitch hangover.

Joshua's father reaches for another beer, tears it from the six-pack's plastic ring. It's a hangover that's lasted me my entire life.

As he drinks, he looks at a framed picture on the table before him—a group of men in battered metal hard hats smiling at the camera, eyes squinting into sunlight, the half shell of a tunnel entrance in the foreground and the blurred suggestion of water shimmering with refracted light like steel—gestures with his beer can toward the image.

It was early October and Joshua and his momma were there waiting. He had a little sister too. Sarah. She's dead now.

He nods and drinks some more.

I walked out the west entrance of the shaft with the other workers carrying the statue of St. Barbara and all the press in San Francisco were there. Newspapermen were snapping photos and there were television cameras as well. Our families were standing behind a gold ribbon waiting for the mayor to cut it. We was all on the news that night, and not just local neither. It was national television.

They took a picture looking back over the bay with our crew and three crew bosses standing before the entrance to the shaft, and then they cut the ribbon, and Joshua, little Sarah, and their mamma came down and had lunch with me on the banks of the bay.

He smiles and turns his head slightly so that the side of his neck is bared. Duncan imagines that in reliving this moment Joshua's father is feeling the sun on him again and how on that day it warmed all of them as they ate their lunch on the bank above the shore and watched men emerging from below the sea into the sharp brightness of day, but he knows that when Joshua's father came west from Boston, he was alone: His wife had left him and Joshua would soon and little Sarah was already dead.

Joshua works—worked—on tunnels too, Duncan says, as he picks up the picture and searches for some resemblance of Joshua in the young man's face.

Yeah?

Duncan nods and puts the picture back on the coffee table next to the six-pack, but Joshua father sweeps it aside when he reaches for another beer and yanks it from the plastic.

What tunnels did he work on?

The San Padre Tunnel—

Shit, heard they canceled funding for that after the accident.

He was also in the army. In Vietnam. He was a war hero—

When you see my Joshua, he says, you give him my best. Tell him his daddy did the best he could. The best he could. And that's no lie. I did the best I could.

Joshua's father gulps from his beer can and then lays his head slowly back on the couch, watches the television through slitted, clouded eyes.

After, Duncan stands on the dirt lawn and watches Joshua's father through the window, the blue flicker of his television in the dark room, and upon the wall behind him, above the couch, the phosphorescent blue nimbus of wings, and he sees an angel there, squatting just over the man's shoulder. A black angel whose giant wings unfurl and spread back blotting out all light in the room, the humerus and carpometacarpus bones built to hold such heavy plumage shattering the plaster from the walls and suddenly sweeping about Joshua's father. And within that blackness what seems to be the convulsive, shuddering ripples of a violent struggle.

A car horn sounds down the street and Joshua's father is sitting upon his couch, staring blankly at the television before him, a can of beer clutched in his hand, and foam dribbling down his fingers.

Through the window the blue of the television flickers ashen and cobalt—a dusk light, as in that moment before night. In this small frame of cobalt-hued light Duncan feels momentarily safe and does not wish to move, yet he knows he has to, and as he thinks about the journey back home across the bridge, the sounds of the neighborhood and of the night come to him, magnified: of shouting and of banging screen doors, a car roaring into life and screeching down the street, its hubcaps a Catherine wheel of fireworks and multicolored light.

Later that night Duncan stares out across the bay at the lights that show through the darkness and crepuscular fog and thinks of Joshua's father sitting alone in the dark before his television imagining his son a boy again and then as the man whom he has never known. Duncan wonders if the medals make a difference in the way he thinks of his son, or merely make their distance and his son's absence all the greater, all the less retrievable, unfamiliar and so strange as to not even be recognizable, familiar, as if his son were not his own and these things happened to someone else's child and occurred in someone else's lifetime.

Perhaps, Duncan thinks, he looks toward the window or stares out at the night just as Duncan is doing now, or stands and turns the knob of the television to another station or adjusts the volume, and then with a beer settles himself back into the deep settee, raising the volume even further so that the thoughts, memories, emotions in his mind might be drowned out, so that he can return to a time of days or weeks before he thought of his son in such a way that threatens each of his nights with sleeplessness and guilt and despair. Or perhaps this is merely what Duncan would wish for if this man were his father, and what he would wish for from his own if he were to find him and call him by his name.

October 1985

DUSK IS FALLING over the street and Maggie is doing her makeup and preparing for, as a memorial to Joshua, a weekend of performances at the Windsor. From their house comes the sound—strange and melancholy—of her practicing her scales and arpeggios. Every morning and evening she opens her throat, preparing it for song, and her music fills the quiet of the street. Duncan sits on the stairs outside listening and lowers his head against the cold wind coming in off the bay. Wind moans beneath the eaves, shears particles of old paint off the clapboard and sends it drifting down the walkway; it whistles across the tops of Maggie's empty liquor bottles stacked in their recycling bin—since the night of Joshua's funeral, when he threw out all of her bottles, she hasn't had a drink, and told him she no longer had the taste for it.

The old parts of the city push and pull and wrestle slowly, inexorably beneath them, and he feels he can almost hear the stone embankments, the pressing asphalt of the bowed street crumbling and widening in the chill. A single gray cloud, like a wispy ball of damp cotton, tumbles slowly across the sky, barely seeming to move, but when he looks moments later, still transfixed by his mother's voice, it has traveled across the horizon and looks shriveled and shrunken in the eastern corner of the sky.

In the corners of the bar, candles flicker from ancient cast-iron candelabras, and at the front of the stage, shaded by scalloped reflectors, small candles glow and cast their golden, yellow light upon Maggie in her blue sequined dress standing before an old microphone stand—their shadows dance upon the ornately painted drop cloth at the back of the stage against which the bar's revolving fans whisper and tremble.

The performance is highlighted by the simple beauty of her voice, even as damaged as it is. For hours she could sustain it. On Friday and Saturday people from Oakland and Santa Clarisa, come over the bridge to listen to her. They sit on the folding chairs that Clay has arranged around the low stage and dream of far-off places and lost lovers as Maggie sing songs of unrequited love from a hundred years before, of dead lovers calling to their darlings from beneath the ground, and how they will wait for them, however many years it takes, before they too give up the mortal coil. And so they wait as the seasons change, as petals fall from blossoms and snow covers the ground and the first warm days of spring bring the green grass from cover once more and hope that they might be reunited. When she begins Sissieretta Jones's "The Last Rose of Summer," she looks to Duncan briefly and smiles, and Duncan knows she is singing this just for Joshua and it does not surprise him when she ends her first set with a strange, sad version of Bill Withers's "Ain't No Sunshine."

And as she sings, Duncan watches his mother's hands, pressed tightly against her dress, then gesturing at the air as her voice rises, and her belly, suddenly exposed, hard and bulging as if with child. But it is her face, her eyes, her voice, with its intense, plaintive yearning, that averts eyes away from her stomach so that, mostly, no one seems to notice, and if they do, and consider it, it passes unconsciously across their faces and disappears just as quickly.

Near the end of her show Maggie moves seamlessly into old revival numbers, those she'd learned as a child, and the audience sways and nods, closes their eyes and reaches out with their arms, almost unconsciously. Ray Cooper and the Hi–Fidelity Blu-Tones strike up the horns. An accordion moans and the Hammond organ harmonizes with the accordion's low, dirgeful notes and the bursts of trumpets. A snare drum fills the silence before the chorus with a frenetically fast, loud, thumping roll, which has the audience singing and moving in their chairs. They are smiling and beaming, shouting aloud the chorus, and Duncan sings with them, imagining Joshua here. When the song ends, many are bright-faced, looking at one another and laughing, and Maggie is laughing also, with joy and happiness and, finally— Duncan likes to believe—some manner of redemption.

IT's RAINING AND Maggie and Duncan are strolling through the nearly deserted fairgrounds at Golden Gate Park. An empty Whirligig spins in alternating parabolas, its lights blurred by speed and rain so that it seems to entwine with itself as each brightly lit arc crisscrosses the other. Giorgio Moroder's "Chase" theme from *Midnight Express* plays loudly from the ride's speakers: whooshing synthesizers, accelerating snare and high hat, bass beats, and looping four-chord sequences— the suggestion of speed and escape and of a strange, thrilling contagion; and of a carnival thronged with shrieking, laughing people.

Mother lifts her skirt to jump the puddles, and as they come closer to the music, she raises her hands and begins clapping. She leans her head back, lets loose her arms, and swings them about her, turning in circles first one way and then the other like some mad disco queen, and then she reaches for him and without pausing takes his hands in her own and begins to spin him about.

I love this song, she says, breathless, as they slow. Here comes the

chorus—are you ready? Quicktime! And they spin off again, splashing through the rust-colored water and through the divets and grooves
gouged out by the tractor trailers and past the stalls and booths and the
fun house mirrors that turn them into ridiculously wide-mouthed
misshapen things and with everything a speeding blur about them—
the faces of the few remaining parkgoers, vendors with open mouths
and weary eyes, the bedraggled performers rolling their painted
drop cloths, watching them and smiling—as they turn and turn and
turn and it begins to rain harder, multicolored windswept darts
spilling down through the Whirligig's bright-lit revolutions, shining brightly on mother's upturned and glistening face, and if she is
saddened by some foreknowledge of what is to come, Duncan has
no sense of it.

The only riders aboard the Whirligig, Mother and Duncan hold
each other's hands and lean their heads back and are flying, laughing, through the low, pulsing cloud-gray sky. The carousel turns
lazily in bright, blinking multicolored arcs while the Whirligig centrifuge spins above them in endless, vacant revolutions. Mother lays
her arms across the back of the chair, stares up at the sky, and sighs
long and deep and content.

Upon the fairground's sound system an old Tangley Calliaphone
plays a medley of old seaside carnival tunes, and the smell of rain: of
damp wood and canvas and soggy, moldering trash, melds with the
lingering odors of disinfectant from the portable toilets, diesel, popcorn, and old cooking grease from the food stalls.

It's getting cold, mother says, and shivers. They say it could even
snow soon. The sky continues to spin about them: A seagull flaps
madly, rising toward a blurred and crooked zenith, and the Calliaphone suddenly begins to play manically and off-key, as if it were
slowly winding down, and when Duncan turns to smile at his mother,
her face looks pale and shaken. Mom? he says and she pulls forward,
letting loose his hand, and clutches at her mouth as if she's about to
be sick.

Duncan looks down for the Whirligig attendant and waves for him to cut the ride. As the sounds of the motors and gears subside, he and mother continue in their slow, lazy orbit above the fair-grounds. Mother lays her head back and closes her eyes, and there is only the sound of the wind sighing through the metal buckets and cantilevered tie-arms, gnawing like invisible rats at the thin metal cables. Gradually the chairs come to a stop upon the ground and the attendant swing theirs forward to the gate and unlocks it. He reaches for mother's hand and he and Duncan help her as she steps off. Her ankles buckle and for a moment it seems as if she will fall, but then she reaches for the guardrail. She closes her eyes again, inhales slow and deep, and as Duncan and the attendant watch her, she vomits, a yellow, strong-smelling bile that spatters against the rail.

Mom, are you okay?

Is everything all right, Ma'am? the attendant asks.

I'm just not built for these things anymore. I'll be okay in a little while.

A fine rheum of vomit greases Mother's mouth and she wipes at it with the back of her hand. Then she attempts to smile but her lips are pressed tight and she squints as if she is having trouble seeing them in the gray light. Her pupils have shrunk to mere pinpricks.

Mother takes his hand and they step across the runoff from the rows of plastic port-a-potties turning the edge of the park to black muck. From somewhere comes the low thumping of diesel genera-tors and there's the constant hum of electricity passing along cables between trailers and tents, and farther, a dog's hesitant bark sound-ing fearful in the encroaching darkness.

On the street, people seem to emerge out of the strange crepus-cular light like milky apparitions, as if they had only the moment before come into existence, footfalls splashing through neon-lit pud-dles. A wide bar of bright yellow light spills across the alley from the Chinese Garden kitchen and from within the rapturous clattering of pots and pans; a radio sputtering jazz, jubilant footfalls on the thin floors as if someone were dancing; and the sudden, violent beauty of a woman's voice in song. Mother pauses and slants her head unconsciously toward the music, then she looks about her, squints as if looking for something that moments before was there and is now gone. She chews on her lower lip, pulls at her hair.

The streets are mostly deserted. Stoops are filled with bulging trash bags and here and there various broken electric devices: a portable television, a stereo turntable, speakers, a toaster, transistor radios, a hair dryer and curling tongs, a typewriter, a fan.

A man coughs—a smoker's cough: first hoarse and then thick and moist with phlegm—in the kitchen over the soft sound of slow-running water and the clatter of dishware. From another window the opening music to *Ironside*, with its three repeating notes of warning, like a clarion. Mother blinks, eyelashes fluttering, and licks her lips savagely as she stares at the city about them.

Do you feel it? she asks, and absently squeezes his arm, harder than she intends.

Feel what?

There's something missing here—can't you feel it? It's all wrong. She shakes her head. I'm sorry, she says. I'm so sorry.

JUST AFTER DAWN gray light filters through the gap beneath the window shades and Duncan wakes and sniffs the stagnant, sulfurous air. The rain must have stopped sometime during the night. A hammer is banging somewhere in the rail yards, a thunk of metal on wood—perhaps driving cross ties into the ground—followed by a loud clanging, and he can hear men's voices calling to one another. He'd been listening to the church bells from St. Mary of the Wharves and as they sounded he was standing crying in his suit and tie at the grave overlooking the bay where they buried an empty coffin in place of Joshua. He sees Joshua flailing far out at sea and the water pulling him down and then Joshua no longer struggling but welcoming this strange peace, and his mouth opening and closing soundlessly as if he were still singing.

Duncan shifts and the mattress groans. Mother is breathing softly next to him; her breath sour on his face. Her skin is sallow and gaunt in the nether light, and as he watches her, he mouths a prayer

379

thanking God for everything He has given him and asking that his mother be well and strong and happy and kept in His care. Mother's breath catches, and she wakes, eyes open wide, as if startled. She looks at Duncan and about the room. After a moment, relaxes. What are you doing, my Duncan? she says tenderly.

Nothing. Just saying a prayer.

Well, prayers never hurt. And neither does coffee and cigarettes. Hand me my bag, would you?

Duncan climbs from the bed and fetches her bag from the table in the kitchen, the floor bowing and creaking under his footsteps. Mother pulls herself upright, leans back against the bed frame as Duncan bunches tobacco from her pouch onto a rolling paper.

Joshua teach you that?

Duncan nods as he licks the edge of the paper, lights the cigarette, and hands it to her, watches as she sucks on it weakly. You'll go to the doctor today, he says firmly and stares at her until she looks at him.

I'll make an appointment for later in the week. After Joshua's memorial, okay? She smiles feebly, lifts the cigarette in her hand. See? I feel better already, but Duncan continues to look at her and she says: After Joshua's memorial, I promise.

October 1985

THE LAST NIGHT of Joshua's memorial Maggie begins her final set by singing the mad scene from Donizetti's *Lucia di Lammermoor*, a song Duncan knows she no longer has the ability to sing, but her first note—a rising, startling B, sustained and lengthened by playful flourishes—is like no other she has sounded. The audience stares at her, and their mouths open unconsciously. The note falters and then Maggie catches it shakily again.

Her voice rises quickly up the scale—and up up up the audience rises with it—and crescendos at that elusive C, held until it is one pleading pitch, shaking but sustained at such a height that it does not seem possible any person could be capable of sustaining it, and then falling slowly back to the middle range with twirling, spiraling or-namentation, so that her voice resembles the broken sound of the plunge itself and of a flock of starlings at twilight. Duncan sees Lucia's madness and her loss. Her pleading to her lover to believe that she is not mad, to not condemn or imprison her. He sees Joshua swimming out into the bay, his thrashing strokes leaving spears of white froth upon the black surface.

As twilight creeps across city from the east, turning the glass of the city a fiery purplish orange, the inside of the bar darkens and candles flickering in the candelabras surrounding the stage cast Maggie's misshapen shadow upon the backdrop and the walls.

Duncan watches as his mother sings and holds nothing back—she sings as if this were the End, sings as she did during those years before her performance at Symphony Hall. And the crowd knows it, and because of this, they believe in her, and they give themselves to her, and she takes them with her. And in that place, every note is perfect.

Maggie begins to sing "Senza mamma," from Puccini's *Suor Angelica*, which Duncan has only ever heard sung in broken fragments before. Sister Angelica, who was put away in a convent after giving birth to an illegitimate child, learns after seven years without news of her son that he died in infancy. She sings of not being able to forgive herself for abandoning him and wishing that she could be together with him in heaven.

Senza mamma,
o bimbo, tu sei morto!
Le tue labbra, senza i baci miei,
scolorriron fredde!
e chiudesti, o bimbo, gli occhi belli!

Non potendo carezzarmi,
le manine componesti in croce!
E tu sei morto senza sapere
quanto t'mava questa tua mamma.

Ora che sei un angelo del cielo,
ora tu puoi vederla la tua mamma,
tu puoi sendere giù pel firmamento
ed aleggiare in torno a me ti sento
Sei qui, mi baci e m'accarezzi.

Ah! Dimmi, quando in ciel potrò verderti?
Quando potrò baciarti?

Oh! Dolce fine d'ogni mio dolore,
quando in ciel potró salire?
Quando potró morire?

Dillo alla mamma, creatura bella,
con un leggiero scintillar di stella,
Parlami, parlami,
amore, amore, amore!

My baby, you died without your mama!
Your lips, without my kisses, grew pale and cold!
And your lovely eyes closed, my baby!

I could not caress you,
your little hands folded in a cross!
And you died without knowing
how much your mama loved you!

Now you are an angel in heaven,
now you can see your mama,
you can come down from heaven
and let our fragrance linger about me.
You are here to feel my kisses and caresses.

Ah! Tell me, when will I see you in heaven?
When can I kiss you?

Oh! Sweet end to all my grieving,
when can I greet you in heaven?
When can I greet death?

O creature of beauty, tell your mama,
by a small twinkle of a star.

Speak, speak, speak to me,
my love, my love, my love!

A cigarette lies bent in a tin ashtray upon the piano's edge and a string of gray-white smoke churns slowly upward from it. The musicians sit silently on chairs watching her performance. Maggie's voice echoes and resonates with such vibrating pitch, resonance, and harmony that it is as if she were singer and tenor and chorus intermingled as one emerging slowly from the darkness and rising, surging quickly together toward the end. And Duncan feels God turning slowly toward them with the last of the sun descending into the hills and the glass and metal valleys and the darkness above sweeping its vast shadow across the bay.

In listening to his mother he knows that on this night, this rare, particular, star-aligned, tumid night, she has been granted a reprieve. She stands in another time, before an audience at Symphony Hall in Boston; she is nineteen and immune to the world of pain, before one note fractures the membrane in her throat, swelling her voice box, and causing her larynx to harden with coarse cartilage, a time before he was born.

After her performance she will race to North Station through the snow toward the man who will become his father and it will feel as if it is snowing just for her, as if the world has momentarily stopped and His great gaze has paused from its cosmic ruminations and a light has shot the bow of the universe and materialized out of the darkness merely to consider the wonder of her. Maggie will raise her face, her chilled cheeks to the tumbling snow and to the invisible glittering stars beyond the billowing white of the sky, and briefly understand her part in everything. Her life will begin and end here in the brief time before Duncan is born, while she is still very much a young girl and while the promise of all manner of dreams lie before her. And he knows that when his mother stops singing, there *never* will be another like her.

THE SHOW IS over; the candles are extinguished and the musicians and Mother are in darkness. Beer bottles clatter and chairs scrape against wood. Clay calls out to them, says, Great job, Maggie! and begins to stack the chairs and the patrons slowly trudge out to the street. Ray Cooper and the Hi–Fidelity Blu–Tones break down their equipment. A Harley backfires and roars violently up the avenue. Then the footfalls of the musicians on the steps of the stage, Clay hollering for them to lock up after themselves, and after a long while mother's blue sequined dress shimmering through the dark toward him.

Hey, you, she says. How's my biggest fan? And Duncan grins.

In the alleyway behind the bar a radio is playing big band music by Tommy Dorsey, the horns blowing slow and melancholy. Duncan watches his mother's gaunt face, hears in the silent space between them her voice still resonating from her performance. He is sitting upon a hard-backed, fold-up chair, with shadows shifting upon the back of the bar wall, and they are all alone.

Maggie smells of sweat, cigarette smoke, and skin cream. One arm folded across her middle, she sucks hungrily on her cigarette, pauses to purse her lips and pick a fleck of tobacco from her lower lip. Slowly, she touches the side of her head.

What is it? Duncan asks.

Nothing, sweetie. Just got a headache. I think everything is finally catching up with me. I just need to sit for a while. She looks about the dark bar.

You know this—tonight—it's not what I thought it would be.

No. Duncan grins. Me either.

But that's all right too.

Yes, it is, Duncan agrees.

I'm done, you know, Maggie says, and clutches her belly unconsciously. Duncan nods. Anyone could see the toll the last week had taken on her.

She laughs softly. No, she says. I'm really done. I can't sing, Duncan. There isn't anything left. I tried, just now in the bathroom. My voice is gone. She opens her mouth and shapes it as if to sing, but when she exhales, only a whistle emerges, cracked and broken from her larynx.

Her voice is truly gone.

As they sit and he waits for her to say something more, she gradually leans against him, and she feels weightless, so tall and big boned yet weightless. He has no idea how much time passes but has the sense that the two of them have dozed. The lights are coming up slowly like filaments warming with heat, and a theater is taking shape about them. At the back of the Windsor stage a proscenium shimmers out of the darkness. Above the proscenium gilded balconies emerges. The blurred, dark shapes of people rise here and there, shuffling and whispering in mute, unintelligible voices, much like distant echoes piled one atop the other, as they find their seats.

Maggie sighs and then smiles slowly. The last place I performed, she says and raises her eyes to the shattered galleries.

It didn't look like this then, she says. The production was sometimes terrible but still . . . this place . . . you could almost see and
feel what it wanted it to be—you could feel the small part of the
opera that it had reached for, had wanted so badly to be.

The smell of grease and tobacco comes off the satin and velvet
chairs, once red but now faded to a burnt umber and shimmering
black in places where the felt has been worn away.

Let's stay here for a while, shall we? I'm feeling very tired, sweetie.

Maggie places her hands upon her stomach and Duncan lays his
head against her shoulder and together they stare toward the front of
the opera house. Slowly, so slowly that he imagines he must be
dreaming, in the darkening light, as if a film is about to begin, flickering upon a invisible screen, there emerges a shimmering about
them, in the seats, along the bas-relief of the proscenium, and upon
the stage, where a young pale-faced soprano now stands in a white
gown.

Maggie smiles. I forgot how young I was, how young I was when
it all ended.

On the stage the young woman bows and Duncan hears applause,
subdued and distant, like the rhythmic chattering of a far-off
train. And then the woman lifts her face to the mezzanine and
clerestory, a face unmarred by lines of pain and years of frustration
and regret. Her red hair spills in tightly wound curls down her back.
Duncan's mouth is open and he realizes that he's not breathing.
You're beautiful, Mom, he says. You're so beautiful.

He senses the presence of the people about them—shades of
people, shadowed angles and planes and strange coronas of light—a
burning luminosity at the edges of black, shifting outlines, becoming more distinct and recognizable. There is movement in the seats,
the low timbre of men and women speaking, the smell of pomade
and Fragonard, the musk of rich perfume and cologne, and the settling of the opera house as it fits itself to contain the glittering
memories of the past. The faded, decrepit paneling and bar stools of

the Windsor Tap are gone and in their place is ornate, gold-leaf filigree and the sculpted booths of the mezzanine, in which long-dead men and women sit in silent splendor, entranced by his mother's performance. The stairs to the foyer are enclosed by red marble balusters supporting a balustrade of onyx. Twenty monolithic columns of a pale opal-like marble, honeycombed with arabesques and ornaments and surrounded by smaller pilasters of peach and violet stone, rise to the panorama of the ceiling.

Duncan stares at the raised Italian plasterwork, the golden tiled sections of the orchestra, the elaborately painted ceiling, with dryads and nymphs playing music in Greek pastures, and suspended a hundred feet above them the shimmering grand chandelier and its thousand cut-crystal diamond tapers, through which electric flames revolve and refract in twirling hollow points of light. And below this and encircling the clerestory, a dozen gold painted statues: the muses of the arts.

What do you think, Duncan? Mother says. It's not the Palais Garnier, I know, but it's not so bad, is it?

No, he shakes his head and clutches her hand in all its feverish strength as the soprano's voice surges through them, vibrating in a crescendo that he can feel trembling in the nerve endings beneath his skin. *No, it's not so bad at all.*

After a moment, he asks her: Is this the end then?

I suppose it is, Duncan.

For a while they stare at the stage. It really is a beautiful show. Mother reaches the heights of her range with such force of violence and pain, anguish and desperation and loss—and in this is the happiness that comes with the power of her abilities, when everything that is her essence pours forth from her heart—and with such seeming effortlessness the audience shimmers in appreciation. Upon the stage, beneath the bas-relief of the golden proscenium, Duncan's mother performs her final aria as the Queen of the Night, her arms outstretched toward the audience in pleading, in joy.

At its end she bows and then lifts her face to the clamouring audience, a sight that she will never see again. But for now she is momentarily illuminated and held, transfigured by the lights of the stage.

Disowned may you be forever, Abandoned may you be forever, Destroyed be forever.

Heads turn in their direction. Elaborately dressed men and women nod and silently mouth the words, Brava! Brava! Magnifico! and clap the tops of their hands in restrained and respectful applause.

Duncan senses Maggie smiling. I love you, Duncan, she says.

I love you too, Mom.

Cherry blossom petals, turned opaque and pearl by the stage lights, rain slowly from behind the curtains—the suggestion of pink-tinged snow in May, glinting in slow spirals to the stage as if they were falling onto a grave.

It's like the Festival of Lights, he whispers, and mother nods knowingly. The Festival of Lights Holiday Train, she echoes. How long ago it seems. Like this. Like a dream.

And he wonders how she can know about the Festival of Lights Holiday Train. It froze on the tracks the night I was born, he says, and everyone died. The night you left me at the Home. That's what they told me, what Brother Canice always said.

Mother nods sleepily. But we didn't die, did we sweetie? We didn't die. We should have died but we didn't. We were like Joshua and his angel, flying above it all.

No. Only the people on the train died.

We were on the train, my Duncan. *We* were the only survivors. I took us through the snow and walked until I couldn't walk anymore. It was so cold and everything was lost in the white and I prayed that God would take us.

Duncan turns and looks at her.

You weren't breathing. It was such a strange thing, an odd lurching in your throat, a little gasp of air and you were gone from me and I was sure that we'd both die there in the snow miles from any-where and I lay down with you, wrapped you up in my clothes, and fell asleep. Your heart had stopped Duncan, and I didn't want to live anymore. I never intended for us to wake up again.

When they found me, you were dead. But then your heart began beating again and I knew it was a miracle, a sign from God. I remem-ber looking up at one point as they carried me over the snow and rockets were shooting through the air.

It was a meteor shower, he says.

Mother nods. A meteor shower, she says dreamily. I looked up through the snow and there in a tear of clearest dark starlit sky I saw hundreds of rockets arcing and sputtering and I knew that at any moment you would be born and that you would be special. My spe-cial Duncan.

Then I was never here with you?

I was in a delirium for days, sweetie, and when I finally came through I couldn't manage a baby, I couldn't look after a child. And then *he* came, because they'd called him and he said he'd take me back and everything would be right again, that we could start over. He said that we couldn't be on the road with a child, that if I didn't leave you, he'd go and never come back . . . He promised that we'd be together, that he'd take me back west and we'd get married, in a couple of years we'd start a real family.

Who Mom? Who are you talking about?

Your father.

I gave you up almost immediately and they took you without question. I think they knew that, after everything that had hap-pened, I was in no fit state to look after a child. It was as if you were meant to be with them, as if the storm was merely part of some di-vine plan, as if it had been engineered to bring you to them. I knew you would be safe—I hoped you would be safe. I'm so sorry that I left with him, I'm so sorry I left you.

What about the pictures? I'm in them and you're holding my

hand. That had to be from a time before. And someone had to take those pictures.

No, Duncan. His mother shakes her head. That's not me. And I don't know who took the pictures.

He stares at her.

They're made up, Duncan. They're not really us. They're pictures of other people, not us.

The boy—

It's not you, Duncan. O my sweet, I'm so sorry, but the boy, he isn't you either. I don't know who he is. They were four for a dollar at the St. Vincent De Paul. They came out of a box filled with hundreds of other pictures.

You mean they're dead people.

I don't who they are, Duncan.

But those are dead people's photographs. The St. Vincent De Paul takes them when there's no one else to. Why? Why did you tell me that we'd lived together?

Mother sighs contently, as if the burden of fourteen years of lies has suddenly been lifted from her, as if she is fading, disappearing in the light.

I was so filled with guilt and shame, she says. I didn't want you to think that I was the type of mother who would abandon her child. When he left me, I wanted to come back but I was too weak. I've failed so much in life, made decisions I never thought I could make right again. When I came to get you, I was so frightened. I wanted you to believe in me.

But I do, he says. I do believe in you. I've always believed in you.

I never wanted to leave you, she says, never . . . I made a choice, one I've regretted my entire life . . .

It's okay, Mom. It's okay. We're together now.

She smiles toward the stage, waves her wrist weakly at the air. So long ago, she says. So long ago.

Don't leave me, Mom, Duncan says. You promised. You promised to never leave me again.

No, honey. Maggie shakes her head. I'll never leave you again. Never. I promise.

Cherry blossoms continue to fall on the stage like snow and suddenly he's cold. Maggie reaches for his hand, and missing, clasps her own and holds them to her breast, and Duncan takes them, works his own fingers amongst hers and holds to them tightly. The show is almost over. He sees Mother rushing through Scollay Square, and snow, white and thick, tumbling down around her. At a street corner she pauses to watch two lovers, arm in arm, kiss and their kiss floats, rises up to the rooftops, above crumbling lofts and soon-to-be-demolished tenements. The kiss rising upon the final notes of her performance, which still ring in her head, and the crowd rising to their feet, and mother bowing before them as the Queen of the Night and she blinks now into the snow coming upon her upturned face, like darts of soft yet brilliant light. Up, up into such white light. She is rising with the kiss up into the night above Boston, a night filled with the music of her, and into the white churning snow clouds, up up up—she is the woman in the snow from his dreams, the woman standing before the Festival of Lights Holiday Train, and the snow is coming harder now, blinding and white, and Mother moves into its whiteness and toward the divine music only she can hear.

Please, Mom.

My Duncan, Maggie says, and then her body seems to be leaning, yearning to rise, as if invisible strings were pulling her upright. A smile flickers on her face, her eyes shine so brightly that he imagines if he looks hard enough into them, he might see what she sees—and a thin, single drop of dark blood trickles from her nose. Her body settles back in the chair and her eyes look blindly and unblinking at the stage before them. He watches as slowly her eyes cloud and both color and fire are extinguished.

Mom? he calls to her. Mom? But he realizes even as he takes her

393

limp hand in his that she is gone. Leaning his head against her shoulder, he tries to force his own life back into her, pretends that he can hear her heartbeat, the pulse of blood in her hand beneath his own, the rise and fall of her chest, and the reassuring warm exhale of her breath. There is the smell of her skin and of her clothes and he clings to this. And she remains warm for a long time, and when her warmth begins to fade, he presses himself closer to her and sits there weeping and then falls asleep and wakes with his hands in hers and she is cold and stiff and it is dark. He calls her name softly in the darkness, whispering to her as she used to whisper to him in the night when the nightmares came, and the hours pass in the resuscitation of her name like a prayer.

In the early hours of the morning a light flickers through the dark, the short diffuse beam of a small flashlight through which dust motes shudder as it sweeps slowly across the back of the theater and across the seats. When the beam reaches them, Clay's voice sounds at his shoulder: *Duncan? Maggie? Are you okay?* But Duncan is walking arm in arm with his mother through the snow of Scollay Square now. When he looks back, he sees his mother and himself sitting amongst the empty rows of seats staring blankly up at the stage, and Clay's flashlight searching the dark for them.

Upon the stage snow falls unabated. Mother and Duncan look at each other and smile. He stares at the paleness of her face, the intensity of her blue eyes, sharpened now by the white snow that surrounds them. He feels the weight of her pressed against him and his arm looped warmly through hers. The snow is falling upon their faces, pelting cold upon the skin, caught perfectly formed and then slowly melting in his mother's hair as they move through old Scollay Square, *Duncan?* farther and farther into the snow-whitened alleys until, *Duncan, are you okay?* there is nothing to see of them—all sight and sound is obliterated: He and mother are together and then they are no more and then they are gone.

It is 1972 and Duncan sees the Festival of Lights Holiday Train, a 1928 GNR Empire Builder steam engine streaking along the snow-blown Minnesota tracks, with coal roaring in the engine's coal port and spilling in fiery embers from the tender in the way that he remembers embers tumbling from the kitchen woodstove when Brother Canice stoked the ashes before telling his stories. Aboard the train one of the performers—his mother as a young woman—passes Father Magnusson and glances at him briefly and then pauses before his chair, transfixed by and in awe of the storm beyond the glass. The light in the carriage flickers and then dims and the swaying, trembling car is in darkness. The electric Christmas lights upon the exterior of the carriage continue to burn and their phosphorescent glow shows the rills of snow beyond the blurred rails, and in the dark the vast and inexorable sense of such snow hurtling down.

Father Magnusson stirs and glances up at Mother, who continues to stare beyond the glass.

My, it's some storm, Father, she says. Do you think we'll be all right? Instinctively, something she has done since her belly became so prominent and vulnerably exposed to every doorway, wall, passerby, Mother clutches her stomach and cradles it with both hands.

I think we'll be fine, child. Don't you worry. And as if to reassure her, he reaches out and briefly touches his hand upon hers. You'll both be fine.

Mother looks out at the night. The lights within the carriage slowly burn up to their peak, and the car is lit once more. Father Magnusson lays his head back upon the pillow. She nods and glances at the priest, but he has already closed his eyes and turned away, his old head lolling toward the whispers and sighs of the storm. Goodnight, Father, she whispers and moves toward the vestibule.

Beyond the plate glass window the landscape is lost in snowfall; it swirls and presses against the glass, and the wind pushes it beneath the sill, where it moans and sighs and then sweeps the sides and tops of the carriage, down, down, down the length of its fifteen cars and at the train's end the snow and ice form a great tail: a comet shooting along the tracks.

Duncan sees the rescuers moving through the frozen vestibules of the train, their flashlights and lamps flickering. Over here! a man hollers. There's footprints! One of them is out in the storm! and then comes the sound of pounding footfalls banging the hard metal dividers between the carriages, as other men, already exhausted and numbed by their daylong trek through the cold and by experiencing the sensation of death everywhere before them, come running, their lanterncaps sweeping the carriages frantically.

Mother is struggling through the snow, stumbling, blinded by the wind and the cold, and her strength is fading, her heartbeat sluggish in her chest, the air seeming to freeze the breath in her throat. With her arms wrapped about her newborn child, she can feel that other heart now slowing and becoming so soft she can barely detect it and then it stops completely. Gritting her teeth, she falters, sinks to her waist, and wrestles forward and up again—she and her child cannot die here like this.

They track Mother's footsteps for what seems hours, disappearing out over the white, windswept plains, farther and farther from the train, and finally find her, partially covered in a snowdrift. A doctor holds her wrist and listens through a stethoscope to her heart and from mother's nostrils a meager tendril of breath smokes the air. Her skin is ashen and pale, icicles hang from her closed eyelashes; and only when they've pulled her from the snow do they discover Duncan beneath her and the doctor hushes the men so that he might hear Duncan's heartbeat, faint and almost imperceptible. They cover them in blankets and, returning to the train carriage, carry in industrial heaters to warm them until the doctor decides they are ready to be moved onto one of the snowcats. Every twenty minutes the doctor presses a warm solution through a small incision he's made in Duncan's stomach, and as his core temperature rises, the men nod to one another, touch one another's backs and shoulders reassuringly, almost tenderly. More than one man cries but the cold immediately freezes the tears upon their cheeks.

Although Duncan is alive, his heartbeat is almost too weak to be heard, and they pray before they wrap him in blankets and transport him outside. And now they are taking him and Mother through the swirling snow and above them the storm momentarily pauses, the sky clears, and he sees the stars falling from the heavens. The brightness collapses and the storm rages on and he is carried through the blizzard, and in the cold and coming darkness he turns toward his mother but can no longer see her face.

Maggie? Duncan? Are you okay?

We shall find peace. We shall hear angels.
We shall see the sky sparkling with diamonds.
—ANTON CHEKOV

BEYOND THE RAIL yards and the rented house on Ipswich Street, the first strakes of freewheeling snow drifts across the railway tracks, dusting the metal with a fine white powder, and Duncan pulls the collar of his jacket tighter about his neck. The siren from the Edison plant bellows as twilight fades and his stomach cramps with hunger. The ground is cold and wet and the pressing darkness has turned the sky the color of a plum halved in two. For a moment he is caught in that strange going-down of light: dark clouds pressing with the night from above but through the tree line the slivered impression of everything in flame, and beyond the trees and hills, and far away in the distance, so far it might even be another country, the suggestion of light like dawn. The voices of workmen come to him, cajoling and distant, their lanterns trembling like small flames as they traverse the tracks. Foghorns sound out in the bay. The distant bridge is a flickering band of bowed, unceasing light, the beams of car headlights merging and coalescing, sparkling through the crystals of snow.

When the train comes, its lights shuddering through the dusk, he sees the snakelike silhouette of its load: a hundred or more dump cars swaying upon the rails, and it is moving so slowly from the yard that he is able to climb aboard easily, his heart hammering in his chest and his breath smoking the air relentlessly. Searching behind him, he pauses on the ladder, as if his mother might suddenly reach her hand out of the dark to him, but there is only the trembling impression of things passing darkly before his eyes as the train picks up speed, and he climbs the ladder and drops down into the tin.

The car rocks from side to side, bangs and thumps on the rails as the engineer opens the valves. Duncan closes his eyes and dreams and then wakes again and it is still dark. He is riding all the points of the compass, traversing all the great and strange meridians of the wide earth to a place where he might finally see those things that his mother dreamed of seeing, her red hair whipping about her face as she peered over the lip of an open dump car out upon the vast expanse of America: goldenrod and larkspur trembling at the edges of the tracks and the land falling away behind her in one endless, spiraling revolution.

The train lurches forward and into the dump car comes snow. Duncan can feel it on his face and in his hair. He holds out his tongue to taste it. Through scattered storm clouds the stars are glittering, and crumbling satellites spin through their lonely orbits. A hundred astronauts are floating up there, at the edge of night, arms outstretched like the wings of angels. Michael Collins stares down upon the moon from the command module *Columbia* and listens to the mission's audio files. Father Magnusson stands upon the edge of the great, striated mare, the Sea of Tranquility, scattering the ashes of the stranded astronauts and commending their souls to the deepest of the deep. Billy and Julie are there as well, lowering their heads as Father Magnusson prays, and holding each other's hands like small paper dolls. Joshua is sitting before the sea, dangling his feet over the edge of its precipice. He's wearing his olive field jacket and his blue bandanna and Maggie stands above him, softly kneading his shoulders. She bends to his ear, whispers something, and Joshua nods, reaches back and takes her hand. She's wearing her blue sequined dress from the Windsor Tap, and though it is stretched across the protuberance of her cancerous belly, it sparkles with starlight, the fading iridescence of a passing comet. And Duncan looks up at them and smiles and tells them that everything will be okay, that he is okay, and somewhere out in the dark, like a spark of dimming light, Elvis begins to sing a halting version of "Blue Moon."

Michael Collins touches his intercom console, clicks the Play button, and through the vacuum of space, comes a ghostly static followed by the "Star-Spangled Banner" and the audio files of Buzz and Armstrong from twenty years before, looping over and over and over, and always he is spinning, spiraling farther and farther away through all the dark, silent corridors of space where night begins but there is also light and everything that God made possible in his slow turn toward them.

109:43:16 ALDRIN: Beautiful view!

109:43:18 ARMSTRONG: Isn't that something! Magnificent sight out here.

109:43:24 ALDRIN: Magnificent desolation.

109:43:16 ALDRIN: Beautiful view!

109:43:18 ARMSTRONG: Isn't that something! Magnificent sight out here.

109:43:24 ALDRIN: Magnificent desolation.

109:43:16 ALDRIN: Beautiful view!

109:43:18 ARMSTRONG: Isn't that something! Magnificent sight out here.

109:43:24 ALDRIN: Magnificent desolation.

000:00:00 Tranquility to Columbia. Michael, are you there? Over. My God, Michael, you should see this. What a sight!

000:00:00 Are you there?

000:00:00 Michael? Are you there?

000:00:00 Michael?

000:00:00 Michael?

000:00:00: Michael?

Are you there?

Acknowledgments

With thanks and appreciation for funding provided by the Burke Foundation and the Walter and Constance Burke Award, which contributed greatly to the completion of this book.

To my agent, Richard Abate, for his unwavering faith. To my colleagues at Dartmouth, and specifically to Darsie Riccio, Andrew McCann, Michael Chaney, and Patricia McKee.

To Douglas Purdy, with respect and admiration, for his inspiration, friendship, and brotherhood.

To my daughter, Colette Gráinne, who always makes me remember what is most important and who keeps me real.

And with love and gratitude to Jen Purdy, for all the things you make seem possible and for the beauty of your wild heart.

Thank you, and bless you all.

A Note on the Author

Thomas O'Malley is a graduate of the University of Massachusetts at Boston and the Iowa Writers' Workshop, and is currently on the faculty of Dartmouth College's creative writing program. He lives in the Boston area.